Emma

A Widow Among the Amish

Also by Ervin R. Stutzman

Tobias of the Amish (2001)

Emma

A Widow Among the Amish

A true story woven by strands of faith, family, and community

Ervin R. Stutzman

Foreword by
Rachel Nafziger Hartzler

HERALD
P R E S S

Harrisonburg, Virginia

Herald Press
PO Box 866, Harrisonburg, Virginia 22803
www.HeraldPress.com

Library of Congress Cataloging-in-Publication Data
Stutzman, Ervin R., 1953-
   Emma: a widow among the Amish : a true story woven by strands of
faith, family, and community / Ervin R. Stutzman.
      p. cm.
   ISBN-13: 978-0-8361-9394-7 (pbk. : alk. paper)
      1. Stutzman, Emma, 1916-1989—Fiction. 2. Amish—Fiction.
3. Widows—Fiction. 4. Kansas—Fiction. 5. Domestic fiction.
I. Title.

   PS3619.T88E46 2007
   813'.6—dc22

                                        2007028473

EMMA: A WIDOW AMONG THE AMISH
© 2007 by Herald Press, Harrisonburg, Virginia 22803.
      800-245-7894. All rights reserved.
Library of Congress Catalog Card Number: 2007028473
International Standard Book Number: 978-0-8361-9394-7 (paperback)
International Standard Book Number: 978-0-8361-9412-8 (hardback)
Printed in the United States of America
Book design by Merrill Miller and Joshua Byler
Cover art by Allan M. Burch

21 20 19 18 17   10 9 8 7

To my daughter,
Emma Ruth (Stutzman) Dawson
with the hope that she will carry on, in her own way, the legacy
of the grandmother for whom she is named

Contents

Foreword

I was making a blueberry pie when my husband left for his daily jog along the canal near our home. When the pie was out of the oven and Harold had not yet returned, I became concerned. Eventually I called the hospital and learned that his body was there. He had had a deadly heart attack within two blocks of home as he was returning from his run.

Tobe Stutzman drove his children to Bible school, stopped at home to give Emma some grocery money, and then went to a neighboring town on business. A few hours later, as Emma was walking to town with one of her six children, their minister drove up beside her, rolled down his window, and said, "I have something I need to tell you." Emma and her son got in the car, and the minister drove them to the funeral home, where the funeral director confirmed her worst fears: "I'm so sorry to tell you that your husband was killed in a car accident today."

Each of these men died while they had dependent children, suddenly and unexpectedly leaving a widow with the immense tasks of mourning the death of a life partner, caring for grieving children, becoming the single head of the household, and searching for a new identity.

Life has gone on for us twenty-first-century widows as it did for Emma Stutzman in the 1950s. We each have been surrounded by a compassionate community, whose loving care has wrapped us like a blanket and has been an expression of God's gracious, steadfast love. However, the journey for each of us has included periods of almost overwhelming grief, episodes of nearly insurmountable challenges of parenting and householding, and occasions of facing new and disquieting questions about God. Coinciding with these difficulties were times of feeling no energy to face the day ahead. But we survived—by the grace of God and loving human support and encouragement.

Some widowed people find courage to go on in the stories of others who survive similar circumstances. Some of us repeatedly tell the story of our loss, some of us journal, and some of us cry out our laments to God. Lamenting in some way is a necessary ingredient to eventually living well again. Telling and retelling helps us to confirm the reality of the horrible loss and assists us in trying to make sense out of life. Listening to others' stories of loss helps us to place ourselves in the arena of those who have suffered, struggled, and survived. Knowing that widows around the world and throughout the ages have faced similar or even greater challenges than our own, we discover hope! *Emma: A Widow Among the Amish* is a story of hope.

In some ways this book is Ervin Stutzman's story about growing up Amish. But it is much more than that.

It is a historical account of life among Amish folks in Kansas during the third quarter of the twentieth century. Many will be interested in the facts about life on a small farm in an Amish community, and life during a time of significant changes in the church, but this narrative is also more than that.

It is the story of a remarkable woman written through the eyes of her youngest son, whose credentials and experience include ordained Mennonite minister, pastor, preacher, teacher, theologian, church administrator, and student of the church past and present.

The historical data woven into the story continue to remind the reader that this is a true story, if not in all the details of activities and spoken words, at least in the setting where experiences and conversations attributed to Emma and her family really did happen.

In some ways this story includes a critique of a widow's life. Amish folks take seriously the biblical call to care for the widows and orphans. Emma's parents and siblings and Tobe's parents and siblings are supportive as well as brothers and sisters in the church. Although many widows say that they could not survive without this kind of support, it may come with a price. Stutzman makes an astute observation: "The safety net that kept widows from plummeting to ruin also restricted their movements."

This is indeed a dilemma that some widows encounter, even those of us who aren't Amish. Some widows (and even widowers) today feel as though they live in a fishbowl. After being the recipients of generosity, for which they are grateful, they realize that people are watching. When one's choices do not please one's benefactors, will the needy be cut off? What about the widow who declines to marry a widower who would care for her and relieve the church of the responsibility they are expected to carry? Stutzman does not shy away from these difficult questions. In the description of his mother's struggles, he opens up agenda that twenty-first-century people face. How can we live in community and at the same time make choices that best serve our own needs and those of our children?

Emma: A Widow Among the Amish is also a story of community and forgiveness. Reading John Ruth's *Forgiveness: A Legacy of the West Nickel Mines Amish School* alongside Emma may help the person unfamiliar with Anabaptist theology to better understand the importance of community and the concept of forgiveness.

Many widowed people find themselves grieving not only the death of a spouse, but also the loss of the dream of an imperfect marriage becoming better in the future. With the death comes the end of aspirations for that marriage. Some widowed people need to forgive their spouses for not becoming what they had always hoped for, and perhaps to forgive themselves for not loving differently, trying harder, or learning to accept the deficiencies or limitations of the one who died. Sometimes there are other parties to forgive.

Before you is a story of community, forgiveness, grace, and hope. Emma Stutzman is a model for living well after the death of a spouse, and her son has given us a vivid picture of a real woman who suffered many losses and hardships, but engaged in a courageous struggle, found joy in living, and died in peace.

Rachel Nafziger Hartzler
Goshen, Indiana
Author of *Grief and Sexuality: Life After Losing a Spouse*

Author's Preface

The writing of this book about my mother was prompted by the many personal responses I received from readers of *Tobias of the Amish*, a book about my father. I was surprised and delighted by the many men who responded to *Tobias*, especially those who do not by habit read for pleasure. Reading about my father's life sparked in many of them the desire to connect more intimately with their fathers, to plumb the depths of their family lore. I have been profoundly touched by their stories of discovery, sometimes through the awkward search for accounts of family history purposely hidden from public view.

Some of the women who read *Tobias*, however, wished to hear more about my mother as she stood alongside her husband through his entrepreneurial ventures. Their questions stirred in me the restless desire to sift through the pages of family lore again, to examine the evidence through a different set of lenses. What kind of person was Emma? What sustained her through the stresses of life on the roller coaster with Tobe? How did she gather up the strength to rear her family following his tragic death? These questions have guided my quest.

Chronologically, *Emma* is a sequel to *Tobias of the Amish*. It begins where Tobias ends. Although the book can stand on its own, the reader will gain a richer sense of Emma's story by reading *Tobias* as well.

Since I have no personal recollections of my father, the writing of *Tobias* was a genuine journey of discovery. Each new anecdote I gathered in my research became a new entry in the journal that served as the background for *Tobias*. Because I knew my mother well—or so I thought, having grown up in her home—I naively anticipated that the research task would consist primarily of recall and organization of existing knowledge. As it turned out, the writing of this book became a long journey of genuine discovery. I found it deeply instructive to scrutinize the memories of my childhood and adolescence with adult eyes. As I near the end of this journey, I feel both chastened and blessed. I feel chastised by the evidence because I recognize now how oblivious I was to so much that my mother passed on to me. Yet I feel deeply blessed because of the insights I have gained.

While most of the events portrayed in this book happened in the order portrayed here, I have not intended a strict chronology or a rigorously factual account. For the most part, I have tried to orient the reader to the time frame by providing some dates in the text in addition to occasional references to seasons of the year or events in the community or nation. This narrative is first of all a story, not a history book.

I took two primary liberties in fictionalizing this story. The first was to create dialogue. Some of the speech portrayed here represents the exact words as I or my informants recall them. I have also drawn from letters and other written sources to imitate the dialect of mother's community. Beyond that, I have drawn on my imagination, informed by the memory of the way people talked to each other.

The second freedom that I exercised was to interpret my mother's thoughts. Here, of course, I found myself skating on thin ice on an isolated pond. In the first draft of this manuscript, I skated close to shore. What I feared most, as I see it now, was that I might not interpret mother fairly. All of my relatives and family members would be quick to say that if my mother had played cards, she would have kept them close to her chest. She readily listened to the laments and woes of others, but rarely chose to write or speak of her own. How could I dare to pretend that I understand the swirl of emotions that she felt throughout her difficult life? In what sense could I profess to be writing a true story without the certainty of direct knowledge conveyed by my mother or one of her confidants?

I chose to face into my fears when several readers of my first draft, particularly women, voiced the hope for more glimpses of Emma's inner life, the interior conflicts that remained largely hidden from public view. As I tested subsequent efforts motivated by their prodding, I received assurance that my interpretation rings true. The verisimilitude in this story, then, is assured not by factual proof but by the testimony of the people who knew her best. Her siblings, in-laws, and a few other friends—along with my own siblings—have confirmed that this account rings true to mother's life as they knew it.

When it comes to the telling of events that occurred in mother's life, I tried to hew closely to an account of reality as I experienced it. In that attempt, I struggled with the natural temptations to color the events in the ways most favorable to me as a writer or to give a primary account of the events I recalled rather than seeking out the meaning of events recalled only by others. To a considerable extent, I am now convinced, my mind selected what it wished to retain. I am humbled by the lapses of memory exposed through research. I am left wondering how my perspectives on my family would be different if I were to remember all of the household incidents my siblings readily recall.

Every name in this book is the one carried by the characters in real life. Some readers may find the many different proper names to be distracting, even confusing. Others—especially those acquainted with these people and places—will be gratified by the connections they provide. I employed this means to ground my mother's story in the particularities of a unique people in their time and place.

You will note that some of the characters show up in many places throughout the book. Other names show up once or twice. In the latter case, I advise the reader to see them as supporting characters in a cast, adding a bit of color.

To keep from confusing the identities of people with the same names, I chose to use an initial or some other way of distinguishing them from each other. For example, I depicted two of my Stutzman uncles as "L. Perry" and "Ervin J." to keep their identities separate from my brother and me, even though we rarely referred to them in that way. In a few places, I have employed the common convention of identifying an entire family by the father's name, such as "Raymonds invited us to their house."

On the other hand, I have limited my use of the most common naming convention for women, whereby spouses were identified by their husband's first names, such as Tobe's Emma (often shortened to Tobe Emma). Most of the people in my community referred to my Grandmother Mary Nisly as Noah Mary and my aunt Mary Nisly as Raymond Mary. Also, at that time it was common for women to use only their husband's names for identification, such as when my mother signed her name as Mrs. Tobe Stutzman.

During the first years portrayed in this book, my mother's congregation spoke German in their Sunday worship services. They sang hymns composed mostly by German-speaking authors from Europe and read from Martin Luther's translation of the Bible. Part of the communal journey portrayed in these pages is the move away from the German language in worship toward the nearly exclusive use of the English. Since language profoundly shapes one's identity and perception of reality, this journey represents a gradual shift toward acculturation.

However, most of the Amish community retained the use of Pennsylvania German for everyday conversation. Not only was Pennsylvania German more familiar; the dialect also provided an important separator between the Amish Mennonites and their neighbors in Christian faith. Although my mother spoke English without a noticeable German accent, Pennsylvania German was the language of her heart all her life. To remind the reader that much of the original dialogue occurred in Pennsylvania German, I have included words and phrases in the dialect with the English translation of these words following immediately after. Although there is no standard spelling for Pennsylvania German words, I have relied for the most part on C. Richard Beam's *Pennsylvania German Dictionary* as a guide.

This book is first of all the story of my mother, an Amish widow rearing six children in the aftermath of her husband's recent business failures and tragic death. While she did nothing to earn notoriety, she was "heroic in the quotidian," as the publisher put it. That is, she lived day by day, trying to be faithful to God and providing for her children. Second, the book is an account of the Amish Mennonite response over time to pressures of modernization and accommodation to mainstream culture. I have not celebrated any heroes in this account, save the Holy One whose plans are mysterious beyond understanding, whose ways are beyond finding out.

This venture has given me the opportunity to connect or reconnect with many people during my process of research. Collecting the myriad details for this book has provided a wonderful excuse to ask probing questions of the people who knew my mother. In the process, it helped me forge deeper connections with each of my siblings.

My writing often transported me in spirit and memory to the times and places where I lived as a child. For the most part, I found these memories to be comforting and assuring.

I am grateful to God for the heritage of faith that my mother passed on to me. I pray to God that my descendants can say the same for me.

I hope that this story will prompt you to embark on a search for meaning in your own family history. If this book prompts that kind of thoughtful reflection, I will count my efforts well worthwhile.

Ervin R. Stutzman
Harrisonburg, Virginia

Acknowledgments

This book marks the culmination of several years of work with much encouragement from others along the way. It is my pleasure to recognize a few of them for their contribution. First of all, I offer thanks to my wife, Bonita, for the immense patience she exercised in allowing me the time and space to do this writing. Perhaps her most important contribution was the emotional support for the project, including the sympathetic perception that my imagination was at times preoccupied with musings far removed from our shared haunts of bed and board.

Second, I am grateful for the interest and involvement of my two sons, Daniel and Benjamin, who offered valuable assistance. Daniel read the first draft and offered many helpful suggestions, including the bold assertion that I needed to take the time to do extensive revision. Benjamin created a Web page—www.ervinstutzman.com—which offers important supplements to this book, including more-detailed acknowledgments.

I am deeply indebted to the many people who comprised the community of memory from which I drew the material for this narrative. I depended on many people to provide both general and specific information. My brothers and sisters, my childhood friends, my uncles and aunts, and friends of my mother all shared generously and openly with me. As the manuscript grew to full length, I shared it with a number of readers, who provided both encouragement and counsel. Their comments led to some important revisions.

I came upon a treasure trove of detail in the diaries and journals of my late sister Mary (Stutzman) Yoder, generously shared with me by her husband, Menno. I also gained valuable perspective by reading letters written by Mary to various individuals. I drew from diary entries written by my brother Perry L. Stutzman, my mother, Emma Stutzman, and some that I wrote as a teenager. These sources helped to provide depth and perspective, as well as a time frame for the events in this book. A number of people shared generously in a photo harvest that helped me to picture many of the scenes in this book. A few of these photographs are included at the back of this book.

I am also grateful for the contribution that others made to me along the way, particularly people who never knew my mother. In this vein, my thanks go to Lucy O'Meara, a spiritual director who helps me to see God's hand in the midst of ordinary life. My thanks too go to Owen Burkholder, a spiritual companion with whom I experience deep freedom to talk about issues of faith and family.

I am grateful too for the way that my colleagues at work encourage me to write about family. My supervisors at Eastern Mennonite University—President Loren Swartzendruber and Provost Beryl Brubaker—were particularly encouraging. They support my conviction that my effectiveness as a church leader and seminary dean is enhanced by research regarding my family of origin. In that vein, they generously granted permission for me to use sabbatical time from the university to do the final editing. My thanks also go to Joanna Swartley, who read carefully through the manuscript.

I appreciate the good counsel of David L. Miller, an

ordained minister of the church in which I was baptized. His extensive knowledge of Amish history and community enabled him to critique my work with an eye for nuances of fact as well as tone. I am grateful for his helpful insights and suggestions. In a similar way, Linda Rose Miller of the same community helped to assure that the spelling of names and other local details were accurate. I am grateful for her attention to detail.

I am particularly indebted to Sara Wenger Shenk, my colleague who serves as the Associate Dean at Eastern Mennonite Seminary. She provided both encouragement and helpful literary critique as a reader of the manuscript. Her perceptive feedback helped to make the book a better literary piece.

Since I have chosen not to include reference notes in this text, I will acknowledge some of my written sources here. I drew general information from many written sources, including published works such as the *Hutchinson News*, the *Calvary Messenger*, *The Budget* (Sugarcreek, Ohio), and the *Gospel Herald*. I found valuable historical material in an essay written by David Wagler as an assignment for Bethel College, North Newton, Kansas, in 1968. I discovered valuable legal information in the Reno County Courthouse in Hutchinson, Kansas. I also found helpful reflections on widowhood in a variety of books, including the writings of Katie Funk Wiebe and Rachel Nafziger Hartzler.

Most important, I thank God through Jesus Christ, who has called me into the eternal family of faith that embraces people from every tongue, people, and nation who call on his name. My faith in him provides the impetus to use insights from my family of origin to encourage people everywhere to become a part of God's greater family. *Soli Deo gloria.*

1

Lost Ground

Emma Stutzman plied her hoe between two rows of peas in her large garden patch. The black soil warmed her bare feet as she chopped at the small weeds poking their way into the May sunlight. "*Ich hasse die Rewwer Bodde Grund.* I hate this river bottom soil," she mumbled to herself in Pennsylvania German as she pushed back a strand of brown hair from her forehead. "It must have been too wet when we plowed it." She whacked at a large clod with her hoe. "The ground back home isn't hard like this."

The Stutzman's dwelling lay not far from the English River that ran through Kalona, Iowa. The rich gumbo soil on the flood plain was easy enough to till when there was adequate rain. But when it was dry, hoeing could be like whacking at a rubber tractor tire. In contrast, the soil in Emma's native Kansas was sandy and light.

Emma straightened up to survey her vegetables. She couldn't really complain about the way things were growing. The corn was pushing up shoots to join company with long rows of carrots, beans, and potatoes.

"It's time to get these tomatoes staked," she said aloud to herself. She made her way to the storage shed and found a dozen collapsible tomato racks that her husband, Tobe, had fabricated in his metal shop. She unfolded them and pushed the four-cornered wire supports into the soil around the foot-high tomato plants.

"And I must dust these potatoes," Emma lamented as she looked at the leafy vegetation. "Those potato bugs will soon take over."

"If it weren't for this garden," Emma mused, "I'm afraid I wouldn't be able to put food on the table. We just don't have the cash. But I must buy potatoes. There are none left in the cellar. It'll be more than a month before these are ready to dig."

She took a break from hoeing to harvest several handfuls of radishes and onions. Then she cut off two heads of lettuce and put them in her dishpan with the other cuttings. These would make the salad for Sunday dinner.

Not since the Depression years could Emma remember thinking so much about money. It was a constant worry. Emma's seven siblings seemed to be doing well. Three years earlier, in 1953, each of them had received an inheritance— a choice of forty acres of land or the same value in cash. But to keep Tobe from getting his desperate hands on Emma's inheritance, Emma's father deeded it to her younger brother Raymond Nisly. Raymond lived on the home farm next to Emma's promised forty acres in Kansas, so he agreed to farm Emma's promised acreage in return for a share of the crop.

Emma hoped that she and Tobe would be able to pass on an inheritance to their children. But at the rate things were going now, they would only pass on a debt. After having grown up to believe that one should avoid debt whenever possible, she felt deeply shamed by her husband's recent bankruptcy proceedings.

Money problems didn't seem to bother Tobe in the same way. Even through the legal process, he'd expressed optimism. Not long after he lost the ownership of Kalona Products

Company in May of 1955, he started a new business. With the financial sponsorship of an Amish neighbor named Harvey Bender, Tobe built a thirty-by-fifty-six-foot block building for a manufacturing shop. As a member of the creditors' committee of the bankrupt business, Harvey helped Tobe equip the new shop and get started.

Not long afterward, Tobe talked Harvey into letting him build thirty-by-thirty-six-foot living quarters onto the end of the shop. Harvey agreed to put up the money, and Tobe supplied most of the labor. All this happened after Harvey had lost parts of four fingers in the shop's metal punch press. Emma marveled at the man's trust and generosity.

Emma didn't enjoy living in an unfinished house, but she consoled herself that it would soon be done. Perhaps even this week, Tobe would finish laying the linoleum in the kitchen. And he had promised he would put up the ceiling and install the inside doors soon. Until then, she'd need to be content to look up at the rafters. And she would manage with privacy curtains in the doorways.

Sometimes Emma felt a bit guilty about expecting Tobe to get things done on the house when he desperately needed to get his work done in the shop. If the metal parts weren't fabricated, they couldn't be sold. And if Tobe didn't have time to make his sales calls, he wouldn't get the orders he needed.

Emma had never met anyone who matched Tobe's energy and drive. He built the business at the same time that he was building the house. Between shop management, sales trips, and house construction, Tobe was busy from early morning till late at night.

The children and Emma helped in the shop whenever they could. On most days, the three older children worked in the shop after school. At urgent times, Tobe kept them home on school days to help get products out the door. At this point, he couldn't afford full-time employees.

Emma wondered if life would ever be normal in the Stutzman household. Would Tobe ever be content to live like other people? Would he settle for a regular job with a steady income and a relaxed family life? At times she felt like she was riding in a buggy hitched to an ill-tamed horse.

After Tobe had dragged the family from Kansas to Iowa in 1951 to take up metal fabricating, Emma had hinted to him that someone else might better manage the shop finances. She'd suggested that he pay more attention to the counsel of his investors. She'd urged him to pay back his outstanding loans before borrowing even more. In the end, he hadn't paid much attention to her suggestions—as though to say that women didn't understand business.

How Emma longed for Tobe to change his course now, in the face of the deepening debt! Why couldn't he be content to be a farmer like her brothers back in Kansas, or to take on a day job with an hourly wage? What was she to do when he gave no heed to her counsel? She sensed that Tobe was driven by a compelling ambition that she could not fully comprehend.

Emma worried that if the business didn't turn around soon, they could lose their right to stay in the house. She shuddered to recall their eviction from a property in July 1954, when they couldn't come up with the balloon mortgage payment. Emma never could have imagined that she'd have to sign legal papers delivered by a sheriff.

The family had moved five times since coming to Iowa from Kansas five years ago. Most of the landowners gave them cheap rent or allowed them to pay with some kind of work. But moving frequently meant that it was difficult to develop a really productive garden. There was no time to build up the soil or get plants like asparagus growing. It also meant that the children had attended three different country schools—Prairie Dale, Evergreen, and Pleasant Hill—and finally the town school in Kalona. At least Mary Edna was out of school now, having finished the eighth grade just last Tuesday.

Since participation in the Amish church districts depended on one's place of residence, their moves had also meant a change in church attendance. Each district had its own bishop, with his idiosyncrasies and differing ways of interpreting the Ordnung, or church discipline, the guidelines for Christian conduct. Emma felt rootless, numbed by transplant shock. She wished they could live back home in the house they had built in Kansas.

Tobe felt differently. As long as they had a roof overhead, he was satisfied. And he was always optimistic that things would eventually turn out for the better. Rather than argue or try to change her husband of fifteen years, Emma determined to concentrate on keeping food on the table. Even though Tobe at times lost money by the shovelful, she would do her part to save by the spoonful. "That's where a good garden makes all the difference," she mused as she leaned her hoe against the garden fence and walked toward the house, with her vegetables in hand.

Emma put the vegetables onto the kitchen counter and stepped into the living room, where Mary Edna was ironing. The three-year-old twins, Ervin and Erma, were playing on the floor nearby. Eight-year-old Edith, slowed by a mental handicap, was mumbling to herself in a nearby chair. "Thanks for watching the children," Emma said to Mary Edna. "It's good to have you home from school."

"Dad says he wants me to help the boys weld up some hangers today," Mary Edna replied. "I'll do that as soon as I get done with this ironing."

Emma washed and trimmed the vegetables and put them into the refrigerator. Then she stepped into the shop, where Perry and Glenn were working. "What are you working on?" she asked.

"Dad asked us to weld up these seven bundles of steel while he went to town," Perry said. Although Perry was only going into the eighth grade, he stood much taller than Emma's five-foot, two-inch frame. With the way he was growing, Emma expected that he would reach the six-foot, one-inch height of his dad before long.

Glenn was about sixteen months younger, shorter, and less stocky than his older brother. And he found it more difficult to concentrate on the task at hand. At least the boys were out of school for the summer now, so they wouldn't have to miss classes to get the shop work done.

Emma surveyed the shop with its saw, press, bender, roller, welder, and other heavy tools. She was amazed that Tobe had managed to assemble all of this equipment so soon after losing everything in the bankruptcy case. During his trips to Chicago and elsewhere, he often took the opportunity to buy good used equipment. Although Harvey Bender owned the things now, Tobe expected to pay for them when he got back on his feet.

She glanced at the stock of tin hog feeders and feed scoops that Tobe had recently made. Soon, she hoped, they could be sold for a bit of income.

Emma was preparing supper when Tobe got back to the shop. He helped finish the last of the bending and welding for the day, filling an order for hangers from a company in the nearby town of Fairfield. The Fairfield company used the hangers to make garment bags for closet storage. The bags were large enough to protect a dozen full-sized garments.

As soon as the quota of hangers was finished for that day,

Tobe worked on his latest idea, a rack to display gloves for retail sales. He called Emma into the shop as he put the finishing touches on the prototype. "I'm going to take this with me the next time I go to Chicago," he said. "I've been to a lot of places that could use a better way to display their gloves."

Emma nodded politely and then went back into the house. More than anything else, Tobe loved to exercise his inventive mind by creating new products. If the buyers were as excited as he, the new shop would soon turn a profit. But Emma wasn't convinced that would happen anytime soon.

2

Wrecked Hopes

The following Sunday morning, the Stutzman family attended services at the Sharon Bethel Amish Mennonite Church, located in a meetinghouse five miles north of Kalona. They were new members, having attended for less than a year. Part of the motivation for joining this more-progressive church, Tobe was quick to admit, was that the congregation allowed members to own automobiles. After years of hiring drivers to take him to distant cities in pursuit of his business, Tobe was convinced that he needed his own vehicle to make a go of it. So he purchased a 1941 Ford, which he traded in soon afterward for a blue 1947 Plymouth sedan. Emma wasn't as convinced as Tobe that it was necessary to own a car, but she went along with it. Like many of the women in the congregation, she let her husband do the driving. Driving could be dangerous.

It took longer to gain official membership in the Sharon Bethel church than Tobe and Emma had anticipated. But a couple of members at Sharon Bethel were creditors from Tobe's bankrupt business. They were determined to block their acceptance as members without some confession on Tobe's part or some structured accountability. The ministers, John Helmuth, Mose Yoder and Jonathan Miller, struggled to work through the issue. Emma was particularly appreciative of Mose and Cora Yoder's acceptance. Cora was as supportive as Emma could imagine a minister's wife might be. After Cora went out of her way to help the Stutzmans find a place of fellowship in the church, Emma cherished their friendship.

Tobe purchased his car while he was still a member of the Old Order Amish Church, so the delay in new church membership put the Stutzmans in a vulnerable spot. When the time came for the biannual Amish communion service, they didn't feel free to participate. So Tobe and Emma chose to make a trip back to the Amish church in Kansas for communion. Because they owned a car, which was against the *Ordnung*, they were told they would need to make a confession in the worship service. Emma was particularly embarrassed to admit their infraction of church rules in front of her extended family, but it was better than missing the Lord's Supper.

Like more-traditional Amish congregations, the Sharon Bethel Church worshipped together only every other Sunday morning. Unlike the strict Amish, however, they offered a Sunday school program on the alternating weeks. Sunday school made room for lay members to study the Scriptures, share insights, and make comments in the congregational setting. The congregants worshipped in both the English and German languages, with most of the sermons preached in the German tongue.

After the membership issue was resolved, the family seemed to thrive in the new church environment. Emma sensed that Tobe was taking increased interest in Bible study and discussions of a spiritual nature. Tobe enjoyed the singing too, much more than the chanting of the slow tunes in the more-traditional church. He often suggested hymns to sing and led them in the church service, particularly in the Sunday evening service, a new thing among the Amish. Parents with cars found it much more practical to take their families to evening services, whether on Sunday evening or for a Wednesday evening prayer meeting. The Stutzman family adopted the rhythm of going to both evening services most weeks, even when work was pressing.

As Emma entered the sanctuary on that last Sunday evening in May, she noticed that the remodeling work on the building was complete. Although the building was only five years old, the congregation had decided to install double doors in the back to make it easier to bring caskets through for funeral services. She looked for a spot on the woman's side of the meetinghouse and then moved toward it with a twin on each side.

Because Mary Edna was old enough to sit on a separate bench with other adolescent girls, she sat with Martha Miller, the preacher's daughter, who had quickly become her best friend. Tobe moved to a place on the men's side, accompanied by Perry, Glenn, and Edith. Emma was relieved that Tobe was willing to have Edith sit with him. While Emma was easily overwhelmed by the young girl's wiggling and whining, Tobe's strict manner combined with an empathic touch kept Edith in line during the church services.

During the time of singing, Tobe called out the page number of one of his recent favorites. Emma thrilled to hear him lead out in his confident tenor voice:

> Death shall not destroy my comfort.
> Christ shall guide me through the gloom;
> Down he'll send some angel convoy
> To convey my spirit home.
>
> Soon with angels I'll be marching,
> With bright glory on my brow;

Who will share my blissful portion,
Who will love my Savior now?

"Is it my imagination?" Emma asked herself, "or is Tobe freer in recent weeks to speak about death?" Perhaps he was becoming more like his mother, Anna, who loved to sing gospel songs about heaven. Or perhaps he was studying the Bible in a more-personal way. Whatever the reason, Emma was happy to see Tobe focus on something other than business for a few hours a week.

The next day, Tobe stepped back from his work long enough to ferry the three older children back and forth to the vacation Bible school offered by Sharon Bethel. On Tuesday, however, Tobe went to Chicago for business. When he got back on Wednesday, he told Emma about his latest plans for making products in the shop.

Emma listened as he talked about how pressed they were for cash at the moment, and then lost her patience. "I must get groceries this week," she insisted. "And Glenn needs a straw hat." Like most of the men in the Amish Church, Tobe took charge of the family's cash supply. Emma tried to restrain herself from asking for money unless she really needed it. She wished that he would give her money without her needing to ask, but it didn't often happen that way.

"I'll get some cash for you by tomorrow morning," Tobe promised.

Emma sighed. She wondered where he would find it.

The next day, after Tobe returned from taking the children to Bible school, he handed Emma a five-dollar bill. "I sold a couple of hog feeders to Mose Yoder for ten dollars," he said. "I'll need to use the other five to get gas for the car. I'm leaving for Wapello today to get some metal for the shop. I'll be back by suppertime."

Emma nodded impatiently.

"*Ich hab en Koppweh.* I have a headache," Tobe said as he handed her the five-dollar bill. "*Hen mir ennich aspirin dorum?* Do we have any aspirin around here?"

"*Ich kann mol gucke.* I can look once." Emma stepped in to check the cabinet. "*Nee, awwer ich kann wennich griege wann ich zu die Schtadt denochmiddaag geh.* No, but I can get some when I go to town this afternoon."

"*Nee*, that's okay," Tobe assured her. "*Ich kann duh ohne.* I can do without." A few minutes later, he got into his car and left for Wapello.

A couple of hours later, Emma asked Glenn to accompany her to town. Together they walked the short distance from their home to Kalona. She adjusted her black bonnet to shade her eyes from the late May sunshine as they came to the edge of town. She looked at Glenn's straw hat, which was badly frayed.

"We'll get your new hat at Reif's store first," she said, "then we'll pick up a few groceries."

The boy grinned. "I can't wait to show it to Dad."

They were heading for the store when a car approached them. The driver rolled down his window. It was Mose Yoder, the minister. "I have something I need to tell you," he said. "Do you want to get inside?"

Emma nodded and got into the back seat with Glenn.

"The funeral director said he has a message for you," he said. "I can take you there."

Emma nodded wordlessly. Her face paled with dread as she anticipated what the message might be.

Mose drove the few blocks to the large mansion that served as the Herman Yoder residence as well as a funeral home.

Mose pulled up to the door of the funeral home.

"You wait out here," Emma told Glenn as she made her

way toward the door. She took a deep breath and turned the knob.

A few moments later the funeral director confirmed her worst fears. "I'm so sorry to tell you that your husband was killed in a car accident today," Mr. Yoder said.

Emma sat stunned for a long moment. "Did he suffer much?" she managed to ask.

"No, Ma'am. I'm sure he died instantly. The top and side of the car were torn off."

She paused to take this in. "Was anyone else hurt?"

"No, Ma'am, he was hit by a big concrete truck. It turned over but neither of the two people in it were hurt."

"Can I see Tobe?"

"I think not. He was done up pretty bad. Let us work on the body first."

"When will I get to see him?"

"We'll bring the body out to your home tomorrow evening. The ministers will help you with funeral plans."

Emma sighed heavily. Her legs trembled as she forced herself to move toward the door.

"*Oh, die grosse Shulde!* Oh, the huge debt!" she cried out as the door closed behind her.

Slowly she moved toward Glenn, who was waiting near the car. It wasn't easy to meet his eyes.

"Dad was killed this afternoon," Emma said with ashen face. Her hands trembled as she spoke.

"What happened?" Glenn asked, pulling his tattered hat to his chest. His face grew dark with concern.

Emma choked back tears. "Dad was killed. A concrete truck hit his car."

"Now what are we going to do?" he asked plaintively.

"Mose will take us home. People will help us."

As the minister steered his car toward Emma's home, her

breath came in short gasps. Questions flitted through her mind like the barn swallows on her childhood farm. "Was Tobe driving too fast? Did he fall asleep at the wheel? Did he see the truck before it happened? Did he try to stop?"

"Mom?" Glenn's voice shook with emotion.

"Yes?"

"I was going to go along with Dad today. He told me I had to wait till some other time. It's good I didn't go."

Emma shuddered to think that she could have lost her husband and a son on the same day.

Mose dropped the two of them off at the house and said, "I'll be back before long to help make funeral plans."

"Thank you," Emma said as she dragged herself out of the car. She walked into the house, hung up her bonnet, and sank into an armchair. Glenn stood nearby, sober faced and silent. He held his worn hat in his hand.

The other five children quickly gathered around Emma's chair. The twins clung to Emma's dress as she explained what had happened. The others stood nearby, wide-eyed and worried.

"*Wo is da Datt*? Where is Dad?" Edith was trying to catch up with the conversation.

"*Da Datt is dot*. Dad is dead," Mary Edna explained. "They're going to bring him here in a coffin."

"To our house? Today?"

"Not today," Mary Edna replied. "Tomorrow."

Edith shook her head, her thin lips in a pout.

Emma glanced around at the unfinished house with some embarrassment. "We should do a little straightening up around here," Emma said. "There'll be people coming here before long. Let's get these toys off the floor."

A few moments later Fred Nisly knocked at the door. He was Emma's well-loved uncle, who served as an Amish minister. Although it was Thursday afternoon, he was dressed in his Sunday suit and wore his black hat. Emma invited him in and offered to take his hat.

Fred offered a few words of consolation and then said, "I went with the funeral director to pick up the body where the accident happened. Now I'm here to help make funeral arrangements."

Emma's family looked on as she gathered the strength to reply. "I don't know what to do. I feel completely helpless."

"Don't worry about anything," Fred said. "We'll take care of everything."

Emma breathed a sigh of relief. As a farmer-preacher in the Amish Church, Fred had long experience with funerals. Although Tobe and Emma had left the Old Order Amish Church, she was confident that Fred wouldn't abandon them at a time like this. He knew her dire financial situation, too. Fred and his wife, Katie, had invested money in Tobe's business.

After they were seated at the dining room table, Fred said, "I've been thinking you might want to have a funeral in both Iowa and Kansas."

Emma nodded. She certainly wanted to have Tobe buried back home. But now that their family had lived in Iowa for five years, Tobe was well known here. Surely many of his friends and business associates would want to pay their last respects to him in the Kalona area.

"But won't that make too much expense? I don't have any money."

"Don't worry about the expense."

"Thank you." She brushed the tears off her cheeks with her hankie. "When can we call the folks in Kansas?" she asked. "I'm sure that Tobe's family will want to know as soon as possible. And my family too."

"Let's wait to call them until we have the funeral arrangements made. That way we can tell them all the details with only one long-distance call."

"I hope some of my relatives can come."

"We will call them this evening, as soon as we know the details." The grace and ease with which he spoke belied the authority in his voice.

Emma's shoulders sank. Long-distance calls were expensive, but it seemed important to call right away.

"I want my bottle," Erma begged as she tugged at Emma's skirt.

Emma turned toward her oldest daughter. "Mary Edna, could you please take the babies to the other room? Or maybe you can take them outside to play."

"Okay, Mom." The fourteen-year-old took the twins by the hand. "Erma, I'll get you a bottle."

"Take Edith too." Emma's voice was weary.

Mary Edna nodded. "Come, Edith. Let's go outside."

The children were going out the door when Mose Yoder returned. Fred Nisly rose from his seat and greeted his fellow minister. They sat together at the table.

"I suppose you'll want to have the funeral at Sharon Bethel," Fred said to Mose.

"Yes, I think we should have it at our church since Tobe and Emma are members with us," Moses said. "I suppose the service should be mostly in English, with some German."

Emma nodded in agreement. She anticipated, however, that the folks in Kansas would insist on a German service there. Tobe's mother Anna was a stickler for German. At times she taught German classes for the young.

Emma listened as the two men planned the service. She gave an occasional nod or spoke as requested. She felt she had little to say.

It was suppertime when the two men rose to leave. "I'll check with all of the people that we've chosen to take part in the service," Mose said as he moved toward the door.

"Let's finalize the plans as soon as we can," Fred said as he reached for his hat. "We want to make a call to Kansas yet this evening."

Soon after the two men left, other folks from the neighborhood arrived to offer condolences and assistance. Several women greeted Emma with a hug. It was a rare show of empathy, since the Amish community frowned on displays of physical affection even between parents and children. Hugging was reserved for moments such as this.

A number of women came with dishes of food in hand. Emma forced herself to eat a few bites with the children for supper as her neighbors scurried around the unfinished kitchen.

Sympathizers came and went throughout the evening. The sun had long set when Fred Nisly made the long-distance phone call to notify Tobe and Emma's relatives in Kansas. He called Emma's brother Raymond Nisly and asked him to relay the news to others. Unlike Tobe or Emma's parents, Raymond was part of a church that allowed a telephone. Since Raymond lived less than two miles from the place where Tobe's parents were staying, he promised to notify them as well as the rest of Emma and Tobe's close relatives.

The next morning, Emma learned that a carload of mourners from Kansas was on the way to Iowa. All three of Tobe's brothers were coming, she was told, as well as Emma's mother and one of Emma's sisters. She breathed a deep sigh of anticipation.

The group of mourners in Emma's home thinned out as the night advanced. It was near midnight when she finally got all of the children settled in bed. The thin curtains and open ceilings allowed for little privacy from the hum of conversation among sympathizers. A friend offered to keep watch throughout the night. Emma thanked her and headed for her bed.

She lay quietly, longing for the comfort of sleep. Instead her mind churned over the day's events. Was it only at noon today that Tobe had picked up the children from vacation Bible school? Or was it yesterday?

"I know the men said that Tobe had an accident, but maybe it was someone else. If the man was badly hurt, maybe they got the wrong person. Maybe it just looked like Tobe. Maybe Tobe forgot to tell me that he was going to New York or somewhere and he'll come back tomorrow. He was just in Chicago a couple of days ago.

"But Uncle Fred said he went along with the undertaker to pick up the body. He knows Tobe and he knows the car. And I suppose they looked in Tobe's billfold for identification. I wonder if he had any money in his pocket. He said he was out of cash. We're going to need money for groceries soon."

Emma prayed for sleep, but it would not come. A cacophony of voices from the evening's guests echoed in her head.

"Tobe was such a strong man. It doesn't seem possible that he's gone."

"I'll always remember Tobe for those cabinets he made for me. I really like them."

"I enjoyed working for Tobe. He always looked on the bright side, even if things weren't going like he thought they should."

"Those big companies in Chicago should have been more patient. Tobe would eventually have found a way to pay them back."

"I never met anyone else like Tobe. He was a genius at inventing things. And he had such a good eye for measurements."

"I loved to visit with Tobe. He was quite a talker."

"It must have been the other driver's fault. Tobe wasn't a careless driver."

"Just forget about that money you owed us. It wasn't that much, and I'm sure the Lord will provide for us without it."

"I've noticed that Tobe seemed to be more spiritual lately."

"We all know that he's in a better place now."

"I'm sure that God meant it for the good."

"God will take care of you."

Emma wondered what she was to say in the face of all the comments people made. The natural thing for her to do was to nod or smile. She had always depended on Tobe to carry the burden of conversation, particularly in groups. While words came easily for Tobe, she enjoyed listening more than talking. It was one of the reasons she'd felt drawn to him in the first place. She'd been captured by Tobe's visionary plans, his entertaining accounts of encounters with strangers, his quick retorts to challengers.

Others had been captivated by Tobe's talk as well. How else could Tobe have persuaded hard-nosed businessmen to loan him cash for his enterprise with only a handshake to close the deal? With Tobe gone, the burden of speaking for the family would fall on her.

Tears ran down her cheeks and onto her pillow as she considered the journey ahead. How was she to rear the children by herself? It took much of her energy just to care for Edith, with all of her special needs.

She surely couldn't run the business. And with no regular income, she wouldn't be able to pay rent. She'd probably need to move out of this house soon.

Emma wondered what was in Tobe's mind just before the accident happened. Was he thinking about the business? About her? Or the children? Maybe he was daydreaming and forgot to watch the road. Or maybe his headache got so bad that he couldn't concentrate. Perhaps if she would have had aspirin in the house, this wouldn't have happened.

She wished she had said a last goodbye before he left for Wapello. If she'd only have known what was to happen, she would have pressed a kiss to his lips and assured him of her love.

Emma heard one of the children mumble in sleep. Were the children dreaming of Tobe? How would they get along without their father?

Although it was two o'clock before Emma managed to sleep, she awoke to the brightness of the early June sun. She had hardly finished breakfast with the children when neighbors began to drop by. Many brought food. Several offered to help with the children. There were a dozen people in the house when Emma's relatives arrived from Kansas. After greetings all around, Emma showed her relatives a copy of the obituary the funeral home had brought to the house.

> Tobias J. Stutzman, son of John and Anna (Miller) Stutzman, was born at Thomas, Oklahoma, October 21, 1918, and died May 31, 1956, at the age of 37 years, 6 months, and 10 days. He was married to Emma Nisly in Hutchinson, Kansas, October 10, 1940. Survivors included his widow, three daughters, and three sons: Mary, 14, Perry, 13, Glenn, 11, Edith, 8, and twins Ervin and Erma, 3. Also his parents and three brothers, Ervin, Clarence, and Perry, all of Hutchinson, Kansas.

> The call was sudden, the shock severe;
> Little did we think his end so near.

Only those bereft can tell
The sadness of parting without a farewell.

Tears trickled onto her cheeks as she watched her family read the short script. It seemed unreal, as though it were happening to someone else.

At noon, the kitchen helpers served a sumptuous dinner—not that Emma ate much. The gnawing inside robbed her of any appetite. She picked at her food while listening to conversations among the others.

Immediately after dinner, Tobe's three brothers drove to the site of the accident. "We want to learn more about how the accident happened," Tobe's brother Ervin J. said.

Clarence nodded, "We're going to talk to the sheriff if possible."

"And arrange to get the car back into town," L. Perry added.

After supper that evening, nearly thirty mourners joined Emma and her relatives for the wake. Together they awaited the arrival of Tobe's body from the funeral home. Mose and Cora distributed hymnals from the Sharon Bethel Church. "Let's begin with number 496," someone called out. The group sang a cappella, blending their voices in four-part harmony:

We are going down the valley, one by one,
With our faces tow'rd the setting of the sun;
Down the valley where the mournful cypress grows,
Where the stream of death in silence onward flows.

Emma had sung the song many times, but this time when she tried to join in, the words caught in her throat:

We are going down the valley, one by one,
When the labors of the weary day are done;
One by one, the cares of earth forever past,
We shall stand upon the river bank at last.

We are going down the valley, one by one,
Human comrade you or I will there have none;
But a tender hand will guide us lest we fall,
Christ is going down the valley with us all.

"Yes," Emma assured herself, "Tobe had believed in Christ. He had been baptized and joined the church." She took particular comfort in hearing about Tobe's parting words to a friend, Harlan Stubbs, on the morning of the accident: "If I don't see you again, I'll see you in heaven." Tobe wasn't quick to use such words.

It was nearly 9:30 p.m. when the hearse from Yoder's Funeral Home pulled into the driveway. The room turned silent as the funeral director and a helper carried the casket into the room. "How about putting the casket right here, Mrs. Stutzman?" Mr. Yoder asked.

Emma nodded.

Clarence and L. Perry quickly made room by moving two of the backless benches brought from the church. The funeral attendants set the casket in place and propped open the lid. The coffin was made of mahogany wood crafted by a local artisan. It was the moment that Emma had been longing for. But now that everyone's eyes were on her, she hesitated. Did she really want to see Tobe in this condition? What if she was really disappointed by what she saw? What if she lost her composure while everyone was watching?

Emma's mother, Mary, made the first move. She took Emma's arm and stepped toward the casket. Together they stood gazing at Tobe's disfigured body. The funeral director's craft only partly hid the damage wreaked by shattered glass and ripping metal. The mourners resumed their singing as Emma reached out to stroke Tobe's chest.

> When my life work is ended, and I cross the
> swelling tide,
> When the bright and glorious morning I shall see;
> I shall know my Redeemer when I reach the other
> side,
> And his smile will be the first to welcome me.

> I shall know him, I shall know him,
> And redeem'd by his side I shall stand,
> I shall know him, I shall know him,
> By the prints of the nails in his hand.

A chill ran through Emma's being as she touched Tobe's body. This was not like the man she had known and loved.

"Mom, I want to see." Three year old Ervin tugged at her skirt.

She picked up the young child and held him over Tobe's lifeless body. The child reached out a curious hand and touched his father's face and neck. He frowned and pulled back his hand. "*Er schpiert grimmlich*. He feels crumbly," he said.

Emma set Ervin back down on the floor. "It's past time for the children to be in bed," she said to Mary Edna, who had joined her at the casket.

"I'll take them," Mary Edna offered.

"I'll help too," Emma's mother said.

Emma sat down close to the casket and drew a long breath. She watched numbly as the mourners took turns at the open casket.

By eleven o'clock, everyone but the family had left. "Uncle Fred and Katie said they'd have room for several of you to sleep at their house," Emma told her brothers.

"We have other places to stay," Clarence said. "I'll drop everybody off with my car."

"I'm going to stay here with you," Emma's mother Mary said. "I can sleep on the sofa. Emma, you need your rest. Right after the funeral tomorrow, we'll be driving to Kansas."

Emma took a deep breath as she headed for her bedroom. Tomorrow was sure to be a very long day.

3

A Sad Farewell

The next morning dawned bright and clear. By 9:30 a.m. a congregation of nearly five hundred mourners had crowded into the church building at Sharon Bethel. The parking lot was full of cars and buggies.

Emma sat on the front bench on the right-hand side of the meetinghouse, accompanied by her children. Mose Yoder took charge of the service. He was assisted by two other ministers, including Tobe's uncle David A. Miller from Oklahoma. Brother Yoder opened the service and called for congregational singing. The audience sang in both German and English. An octet of four men and four women sang from the rear of the audience; funerals provided the rare occasion when special music was permitted. The sermon and eulogy were presented in English, favoring the attendees who could not understand German.

Following the service, the undertaker loaded the body into the waiting hearse and took it to the train station for shipment to Kansas. Not long afterward, Emma and her family climbed into Mose and Cora Yoder's car to leave for Hutchinson, Kansas. Since Edith had suffered an unusual number of epileptic seizures in the two days since Tobe's death, Emma was overwhelmed with the prospect of thirteen hours of travel with Edith in the car. Emma deemed it best to leave her behind with nearby neighbors named Noah and Sarah Weaver.

Noah and Sarah knew Edith well. Emma's older children had spent many hours on their farm, which was only a half mile away. They had even stayed overnight at times when Tobe and Emma were traveling. Their maiden daughter Arvilla was thoroughly familiar with Tobe's business, having served for a time as his bookkeeper. All three members of the Weaver family demonstrated compassion for Edith, so Emma felt quite comfortable in leaving her eight-year-old daughter there.

When Emma and her children arrived in Hutchinson the next morning, they went to the home of Mattie Miller, where Tobe's parents were staying. It was also the home where Tobe's body had been taken. By an ironic coincidence, Tobe's body lay in the casket next to the room where Tobe and Emma had been married.

After lunch several attendants transported the body a few miles to the Albert Yoder residence, where they placed it inside a tin farm shed known to locals as a round top. This is where the Old Order Amish funeral was to be held on Sunday afternoon. The host, Albert Yoder, had made careful preparations. The concrete floor was swept clean. Most of the farm machinery had been moved outside, leaving room for several dozen rows of backless gray benches. Mourners began to arrive in cars as well as buggies. They parked on the sandy surface of the farmyard or on the browning grass and then huddled in small groups or made their way quietly to the round top.

The afternoon sun blazed like an overhead furnace. Emma stood outside under a shade tree, near her aunt Lizzie.

"Raising children alone is such a responsibility," Emma

said to Lizzie. To rear children to walk in the plain and simple way of the Amish was what she thought of as her highest calling in life. But nothing weighed on her more than the thought that Tobe would not be able to help bring up their offspring. She had always assumed that leading a family was meant to be a man's job.

Lizzie nodded and squeezed her hand as tears sprang to her eyes. After some moments, they both made their way to the round top. Ervin wiggled in Emma's arms, begging to walk on his own. His white shirt was soaked with sweat.

Cora Yoder stepped forward. "I'll take him into the house."

Emma sighed. "Thank you. He needs a nap."

Emma walked to the front row and sat near the casket in the bare shed. There were no flowers. Several ministers walked to the front and sat down on a backless bench. They watched as John D. Yoder, the white-bearded Amish bishop, rose to address the congregation. He greeted the congregation in German, acknowledging the solemnity of the occasion. He then read a portion of Scripture and made a number of comments in English. Unlike the service in Iowa, the Kansas Amish did not sing. While singing at the wake was customary, funerals were a time of mourning without song.

The heat in the tin shed was sweltering. Although the wide implement doors were left open, there was little air movement. A baby cried in the mother's arms, exhausted by the heat. Boys and girls squirmed in their seats, worn out by the unforgiving surface of wooden benches. Women fanned themselves with their handkerchiefs. Sweat beaded on the men's bearded faces and wet their broad backs. In the Amish community, a funeral was an event for all ages, just like their worship services.

Stirred by a slight breeze, the branches of the elm trees outside scratched rudely against the tin roof of the round top. A train whistled its warning as it approached the near-by crossing on the railroad that angled out of Hutchinson toward the small town of Partridge, carrying passengers and freight into the Southwest. The railroad ran just a few hundred yards to the north of the homestead, so the long train's rumbling made it hard to hear the words being spoken in the service. Tractor-trailers roared by on Highway 61, paralleling the railroad track.

In the main sermon, David A. Miller quoted several verses from the Bible, then expounded on them. He assured the congregation of a better life beyond the grave for those who came to God through Jesus Christ. He explained that it was not through personal merit or good works that one found salvation and eternal life. Only God's grace made it possible to enter heaven.

David spoke favorably about his deceased nephew. He lauded Tobe's natural abilities, his high energy level, and his willingness to help others. Then he posed a question to the congregation: "If Tobias had put that same kind of energy into spiritual work and preaching, would he have been accepted among his people?"

Emma wondered if the question might not apply just as aptly to David's own ministry. Detractors sometimes responded to his enthusiastic preaching with caustic criticism.

David also praised Tobe's unique ability to work and design products. He extolled Tobe's care for others and asserted, "I have never seen him angry." Then he dropped his voice and admitted that Tobe had some difficulty managing money in his business. But in a bold voice he proclaimed, "If Tobe had lived, he would likely have become a millionaire."

Emma was grateful for David's confidence. He himself was a good manager of money.

When the preaching service ended, people paid their

last respects. An attendant lifted the lid of the casket and braced it open. Ushers released the congregants row by row to file by the coffin. The family silently observed from the front rows. Young and old paused by the bier, each paying silent respect. Several men plunged their calloused hands into the pockets of their handmade trousers to pull out huge white handkerchiefs. They blew their noses and wiped the tears off their weather-beaten faces as they stepped outside the building. Women dabbed at tears with handkerchiefs as they greeted Emma with a handshake.

After the crowd of 625 mourners had filed by, the family gathered around for a final farewell before the ushers closed the lid. Emma reached to stroke Tobe's body a final time before an attendant stepped forward to close the lid and put several screws in the wooden top. Then six pallbearers lifted the casket and gently carried it to a wooden wagon. The spring wagon would need to go slowly, lest the ride be too bumpy. The horse switched its tail at a group of pesky flies.

Tobe's brothers had suggested that an automotive hearse be employed. Tobe's mother wouldn't hear of it. She said it wouldn't do to have a hearse at an Old Order Amish funeral, even if her son had recently joined a more-progressive church.

Emma climbed into a buggy with her family. They followed the hearse west on the gravel road the short distance to the West Center Amish Cemetery. White foam flecked the corners of the horse's bridle and dropped to the browning grass as they approached the entrance. An attendant slid off the spring wagon to open the gates. He uncoupled the short chain and swung open the two hinged gates made of woven wire stretched over metal-pipe frames.

Many grave markers lined the graveyard. Nearly all the monuments looked alike—round-topped slabs made of poured concrete. Some engravings were badly faded, the words

rendered illegible by exposure to the elements. A few grave-
stones kept vigil at the head of shrinking mounds, evidence of
recent burials. Without the benefit of concrete vaults or water-
proof caskets, the rounded soil gradually sank until it was level
with its surroundings.

Knotted ropes soon choked the rusty hitching rail that
bordered the burial ground. The horses drew up quickly, eager
to stand in the shade of the hedge trees planted by early set-
tlers along the fencerow. Buggies tipped sharply as passengers
disembarked. Cars pulled off into the shallow ditches on both
sides of the gravel road. Emma wiped the sweat off her face as
the crowd of mourners swelled around her. Soon there were
more than a hundred.

The pallbearers slid the casket off the back of the wagon
and carried it toward the grave. Emma followed close behind.
Dry prairie sod mixed with clay lay beside the yawning hole,
hand-dug by volunteers the day before. Several spades angled
out of the earthen pile. Three wooden boards spanned the top
of the grave. Emma watched as the pallbearers gently laid the
casket onto the boards. Bishop Yoder motioned the mourners
toward one side of the cavity. Emma silently stepped up to the
grave, with her extended family standing nearby.

Emma glanced over at Ervin, who squirmed restlessly in
Cora Yoder's arms. The young boy pointed toward the grave.
Noah Nisly, Emma's stepfather, admonished the woman, "*Du
kannscht ihn annestelle; er kann selwert schteh.* You can let him
down; he can stand by himself." Cora nodded and released the
wiggling toddler. The young boy edged toward the wooden
box that held his father's still body.

The assembly listened reverently as a small ensemble raised
its voice in song. Then the bishop stepped forward, perspiration beading his broad forehead. He was dressed in black
trousers, a long-sleeved white shirt, and a black suit coat fas-

tened with small hooks and eyes. After he comforted the mourners with words from several passages of Scripture, he quoted the familiar words of the committal:

> Forasmuch as it has pleased Almighty God, in his wise providence, to take out of this world the soul of the departed, we commit the body to the ground; earth to earth, ashes to ashes, dust to dust, and commit the soul to God who gave it. . . .

The men removed their hats as the minister bowed his head to pray. In the brief silence, a meadowlark sang from the fence at the edge of the yard. The preacher's "Amen" was accented by the whistle of an approaching train on the tracks that ran close by.

Emma stepped back as the attendants prepared for the burial. Holding opposite ends of two braided hemp ropes, four men swung the loops under the wooden coffin. As they hoisted it off its wooden supports, two assistants drew away the boards that spanned the grave. The men lowered the coffin into the rough wooden box that lined the grave, playing out the ropes hand over hand. The bier sank unevenly into the rough box and then leveled as the ropes slackened against the bottom. On silent cue, the men on one side dropped their ends of the ropes. The other pair tugged on the remaining ends, dragging the ropes out of the hole. After they had laid planks over the box to keep out the soil, several men picked up spades and began shoveling earth into the hole. After a few minutes, others stepped forward to take a turn with the spades. All the mourners watched as they piled the dirt onto the grave until it stood as a heap, with pieces of sod on top.

Emma watched numbly as the men tossed the last few clods of dirt onto Tobe's final resting place. She wiped her face with her embroidered white handkerchief as she turned from the grave and walked away.

The parched grass crunched beneath Emma's feet as she walked the two dozen yards from the gravesite back to the gravel road. Heat waves shimmered across the Kansas prairie as she hoisted the twins into the backseat of the buggy. Perry, her oldest son, unhitched the horse and took the reins as Emma stepped up into the buggy.

As the many mourners left the graveyard, most made their way east, toward the heart of the Amish settlement. Emma's family turned toward the west. She sighed deeply as they pulled away from the burial ground. She was relieved that the two funerals were behind her now, as were the long vigils by the open casket. Tobe's body lay still now, at rest after years of frenetic efforts to establish a business. Emma reflected that she had found little time to rest during those years. There would likely be even less now. As the buggy reached the first intersection, Emma took a long look to her left. She surveyed the site where she and Tobe had taken up housekeeping and the four oldest children had been born. It was the place where Tobe had started his woodworking business before moving the shop and the family a couple of miles further east along Highway 61. The weathered two-story clapboard house and other outbuildings were all gone now, torn down by a farmer expanding his tillable land. Only a pile of cement slabs remained. As she looked over the debris, Emma felt as though her own life had been reduced to rubble.

As the family rode along in silence, difficult questions pestered her mind like flies at a sweet-corn husking. The biggest questions had to do with location. Where was she going to live? She would need to make that decision in the next few days. It only seemed logical for her to move back to Kansas, to be close to her extended family.

Emma hadn't favored the move to Iowa in the first place. Tobe had convinced her that the move was necessary to help Edith find specialized medical care. Somehow that reason seemed more acceptable than the draw of better business contacts during a time when financial loans were more difficult to secure in Kansas.

More than once during their stay in Iowa, Emma had hinted that it might be time to move back to Kansas. Tobe countered with his sense that it was God's will to stay. Emma didn't argue with Tobe, not wanting to offend God by stepping out of submission to her husband.

Now that Tobe was gone, Emma had little desire to stay in Iowa. But where was she to find the money to move? It was true that she still owned half of the small property that Tobe and she had purchased in 1948 along Highway 61 in Kansas. As part of the bankruptcy proceedings forced on Tobe in 1954, a compassionate judge and a competent attorney had allowed the property to be divided. Tobe's brother Ervin had purchased one-half interest. Those proceeds were now in the court's hands, waiting to be distributed among Tobe's creditors. Emma reckoned that her half might be worth about $4,000.

Also, Emma anticipated an annual payment from the rent of forty acres of ground as a distribution from her father's estate. She recalled Tobe's anger at the time when it had been willed to her brother Raymond. Now she could be grateful that they hadn't lost it to hungry creditors searching for assets.

Emma worried most about her six children. How could she possibly care for them by herself? How could she help them grow up to behave like responsible adults? Tobe had always been the one to carry out parental discipline in the household.

Emma worried most about Edith. Her mental retardation

and speech impediment sometimes led the other children to tease her until her sunny disposition turned dark. At times she reacted to Emma's attempts at discipline with obstinate stubbornness. Since it tore at Emma's heart to speak sternly to Edith, she had relied on Tobe to subdue their daughter's childish will.

Edith seemed to sense her father's compassion even when his manner turned stern. Tobe was the one who had insisted that they find a surgeon to straighten out Emma's crossed left eye. Though their search proved fruitless, they found a chiropractor in eastern Iowa who promised to help the child through alternative means. The doctor's promises proved hollow; Edith went on to develop grand mal epileptic seizures.

Like Edith, Emma's three-year-old twins often taxed Emma's patience. They seemed even more energetic and demanding than their older siblings had been. The older children often doted on the young twins, but at other times their persistent teasing pushed Emma's patience to the limit.

A move back to Kansas would mean that the family would need to adjust back into the Old Order Amish Church. Although Emma didn't drive, she had gotten used to having a car available for transportation. Since Tobe had sold the horse, she'd need to buy or borrow another one to pull their family-sized buggy.

How was she to decide what to do? Perhaps tomorrow evening, at a meeting planned by her siblings and in-laws, she would find the guidance she needed. Now that Tobe's death had nearly knocked Emma's feet out from under her, she instinctively reached out to her family so they could steady her.

The next morning dawned warm and clear—a perfect day for baling the alfalfa hay lying mown in the fields. For most church members, however, haymaking would have to wait until the afternoon. Although it was Monday, a church service was being held at the Albert Yoder residence in honor of several visiting ministers in the area. The church benches used for Tobe's funeral now doubled for a preaching meeting, again in the round topped storage shed.

Emma dragged herself to the church service along with her children. She found some small comfort in the kisses of greeting, the empathic looks, and the heartfelt expressions of sympathy. But she was relieved when the service was over. She felt exhausted.

Because it was a workday, the congregation did not linger after the service. Shortly after the bishop pronounced the benediction, the men hurried off to hitch the horses. "Gotta make hay while the suns shines," one of the men commented as he left the service.

After a relaxed dinner at a friend's home, Emma went to her mother's home for the remainder of the afternoon. Mother Mary Nisly was a much-loved matriarch in the church, her door unlatched to friend and stranger alike. After her first husband's death in 1953, Mary had married Noah Nisly. Although Noah was a double first cousin of Mary's first husband, Levi Nisly, he was much more abrupt in his manner. Emma was still adjusting to him as a stepfather.

Mother Nisly showed the children to the toy closet and then motioned Emma to an armchair.

"How have you been sleeping?" Mother Nisly asked gently.

"Not so good."

"I'll watch the children. You go take a nap. The bed in the basement is the coolest spot in the house today."

"Thank you. I'll do that."

Emma made her way down the stairs and sank into the bed. In a few moments she fell asleep.

Later, after the supper dishes were done, all of Emma's brothers and sisters dropped by. They joined kitchen chairs with the stuffed sofa, living room chairs, and rocker to form a circle around the perimeter of the living room. Emma leaned forward with anticipation. Now was the time to gather counsel on hard questions.

After a few pleasantries, her brother Raymond spoke to the most important issue: "I think it would be best if you could move back to Kansas."

"I agree," said Emma's brother Henry. "We could help you so much better if you were here."

"But I don't know how I can afford to move," Emma worried aloud.

"Uncle Fred spoke to me about that," Raymond responded. "He said he would be willing to help you. I can haul a load with my truck."

Emma pursed her lips. "Tobe's parents said we could live in their house for a few months since they are living with Mattie Miller for now. But I don't know what we would do after that."

Mother Nisly spoke up. "I'm willing to give you some acreage at the front of the shelterbelt if you want to live there."

Emma reflected on that for a moment and then nodded in appreciation. The idea pleased her a lot. The belt of trees occupied a strip along the southern edge of the eighty-acre home farm, now tilled by Emma's brother Raymond. As a teenager, Emma had helped to water the seedlings planted by the federal government as a conservation project during the Depression years in the 1930s.

"But I don't see how I could afford a house," she worried out loud.

"You might be able to buy one of the homes that are up for sale in South Hutchinson," Henry suggested. "They're going to move a bunch of houses to make room for the new Woody Seat Freeway. They'll probably go pretty cheap." Henry always kept a sharp eye on the latest construction developments as well as the real estate market.

"But wouldn't it be expensive to move one of those homes six miles from South Hutch to there?" Emma asked.

"Maybe so, but if you got the house cheap enough, it might be well worth it," Henry ventured.

"Don't you still have part interest in the house and shop at Stutzman Brothers?" Raymond inquired.

"Yes."

"The business is doing well there. He might be able to buy out your half. That would give you some cash to buy a house," Raymond suggested.

"I'd be willing to give some of my labor to help build a house," Alvin volunteered. He was married to Emma's younger sister Barbara. "We could build a cement-block house for a real reasonable price. I'm sure that we could find men who would donate some of their time to help build it."

"I imagine that Clarence Stutzman would be willing to put his building crew to work on the house," Raymond suggested. "He could help design it and get materials at a good price."

It was true. Tobe's brother Clarence was building new homes in Hutchinson.

"Whether we move a house from town or build one," Alvin said, "if we get started soon, we could be done before the snow falls."

Heads nodded around the circle.

Emma breathed a sigh of relief. It would feel so good to come back to Kansas. "I'll need to go back to Iowa soon to finish up things there," she observed. "Clarence said he'd take me."

In the silence that followed, Emma wrung her white handkerchief with the embroidered corners. Then she voiced the concern that most worried her the most. "I'm not sure what to do with Edith," she said. "I don't see how I'm going to be able to take care of her."

The question hung in the air for a time until Barbara spoke. "I could help take care of her sometimes."

A couple of the other women nodded, as though to volunteer their own services.

"I'm definitely going to need some help." Emma looked down as she spoke.

Although they talked a bit longer, the matter wasn't settled in Emma's mind when everyone got up to leave. Her shoulders sagged with the weight of the decision. She mulled over the question of what to do with Edith for the next few days as she visited with friends and family.

4

Leaving Iowa

The following Monday, Emma and her five children piled into Clarence's midsized sedan at 4:00 a.m. for the trip back to Iowa. It was the second trip that Clarence was making to Iowa on behalf of his deceased brother.

"Have you decided for sure where you're going to live?" Clarence asked Emma as they drove along.

"Yes, I'm going to move back to Kansas by the end of this month. Tobe's folks said we could live in their house for a little while, since they're staying with Mattie."

"Good. I'm sure there's plenty for the boys to do around here."

"Raymond said the boys can help on the farm. And they might be able to help at the Stutzman Brothers' shop. Or the produce patch."

"Good." Clarence opened the cozy wing window as he spoke, adjusting it so that a stream of the cool morning air flowed across his face. "Do you know yet where you'll live after that?"

"My mother is giving me an acre at the front of the shelterbelt. We'll build there or move something in."

Clarence nodded approval. "My crew could build you a nice little house in there," he said.

Although the rest of the trip seemed long in the summer heat, the travelers made good time, arriving in Iowa a little after 5:00 p.m. After a quick supper, Emma and the older children made their way to the garden.

"My, these weeds have grown since we were gone," Emma clucked as she surveyed the garden. "The strawberries and the peas must be picked. Mary Edna, go get a bucket."

The children picked the ripe produce while Clarence drove Emma to the Weaver home to pick up her daughter Edith. "I'll just stay in the car," he said as he pulled up to the house.

Edith spied Emma and came running across the corner of the yard. "Hi, Mama," she said. "*Tschell* I go *wit chue*? Shall I go with you?" Edith often mixed English with German in her own way of speaking.

"Yes, Edith, you will come home with me," Emma replied as she squeezed the child to her chest.

Just then Sarah Weaver appeared at the front door. "Come in." She beckoned with one hand while holding the screen door open with the other.

Emma stepped inside the house and shook Sarah's outstretched hand.

"How did Edith do?" Emma asked.

"She did really well. She only had two seizures while you were gone."

Arvilla stepped in from the kitchen. "I think Edith likes it here."

"Thank you for taking care of her." Emma paused for a moment and then spoke with a slight tremble in her voice. "I've decided to move to Kansas."

"Oh," said Sarah. "We will surely miss you. But I can't blame you for wanting to move since your family lives there."

"Yes, it's best to be near them. I don't . . . ," Emma paused. She wasn't yet sure what to say about Edith.

"Well," said Sarah. "If there's anything we can do to help you get ready to move, just let us know."

"Thank you," Emma said. "I think we'd better go now. Clarence is waiting in the car."

She stepped back into the dimming daylight to see Edith cradling a kitty in her arms.

"Put it down, it's time to go," Emma said.

Edith's lips curled into a frown as she dropped the cat to the ground. "*Otay, dann.* Okay then," she said. She waved to the cat as it made its way toward the barn. "*Bei, bei, tittie tat. Ich muss geh nau.* Bye, bye, kittie cat. I must go now." Edith climbed into the backseat of the car as Clarence started the engine. Emma waved to Sarah and Arvilla through the open window as they drove out the lane.

That evening as Emma washed the dishes that had been stacked after supper, she heard Edith and Glenn playing in the other room.

"I'm going to get your tittie tat," Glenn teased.

"*No, Den! Es mei tittie tat.* No, Glenn. It's my kittie cat."

"I'm going to pull its tail."

"*Nee! Doh away!* No, go away!"

"I'm going to pull your dolly's hair."

"*Nee! Mollie is mei dollie.*"

There was a brief silence and then a thump on the floor.

"Mom, come quick!" Glenn shouted.

Emma dried her hands on her apron as she headed for the bedroom. Edith was on the floor, her arms flailing and feet thrashing. Emma knelt over the child and stroked her body. "It's okay, Edith, I'm here."

After a minute or so, Edith quieted down and opened her eyes.

"Mom."

"Yes, Edith."

"I don't *fiehl doot. Ich bin nass.* I don't feel good. I wet myself."

"*Ich wisse. Kumm zu die Kammer.* I know. Come to the bedroom." Emma helped Edith up from the floor. Then she reached down to pick up the eyeglasses that Edith had unintentionally flung from her face."

Edith put them on and headed for the bedroom.

After helping to change Edith's underclothes, Emma headed back to the kitchen.

"Glenn, I wish you'd stop teasing her."

"Okay, Mom," he said in a chastened tone as Emma put her hands back into the dishwater.

Erma toddled up to Emma and tugged on her skirt. "*Boddel, Boddel.* Bottle, bottle."

"*Du bischt zu alt fer en Boddel.* You're too old for a bottle," said Glenn, who was within earshot.

"Oh, go ahead and give it to her." Emma motioned to Mary Edna. She couldn't bear to hear the child whine.

Emma felt the strength draining from her arms as she scrubbed the stainless-steel pot she had used to cook the potatoes. "Why do the boys tease Edith so? Don't they realize how wrong it is to take advantage of her handicap? Don't they know that they might be causing her seizures?" Her lips moved in an unspoken prayer as she wrung out the dishrag and wiped off the countertop.

• • • •

The next day, before Clarence left for Kansas, Emma asked if he might help carry the washing machine up from the basement. "I'm tired of carrying water up and down the stairs to do my wash," she said, "but for some reason, Tobe thought I should do my wash down here."

"Well, hey," Clarence said, "let's make it as easy as we can."

When they had the machine in its new place upstairs, Clarence surprised Emma with a proposal. "I've been doing a little research," he said. "I learned that you could collect Social Security."

"How would that work?" she asked. She had not thought of such a thing.

"Tobe paid Social Security taxes for the business," Clarence explained. "Now as his widow, you can collect. You could get a monthly check for the rest of your life. And you can get an amount for each of the children until they turn eighteen years old. Since Edith is retarded, you might be able to collect for her the rest of her life."

Emma's mouth dropped. "How much would I get?"

"I'm not sure yet. First we'll need to pay the amount that Tobe owed in back taxes. The people at the Social Security office will let us know."

"What do I need to do to get started?"

"Just let me know if you want to apply, and I'll work it out."

"I suppose I should talk to my brother Raymond first. He knows about these kinds of things."

Emma was excited by the possibility that she could get a monthly support check. A regular check, even if small, would be a relief.

She was pondering her good fortune when Sarah Weaver dropped by later that afternoon. "Are you taking Edith with you to Kansas?" Sarah asked.

"I guess so," Emma said. "I don't know what else to do. Someone thought maybe I could put her in a home. But I can't afford that."

Sarah laid her hand on Emma's arm. "It would be nice if she could stay here in Iowa. We wouldn't want you to put her into a state home. Don't put her anywhere until I have time to talk to Arvilla about it. She might agree to take care of her for a while."

Emma shook her head. "I can't ask you to do that."

Sarah turned to go. "I'll talk to Arvilla this evening. If she's interested, I'll let you know." With that, she stepped outside into the sunshine.

Emma's stomach churned as she prepared supper. On the one hand, it would be a relief to give Edith into the Weaver family's care. Her deep weariness bordered on panic as she thought of caring for Edith while setting up a new household in Kansas. Edith might do better at the Weaver's house.

On the other hand, how could she give up her own flesh and blood? What would Tobe think if he were alive? What would the people in Kansas think? Might their pity turn to contempt? Besides, the Weaver family was poor. They weren't even relatives. They had little money for the doctor bills. She couldn't expect them to care for Edith with no pay, yet she had no way to reimburse them. That is, unless she did manage to get Social Security payments.

These thoughts were still heavy on her mind when Sarah dropped by the next day. This time, Arvilla was with her. After Emma welcomed them into the house, Arvilla got right to the point: "We are willing to take Edith for a while. I'll do most of the work."

"But I don't see how I can pay you," Emma objected.

"Don't worry about the pay," Sarah replied. "God will provide for us. He has always taken care of our needs."

Arvilla added, "I feel that it's my calling in life to take care of children, so I'd like to help you out."

Emma took a deep breath. "Is this your will, Lord?" she prayed under her breath. She paused for a moment. "I want to think a little more about it," she replied. "I'll let you know by Friday what I've decided."

That evening after the dishes were done, Emma gathered her children in the living room. She couldn't give up Edith without saying something to the family about it.

"Sara and Arvilla would like to keep Edith at their house for awhile," she began.

"You mean until we move to Kansas?" Perry asked.

"No, she would stay here in Iowa."

There was a long silence. "You mean Edith wouldn't live with us anymore?" Mary Edna asked.

"At least not for now."

"How often would we get to see Edith?" Glenn worried aloud.

"We would come to visit her as often as we could," Emma assured him.

Emma glanced at Edith, who was playing with a doll on one end of the couch. She was murmuring to herself, oblivious to the conversation.

"Edith."

The girl looked up, gave a nervous laugh, and then returned to her play.

Glenn poked her. "Edith, Mom is talking to you. Listen."

Edith looked up again.

"Edith, how would you like to go to Sara and Arvilla's house to live?"

"*Doh to Arvilla's Haus mit der billie doat?* Go to Arvilla's house with the billy goat?"

"Yes, to stay for awhile."

"*Yah, ich kann geh.* Yes, I can go."

Emma wasn't sure the young girl grasped the import of the decision. But further explanation now wasn't likely to help.

• • • •

To let her scattered relatives and acquaintances know about her plans, Emma prepared a note for *The Budget*, a weekly newspaper for Amish communities. It seemed like the most efficient way to notify the broader Amish community about the news. Emma sat down and wrote:

June 18, 1956

We came back home from Kansas Monday evening after burying our dear husband and father. Funeral was here in Iowa June 2, in a.m., then funeral in Kansas was on Sunday p.m., where we laid him to rest. Now we want to make our home in Kansas. Want to leave here in 2 or 3 weeks. Our address then will be Hutchinson, Kansas, R. 1.

We want to take this way to thank all the people for what they have done for me, all the cards, letters, money, and comforting words.

I want to thank you all for the visits and your help during the funeral and afterward. Obituary will be found elsewhere.

Mrs. Tobe Stutzman

She paused before she put the letter in the envelope. "Should I say something about Edith?" she asked herself. "People might be interested to know that Edith will stay in Iowa." "No," she decided, "it is best to leave that part out. It's too hard to say in a few words."

Emma felt a lump rise in her throat as she sealed the letter and carried it to the mailbox. There were indeed many people who had reached out to help. Besides all the assistance with meals, funeral arrangements, and canned goods, more than twenty people had given cash. Most were gifts of five or ten dollars, with a few larger ones.

Emma was packing her best dishes in a box when a knock came at the door. She opened it to find two women from the Sharon Bethel congregation. One of them held out a folded piece of fabric. "We have something for you," she said.

Emma reached out for the gift. "Thank you. Let's see what this is." She unfolded the fabric to reveal a large quilt top made up of twenty white squares of fabric joined by green and white strips. On each square was a painted design, a family name, and a short inspirational phrase. A large strip of white fabric made up the outside border.

Emma scanned the first few names: William Helmuths, Mr. and Mrs. Chris Gingrich, Mr. and Mrs. Daniel B. Miller.

"It's a memory quilt, something to help you remember your years in Iowa."

"Thank you! This is so kind of you." Emma glanced at a number of the short sayings that people had inscribed on their squares: "Only trust Him." "Be of good courage." "He careth for you." "Trust and Obey."

"You must have worked hard to get this done so soon."

"Yes, we did. If you want, we'll help quilt it for you before you leave for Kansas. We can do it here at your house."

Emma nodded assent. "We have a few days left before we move."

Over the next few days, a stream of women came and went from Emma's home. Some quilted or helped pack her belongings. Others helped to can the cherries that the church youth group picked for Emma's family at a member's home. Mary Edna and her friends packed the cherry jars into boxes alongside other canned goods shared by folks from the church.

The women finished the quilt the day before the move. Emma stretched it out for all to see. "I'll think of you whenever I have this quilt on my bed," she said as tears welled up in her eyes.

That evening Emma packed her clothing for the move. Pain gripped her as she stood in front of the rack that held Tobe's clothing. She hadn't touched his things since his death. Now she had to do something with them. She pulled a shirt off the hanger. She could almost feel Tobe's arm around her as she hugged the familiar garment to her chest.

Emma put the shirt back on the hanger and bent down to pick up one of Tobe's work shoes. The rough leather bore witness to the stress of hard labor. She rubbed at the traces of concrete left from the recent construction of the house. She turned it over and felt a weak spot in the sole. "These shoes could be resoled," she thought. "Maybe one of the boys can wear them when they get older."

She set down the shoe and pulled Tobe's work suspenders off the hook. Fresh tears coursed onto her cheeks as she smelled his familiar scent on them. "What shall I do with these?" she asked herself. "It will be awhile before the boys will grow into them."

Finally, after the wave of grief subsided, Emma took a deep breath and put Tobe's clothing and shoes on a separate pile. "I'll leave them here in Iowa," she decided. "Someone might be able to use them."

The next morning, Emma's brother Raymond arrived with his farm truck to help with the move. Like Tobe's brother Clarence, Raymond belonged to a progressive congregation that allowed him to own a truck. To hear him talk, occasions such as these provided ample confirmation that it was right for him to have left the Amish church.

Throughout the day, neighbors dropped by to help the family load boxes and furniture. Glenn paused as he finished packing a suitcase. "Erma wants to put her bottle in here," he said to Emma. "I think she's too old to have a bottle."

Emma winced. "Okay," she said. "Let's leave it here."

Emma knew Glenn was right. It was time to wean the three-year-old, but she couldn't bring herself to do it. It was easier to keep the child content with something in her mouth. It might even keep her from missing her daddy so much.

By early evening, all but a few of the household goods were loaded onto the trucks. Then a pickup truck pulled into the yard pulling the wagon used to haul church benches from one worship location to another. Several men pulled the backless benches from the wagon and set them up in the living room. Group singing seemed to be the best way to say goodbye.

The sun was low in the west as friends and acquaintances from different churches streamed into the room. They sang for more than an hour, raising their voices in rich harmony. Some started songs from memory; others called out numbers from the hymnbook for someone else to start. The melodies echoed against the bare walls and penetrated Emma's soul. How she wished that Tobe could somehow hear them sing.

It was after 9:00 p.m. when everyone stood to sing the familiar hymn "God be with You Till We Meet Again" (J. E. Rankin). The men folded up the benches and loaded them back into the wagon. Friends lingered as Emma shook hands with the men and greeted each woman with a kiss and a handshake. A few gave her a light embrace.

It was 11:00 p.m. when the family carried the last few items from the house to one of three vehicles. Raymond Nisly's farm truck was loaded with household furniture goods. Preacher Jonathan Miller's pickup held the family buggy. Most of the family would ride in Clarence Stutzman's car. The family chose to travel in the coolness of the night, a common practice in the heat of summer. They hoped to arrive not long after noon the next day.

She lingered at the door as a deep sadness welled up and

washed over her. Would it ever be different? Would there ever be a time when she could feel settled, rooted, secure? Slowly she closed the door behind her.

Emma slipped into Clarence's car after making sure that all of her children were in one of the vehicles. Since Edith and her things had been taken to Noah Weaver's home earlier that day, Mary Edna's friend Martha Miller crowded into what would have been Edith's spot.

Emma swallowed hard as she thought of leaving Edith behind. Could God approve it? What would the neighbors think? She consoled herself with the thought that she needed time to adjust to life as a widow.

Raymond started his truck and pulled out of the driveway first, turning toward Kalona and Route 1. Jonathan and Clarence followed close behind, hoping to stay behind Raymond as a caravan.

Emma breathed a deep sigh and then whispered mostly to herself: "I'm going home."

5

Building Hope

Mary Edna and Martha were too excited to sleep, so they sang. Emma joined in from time to time, but preferred to listen in silence. The familiar music nurtured her soul. The girls sang mostly from memory, with the occasional foray into the *Church and Sunday School Hymnal*. A flashlight helped to light the pages in the darkness of the night. Emma sobbed inside as they sang one of Tobe's recent favorites. She recalled that Tobe had led the song (no. 191) at Sharon Bethel on the Sunday before he died.

> Death shall not destroy my comfort.
> Christ shall guide me thro' the gloom;
> Down he'll send some angel convoy
> To convey my spirit home.

Emma pondered many questions: "Was Tobe with the angels now? What kind of body did he have? Was he happy? Could he see the family driving in the car? When would she see him again?"

It was half past noon the next day when they pulled into the driveway at John and Anna Stutzman's home. Tobe's parents were there to greet them. The children jumped out of the car and raced around the outside of the house to stretch their legs. It was a large two-story frame structure coated with whitewashed stucco. The noonday sun glared down on the large roof overhangs, casting long shadows on the outside walls. The house was located near Whiteside, the site of a few houses and a grain elevator. It was bordered along the back by the railroad track that paralleled Route 61, the road that angled southwest from Hutchinson. The manufacturing shop that Tobe had built in 1948 was located another mile and a half southwest on Route 61 as it headed toward Partridge.

Emma breathed a prayer of thanks that this house was temporarily available. At least she wouldn't need to worry about a place to live for the next several months. The house had been standing empty for some months now, since Tobe's parents were living with a newly widowed lady who hated to live alone. By granting their home to Emma for a time, the elder Stutzmans were able to accommodate two widows' needs at the same time. It would do her mother-in-law's heart good, Emma thought to herself. Anna was a compassionate woman who often wished to give more to charity than she was able. John and Anna had not prospered financially like Anna's siblings, but they were generous with what they had.

Emma swung open the door to the enclosed back porch and stepped inside. The twins hovered nearby as she made her way through the kitchen into the main part of the house. The wooden floors creaked as she crossed through the living room toward the large wooden stairway. She stopped to admire the leaded glass in the wooden double doors that led to the front porch. She couldn't remember ever seeing them opened.

Emma made her way up the steps, holding on to the large curved handrail. She peeked into each of the three bedrooms that lay at the top of the stairs. Some of the rooms had furniture in them. These would be good accommodations for her family.

Emma made her way back down the stairs just as the men began carrying furniture through the kitchen. "Where shall we put this table?" they asked. Emma pointed to a spot in the small room off the kitchen. Then she walked through the dining room to the bay window facing the driveway they would share with the next door neighbor. Sunlight streaked into the room, filtered through the leaves in the large elm trees west of the house.

Emma walked into the main living room and wiped the dust off the fireplace mantel with a cloth. It was the obvious place to put her Seth Thomas mantel clock.

Within an hour, a number of Emma's siblings and in-laws arrived to help unload the trucks. The sun blazed hot on their backs as they carried items from the vehicles. The men's shirts were soon soaked with perspiration. Sweat dripped from Emma's brow as she scurried around the house.

By late afternoon the household goods were unloaded and placed in one of the rooms. At the potluck dinner that followed, Emma's brother Fred commented; "It must have gotten over 100 degrees today."

"Yes," Henry replied. "The thermometer showed 110 degrees at 5:00 this afternoon."

"Then I don't need to feel bad for feeling so hot today," Fred grinned.

Henry flashed a wry smile. "Did you think it was because you were working harder than anyone else?"

Fred grinned broadly in response to the laughter that followed.

The next morning, Emma awoke as the first rays of the sun streamed through the bedroom window. It was the Lord's day, so she would get a break for her tired muscles after the exertion of moving and unpacking. She looked forward to seeing relatives and friends at the church gathering.

Most of Emma's relatives, though they worshipped in several different congregations, were Mennonites or Amish, spiritual descendants of the sixteenth-century Anabaptists who worshipped in several different congregations. All believed in similar doctrines such as nonresistance (or pacifism) and nonconformity to the world. All thought of themselves as "plain people." But they distinguished themselves from each other by differences in practice, both in worship and in daily life.

On the spectrum of practice, the Old Order Amish were the most conservative. Their worship services in the German language were the most traditional too. Their nonconformity was most visible to the outside observer, particularly in their attire. The men wore long, full beards. They had simple haircuts, with bangs on their foreheads and thick hair in the back. They wore hooks and eyes on their dress suits along with suspenders for their trousers. All of their clothing was homemade. The women wore their uncut hair under a prayer covering. They wore plain dresses with capes, pinned together, and bonnets and shawls for formal public occasions or when shopping in town.

The Amish worshipped in the homes of their members and used horse-drawn vehicles for transportation. They met every other Sunday for worship. They had no telephones or modern appliances such as radio or television. Although they considered themselves Old Order Amish, the folks in Emma's home community in Hutchinson and Partridge at times referred to themselves as Amish Mennonites. With some pride, they distinguished themselves from the Amish who lived further east near the towns of Yoder and Haven. They viewed the more-conservative Haven Amish as being less spiritual since they shunned Sunday school, lay Bible study, and other evangelical expressions of faith.

Most of Emma's close kin worshipped with the Old Order Amish church. This church community best expressed their beliefs and simple way of life, including dress, speech, and the homes in which they lived.

A few of Emma's relatives worshipped in a more-progressive church called the Plainview Conservative Mennonite Church. Emma's brother Raymond was a charter member who had pressed for the formation of the group six years earlier, in 1948. Tobe's brother Clarence was a member too. The congregation was affiliated with a scattered network of churches called the Conservative Mennonite Conference. Unlike most Amish folks, they worshipped in church buildings, held Sunday school meetings and worship services every Sunday, as well as Sunday evening services. They used the English language for all church activities. They hosted revival meetings with guest speakers.

The men wore their hair and dressed much like their more-worldly neighbors. At church, however, they wore plain suits that buttoned all the way up to the chin. No neckties were allowed. Each woman wore a homemade dress with a cape. Unlike the Amish, they had the freedom to make dresses that closed with zippers and snaps, rather than fastening them together with pins. Their prayer coverings were smaller than that of their Amish neighbors. They used many modern conveniences. They listened to music on their car radios and phonographs in their homes.

Tobe's brother L. Perry worshipped in a yet more-progressive church. It was called the Yoder Mennonite Church, named for the town of Yoder, Kansas. It belonged to the South Central Mennonite Conference, affiliated with a larger network often referred to as the Old Mennonite Church. Except for the women's uncut hair and prayer coverings, it was more difficult for the uninformed observer to distinguish these believers from their neighbors who were not Mennonite.

The Old Order Amish who lived near the towns of Hutchinson and Partridge belonged to one of three church districts, according to their place of residence. The folks in the area closer to Hutchinson were assigned to the east district. Their bishop was named Levi Helmuth. The folks who lived closer to Partridge belonged to districts further west, comprising the north and south districts. Bishop John D. Yoder and several ministers served in both of these districts, rotating their attendance from one Sunday to the next as needed.

In each district, the bishop was the final authority in church governance. He was the full minister, so to speak, who led in the rituals of baptism, communion, and marriage. Yet he depended on the counsel and assistance of the preachers and a deacon. Together they formed the leadership team called the ministers. The bishop was deemed responsible before God to keep house by maintaining order in the house of God. Scripture and the Ordnung or church discipline, were his guides. If members did not submit to his discipline, they could be excommunicated and shunned by the remaining members. If the bishop called for an offender to be shunned, members were expected to refrain from social interaction such as eating together or making business deals with the deviant member.

Although the Amish in the Hutchinson, Kansas, area accepted the biblical basis for shunning, they rarely practiced it. Emma recalled with relief that the church had not shunned the members who left the Amish church in 1948 to start the Plainview Church. It would have been very complicated to try to enforce shunning in such situations. For example, she would not have been able to accept rides in their vehicles. How would she have managed after Tobe's death? It was Raymond and Clarence who volunteered their vehicles to help move her things.

Now that Emma had made the decision to return to the Old Order Amish Church, she looked forward to the fellowship. She was sure the folks would understand her situation. She didn't anticipate that anyone would be standoffish just because she had been a part of the more progressive church in Iowa. She reasoned that at least some of these people would have done the same thing in her circumstances.

Since the Amish defined membership by district, it was considered taboo to seek church membership outside one's place of residence. Emma lived in her Stutzman in-laws' home, so she would normally have been expected to join the east district. However, she felt far more affinity with the other two districts, where most of her Nisly relatives belonged and where she had grown up. And when she moved to the shelterbelt property, she would be in the north district. So Emma decided to attend the worship service at her Uncle Ed Nisly's home, part of the north district.

After breakfast with the family, Emma sent Perry to harness the horse that Mother Nisly had loaned them for the time being. The family rode to church in the two-seated buggy they had brought with them from Iowa.

Emma basked in the warm greetings and expressions of deep sympathy in the women's eyes as she made her way into the house. Her quick smile and cheerful greeting masked a deep weariness of body and soul. Although she fanned herself and put forth a valiant effort to stay awake, she could not keep from nodding off several times during the two-hour service in the summer heat.

In their custom, the entire congregation stayed for the common meal shortly after the worship service. As usual, it was served on oilcloth, with no need for a plate. Emma seated herself and her twin children at the table with other women and children, sitting at the tables made from two backless benches joined together on small wooden stands. Most of the men stood outside, visiting with each other as they awaited their turn at the table.

Emma ate gladly of the standard fare: canned red beets, pickles, homemade bread served with butter and apple butter. As always, there was coffee and cream. It was a simple meal, although different hosts at times added jelly or syrup to mix with peanut butter for a spread.

• • • •

Emma's brother Raymond dropped by her home the next week to make arrangements for Perry and Glenn to help on the farm. "If the boys help with the farmwork," Raymond promised, "I'll give you fresh milk and share part of the milk check."

"I think Perry would enjoy the dairy," Emma replied. "He learned to milk cows in Iowa."

Emma hesitated for a moment and then asked, "You know Tobe always kept the books and took care of the money. I don't know if I can do it. Would you be willing to keep the books for me?"

"Sure, I'll be glad to do that for you."

She paused then added: "Clarence says I should apply for Social Security."

"Yeah, he talked to me about that too, but I doubt that you could get it. Tobe was behind on the tax payments."

"But Clarence talked to the man in the Social Security office," Emma said weakly. "He said I could get Social Security if we pay the back taxes."

Raymond shook his head. "Naw, you shouldn't do that.

If you need help as a widow, the family or the church will help you. The Bible says, 'If any provide not for his own, and specially for those of his own house, he hath denied the faith, and is worse than an infidel' [1 Tim. 5:8]." Raymond was quick to find biblical backing for his opinions.

Emma shrugged and looked down at the floor. "Clarence says we paid for it, so we'd just be getting back what we paid for."

Raymond shook his head. "By law we have to pay Social Security, but that doesn't mean it's right for us to ask the government to support us. We'll help you, Emma," he promised. "We'll see to it that you have what you need."

Emma's shoulders sank as Raymond left the house. It wasn't easy to stand against his convictions. Although he was next to the youngest of Emma's siblings, he readily took leadership in family affairs. She felt trapped, caught between her siblings and her in-laws. Brother-in-law Clarence was open to Social Security, but Raymond was opposed to it. Were the two men extending the friendly competition that had developed between them a dozen years earlier, when the two families had lived across the fields from each other?

Tobe would surely have agreed with Clarence. "Why should we pay into the fund but not draw from it when we have a need?" she thought. "A monthly Social Security check would make a world of difference for us. Why should I turn away monthly support for myself and all of my children?

"It would be especially helpful for Edith," Emma reasoned. "True, the doctor said that Edith might only live to be twenty-one years old, but who could know what medical treatment she might need by then?" Whenever Emma thought of caring for Edith by herself, she felt a tightness in her chest.

To apply for Social Security now that Raymond opposed it would only be asking for trouble. She couldn't afford to put him off at the very time when she desperately needed his help. And before she could even apply for the benefits, she'd have to come up with the cash for the back payments. "Where would I find the money to do that?" she asked herself. "Tobe's parents certainly can't help." In times of poor health and misfortune, they had at times been forced to rely on their sons to keep food on the table. If she were to pursue the route to Social Security, she'd likely have to borrow money from one or more of Tobe's brothers.

But then she thought, "If I were to get Social Security, what would people in the church think of me? Would they look down on me?" It would surely be better to bow at the feet of the church than to seek security in the arms of a government agency.

Over the next few weeks, Emma found it difficult to gather enough hope to face each day. One morning the sun had climbed quite high into the sky before Emma dragged herself out of bed. "*Fer was bin ich so mied?* Why am I so tired?" she asked herself. "*Hab ich net genunk Schlof grickt?* Am I not getting enough sleep?"

She mused about the load she was carrying now. "I guess it's true what Mom used to say, 'A man may work from sun to sun, but woman's work is never done.'" She couldn't remember ever being so exhausted.

Emma shuffled into the kitchen to the sound of a knock on the kitchen door. She glanced at the clock as she stepped toward the door. It was about 10:00 a.m.

"Come in," Emma said, swinging open the door for her sister-in-law Matilda. Clarence called his wife Bunny, but Emma found it hard to adapt. Somehow, "Bunny" just didn't sound right. She preferred to call her by her given name.

"I just thought I'd drop by to see how you're doing," Matilda said.

"I'm fine," responded Emma, hoping that she sounded better than she felt. She motioned toward a chair.

Matilda slid into the chair and set her purse down beside her. "Thank you."

The twins came running from the other room. "Hi, Matilda," Ervin said with excitement as he looked into her face. She reached down and drew him onto her lap.

Emma hoped that Matilda wouldn't comment that the children were still in their pajamas. She simply hadn't found the energy to get them dressed yet.

The two women chatted for a while. Before Matilda got up to leave, she said, "Let me know if there's anything I can do for you."

"Thank you," Emma replied. She thought Matilda looked a bit worried as she walked out the door.

"Come children," Emma said. "Let's get your clothes on."

"At least the older children have something to do," Emma thought to herself. Each weekday, Perry and Glenn helped one of their uncles. On some days, they worked at the back of the property where Tobe's brothers Ervin J. and L. Perry raised produce to sell in local grocery stores. They marketed radishes, tomatoes, and onions.

The truck patch was an effort to build a wholesale produce business. The work was labor intensive, so it provided ideal employment for Emma's sons. She benefited too because it provided vegetables for her table. Because of the timing for the move from Iowa, she had not been able to harvest all of the vegetables in her garden. Although the summer was unusually dry in Kansas, a new irrigation system for the truck patch made it possible to grow good crops.

Mary Edna and the boys also helped at times in the Stutzman Brothers' shop, a mile and a half away. They felt quite at home there, having lived on the site before moving to Iowa five years earlier. It was the place where Tobe had once built truck beds and other wooden products. And it was where he began making storm windows, the product that eventually led him to start a business in Iowa.

At times throughout the summer, her sons Perry and Glenn rode a horse or a bicycle the three miles in another direction to Raymond Nisly's home. There they helped with the chores or worked in the fields. Raymond taught them the fundamentals of farming and let them cultivate his fields with his tractors, a Case and a John Deere Model D.

In early July, Emma formally accepted Mother Nisly's offer to give her a one-acre plot in the shelterbelt on the southwest corner of the Nisly homestead. Since Raymond lived on the home farm, he volunteered to help Emma get a house onto the property. She'd need to decide whether to build a house or to purchase one of the houses being displaced by the construction of the new freeway in South Hutch.

"What do you say? Shall we go out and look at some of those houses next Monday?" Raymond asked her one weekend.

Emma nodded. "Mary Edna can watch the twins."

Raymond dropped by with his car early afternoon. The two of them drove around the area where houses were slated for demolition. For several hours they strolled around the homes advertised for sale. All were single-story, single-family dwellings made of wood. It would not be too difficult to move them the six miles to Emma's new lot. By the time they needed to head home for supper, Emma wrung her hands in frustration. It was hard to make a choice.

"What do you think I should do?" she asked Raymond.

Raymond cleared his throat. "Some of these houses would make a nice home for you. But by the time you pay to have them moved, I think it's going to cost you more than if you build a house yourself. Why don't you just build a new home out of block? It would be cheaper than wood."

Emma hesitated. Clarence had advised her that a new house should be made of wood rather than block. She voiced his concerns: "Wouldn't a block house be harder to heat in the wintertime? What about condensation on the walls?"

"Naw, I don't think that should be such a problem," Raymond retorted. "Tobe built you a block house both in Kansas and in Iowa."

It was true. But Emma recalled that the house in Kansas sometimes had water problems. Of course, it was built partially underground. What would Tobe say about the choice before her now?

It was the second time that she felt caught between Raymond and Clarence. On the one hand, Clarence seemed the better one to decide. He was a builder with his own construction crew. On the other hand, Raymond was more frugal. He would keep the costs down.

After further conversation, Emma decided to take Raymond's advice to build rather than to move a house. She accepted his offer to help prepare the site. Clarence agreed to draw the blueprint for a cement-block house. Emma's brother-in-law Alvin Yoder, also a builder, agreed to oversee the project.

Emma met Raymond at the shelterbelt to decide the placement of the new house. She watched as Raymond stepped off the area where he thought it should stand. He picked up a stick and dragged it through the dry soil to mark the four corners of a rough thirty-by-forty-foot rectangle.

"What do you think of putting the house right here?" Raymond asked as he pointed to the area marked off by the four lines. "We'll need to pull out some of the trees from these five rows." He pointed to the rows of cottonwood, American elm, black locust, hackberry, and mulberry.

Emma nodded assent. "Maybe we can leave the evergreens and the Russian olive trees there on the south end of the house. That will give some shade from the south sun."

Raymond agreed. "I'll start pulling out these other trees today. Can you send the boys over to help me?"

"Yes, Perry and Glenn can help."

After two weeks of pulling trees, both Perry and Glenn were drooping. "We're just about done," Perry declared one Saturday evening at the end of July. We have just one more stubborn old hackberry to go. Those taproots are awful."

"The ground is so dry," Glenn complained. "It would be a lot easier if we had some moisture in the ground."

Emma wiped her brow in sympathy. "It hasn't been so hot and dry for a long time."

"We have to chop off so many roots," Perry went on. "The tractors just don't have enough horsepower to pull those hackberries."

Glenn joined in. "Today Raymond used the winch on his truck. He hooked up the cable to the taproot. Then he revved up the truck and wound up the cable. Sometimes that works better than using the tractor."

"We want to get done by next Wednesday, because that's when the digger is coming to do the basement," Perry added.

The digger came on schedule, but it took him longer than he had predicted to dig the hole for the basement. The hot sun and the tree roots had sucked much of the moisture out of the soil. As soon as the man was finished, Alvin Yoder poured the footers. After the concrete set, he laid up the blocks for the walls of the small basement. Next he backfilled the dry soil against the walls and poured the floor for the house.

Emma felt excitement for the first time when the men starting building the walls. Several volunteers helped Alvin lay block while Perry and Glenn mixed the mortar. They were used to handling the ninety-pound bags of cement since they had helped Tobe build the shop and house in Kalona. In spite of the intense heat, the project moved at a good pace.

Each day, Emma and Mary Edna brought dinner to the men working on the house. Each evening, Emma recorded the names of the volunteers. She hoped to pay them back in some small way, perhaps by inviting their families to Sunday dinner.

Along with her support for the builders, Emma gave herself to the gardening and housekeeping tasks at home. Several sewing projects begged for her attention. For one, Mary Edna needed a new black dress for the baptism and communion services, which were coming up shortly. Because these were such somber rituals, most women wore black. Mary Edna was being baptized, so it would be her first communion.

Everyone stepped back from the building project on the third Friday in August, the day set aside for the Abraham C. Nisly reunion. July and August were reputed to be the hottest months of the year in Kansas, but it proved to be the best time for family reunions. Since Emma took particular interest in genealogy and family connections, she looked forward with fondness to the large gathering. On this occasion, Emma's sister Elizabeth came from Mississippi along with her husband John Bender and their two daughters. Emma's brother John Nisly came from Indiana, along with his family.

Altogether, the reunion brought together 260 descendants of Abraham C. Nisly and Dinah Yoder to celebrate the memory of these ancestors. Emma was a descendant, as were many of the people in the nearby Amish Church districts. The stature and respect of Abraham's family was not hard to see; three of the four ministers or their spouses in the church district were Abraham's direct descendants. Abraham's son Daniel was Emma's grandfather. He had been ordained as a minister in the Amish church, just as Emma's father, Levi, had been. Emma was the oldest of Levi's children, followed by John, Henry, Barbara, Elizabeth, Fred, Raymond, and Rufus.

Emma's new home in the shelterbelt stood just a mile east and a half mile north of the site of the original Abraham Nisly homestead, settled in 1883. Many of the out-of-town guests drove by or joined Emma at her building site, where block walls now rose on all four sides of her new house. Their sympathetic demeanor confirmed that she had made the right decision to leave Iowa. She tired, however, of explaining Edith's absence. She wondered about her relatives' unspoken thoughts.

Having out-of-town guests gave good reason for Emma to visit Tobe's grave. She felt self-conscious going there by herself or with the children by her side. Hosting guests who'd not yet seen the grave provided an opportunity to talk about Tobe. She always waited for others to bring up the subject. She wasn't about to complain or bore other people by talking too much about Tobe.

A few days after the reunion, the crew completed the walls of Emma's new house. Then Clarence moved in with his construction crew to put up the rafters. Two of the men laid out the two-by-fours and cut them at the angles Clarence specified. Another two nailed the pieces together to form the trusses that spanned the thirty and a half feet over the east and west walls. As the men finished each truss, they hoisted it up to the three men who walked on top of the walls.

The sun bore down mercilessly as they worked under the cloudless sky. Their only relief was a glass jug of water, insulated by a burlap bag soaked with water. At two o'clock in the afternoon, the thermometer showed 102 degrees in the shade.

By the end of the week, the men had finished the roof, including the sheeting and the wooden shingles—not that anyone was worried about closing off the house against rain. It hadn't rained for so long that the fields were too dry to till. And there was no rain in sight.

As Emma looked forward to settling into her new home, her two oldest children prepared to settle into the church. Both Mary Edna and Perry joined the membership class in the Old Order Amish Church in preparation for baptism in the fall. Mary Edna was fourteen years old, Perry was thirteen. Emma recalled that she and Tobe had been much older when they were baptized. In Amish Church districts across the nation, most young people delayed baptism until their late teens or early twenties, often waiting until the time of marriage. The delay gave opportunity for young people in some Amish communities to "sow their wild oats" and consider carefully the lifelong implications of keeping the church discipline.

It was not that way in the Amish Church near Partridge and Hutchinson. Two values served the church to lower the age for baptism since Emma's youth. First, the young people began to emphasize strongly the importance of sexual chastity (or purity, as they called it) in courtship. Young people who had been baptized seemed to take this teaching more seriously. Second, the church taught the importance of personal conversion leading to a holy life. Young teenagers now professed readiness to accept God's call to salvation.

The day of the baptism dawned partly cloudy. The service was to be held only a mile and a half away at the Enos Miller residence, a short buggy ride in the crisp September air. The worship service proceeded like most others except that the baptismal ceremony followed a sermon focused on the biblical teaching about baptism.

At the appointed time, Bishop John D. Yoder called for the baptismal class to come forward—Melvin Herald Nisly, Menno Yoder, Larry Nisly, Daniel Miller, Perry Stutzman, Mary Edna Stutzman, and Alma Miller. All seven knelt at the bishop's feet, their backs to the congregation. The bishop opened his black minister's manual and asked each candidate several questions that constituted a vow. Each answered the questions in the affirmative, pledging faithfulness to God and the church. They also repeated aloud a sentence confessing their belief in Jesus Christ as Lord.

Emma watched with interest as the bishop prepared to baptize each one. She leaned forward as he cupped his hands over Perry's head and intoned: "*Auf deinen Glauben dass du bekennt hast vor Gott und viele Zeugen wirst du getauft in Namen des Vaters, des Sohnes, und des Heiligen Geistes. Amen.* Upon your faith, which you have confessed before God and these many witnesses, you are baptized in the name of the Father, the Son, and the Holy Ghost. Amen." As each person of the Trinity was named, an assisting minister poured a small amount of water into the bishop's cupped hands. Then the bishop emptied his cupped hands over Perry's head. The water ran down onto Perry's white shirt and dripped onto the wooden floor. After baptizing each one in a similar manner, the bishop prepared to formally receive each one into the church. He grasped each one's hand and said: "*Im Namen des Herrn und der Gemeinde wollen wir die Hand dir geboten, so steh auf.* In the name of the Lord and the church, we are pleased to extend to you the hand of fellowship, so stand up." He helped each of the young men to his feet and greeted them on the lips with the "holy kiss" commanded in

Scripture. Likewise, he grasped the young women's hands and helped them rise. But as they stood, the bishop's wife, Katie, stepped forward to greet them with the kiss of fellowship. The ritual "holy kiss" or "kiss of charity" exchanged between believers in each formal church gathering was never shared between the sexes.

Tears of joy coursed onto Emma's cheeks as the bishop read a benediction from the prayer book. How she wished that Tobe could have been present to witness the event. She reached for her hankie as the bishop announced the place of the next meeting. The congregation joined in a final song and then sat down. Emma gazed quietly at the floor as the children and young people began to file out of the house. Then she stood with the other women to begin preparation for the common meal.

• • • •

The fall season brought a change of pace for the Stutzman family. Both Perry and Glenn prepared to go back to school. Since Mary Edna had finished the eighth grade, she would stay at home.

Emma wondered if the children minded having been to so many different schools. In Iowa, the children had not been able to settle down and make friends at school as Emma would have wished. Emma resolved that it was going to be different for the twins.

Raymond's daughter Janice was ready to begin first grade, so Raymond offered to let Perry and Glenn use a stripped-down old car in exchange for giving Janice a ride to school. He didn't mind that neither of the boys had a driver's license. The hot rod, as he called it, certainly wouldn't lose much value if it got a few scrapes and dents. Besides, it was only three miles to school, all by lightly traveled gravel roads. In the hot, dusty weather, clouds of dust made it easy to tell when a car was approaching.

The boys drove to school each day and parked the hot rod at Clarence's home, just a few steps from the one-room school. It kept them from needing to explain their transportation arrangements to the teacher.

• • • •

The long dry spell stretched out until the weather suddenly turned rather cold. The change in the weather caught Emma off guard. She hadn't realized that the butane tank supplying the heating stove was low on fuel until the house turned cold. It was a Saturday, so there was no way to get butane delivered. The children shivered and complained until Grandpa Stutzman brought an unvented oil stove to take the chill out of the air. It wasn't long before Mary Edna complained of a headache from the fumes. Emma went to bed fretting about the dry weather and the lack of heat. "Why didn't one of the men warn me about the low fuel in the tank? Tobe wouldn't have let that happen," she told herself. "Taking care of the family with Tobe gone is like a single workhorse pulling a heavy wagon with a hitch designed for a team."

The next morning, Emma awoke to find puddles on the sidewalk outside the kitchen window. She breathed a prayer of thanks for the rain that had fallen during the night, the first moisture since July 29. Few things were as refreshing to Emma's spirit. She reveled in the smell of rain on the dry earth. Emma felt guilty about her ungrateful thoughts the day before. She told herself that she needed to trust God more deeply, to surrender more fully. It would not be right to complain, even to God. Surely there were others far worse off than she.

After the Sunday service that morning, someone commented to Emma that God's good hand was in the timing of the rain. Because of the long dry season, men had been free to volunteer in the building of her home. Now that the men had finished their task, the rain had come. Tears spilled onto Emma's cheeks as she pondered this "coincidence." God had indeed been good to her. And even though her vegetable garden hadn't done well through the drought, she had plenty of vegetables from the irrigated produce patch.

Now that the men were finished with the main construction on Emma's house, women came to assist. Mary Edna took care of the twins while Emma and others painted the walls and trim. As soon as the painting was done, Emma made curtains for the windows. With the move so near, she felt new energy and hope.

By the last Saturday in October, Emma was ready to move into her new house. A glad anticipation helped to mitigate the weariness she felt as she packed boxes for the move. It would be her third move in six months. She watched with gratefulness as relatives and friends once again helped load furniture and boxes into the trucks. She felt a surge of excitement as the trucks made their way toward the shelterbelt. This would be a place she could really call her own. Having occupied eight different homes in less than six years, she savored the prospect that this might be the last time she'd need to move—ever.

6

Settling In

The truck pulled into the gravel driveway and up to the new house. Emma got out and watched as Tippy, their rat terrier, explored his new territory. Perry and Glenn began to carry boxes into the house. Throughout the afternoon, several of Emma's neighbors and relatives joined in to help. By suppertime, all of the furniture was in place, with many of the boxes unpacked. The family took a short break from the work to eat a meal prepared by Emma's aunt Lizzie, who lived just a mile to the south.

After supper, a middle-aged couple from Kalona, Iowa, dropped by to pay a short visit. Emma honored her drop-in guests by showing them through her new house room by room. "*Es is net en gross Haus*. It's not a big house," Emma commented, "*awwer es is gut genunk fer uns*. But it's good enough for us."

"I think it will make a very good home for you," they said. "We'll tell the folks back at Kalona that you're doing well here."

"Thank you," Emma replied, as the couple reached for their coats. She bid them goodbye as they stepped into the autumn chill stirred by a steady breeze. Emma waved through the window of the porch as her visitors backed out of the driveway. She mused that it was good to have guests from Iowa. Somehow it seemed much longer than four months since she'd left Iowa. She felt truly at home back here in Kansas.

As Emma turned off the porch light and stepped back into the house, she noticed that nearly every room of the house had lights on. "What a change from the time Tobe and I lived in this community five years ago," she thought to herself. "Then, we weren't allowed to have electricity."

The change to allow the use of electricity had come slowly. Dairy farmers pled with their ministers for a change in the church rules. Only Grade A milk could be sold for human consumption. To earn Grade A status, they needed electricity to cool their milk. The difference in price between Grade A and B was significant enough that the issue wouldn't die. The ministers called special meetings to discuss the sensitive matter. Some members saw the use of electricity as an accommodation to the world that did not befit plain people, so feelings ran high. One member declared that it would lead down the road to hell. Yet, in spite of differing opinions, the ministers made the decision to allow electricity in September of 1954.

It wasn't long until women begin profiting inside the house as well, since the rules allowed appliances such as freezers, washers, and irons. Air conditioners were seen as a luxury, allowed only if recommended by a doctor for health reasons. Emma was glad the issue had been resolved while she and Tobe were in Iowa. Now she had the benefit of electricity in her new house.

"Nevertheless," she thought to herself, "we shouldn't be wasting it by leaving the lights on." She went from room to room, turning out unneeded lights, before she turned toward the task of putting the twins to bed. It was Saturday night, time for their weekly bath.

"I'll give the twins their bath and wash their hair," Mary Edna volunteered.

"Thank you. Just leave the water in for me," Emma reminded her. "Let's not waste water."

As soon as Emma got the freshly bathed twins settled into their cribs, she picked up her night clothing and headed for the bathroom. The smell of fresh paint and varnish hovered in the small room as she undressed. She tossed her dress into the new wall hamper and then stepped into the tub. She leaned back and soaked in the warm water.

Emma's mind went back to the house where they'd lived north of Kalona, Iowa. Tobe had struck a deal with Jason Boller to live there rent free in exchange for doing some chores. But the frame house was so drafty in the winter that the heat from the potbellied stove barely reached beyond the living room. The children shivered under the covers on windy nights when snow slipped through the loose fitting windows and fell onto the beds. At times they could hear rats and squirrels run above the ceilings and through the walls. She turned on the faucet to add a bit of hot water as she shivered with the memory.

After washing her long hair, Emma got out of the tub and dried herself. She pulled on her nightgown and wrung her long hair with a towel. She combed out the tangles with a large plastic comb. It could finish drying in bed.

With a large dipper, she took water from the tub and poured it into the toilet until it flushed. Then she pulled the tub's rubber stopper, rinsed the tub, and headed for the bedroom.

As Emma prepared for bed she opened a dresser drawer and pulled out her nightcap. She always kept her head covered, even during sleep. The church taught that it was important for women to have their heads covered any time that they prayed, including nighttime.

The covering symbolized Emma's submission to God's authority. With Tobe gone, however, the matter of spiritual authority seemed ill-defined and confusing. In obedience to scriptural teaching, she had lived in loyal submission to a man all her life, first to her father, Levi, and then to Tobe. Having practiced deference for so long, she felt ill-equipped to take charge of her household affairs. It would take willful self-exertion to strengthen the mental muscles left atrophied by disuse.

Sitting on the edge of her bed, Emma paused to review the Sunday school lesson for the next day. She leafed to the passage where her bookmark was placed and read it silently, her finger following the words across the page. Then she closed the Bible, laid it on the dresser, and turned off the overhead light. She knelt beside her bed to pray, her elbows propped on the mattress. She prayed in a whisper to avoid waking her son Ervin in the crib nearby.

Emma prayed in German, following her custom from childhood. She began by thanking God for her new home. Tears of gratefulness welled up as she thanked God for her mother's generosity in granting her the plot of land. She gave thanks for Raymond, Alvin, Clarence, and the many volunteers who had assisted with the project. She gave thanks that no one had been injured during the construction. She asked for God's protection over the members of her family. Then, in closing, she prayed for the ones who would lead in the next day's Sunday school lesson. After a heartfelt "Amen," she reached for the handkerchief on her dresser to wipe the tears from her cheeks. Then she pulled back the covers and crawled into bed.

She lay in bed tired but content. What would Tobe say if he saw her now? Would he be proud of her? She mused that he would probably have something witty to say—surely an encouraging word to keep her going. With this on her mind, she fell asleep.

The next morning as Emma prepared breakfast, she looked out the east kitchen window. It would take a lot of work to make this place a home. There was no shelter for a horse or other livestock. She hoped to erect some kind of out-building before the first snowfall. "I'll ask Alvin if we can build a small barn," she thought to herself as she plopped mush into the black skillet. It sizzled in the hot oil and turned a golden brown.

"*Welle esse*. Let's eat," she called to the family.

It didn't take long for every one of the children to sit up to the first breakfast in their new home. Emma sat at the head of the table, her two older boys seated on a backless wooden bench on one the side of the table and Mary Edna on the other. Ervin and Erma sat within arm's reach, one on each side.

Emma reached over to the countertop on her right and put two slices of bread into the toaster before nodding to Perry, who sat close to the three-dimensional wall motto produced by the Stutzman Brother's shop: "The family that prays together stays together."

They all bowed their heads as Perry led in a spoken prayer. Since Tobe's death, it only seemed right that the eldest son should lead in prayer. Perry had scarcely voiced the "Amen" when Glenn said "Pop!" As if on cue, the toaster popped up the bread slices. Mary Edna smiled as the boys snickered.

"Boys!" Emma's unspoken admiration for Glenn's impeccable timing took any sting out of her rebuke. But how could the boys pay attention to the prayer when they were counting the seconds for the toast?

The fare was simple: tomato gravy, French toast, and fried mush. After breakfast, they rose from the table to get ready for Sunday school. After Emma had the twins dressed and ready, she changed into her Sunday clothing. Then she went to the chest of drawers in the hallway next to the bathroom. It was a piece that Tobe had made early in their marriage. She pulled open the long middle drawer and looked over her collection of head coverings. The handmade coverings were made of white organdy, a stiff transparent cotton fabric. The newer prayer coverings in Emma's collection followed the pattern prescribed by the church in Iowa. Now that she was back in Kansas, she would make them to fit with the form the women followed in Kansas. The coverings served not only as a prayer cap, but also as a point of identification with a particular church fellowship.

Emma's coverings were neatly arranged in two rows, from one side of the long drawer to the other. She selected one of the newer ones, slipped it onto her head, and looked into the small mirror in the bathroom to make sure that her covering was properly placed. She secured it with a couple of pins in the fore piece and tied the ribbons loosely under her chin.

Emma opened another drawer in the top row of the dresser. She glanced inside, chose a handkerchief with an embroidered edge, and stuffed it into the cape of her dress. The cape was an expression of modesty required by the church. It was an extra piece of fabric designed to "hide the female form," as the ministers sometimes said.

After helping the twins with their coats, Emma donned her black woolen shawl and led the family outside, where Perry was waiting with the horse and buggy. When the six of them were settled into their places, Emma threw a lap robe over their knees. Perry slapped the reins on the horse's back, and they were off.

On the way, the family spoke about Sunday school. In the Amish church in Haven, Kansas, not far east of Hutchinson, Sunday school was seen as a threatening modern innovation.

There the church members used the alternative Sundays to visit each other in their home. In the area of Kansas where Emma now lived, the Amish church conducted Sunday school on the alternate weeks when there were no church services.

Emma recalled that her great grandfather Daniel E. Mast had advocated for the adoption of a Sunday school program in the face of considerable resistance. Now the Sunday school program was well established; nearly all the members of the Amish district participated. They believed that Sunday school met two important goals for the church. First, it provided an opportunity for adults to discuss biblical passages in groups separated by age and gender. Second, it provided an opportunity for the children to study the German language. Using a small primer, they studied the alphabet and learned to read verses. Most learned German well enough to read Luther's translation of the Bible, the version used in the church services. In contrast to some Amish congregations, the Partridge districts encouraged members to carry their Bibles for both worship and Sunday school.

Both the Sunday school and the Wednesday evening Bible study were held in a building dedicated for this purpose, while the worship services were held in members' homes. They called their meetingplace the German Schoolhouse, since they used it to teach the German language to their children. The building had served as a one-room schoolhouse before being moved to the intersection just a mile and a half south of the place where Emma now lived.

Emma recalled that when the building was about to be moved to that spot, some thought a basement should be dug for it. Others disagreed. Since further discussion yielded no agreement, Bishop John D. Yoder suggested the use of the lot to discern God's will in the matter. After committing the matter to God in prayer, he cast the lot, which indicated that they were to dig a basement. This brought peace to the fellowship. Later, members expressed appreciation for the extra space provided by the lower level.

The German Schoolhouse provided freedom to explore practices that could not be readily tried in the regular worship service held in members' homes. The most obvious change was that men other than the ministers helped to provide spiritual leadership. They taught Bible classes, led devotional meditations, and gave leadership to the discussion of topics.

Emma recalled that Tobe had presented a "topic" in July of 1949, the second year such meetings were held. The church occasionally invited speakers from outside the fellowship. Guests like Peter Dyck of Mennonite Central Committee and Elmer Ediger of the Prairie View Mental Health Center opened new windows to the world.

In the Sunday morning service, the church used only the German Ausbund. It contained hymn texts dating back to the sixteenth century. Some were martyr accounts, reminding congregants that believers in the state-church tradition had persecuted their ancestors. To add to the deep sense of sobriety, many hymns were chanted in a minor key. In the Wednesday evening service, the congregation used different hymnals, allowing for an occasional song in English. Emma preferred the joyful mood of the English gospel songs in the newer hymnal.

The members were careful never to refer to the meetinghouse as a church or even a church building. The only biblical use of church, they averred, was to refer to God's people. Thus they eschewed the German word *Kirche* and spoke instead of *Gemeinde*—the fellowship. In common parlance they called it *Gemee*—a form of fellowship that could take place in Sunday school, Wednesday evening prayer meetings, worship services in member homes, and even when members visited each other or shared meals in one another's homes.

Because the German Schoolhouse was fairly small, two

Amish church districts used it on alternative Sundays. Today was the time for the north district to use the Sunday school building while the south district had a church gathering in someone's home.

Perry guided the horse into the yard and stopped at the hitching rail. He got out and tied the horse while Emma and the others made their way into the building. Emma got settled on the women's side, with the twins around her, while the three older children found their way to sit with friends. Emma's mother slipped into the bench beside her to help care for the twins. Emma flashed a smile of appreciation.

The children sometimes complained that Sunday school seemed long. That wasn't true for Emma, even if they had to sit for two hours. That is, unless the twins were tired or fussy. Emma didn't have Tobe's knack of keeping the children quiet. But Mary Edna or some other woman was always ready to watch one of the twins if she needed assistance.

The Sunday school followed the usual form—a cappella group singing followed by an adult Sunday school lesson in two parts. While the school-aged children went off to German classes, the adults divided into smaller classes to study an assigned passage of Scripture. Emma met with the women's class. Although her class was always taught by a man, the women felt freer to contribute to the lesson that way. Women weren't expected to speak in public at church gatherings with both men and women present except when a man was teaching a women's class.

After discussion in smaller classes, all of the adults got together in one large class led by one of the ministers. Since the smaller classes were taught by lay members, the large group arrangement was a way to assure that the ministers had their say in the interpretation of the text being studied.

After Sunday school was over, the family came home for

dinner. In the afternoon, Emma gave Mary Edna the task of putting down the twins for a nap. Then she lay down to seek a few moments of quiet. After a short nap, she heard Mary Edna call out to Ervin in disgust.

"No, you can't have a drink. You already had a drink."

"Why won't you go to sleep?" Mary Edna complained aloud.

"I'm not sleepy." Ervin's high-pitched voice came through the door, opened just a crack.

"Of course you won't be sleepy if you keep talking and bouncing in bed," Mary Edna protested. "Now lie down and be quiet like Erma. If you can't go to sleep, you can at least lie quiet for thirty minutes."

"How long has it been so far?"

"About twenty minutes."

Mary Edna turned to her mother. "I don't know what else to do. I thought he'd be ready for a nap. I'd be tired if I wiggled as much as he does."

Emma grunted in sympathy as she sat up, yawned loudly, and straightened out her head covering, which had been pushed askew. She would gladly have slept longer.

That evening, Emma had invited three single women as guests for supper. One was Elva Bender, a friend from Iowa. Elva's father, Harvey, was the one who had funded the new shop on his property after Tobe lost his assets through bankruptcy. Elva had worked for wages in the shop from time to time.

Emma felt a sense of closeness to Elva as they ate together that evening. She sensed no blame from her for Tobe's financial failures. She felt badly that the empty shop and house in Iowa were now a drain on the Bender family's assets.

"Would you like to show us around your house?" Elva asked as they finished drying the dishes.

"Oh, yes," Emma smiled. "Let's start with the bedrooms."

The three women followed her from the kitchen. "The bedrooms are back here," Emma said, moving out of the living room into a short hallway. "Mary Edna's is here on the left." Emma and her company stepped inside, where Mary Edna was sitting on her single bed and sorting through some small boxes.

"It's my room," Mary Edna smiled. "But that's Mom's desk. And Erma sleeps in the crib."

Emma nodded and motioned toward a tall piece of furniture with curved glass on both sides and a fold-down desk lid in the middle. "Yes, Mary Edna uses the glass part, and I use the center for my business things," Emma said.

"Oh, I see one of the garment bags that Tobe made," Elva said as she glanced through the open closet door on the right. She stepped over to look more closely.

"Yes," Mary Edna answered, rising from the bed and stepping toward the closet. "I helped to make the hanger part in Dad's shop. The company in Fairfield made the fabric part." As she spoke, she pulled on the zipper that ran the length from top to bottom. "It's a good place to store seasonal clothing. It stays nice and clean that way."

"I used to help in the shop," Elva commented to her fellow guests.

Emma stepped back into the hallway. She opened a pair of wooden cabinet doors just to the right of the bedroom door. "This is where we keep our coats and things," she said. "And down below we have these two big drawers for other things."

Ervin, tagging along, stepped forward and pulled open the large bottom drawer. *Die sin mei Schpielsache.* These are my toys," he declared, pulling open the large bottom drawer. He reached in to get a metal car. "Brrrrrrm."

"I see," Elva said as she glanced down at the wooden blocks

and other simple toys in the drawer. A grin crept across her face as she watched the young boy race across the floor with his car. "I see that he's as energetic as ever."

Emma rolled her eyes in acknowledgment. "Perry and Glenn have their bedroom here," she said as she moved further down the hallway to the left. The room had windows to the south and east. A double bed with metal posts stood just inside the doorway.

And then Emma led them into her own bedroom, which lay off to the other side of the hallway.

"Oh, you have your friendship quilt on the bed," Elva exclaimed. The three guests stepped up to admire the quilted cover on the double bed.

Emma smiled widely. "I think of Iowa every day when I have it on my bed." Then she pointed to the crib, which stood in the corner of the pink room. "Ervin sleeps in there," she said.

"I like your nice, big closets," Elva commented.

"I'm so glad to have those. Tobe and I have lived in a few places that didn't have good closets—or big shelves like these."

The visitors followed Emma back toward the living room. "The bathroom is here," she said, reaching inside the door for the light switch. The room was small, with a little corner sink to the right, toilet to the left, and a bathtub at the far end. A large built-in cabinet hung over the tub. Along the side wall, from floor to ceiling, stood a set of built-in cabinets. She opened a door next to the sink, where her medicines were stored—Ungentine, Rolatum, Mercurochrome, Mertiolate, Vicks, and other products. Then she swung open the small cabinet door next to the tub. "This is our hamper for dirty clothes. On the other side it has a door into the washroom."

"That will make it convenient for you," said Elva.

Next Emma led her company through the living room

area and back to the dining area. She pointed to the kitchen cabinets. "My brother-in-law Alvin Yoder built these cabinets," she said as she stroked her hand across the linoleum counter top. "He also laid the block for the house."

"These cabinets look very solid. And they give you lots of shelf space," Elva commented.

"Yes, I'm thankful for that," Emma responded. The smell of fresh varnish tinged the air as she opened several of the solid plywood doors above and below the countertop to reveal her cookware and dishes.

Then Emma opened the door off the kitchen. "This is my washroom," she said, "and I have a small basement for my canned goods down these stairs." She pointed off to the left of the washroom where two steps dropped to a small landing. A set of steps led off the right of the landing downward into the basement. One step up from the landing stood a windowed door to the outside.

Emma felt a deep sense of comradeship with the three women as she bid them goodbye that night. Now that she had been widowed for a few months, she felt closer to those who had never been married. On a couple of occasions since Tobe's passing, she'd felt a slight uneasiness with married couples who came to visit. "Is it my imagination?" she asked herself. "Do some people come to visit because that's what people are supposed to do for widows?" She was thinking of James 1:27.

The next morning, Emma woke up with a slight sense of dread. It was the day that Mary Edna had promised to start working as a nanny for the Lawrence Webb family in Hutchinson. Mrs. Webb was a schoolteacher who needed someone to do housekeeping and watch her young children each school day. The Amish would never have considered such an arrangement for themselves. For a mother to go off to work leaving her small children in the care of others would be to forsake a God-given responsibility. Since the Webbs were *englisch* (non-Amish) folks, they lived by different principles. They did not speak German or understand the Amish practices that kept them separate from "the world."

Emma worried that the Webb home, furnished with a radio and TV, both forbidden by the Amish Church, would surely pose new temptations for Mary Edna. And Emma hated to lose Mary Edna's daily help around the house. It would be stressful to take care of the house and the twins by herself. Yet she desperately needed the income that Mary Edna could provide. Working as a nanny was one of the most common ways for a fourteen-year-old girl to provide income for the family.

Following the custom in the Amish community, Emma made it clear to Mary Edna that she would not be officially "of age" until she became twenty-one years old. Until then, Mary Edna was expected to turn over all of her earnings to help support the family.

Shortly after 9:00 a.m., Mr. Webb came to get Mary Edna. Emma watched and waved as the car backed slowly out of the gravel driveway and onto the road. She swallowed a lump in her throat as she walked back into the house. Mary Edna would be home on Wednesday evenings and weekends, but Emma knew she'd miss her oldest child. The only way to stay in touch was by letter.

The Webbs had asked that Mary Edna work on weekends, but Emma wouldn't allow it. "I need your help with the Saturday work," she told Mary Edna. Saturday was the best time to do the weekly housecleaning, as well as the cooking and baking for Sunday.

Each day, Emma wondered how things were going with Mary Edna. She breathed a sigh of relief when Mr. Webb's car pulled into the driveway at 7:15 on Saturday morning. Mary Edna got out of the car with her small suitcase. Emma opened the door with a wide smile as her daughter came toward the house. "How was it?"

"Okay, I guess. I did a lot of cleaning, washing, and ironing. The boys sure are ornery. Steve went out trick-or-treating on Halloween night. They wanted me to go along. I told them we didn't believe in that."

Emma nodded in agreement.

Mary Edna reached into her suitcase. "Look what I did on Tuesday." She pulled out a piece of fabric and held it up to the light. "I cut out an apron for myself."

"Oh, it looks nice," Emma exclaimed.

"Maybe I can sew it this afternoon."

"Yes, I think you'll have time to do that after we get the house cleaned."

• • • •

Emma had lived in her new house for nearly two weeks when Raymond came by to settle the accounts for its construction. Because of Raymond's careful purchasing and the gift of volunteer labor, the total cost was less than Emma had feared. The final figure for the skilled labor and building materials was just under $4,000, about the same amount as the equity she had in the Stutzman Brothers' property. Most of the labor was volunteer.

Later that week, Tobe's brother Ervin J. and his wife—also named Emma—bought Emma's share of the property in exchange for a clear title and the warranty deed. For Emma, it was a bittersweet moment. It wasn't easy to part with a property that she and Tobe had first called their own. Yet the sale made it possible to pay off her new place in the shelterbelt.

The next day, Emma deposited the check in the bank and paid all of the bills for the house. She smiled with delight to see that she had a little cash left over. Emma was eager to put up a small barn to stable a horse and provide a place to park her buggy. Raymond assured her that her cash in hand would pay for galvanized tin and some lumber. He agreed to promote the project.

Emma was delighted when Alvin Yoder agreed to supervise the building project for a fourteen-by-twenty-foot structure. He assured her that he could locate some salvaged lumber and doors for the project. The church announced a frolic to help build the pole shed. Though a frolic conjured up images of partying and celebration, it was simply a call for volunteers to assist in a work project.

On the first day of the frolic, several men dug post holes and planted eight upright posts on the perimeter of the new structure, with one post in the middle. Next they nailed on the cross members and the rafters that completed the skeleton. Finally they secured sheets of galvanized tin onto the sides and roof.

The next day two men nailed together a frame for an overhead door and covered it with tin. Still others planted posts for a small corral.

In the afternoon, Emma watched two men sawing posts out of Osage orange trees felled on the north edge of the shelterbelt. "These trees make the best posts of any tree in Kansas," one man commented.

"Yes," the other agreed. "My father once told me that this wood won't rot out in fifty years."

"Thanks for helping," Emma told the men.

"We're just glad to help."

The barn was finished by Thanksgiving Day. For Emma, it was indeed a day of thanksgiving. That day, she joined the Miller family—Tobe's uncles, aunts, and cousins on his mother's side—for a gathering at the Joe Miller residence. Even as a widowed in-law, Emma felt at home there. As she sat at the table with her family, she recalled with fondness that Tobe and she had served as waiters at Joe and Catherine's wedding. It had been their first date, so to speak. Now, as an in-law, she savored the warm embrace of the whole Miller family. She also sensed their deep sympathy for her situation as a widow.

Now that Emma was in her own home, she felt a new sense of security and purpose. Life still seemed difficult, sometimes even impossible. There was much work to do to keep the household going. The family ate all their meals together, so she cooked three meals a day. Monday was the day to wash the family clothing and hang it out to dry. Tuesdays lent themselves to sewing and mending. Wednesday brought the weekly evening Bible study. Saturday work consisted of cooking and cleaning. In the summertime, there was gardening to do almost anytime.

On the first Thursday of each month, Emma attended the monthly church sewing. Women spent most of the day working on projects for missions and relief.

In the midst of all the work, Emma savored the sense of tranquility in the domestic routines that defined much of her life. They brought a measure of calm in the turbulent wake of Tobe's death.

• • • •

On the last day of November, Mr. Webb brought Mary Edna home earlier than usual. Tippy, Emma's terrier, announced Mary Edna's coming with his excited barking.

"I got paid today," Mary Edna said as soon as she came in the door. She reached into her purse, pulled out a check, and gave it to Emma, who smiled broadly in return.

"That makes $96 that I've earned at Webbs these five weeks," Mary said with obvious pride in her voice.

"That will really help."

"I get a little tired of working at Webbs. I'm glad that I get some time to myself. This week I read *Little Women* and a Danny Orlis book."

"I'm glad you have time to sew and read."

"What are we going to do for Christmas?" Mary asked.

"We have a family gathering."

"I mean in the house. I helped the Webbs put up a Christmas tree and some lights. Lots of people in town put lights outside their houses."

Emma shook her head. "Those things cost money." Surely Mary Edna knew that the church forbade the display of a Christmas tree because of its pagan origins. And they feared that extravagant Christmas displays would encourage a level of holiday spending not befitting plain people.

"I didn't mean we have to have a tree or lights. But maybe we could display our Christmas cards. We have some nice ones already."

Emma nodded. "That will be okay."

As Emma prepared supper, she dreaded the thought of Christmas without Tobe. It was sure to be a lonely time. And there wouldn't be much money for gifts. "That's nothing new," she reminded herself. "What's new this Christmas is that Tobe is gone."

On Christmas morning, it was so cold in the unheated bedrooms that the children gathered around the stove in the living room to get dressed. Glenn and Perry wrestled on the living room floor, grunting and straining to pin each other to the floor. The two were a good match; Perry was taller and stronger, but Glenn made quicker moves.

"Boys, we're going to have a little Christmas now," Emma said. "Let's sit in the living room."

The two got up, tucked in their shirts, and ran their hands through their tousled hair.

The family sat on the sofa and soft chairs while Emma read the Christmas story from *Egermeier's Bible Story Book*. Then she went to the closet and got an orange for each one, along with some sweets. The older children passed the remainder of the morning playing table games while Emma fixed a dish to carry to the Nisly gathering for dinner.

At noon, the six of them donned their winter clothing and got into the buggy to make their way to the Mose Nisly residence. Mose was Emma's stepbrother, the son of Noah and Rosa Nisly. The gathering brought together both Grandpa Noah and Grandma Mary Nisly's children and their families, so the house was quite full. The Christmas cards, hanging on a string suspended along the wall, served as the only sign of the holiday season.

Emma observed with admiration that her mother demonstrated the same love for her stepchildren as she did for her own. Noah's daughter Ella lived at home with the couple. Mother Nisly appeared to treat Ella with the same kindness and respect that Emma had always known for herself. It was gratifying to see.

Emma wondered whether she would be able to do the same if she were to be remarried to a man with his own children. She quickly put the thought aside. "Why would I want to be remarried? Surely no one could take Tobe's place in my mind and heart."

Several days later, Emma joined Tobe's side of the family for a holiday meal. All of Tobe's siblings gathered at the home of Tobe's parents, who had moved back into their own home. Grandpa Stutzman's table was large enough to hold all the members of their four sons' families, which now included eight grandchildren.

During a lull in the dinner conversation, the talk turned to Emma's new house. "I drove by your new place the other day," Clarence told Emma. "It looks like you're pretty well settled in."

"I'm very happy with it," Emma replied with a large smile.

"She's not the only one settling in," Tobe's brother L. Perry commented. "Emma moved from Grandpa's place to her place in the shelterbelt, Grandpas moved from Dannie Mattie's place back to their own place, and Clarences moved from the Ray Headings place into Dannie Mattie's place. Now we're all getting settled."

Emma nodded. It was true that she wasn't the only one who had some settling in to do. But she was the only one doing so as a widow. That made it quite different.

That evening as Emma tucked the twins into bed, she knelt beside each one and led in a simple eighteenth-century English bedtime prayer: "Now I lay me down to sleep, I pray thee Lord my soul to keep. If I should die before I wake, I pray thee Lord my soul to take." Then she rose, gently stroked the child's cheek, and walked quietly out of the room. There was always a little catch in her breath when she said those words. "If I were to die," she asked herself, "what would happen to the children?" She dreaded the thought of them being orphaned.

Later, as Emma slipped into her own bed, she reflected on L. Perry's comment about settling in. "How could I ever feel settled when I'm alone?" she thought. "I don't think it will ever feel right without Tobe." She sniffed aloud as tears slipped out unbidden, tickling the inside of her nose. She turned onto her side and wiped the tears with the edge of the bedsheet. Then she sat up and blew her nose with the hand-kerchief that had been lying on her dresser.

"What's the matter, Mom?" Ervin asked as he sat up in the small bed in the corner of the room.

"Nothing, Ervin. You lie down and go to sleep now."

"I don't want the children to see me cry," she worried. "It

might make them upset. Besides, crying won't do much good. And I don't want people to think I'm ungrateful."

"I don't know that I can ever thank God for allowing my husband to be taken away," she told herself. "But I can count my blessings. I'm better off than many people in the world. I have a little cash left from the rent of the 40 acres. That should carry us along a few more months, along with Mary Edna's earnings. I have a new house and now a small barn. I have a house with no mortgage."

Emma turned to look out the bedroom window and saw the moonlight glistening on snow that had dusted the evergreen tree. It shone like a glimmer of hope.

Ervin stirred in his crib as Emma continued to muse. "It's so good to be living in my own place. We have plenty of room to start a garden next spring. How could I be ungrateful when I have so much? I think it's about time to have some company over to share our blessings."

7

Hosting Guests

The floor was cold under Emma's feet when she got out of the bed the next Sunday morning. She looked outside through the frosted window. It was clear and cold. Since it was the week for Sunday school, it would be a good day to invite guests for dinner.

That morning as she sat in the Sunday school service, Emma made a mental list of the people that she wanted to invite. Much of the food was already prepared, so she didn't mind waiting to decide on guest invitations until after the service. She decided to invite Perry L. Miller's family as well as Perry's parents, Levi and Clara Miller. Clara was Emma's aunt, so Perry was Emma's cousin. Mary Edna invited her friend Alma to join them as well.

After the service, Emma shepherded her family into the buggy and headed for home a little earlier than usual. It would take some time to finish the food preparation.

As soon as the family got home, Emma hurried into the kitchen and turned on the gas burner under a kettle of water for the potatoes. "You'll want to put all of the boards in the table," Emma said to Mary Edna as she was tying her apron strings.

Mary Edna made her way into the washroom, where the table extension boards were stacked beside the kitchen door. She carried the four boards to the dining room table, where she and Alma set them in place.

Mary Edna counted the places at the table. "I believe we'll be able to seat twelve at the table now," she said. "Now we need to find some places for the children."

"You can put four at the little table that Dad made for the twins," Emma replied.

"That will be enough places for everyone, since we only have sixteen altogether," Mary Edna said. With that, she moved toward the hutch that housed Emma's chinaware.

Emma had just finished peeling the potatoes when she saw the Perry L. Miller family arrive. She glanced out the window to watch Perry L. slowly getting out of his buggy. Before he took a step away from the buggy, he latched the brace on his right leg, shortened by polio. Because this handicap made it difficult to work on the farm, Perry L. had been allowed to go to college. Now he was a schoolteacher, the only person in the church district with a college degree.

Emma watched as Perry L., his wife Judy, and their three children came to the front door. She dried her hands, greeted her guests at the door, shook each one's hand, and invited them to lay their winter coats on the bed in her room. Just then, Levi and Clara pulled into the yard with their buggy, so Emma welcomed them in as well.

"Just make yourself at home," Emma told them. "Dinner will be ready before long."

"We'll help you in the kitchen," Judy said, following Emma back to the kitchen alongside her mother-in-law, Clara.

Perry L. and his father took seats in the living room along with Perry and Glenn, where the conversation turned to the recent community hunt.

"I heard that the men were hunting northeast of Yoder this week," Perry ventured.

"Yes," Perry L. answered, "they got only one coyote. They must be a little scarce this year."

"But they got almost two thousand jackrabbits," Glenn responded.

"That's a lot of jackrabbits," said Levi. "But I think there are fewer cottontails this year."

"We've had good luck with cottontails," Perry said.

"Oh?" Levi cocked his head.

"We trap them," Glen explained. "We made box traps last fall and put them in the shelterbelt. We butcher the rabbits and sell them to Mrs. Gillock."

"How much do you get for them?"

"We charge thirty-five cents apiece for them dressed and soaked in salt brine. She likes 'em that way 'cause the meat turns white."

"Who is this Mrs. Gillock?" the older Perry inquired.

"She runs a group home for about five people on East First Street in Hutch," Glenn replied. "The residents enjoy rabbit meat. We send her a postcard to let her know when we have a dozen or so in brine. She comes to pick them up."

"The weather was so dry I thought there wouldn't be many rabbits," Levi said. "But it sounds like you've been able to find a few."

Just then Emma called out, "We're ready to eat." She laid a hotpad on the table and put the last of the hot dishes on it.

Everyone made their way to the table. Emma pointed each one to a seat. The twins sat at the small table along with two of Perry L.'s boys.

When everyone was seated, Emma looked at Levi and quietly asked, "Would you lead in our prayer?"

Levi nodded as everyone bowed their heads.

When the prayer was ended, Emma said "Just reach and help yourselves." She watched with satisfaction as her guests filled their plates with mashed potatoes slathered with gravy, green beans, carrot salad, and canned beef. She also served her favorite spread—Karo syrup mixed with peanut butter.

It was quiet for a few minutes as the dishes were passed around the table.

Perry L. looked at Emma. "You have a nice home here in the shelterbelt. Is there some acreage with it?"

Emma nodded. "Mother gave me one acre here for the house. And I have the forty acres that I inherited from Dad."

Clara spoke up, "I believe he inherited those forty acres from your grandpa Dan."

"Grandpa Dan gave land to each of his children, didn't he?" Perry Miller asked.

"Yes, he did. He was a good manager," Clara answered.

"But he made his money by horse breeding, not farming," Levi added.

"What kind of horses were they?" Perry asked.

"He owned two or three Percheron stallions for studs," Levi said. "They were good draft horses. Folks came from far and wide to get their mares bred. One of the reasons people came to him is because he gave them a good deal. He didn't charge for the breeding service until the offspring was born healthy. So he had to wait quite a while for his money."

"So he had a lot of customers?" Perry asked.

"Yes, he made a good name for the Nislys."

Perry L. chuckled, "Like we say sometimes, 'If we had the wit of a Yutzy, the humility of a Mast, the moneymaking ability of a Nisly, and the personality of a Miller, we'd really have it made.'" Each of the last names represented one of his great-grandparents.

Emma grinned. There was at least a little truth in the saying. She noticed that the Stutzman name wasn't mentioned. Stutzmans didn't have much status in the neighborhood.

"It would be harder for someone to make a good living by horse breeding these days," Perry L. commented. "Now that farmers are using tractors, there just isn't the market for horses. Except for us Amish, there aren't many people around here who need horses except for pleasure. But in Puerto Rico, there are places where they still use horses instead of cars—up in the mountains, where the roads aren't so good."

Perry L. often spoke of Puerto Rico since he had served there as a volunteer worker for several years. Emma admired his experience and his command of the Spanish language.

Glenn changed the subject. "I met a hoopie on the road the other day," he said. "It looked like William Nisly was driving. I thought he had to get rid of his hoopie before the ministers would let him and Lizzie get married." William was a first cousin to both Perry L. Miller and to Emma.

The adults at the table frowned at the mention of such a sensitive subject at the table. The church allowed the use of tractors but not cars for transportation. Hoopies were stripped-down cars that deliberately blurred the line between the two. There was considerable ferment in the church about what should be done with such offenders. Some wanted vehicles so badly that they risked excommunication from the fellowship.

"It's true that William had to get rid of his hoopie," Perry L. said after deliberation. "That was about a year ago. Now that he's been married for awhile, he decided to get it back. It's too far to go to work with a tractor."

"There are plenty of other people who need cars to get to work," Glenn replied.

It was true. Perry L. Miller used a truck to go to school, but that was because of his handicap.

Emma rose from the table. "I have graham-cracker fluff for dessert," she said. She pulled a serving spoon from a kitchen drawer and pushed it into the sweet dish. She set it in front of Levi and invited him to serve himself and pass it on.

After the meal, Emma's guests scattered into different parts of the house. The men and boys sat in the living room and talked while the women did the dishes. The children played around the toy drawer in the hallway. Both families stayed until the middle of the afternoon.

After Emma bid goodbye to each of her guests she sank into the rocking chair. She was tired but happy. It was hard work to host groups in her home, but farm chores and meal preparation weren't prohibited like most other work on Sunday. Emma wouldn't have dared to make a stitch, balance the checkbook, do the laundry, or work in the garden on the Lord's day. The church had always taught that Sunday was meant to be a day of rest, not to be defiled by ordinary labor.

Suddenly it occurred to her that she should have had her guests write their names in a book. "I'm going to get a guest book by the next time I have company," she vowed to herself. Then she loosened her covering and moved it up on top of her head so that it wouldn't wrinkle when she leaned back in the chair for a nap. She awoke to find Ervin tugging at her skirts.

"Mom, what's a hoopie?"

"Hoopies are cars with the top cut off. People use them like a pickup truck, like Raymond's hot rod. Some put a big wooden box on the back."

"Why do they cut the top off? It's cold to drive in the winter."

Emma nodded, "Yes, it's very cold. They cut the tops off to make them more like pickups." She paused. "Since our church isn't supposed to have cars, some people use hoopies instead. That's how they get around the *Ordnung*."

"Does our church let people have trucks?" the young boy persisted.

124

"Well, not really, but it's not as bad as having cars."

"Uncle Ervin has a truck."

"He needs it to make deliveries."

"Okay." The child seemed to ponder this for a moment and then turned back to his toys.

Emma got out of the chair and brushed the wrinkles out of her apron. Ervin was much too young to be asking about the use of cars in the church. He couldn't possibly comprehend how severely it strained the unity in the church district.

The issue defied an easy solution. A number of young men from the church had gotten used to driving cars while in I-W service. This military draft classification signified one's status as a conscientious objector to war. Many of the Amish young men served in unpopular jobs, such as hospital orderlies, in large cities like Kansas City or Denver. Because horse-drawn carriages could not be used there, the Amish Church allowed them to use cars. Most of these men were not satisfied to return to horse-drawn vehicles after they returned home.

Several members of the church had bought trucks for farm use, a practice forbidden by the *Ordnung*. Five years earlier, in the name of Stutzman Brothers, Tobe's brothers Ervin J. and Clarence had bought a pickup to deliver storm windows. The church said nothing since the registration was in Clarence's name. He was a member of the Plainview Conservative Mennonite Church, which allowed motorized vehicles. But when Ervin J. and Clarence dissolved the partnership in 1955, Ervin J. (though Amish) kept the truck. He felt that his business could not survive without it. While a few people took notice, no one pressed the issue. They knew that Ervin J. was eager to support the church for the most part.

Ervin J.'s Amish brother-in-law Menno Nisly had bought a truck for his butchering business in the fall of 1955, registering it in the name of his brother Jonas, who like Clarence was a member of a church that allowed cars. The next spring, Menno expanded his business by buying a garbage route in Hutchinson. Besides buying several old trucks to haul the garbage, he bought a 1940 Chevrolet car for his brother Jonas to drive to work. To inquiring fellow church members who were farmers, he justified the purchase by saying, "It's like a new tractor for you."

After months went by without any church action, Menno bought a Ford pickup, this time in partnership with his brother Melvin. Both Menno and Melvin were members of the Amish Church. With fall communion just a few weeks away, this action proved to be too much for the church to ignore. Melvin was a farmer. How could he justify the use of a truck?

Emboldened by the Nisly brothers' actions, Emma's neighbor Enos Miller purchased a car for his sons to drive to jobs in town. When confronted with the possible consequences of his transgression, he answered: "I'm not going to beat around the bush by making it a hoopie."

The spring and fall communion seasons were the times when differences of opinion about acceptable practice usually came to a head. The Amish believed that communion was to be shared only by those who were at peace with the church *Ordnung*. Communion implied peace and agreement. To assure such agreement and conformity to the rules, an *Ordnungsgemeinde*, counsel meeting, preceded the communion service by two weeks. There the bishop recited the rules for membership. Every member was expected to give verbal assent to oneness or agreement with the church rules. Those who were not "at one" with the rules were not allowed to take communion. If there were several such individuals, the communion service might be postponed to give time for a broader consensus to emerge. Sometimes, it seemed to

Emma, the oneness attained through the counsel process was a thin veneer. It served as a cover for unforgiving attitudes, underlying tensions, and contrary behavior. At its best, though, the process led to the strongest sense of unity obtainable in a fellowship based on group conformity as disciples of Christ.

Emma's mind drifted back to the time in late 1955 when Tobe and she had made a confession for having bought a car. Emma wouldn't have dreamed of standing back from communion on a matter such as the use of a car. Now Tobe's body lay cold in the church graveyard, mangled to death by that vehicle.

"What if he had not made his confession?" Emma asked herself as she straightened out her covering and moved toward the dining room to take the extension boards out of the table. She pulled off the white tablecloth and shook the crumbs out the backdoor.

"I hope the ministers can work something out," Emma thought to herself as she took the boards out of the table and stood them on end in the washroom. "I know it would be hard on Dad to see this happening." She recalled with some pain the way her father, Levi, had needed to work through church discipline issues as a minister.

The fall counsel meeting in September brought the matter of car ownership to a head. "If we allow pickups and cars, we won't be able to hold the line on other things," one man said with deep conviction. "Our people will want to drive to many places where they shouldn't go—rodeos, fairs, bowling alleys, and other such places. They won't be as tempted if they don't have cars."

"But we need cars and trucks for our businesses," insisted another. "Cars and trucks aren't bad in themselves; it's how they are used that makes a difference. The cars will make it easier for us to get to church services, especially in winter weather."

After discussion, the bishop announced that neither Melvin Nisly nor Enos Miller would be allowed to share in the communion service unless they made a confession regarding their ownership of forbidden vehicles. Both men stood firm in their resolve. They did not believe that they had committed an offense worthy of such sanction. Their wives stood in solidarity with them. The ministers also stood firm, and so it appeared that two of Emma's neighbors would be missing when the church celebrated communion in late October.

Emma sensed that there would be no peace in the fellowship until this issue was resolved. Although the younger ministers seemed sympathetic to the members who wished to own cars, they publicly supported the bishop's decision.

Communion Sunday dawned cloudy and cool. In keeping with tradition for church members, Emma, Perry, and Mary Edna fasted, not eating breakfast. The biannual communion service was called *gross Gmee*, "large congregational assembly." It was the largest and most solemn event of the church year, a joint worship service of the North and South church districts. This time it was held at the Dan M. Nisly residence, just about a mile south of Emma's house.

Emma got the family into the buggy and headed down to the Nisly home just in time for the 9:30 a.m. service. She left the horse in Perry's care and headed for the house with the twins in tow.

Emma greeted a number of women with the customary kiss and then made her way to a seat in the large kitchen. Through the large double door, she could see men assembled in the living room. Just as she sat down on one of the backless benches, the ministers made their way up the stairs to the second floor. The congregation sang an opening hymn from the *Ausbund*, followed by the traditional second hymn, the "*Lob Lied* [Praise Song]" (no. 131). As she sang, she glanced back to see whether or not her two boys had come in. Often the young people dribbled in slowly. She was relieved to see them sitting in the back row.

When the ministers returned, the congregation sang a song of blessing and invocation reserved for use in the communion service. Bishop John D. Yoder opened with a Christian greeting: "We are grateful to be gathered here on this special occasion to celebrate the suffering of our Lord. Today we will share in the bread and the cup. If there is anything that is not right among us or anything that would interfere with this fellowship, you may make it known now. If so, we will not continue until all is made right." He paused for a moment and looked around the room.

Emma sensed that the greeting was a formality, though anyone had the right to speak. Had anyone done so, it would almost surely have been a man. The communion service could be suspended on the spot for reasons of unresolved conflict, bitterness, or someone's blatant disregard for the *Ordnung*.

On this occasion, everyone remained silent. Emma glanced quickly to each side as Bishop Yoder prepared to lead in prayer. Were the two couples who withstood the *Ordnung* on cars in attendance or not? If so, she hadn't seen them. Her heart ached, particularly for the two women.

Shortly after ten o'clock, Preacher Willie Wagler rose to give the *Anfang*, the beginning message. Willie's message was the first part of the day's attempt to recite the *Heilsgeschichte*, God's salvation story woven as a thread through all parts of the Bible. Following long custom, Willie drew from the first few chapters of the book of Genesis. He told of the creation of the world, the judgment of the worldwide flood, and of Noah's faithfulness in building an ark. He ended his message by rehearsing how Noah celebrated God's protection through the flood by building an altar of worship.

Emma shifted wearily on the backless bench as Willie took his seat. Willie always preached good sermons, but it wasn't easy to concentrate with two energetic twins at her side. "If only Tobe were alive," she thought wistfully, "he would help me." She glanced back at the young women seated in the back rows. One of them chewed noisily on a piece of gum.

As Preacher Amos Nisly stood to present the second message, one of the women passed a plate of sugar cookies for the young children. In long services it helped provide a temporary distraction for the youngsters. Emma held the plate while the twins helped themselves. She shook her head in warning when Ervin started to take more than one.

As Brother Nisly wove the next strands into the story of God's redemption, Ervin wiggled in a way that, Emma knew, meant she needed to take him out. "*Ich misse naus geh.* I need to go out," the boy said in a loud whisper. Emma nodded and put a finger to her lips. She laid her sleeping daughter on the floor and then took Ervin's hand. They threaded their way out of the crowded house and walked to the outhouse. On the path, they met a young man who was on the way back in. In long services such as these, it was common to have many people making the trip to the outdoor toilet.

When Emma returned, Amos was describing the forty years when the Israelites were wandering in the wilderness. As Brother Nisly ended his message, Bishop Yoder got up from his seat at the front of the living room and walked to the kitchen. Emma glanced at the mantel clock. It was 11:30 a.m. The bishop would eat a quick lunch and then preach through the lunch hour. The rest of the people would eat in small shifts, starting at noon.

By the time the bishop returned, a guest preacher was

expounding on other themes from the Old Testament—the inheritance of the Promised Land, the time of the judges, the nation's disobedience, and the coming of the prophets. He concluded his message just as the mantel clock struck twelve noon.

Emma shifted wearily in her seat as Bishop Yoder took his place at the front of the room. She glanced into the living room, where the men were seated. A number of them appeared to be sleeping. She also detected the sound of a young man in the back row clipping his fingernails. The bishop began his message by quoting the prophecies in Isaiah regarding the coming Messiah. Then he told the story of Christ's birth from the Gospel of Luke before making his way through an exposition of the Gospel of Matthew. Ervin reached over Emma's lap to aggravate his sister by poking her with his finger. Emma gave him a quick pinch on the thigh. "*Nee, du mich net petze*! No, don't you pinch me!" the boy said, much too loudly for Emma's comfort.

Along with the woman sitting on her bench, Emma soon took her turn at the kitchen counter. The twins followed at her heels. She stepped up to the counter to eat open-faced sandwiches with butter, peanut butter, pickles, and red beets. Emma didn't mind missing a piece of the sermon. She had heard the same texts expounded at communion time since she was a child.

When she returned, the bishop was preaching about Christ's death and resurrection. The twins were more restless now than ever. Erma tugged at the hankie that Emma kept in her cape. "Fold it into a cradle," Erma whispered. Emma rolled, folded, and twisted the cloth until it resembled a pair of twins suspended in a hammock. She handed the cloth to Erma, who hummed softly as she swung it in an arc above the bench.

"I want it," Ervin begged.

"Wait your turn," Emma said quietly.

Long services such as this made it seem impossible for Emma to keep the children's behavior in order. Ervin was particularly energetic. To sit for several hours on a backless bench seemed to be a standard out of reach for him. The church frowned on the use of children's toys or books that didn't readily fit into a small bag. People had little tolerance for children who drew attention to themselves. At times like these, she was greatly relieved when Mother Nisly or a compassionate church member offered to help.

It was nearly two o'clock when the bishop spoke about the ascension of Jesus Christ and his promise to the disciples that they would be filled with power from on high. Then he closed his sermon and announced that it was time to share in the service of communion.

Willie Wagler stepped into the kitchen and returned with the communion emblems. There were two loaves of bread, freshly baked and sliced by Willie's wife, Alma. There was also a glass jug filled with grape juice. Beside it stood a tin cup from Lizzie Nisly's kitchen, which would be used to serve the juice. Willie placed the emblems on a small table at the front of the room and covered them with a white cloth.

After reading a passage of Scripture, Bishop Yoder lifted the cloth and took a slice of bread into his hands. He invited the congregation to stand as he bowed his head for a prayer of thanks and blessing. When he had finished praying, the members remained standing while others sat down. Children and other nonmembers were free to observe, but only members would receive communion.

"Members in good standing," Emma reminded herself. Two couples had considered their cars more dear than the communion of the church. Emma couldn't abide the thought of being excluded from the sacred meal. Surely God's eye was dim toward those who could not commune with other believers.

Bishop Yoder broke off a small portion of the bread, ate it, and then gave a piece to Willie and the other ministers in turn. He began to serve the men in the congregation, breaking off a piece of bread for each one. First the bishop served the elderly men in the front benches, beginning with the oldest. He went from bench to bench, handing a chunk of bread to each member. Each man sat down when he received his portion. The bishop worked his way through each row, moving toward the back where the boys were seated. His assistant stood at attention with a fresh supply of bread.

After he finished serving the men's side, the bishop moved to the kitchen, where Emma was seated. First he served the older women at the front of the room. Then he made his way through the narrow rows toward the back of the room, where the young girls sat. Emma received the bread with an open palm and then bowed slightly at the knee before placing it in her mouth. She chewed it slowly, savoring the taste of fresh bread. Then she sat down.

Emma watched as the bishop served the last of the women's side. He put the remaining bread back on the table and spread the cloth over it. Emma anticipated that Willie's wife would serve it to the family for a noon meal. It would not go to waste.

The bishop then turned to bless the fruit of the vine. Willie picked up the jug, poured grape juice into the tin cup, and handed it to the bishop. He held it up and invited the congregation to stand for the prayer of blessing. Again, those who expected to receive the cup remained standing while others sat down. The bishop made his way through the congregation in the same order by which he had served the bread. He handed the cup to each communicant in turn, extending it to them with the handle exposed. Each time the cup came to the end of a row of seats, Willie wiped the rim with a white cloth. When it became empty, he stepped forward to fill it from the glass jug. When all were served, the bishop gave the cup to Willie, who placed it under the white table cloth at the front of the room.

Brother Nisly then read a passage from the thirteenth chapter of the Gospel of John. The Scripture told the story of Jesus washing the feet of his disciples. The minister read the last several verses with emphasis: "If I then, your Lord and Master, have washed your feet; ye also ought to wash one another's feet. For I have given you an example, that ye should do as I have done to you. . . . If ye know these things, happy are ye if you do them."

Because of the absence of an active deacon, the ministers took up the work of preparing for the ritual of foot washing. Emma watched as the ministers brought galvanized tubs of warm water into the room. Emma sat next to Lydia Yoder, so they would wash each other's feet. Emma stooped down in front of the white porcelain tub and took Lydia's foot in one hand. With her other hand, she splashed a bit of water onto the bare foot and then rubbed it dry with a terry-cloth towel. She repeated the motions with the other foot. Then they exchanged places. When Lydia had finished washing Emma's feet, they greeted each other with a gentle handshake and the kiss of fellowship. Then they returned to their seats to put on their hose and shoes. Emma sat quietly until all had finished washing their feet.

The clock struck three as the ministers collected the tubs and carried them out of the room. Preacher David L. Miller took his place at the door with a small bag to collect *Almose Geld*, money for the alms fund. Then everyone was dismissed. As was the custom, the worshippers left the room by order of age, beginning with the youngest teenagers. As the members filed by the minister at the doorway, most placed money into the bag.

The ministers used the fund to help those in need—members who had suffered loss of health, finances, or property—or at times for a mission project. "It might even be used to aid needy widows," Emma thought to herself as she walked by and slipped a paper bill into the bag.

By the time she got home, it was half past three. She flopped into a chair, exhausted. Mary Edna promised to watch the twins while Emma took a nap. "For mothers with young children," Emma mused, "communion Sunday is anything but a day of rest."

8

Church Troubles

In early spring of 1957, as Emma was preparing to plant the first things in her new garden, she took thankful notice of the way the recent rains had changed the landscape. Little evidence remained of the previous year's long dry season. One day it snowed and rained to the point that water stood in large pools around the yard. That evening, Emma sent Mary Edna downstairs to the basement to get a jar of canned peaches.

Mary Edna called up the stairs, "Mom, we've got water in the basement."

Emma joined her daughter on the steps. The water on the floor came close to the bottom of the first step. "What are we going to do?" Mary Edna asked.

"We'll have to carry it out. Let's go get Perry and Glenn."

Mary Edna trudged up the steps to notify the boys while Emma took off her shoes and hose and stepped into the water.

Perry soon came to survey the scene. "How did this water get in here?" he wondered aloud. Then he answered his own question. "It looks to me like it came in under the outside door and ran down the east wall," he said. "There's no place for the water to get away from the house. The foundation should be up a little higher." As he stood in the open doorway to the outside, the chill of melting snow crept down the stairway to where Mary Edna was standing.

"Close the door," Mary Edna complained. "It's cold in here."

"We need to get the water out of here," Emma said. "We might as well find some buckets and get started." As she spoke, Glenn joined the family in surveying the situation.

"I'll find a couple of buckets," he volunteered.

Meanwhile, Perry took off his shoes and socks, rolled up his pant legs, and stepped into the water. "*Es is kalt*. It's cold," he said. "*Es macht mich schiddle*. It makes me shiver."

Perry began scooping up the water as the rest formed a brigade to pass the buckets up the steps and on to the outside.

After an hour of work, only a small puddle remained at one end of the room.

"I'm hungry. Let's make some popcorn," Mary Edna suggested.

"That's a good idea," Perry agreed.

Emma nodded her assent. Popcorn was the usual fare on Sunday evening.

Mary Edna pulled the corn popper out of the cupboard and put it on the left front burner on the stove. Then she reached for the tin can filled with lard. With a serving spoon she dipped a large spoonful of lard and plopped it into the popper. Smoke rose from the popper as the lard dissolved into liquid. Mary Edna poured a small container full of kernels into the popper and slowly turned the crank on top. As soon as the first kernels began to pop, she cranked faster. The corn popped vigorously, rising in the kettle until it pressed against the lid. Mary Edna turned off the heat and dumped the popcorn into a large stainless-steel bowl. She salted it with the large glass saltshaker on the stove. Mary Edna mixed the salt throughout the popcorn by flipping the bowl up and down with both hands. Only a few kernels spilled onto the floor.

Emma pulled out several small bowls from the cupboard and set them on the countertop. Perry took one and dipped it into the large container. The rest of the family followed suit until the large bowl was empty. Emma carefully picked apart a few kernels. Her dentures didn't work well with popcorn. As was common in the neighborhood, she'd recently had all her teeth pulled after having problems with toothaches.

In spite of a wet spring, Emma managed to get a garden started across the driveway from the house. Since nearly all of Emma's small plot was covered with trees, she set up the garden outside the property line and onto Mother Nisly's land, rented to Raymond. He didn't seem to mind that Emma used that space. "You hafta have a garden, and you can't grow one in the shelterbelt," Raymond agreed.

The wet spring continued through the end of the school year. From New Year's Day to May 16, Emma emptied twenty inches of water out of her rain gauge. "This is Kansas," Emma thought to herself as she recalled the drought of the previous year. "If you don't get much of a crop one year, you might get one the next." Because it was such a wet spring, it took more work than usual to stay ahead of the weeds in the garden plot.

Emma didn't really mind pulling weeds, especially after a rain. Working in the garden breathed oxygen into Emma's soul. The feel of the sandy loam on her bare feet, the rich colors of the flowers, and the taste of fresh vegetables beckoned her to get her hands into the soil. It was also a place to be alone, away from the incessant demands of her two energetic twins. It was a place to think, to clear her mind from the press of duty. It was also a place to explore the many feelings that rose unbidden in her being.

Emma felt a deep sadness as she pushed the steel-wheeled hand cultivator up and down the rows of peas and corn. It would soon be a year that Tobe was gone. Many of the days had simply dragged by, yet so much had changed.

Not a day passed when Emma didn't think about Tobe. There was no end of reminders: conversations with others, comments made by the children, the furnishings in the house, the advertising materials from his business, and a myriad of daily happenings that conjured up memories of their life together. At times she entertained pleasant thoughts, the memories of younger years when she and Tobe were first married. She felt herself swept up again by Tobe's endless supply of energy, his relentless drive to make a big mark in life. Again Emma felt the flush of wellness in the wake of a good laugh together. She reveled again in the joy of Tobe's creations, when his inventive mind yielded yet another new product made of wood or metal. Again she felt Tobe's warm touch and intimate embrace.

Yet those were fleeting moments. Often she tasted bitter disappointment as she mulled over the way things had turned out. She recalled how submissive she'd been to him, how ready to yield to his way even when she disagreed. How hard she had worked to keep the household going with so little income!

The debt still weighed heavily on her mind, but there was little that she could do except forgive Tobe for dragging them into such a deep pit that bankruptcy was the only way out. She didn't intend to speak of the matter to Tobe's creditors; they could bring it up if they thought it necessary.

Emma felt it best not to speak to the children about her disappointments with Tobe. It might shake the ground under their feet. But she determined to teach them to be responsible with their money in order to avoid Tobe's mistakes.

She made a conscious decision not to complain about her lot. People might tire of her coming and close their hands to her needs. Besides, she had much for which she could give thanks. The best way forward, Emma decided, was to give thanks for the good things in life and try to forget the rest.

• • • •

One week before the anniversary of Tobe's death, Emma's stepbrother Will Nisly was killed in Arizona. Will was forty-two years old, the oldest son of Noah Nisly. Will had moved to Arizona with his wife and foster son a few years earlier for the sake of his health. Like Tobe's, his life ended in an instant. He was electrocuted when he accidentally swung an irrigation pipe against a high-voltage wire. Like Emma, Will's young widow shipped her husband's lifeless body back to Kansas for a funeral and burial in the Amish cemetery.

The funeral service was held in the same place as Tobe's—Albert Yoder's round top. As Emma sat through the funeral service, she found it hard to concentrate. Every detail of the funeral brought back memories from the year gone by. It was as though she was experiencing Tobe's funeral all over again. The clammy grip of death tightened itself around her throat, threatening to choke out hope that she would ever feel normal. She felt a dull throb in the back of her skull.

Emma sat absorbed in her thoughts, with her mind wandering far from the service. "How can I feel so lonely when I'm surrounded by so many friends and relatives?" she asked herself. "How can I talk about my loneliness without appearing to be ungrateful? To whom could I speak about such things?"

Emma's thoughts were interrupted by the minister's invitation for the congregation to rise. She stood with the others. Soon the mourners made their way past the casket, bidding their last farewell. As Emma made her way past the bier, her legs turned to jelly. It was as though Tobe were lying there. She was deeply relieved when the burial was over and she was back at home. After putting the children to sleep, she fell exhausted into bed.

Still, Emma couldn't sleep. She shifted onto her side and waved the bedsheet to move air across her tired body. Nighttime seemed to bring little relief from the summer heat. She turned to watch the June bugs thumping against the screen, their bodies casting eerie shadows in the moonlight. A dog howled nearby; a distant neighbor dog howled back. A long freight train rumbled through the neighborhood along Highway 61. Emma usually slept through these night sounds, but now when she most needed sleep, the noises served to keep slumber at bay.

She thought of the events of the day, how Will Nisly had been killed. The electrocution had come about because Will had mistakenly hit a wire with an irrigation pipe. It had been an accident, yet he was clearly at fault. God must have allowed him to make that mistake.

Emma pondered how Tobe had died. The driver of the concrete truck claimed that Tobe had drifted across the center line into his lane. Had Tobe been at fault? Perhaps the truck driver wasn't telling the truth. Clarence and Perry said the man wouldn't answer their questions. Was he trying to hide something? If he was at fault, shouldn't the company admit his wrong?

If the truck driver was telling the truth, why had it happened? Had Tobe fallen ill? Or had he fallen asleep at the wheel? If so, was it because he was working too hard and not getting enough sleep? Then Emma recalled that Glenn had begged to travel with Tobe that fateful day. Perhaps if the boy had gone along, their talking with each other would have kept Tobe awake.

Emma suspected that some of the Amish were thinking that Tobe's death was a judgment from God because he bought a car outside the *Ordnung* of the church. If so, did that mean he wouldn't be in heaven?

It seemed to Emma as though she would never find answers for all her questions. She might just have to be satisfied, she mused, to let them die unanswered. At least she could be confident that God wouldn't have allowed Tobe's death unless it had been his will.

• • • •

In June, Emma traveled to visit her daughter Edith in Iowa. Clarence and Bunny Stutzman had offered to drive. When Emma arrived at the Weaver's house, Edith was playing in the yard. The moment Edith recognized her mother, she came running, followed by her pet Chihuahua.

"*Du bischt*, you are, my Kansas Mama," Edith babbled. "Yes sir." She laughed with excitement. "*Dat* is my *billy doat*. There's my billy goat," she said, pointing toward the farmyard. Two goats romped inside the small corral, where Noah was repairing a wooden fence.

"I see," Emma said with a grin. She took a long look at her daughter. It seemed like some time since she'd last seen her. Edith had the same thin lips, which she so readily twisted into comical expressions to gain attention. Her long brown hair was woven into two thick braids. Her left eye was out of alignment as usual. Emma reckoned that the girl might have grown an inch or two over the last year. She seemed to be doing well on the small farm.

Arvilla Weaver called from the front door, "Come on in." She motioned with her hand.

Emma mounted the two steps to the small landing and greeted the woman who now took care of her daughter. As

Emma stepped inside and set down her suitcase, Sarah came from the kitchen. "Welcome," the older women said in her raspy yet gentle voice. She shook Emma's hand with a firm grip. "Just make yourself at home."

Just then Edith burst through the door and beckoned Emma to follow her. Emma followed her daughter up the stairs and into her room. Edith plopped herself on the bed and began putting together a simple wooden puzzle. Emma watched as Edith put each piece in its proper place. Edith hummed as she worked, nearly oblivious to Emma's presence. When she was finished with the puzzle, she looked up as though she was seeing Emma for the first time. "See there!" she exclaimed, pointing at the completed puzzle. She followed with a string of monosyllables that Emma didn't comprehend.

Emma looked around the room. Everything was neatly organized—magazines, handkerchiefs, dolls, and scrapbooks full of pictures. That part of Edith hadn't changed; she loved to keep everything clean and in order.

Over the next few days, Emma spent time with Edith and helped the women around the house. Arvilla reported that Edith was doing well at the special school that had opened in Washington, Iowa, in the fall after Emma had moved to Kansas. It was the first that Edith had attended school.

It took a bit of adjustment to hear Edith address Sarah as "Mama." Arvilla explained that in order to avoid confusion, she had taught Edith to address Emma as "Kansas Mama."

Emma reflected that it had been nearly a year since she'd left Edith in the Weaver family's care. At that time, Arvilla had agreed to keep her for a while. Now, Arvilla practically considered the girl a daughter.

"If I'm going to keep her," Arvilla said, "I want to keep her the rest of her life."

Having witnessed the bond between Arvilla and Edith, Emma was willing to concede. She was convinced that the Weavers were better suited to care for Edith than she was, particularly now that Edith could go to school.

While Emma was in Kalona, she stopped by to visit the place where she had last lived. She was dismayed to find that the home stood unfinished and empty. The shop stood empty, too; most of the metal-working equipment had been hauled away. Emma blanched to think that Harvey Bender, who owned the land, needed to stand the loss. He wasn't a wealthy man.

She walked out to see the place where she had gardened the year before. Emma noticed with pleasure that the strawberries she had planted were thriving. While she was there, Harvey's daughter Elva came by and invited her to share in the picking. It felt good to help, and she was able to carry fresh strawberries back to the Weaver's house.

It wasn't easy for Emma to face the people in the Kalona neighborhood. The creditors had just conducted their final meeting in the bankruptcy case and the judge was about to make a final settlement for all the creditors.

"Will I ever feel free to look those lenders in the eye?" she asked herself. Emma pondered how things might have turned out differently under slightly different circumstances. If only those big equipment companies hadn't forced Tobe into bankruptcy. If only those house lights would have sold the way Tobe had predicted. If only people who purchased the house lights wouldn't have had to pay a licensed electrician to hook them up. If only we'd never moved to Iowa. If only Tobe would have been given more time. If only he hadn't been killed, he could perhaps have bounced back.

Emma paused and took a deep breath. "I can't keep thinking about the way things might have been," she told herself. "I have to live with the way things are now."

She wondered what God thought about the financial obligations that Tobe had accrued. Did God expect her somehow to pay back those debts? Even though the court had legally released Tobe in the bankruptcy case, she sensed that the church was not of one mind about such obligations. "Owe no man anything," the Bible said, "but to love one another." Would God forgive a debt that was legally dissolved? If not, what was she to do? How could she possibly earn enough to pay it back?

Emma also felt ongoing debt to the Weavers for taking care of Edith. She wasn't able to pay much for their services even though her siblings and the church had arranged to give some aid. Each month, one of her relatives gave a small amount that was matched by the church.

"Will I spend the rest of my life indebted to others?" Emma asked herself. The very thought brought tension to the muscles on the back of her neck. It was hard to relax while carrying a burden of debt.

Yet Emma found ways to compensate. At the end of the year, she sat back in her rocking chair and glanced over the names written in her guest book during 1957. She leafed through the notebook slowly, mentally picturing each one. She'd entertained guests in her home more than thirty times. A few out-of-town guests had dropped by without notice. But most of her guests, well over three hundred in all, had come for a meal by invitation. Emma was a bit tired as she thought of it now, but after having received so much from others, it felt good to give something back.

• • • •

In early April 1958, Mary Edna turned sixteen years old. Because she was working at the Webb's home for the week, Emma would have to wait to see her until the weekend. By community custom, Mary Edna was now old enough to date. And she was old enough to get a driver's license. Even though the church didn't allow the purchase of cars, Emma knew that Mary Edna was determined to drive. She didn't really mind.

Emma's mind drifted back to her own sixteenth birthday. It had been a heady time, a rite of passage. She'd been known as a popular girl, one who'd had many dates, especially with young men who had visited the area from other communities who had different standards of courtship than the one in Kansas. She was embarrassed to recall some of the common practices of the era in Amish communities: dating without lights in the room, sitting on each other's lap in a sofa or chair, or bundling in bed.

Although she had never engaged in bed courtship, Emma had often removed her covering while on a date, since the organdy material wrinkled easily and took a good deal of work to iron. She knew from experience how persistently a young man could press against the boundaries she'd set, how readily their interaction could turn into a quiet contest of wills. "Sowing one's wild oats," as the older ones called it, sometimes resulted in unwanted pregnancies.

Emma was pleased that dating practices had changed considerably since her teenage years. Encouraged by men returning from Civilian Public Service, the youth group had, for the first time, engaged in open conversation about dating standards in the late 1940s. A Wednesday evening Bible Study on Christian Courtship led by David L. Miller in 1949 had lent additional legitimacy to the call for a change in dating practices. Consequently Emma's younger sisters, Barbara and Elizabeth, had reached for higher standards of behavior. In Emma's mind, the changes were all for the good.

Emma was proud that Mary Edna was deeply involved in

personal devotions as well as congregational life. That would help her live more responsibly. She was well liked by the Webbs and others for whom she had kept house. Emma was also grateful for the way that Mary Edna helped care for the rambunctious twins. Mary Edna didn't tire as easily as her mother did when chasing after the youngsters.

The week of Mary Edna's birthday, the Webbs dropped her off at home in time for supper on Friday evening. "Webbs bought me a beautiful cake for my birthday," Mary Edna said. "They got me a gift, too."

Emma's face flushed. She wished she were able to do more for Mary Edna at times like these. But the evening turned out nicely, with Raymond's family sharing the evening meal. Good food would need to be sufficient for a gift on this occasion.

After the meal, Emma told Raymond, "The bishop announced on Sunday that we won't have communion this spring. He says that we're not ready for communion. We don't have peace in the church."

"Did he say what the problem is?"

Emma took a deep breath. "I suppose it's about cars. The ministers can't agree on what should be done."

"I think they should just allow them," Raymond said. "They won't have peace any other way."

"The bishop also announced that there will be an East Eureka school reunion on May 30. After that, they're closing the school, since the county is consolidating the schools."

Raymond nodded. "I heard say they'll close Buckeye, Elmhirst, and East Eureka. All the scholars from there will go to a new school building, along with a few pupils from West Eureka. I think they're going to build it on Menno Yoder's land just south of the Stutzman Greenhouse."

Several weeks later, on the appointed day, Emma joined

her children at the carry-in meal and closing ceremonies at East Eureka. She hated to see the one-room schools close, especially East Eureka, where she'd attended as a child. Emma recalled her six years of grade school there with fondness and appreciation. Now the twins would need to go to the large new school. Was it really better to make schools bigger? In a one-room school the older children could help the younger children with their lessons. And all of the children could learn to know each other.

That evening, Emma and her three oldest children attended a special meeting for church members at the German Schoolhouse. Emma recalled that the building had once been a one-room schoolhouse, now moved to this site for a different use.

The bishop called the special meeting to discuss the *Ordnung*. Because of the recent tension, he thought it wise to call the north and south districts together for a time of discernment. The conversation that evening addressed several topics that threatened the unity of the church.

Emma empathized with the ministers. She understood the difficulty of drawing people toward a common mind and wasn't surprised when the majority of time that evening was spent on the issue of transportation. Clearly the matter hadn't been settled last fall when the two couples stood back from communion. By now, the arguments were familiar. On the one side, some pressed hard to approve the automobile as an acceptable mode of transportation. They gave several reasons. For one, some of the young men were getting jobs in town. It wasn't practical to take a horse and buggy to most job sites. At some locations, there was no place to keep the horse safe from the weather. It wasn't satisfactory to tie up a tractor from the farm all day just to have a vehicle for the road. Further, some of the jobs required travel for some distance.

Again, cars were much more convenient in bad weather. Some of the folks had addressed this problem by using enclosed trailers to pull behind their tractors. But in cold weather, it was still cold inside the trailers. It wasn't practical to heat a trailer.

Finally, allowing cars would enable people to make their own travel plans to conduct business or visit relatives and friends in other states. It was expensive to hire a driver. It would be much more convenient for members to own their own vehicles.

Convenience seemed to be the nub of the issue for both sides. Those who opposed the purchase of cars argued that the added convenience would introduce new temptations, which would eventually undermine the church community. Young people would be drawn to take joy rides and drive to places where they should not be: fairs, skating rinks, rodeos, and other places of questionable entertainment. They would also be tempted to drive to town and mix more readily with people who would compromise their church commitments.

The ownership of vehicles also threatened to blur the church's identity as an Amish Church. It was true that the congregation had named itself as an Amish Mennonite fellowship from its inception in the late 1800s. But they still thought of themselves as Old Order Amish, connected to the larger groups of Amish in Indiana, Ohio, and Pennsylvania. The use of horse-drawn vehicles served as one of the most visible markers of Amish identity. If they adopted the automobile, the folks back east might not think of them as faithful Amish. Were they really prepared to lose this symbol of belonging to the larger Amish community?

Emma was ready to vote for the use of cars. After all, she and Tobe had bought their own car back in Iowa. Tobe had been convinced that his business depended on it. So thought many folks in Kansas, since there were well over a dozen trucks and cars in the fellowship. Like cows that pressed against the fence to reach for greener grass, many church members stretched the rules. Some converted cars into hoopies. Others drove cars owned by a relative or an employee. A few openly defied the rules by buying a car.

That evening Emma left the meeting not knowing how the church would make the decision. But they couldn't go on like this. Surely something would be decided by the time for fall communion.

Mary Edna and the boys freely borrowed Raymond's hot rod, as they called the stripped-down car. Although they wouldn't have dared to drive it to Sunday morning church services, they often drove it to the Wednesday evening Bible study. They parked it alongside the farm tractors with trailers used by fellow church members.

The Wednesday evening services pointed in the direction that the church fellowship was going. What was allowed there was likely to be allowed in the Sunday morning worship at some time in the future, whether mode of transportation, style of music, or standards of dress.

The Wednesday evening Bible study was now ten years old, after beginning in some controversy in 1948. Was it a coincidence that it was born the same year as a group broke off to start the Plainview Conservative Mennonite Church? The weekly study provided a place for young men who had returned from I-W assignments. They were hungry for more interaction than the regular church service afforded, to discuss the Scripture and other elements of their faith. Some of the more-conservative older members registered a quiet protest by their absence, but the majority of the church members in the North and South districts supported the venture. Not many came from the East District.

The weekly meetings were conducted under the watchful

eye of the ministers, but they were planned by an elected committee of three laypersons. Every month, the longest-serving member was replaced by a new member. The planning committee saw to it that most of the men in the church had an opportunity to lead a topic. The congregation did not believe that women should teach in public.

On most weeks, after an opening devotional meditation, the speaker for the evening addressed an assigned topic of particular interest to the congregation. Generally this was followed by some time for group discussion. Although men led the topics, the bolder women among them may have felt free to join in the discussion. But it was always men who led in a time of group prayer in the last fifteen minutes of the meeting.

The Bible study meetings sometimes served as a time of discernment on difficult issues. The topic assigned to Tobe's brother Ervin J. Stutzman in June captured the heart of an issue: "What is our responsibility to our Christian brother?" The Scripture clearly taught that the church was to be a community of disciples. What then was the church to do when they had differing convictions on heartfelt issues?

In the midst of the controversy about vehicles, someone suggested that the ministers draw lots. After all, the use of the lot had helped to settle a controversy about a church basement. And it was regularly used to seek God's will for the leadership of the church. Why not use it as a way to seek God's will regarding the ownership of vehicles? However, Bishop Yoder opposed the idea of using the lot on this occasion, so the discernment meetings went on in the hope of finding a different solution.

The youth group sometimes held separate meetings for discussion and discernment. While the adults discussed the appropriateness of owning vehicles, Mary Edna and Perry attended a meeting in which the youth discussed at some length the appropriateness of wearing a wristwatch. Many of the older members thought of wristwatches as jewelry, unbecoming to a plain church. After all, weren't watches sold in jewelry stores? And since they were quite expensive, didn't they present a temptation for the more-well-to-do members to show off their wealth? In the midst of the discernment, nurses were allowed to wear wristwatches, since they needed a timepiece to help them calculate their patients' heart rates.

It was easy to identify the young people who regularly wore wristwatches even though they took them off for public meetings. The hot sun bronzed their arms and wrists, leaving a white band where watches were worn.

Although the ministers tried to present a united front in the controversy, the differing convictions in the fellowship threatened to fracture the congregation. The ministers spoke of late-night discussions among themselves. Could they find a way forward together, or would some members choose to start a new church?

One evening after supper in early June, Emma and her family headed for Grandpa Nisly's house in Raymond's hot rod. They went to assist, as they often did, with hand-addressing the Amish mission paper called *Witnessing*. The free paper often drew inspiration from writers related to the mission board of the Old Mennonite Church. More important, it told stories of Amish-related mission work. Both Willie Wagler and David L. Miller, ministers in Emma's church district, had helped to initiate the mission movement among the Amish churches. With other mission-minded leaders, they helped to form the Mission Interest Committee in 1952.

The MIC, as they often called the committee, sponsored the Hillcrest Home in Arkansas, a nursing facility where Amish young people could volunteer their time in service. The profits from the Home helped to sponsor MIC missionaries in other places, such as Gulfport, Mississippi, where Emma's sister Elizabeth had served as a rural missionary.

Since David L. Miller served as the treasurer of the publication, the newsletter was mailed from the small post office at Partridge, not far from his home. Emma and the other helpers wrote the addresses on about eight hundred copies of the mimeographed newsletter. It would then be shipped in bulk to Amish congregations, most of them in the more-populous areas east of the Mississippi River.

When she reached home that evening, Emma paged to the *Witnessing* article written by Lydia Mae Schwartz, "Gleaning on the Hillside." Mrs. Schwartz told about the MIC outreach at Mountain View, Arkansas. She gave thanks to God that Mr. Murl, a neighbor professing to be an atheist, had recently attended a church service. "It is not very thickly populated here," she wrote. "Therefore we feel very thankful when the attendance is up to twenty, which has been our average attendance the past month. Pray for all of us and the work here."

"Yes," Emma thought, "they surely need our prayers." A few moments later, she knelt beside her bed and named the Schwartzes in her nighttime petitions to God. She prayed also for Tobe's father, who was mostly confined to bed with an undiagnosed illness.

In late August, the Wednesday evening Bible study topic faced head-on the controversial issue of modes of transportation. Three men from the Plainview Church—Jonas Yoder, Dan Yutzy, and Paul Yutzy—were the speakers. Since all were men who owned cars, Emma sensed that a change was in the making. The ministers surely wouldn't have allowed these men to speak if they were not planning to allow cars in the near future. Or had some members, eager for cars, planned the meeting without consulting with the ministers?

The next week, the new Elreka School opened several

miles southwest of Hutchinson. Because many students did not live within walking distance, the school district provided bus service. Tobe's brother Ervin J. Stutzman and his brother-in-law Eli Helmuth were the drivers. It didn't seem to matter to the church that Ervin J. was Amish and wasn't allowed to own a car. In his role as bus driver, he was performing a service necessary for all.

The twins watched as the yellow school bus passed the house that evening in a cloud of dust. "Look, Mom," Ervin yelled, "Uncle Ervin is driving."

Emma nodded. "Next year you'll be riding the bus."

The following Sunday, Emma sensed a particular tension in the church. She worried that the discussion of the *Ordnung* among the ministers was going badly. At the end of the service, when Bishop Yoder stood to dismiss the congregation, he had difficulty clearing his throat. Emma sensed that he was about to make an important announcement. Others must have sensed it, too, since the room fell unusually silent. Emma leaned forward to hear what he was about to say.

9

Church Split

Emma noticed Bishop Yoder's hands shake slightly as he spoke. "*In zwee Woche*, In two weeks," he said, "*selli es bei mich bleiwe welle, tsella zammer kumme do uns Dan Nissely's. Tsella es nat bei mich bleive welle, tsella zammer kumme uns Schulhaus.* Those who want to remain with me will meet together here at Dan Nisly's for our church service. Those who do not want to stay will meet together themselves at the [German] Schoolhouse." Then he sat down and buried his face in his hands.

"So it has come to this," Emma thought. "The ministers decided to go separate ways."

After the final prayer, Emma lingered in her seat. It was sobering to think that the members would have to take sides. She hoped that the bishop would not call for shunning of those who decided to leave. Knowing Bishop Yoder, it seemed unlikely. He tried hard to keep the peace.

The visiting around the meal tables that day was somewhat strained. No one openly mentioned the parting of ways, but Emma knew there'd be plenty of talk about it when families got home from the service.

The conversation at home later that afternoon made it

clear that her children had no doubts about which church fellowship they would choose.

"Mom, today after church I heard the bishop asking a few people whether they were coming with him or not," Glenn said.

"I hope we go with the ones who drive cars," Perry declared.

"I suppose we will," Emma said.

None of the preachers in the North or South districts chose to side with the bishop. At 72 years of age, the bishop had little incentive to change. It was different for the younger ministers. Willie Wagler was barely 44 years old, Amos Nisly was 34, and David L. Miller was only 30. All three of them had been deeply involved in the Bible studies since their beginning in 1948. All had attended the mission meetings that had started in the early 1950s. They were eager for change.

The ministers called for their supporters to gather at the German Schoolhouse on Wednesday evening of that same week. Emma came with an air of somber anticipation. The ministers began by reading a church letter from the bishop indicating that those who left would not be shunned. Emma was relieved.

The ministers shared briefly about the events that had led to their parting of ways. Then they outlined their vision for a new fellowship—its *Ordnung* and purpose. They closed the meeting with an invitation to meet again the following Wednesday evening.

A few days later, Emma was riding in her buggy with Mary Edna and the twins. As they were heading for home, a car approached them in a cloud of dust. It was traveling much too fast for Emma's comfort. She tugged gently on the reins in an attempt to keep the horse calm.

As the car drew close, the horse shied hard to the right,

yanking the buggy into the ditch with him. Emma held the reins tightly as the buggy tilted onto its right side. Mary Edna grabbed for a hold in the front seat. Erma screamed as she and Ervin smacked hard against a side panel. As the car passed, the horse bolted, yanking the harness from the shafts. Emma lost her grip on the reins as the horse leaped out of the ditch and onto the open road. He loped away, the reins trailing behind him. The mother and children crawled out of the buggy and surveyed the scene.

Emma called for the horse to stop, but to no avail. She hoped that the frightened animal would go back to the house. Emma and the twins waited at the site while Mary Edna walked to Emma's brother Fred's house. Fred came and helped get the buggy out of the ditch. When they finally got home, Mary Edna burst out, "I can't stand that horse. I hope we buy a car soon."

Emma sympathized with her daughter. It wasn't that she minded harnessing up the horse or riding in a buggy. But more times than she wished to recall, she'd had to deal with a balky or frightened horse. It was one thing when Tobe was nearby, since he took pride in training horses. It was quite another thing to deal with an unruly horse on her own. The buggy was not damaged except for scratches and they found the horse at home, but she longed for a safer horse.

The next evening the congregation debated the role of a written discipline. The *Ordnung* in the Amish church was an oral agreement, recited aloud at the counsel meeting preceding each spring and fall communion service. The ministers proposed that from now on the guidelines be written.

After providing the background for their recommendation, the ministers took the counsel of those who had come. The ministers walked between the rows of members, listening to each one. When all had been heard, the ministers reported back the contours of the counsel. It was becoming clear that the fellowship should establish its own identity, with its own written discipline.

The next time the emerging congregation met, the ministers read a copy of the prospective discipline. The ministers began by stressing that their hope was to have a congregation in complete harmony with the Scriptures. It was to be a church "composed of members who had been born anew through faith in Christ Jesus, their sins washed in the blood of the Lamb, and have the witness of God's Spirit to their spirits that they are children of God."

Further, the ministers hoped to establish a congregation that maintained principles of Christian living such as nonresistance and nonconformity. While God had left the matter of interpretation and application of the principles to his people, it was reasonable to expect some degree of uniformity, given the times and circumstances. The ministers averred that without some degree of uniformity in each congregation, the principle itself was soon lost. That's why it was necessary to have a written and agreed-upon discipline.

Emma glanced over the first draft of the discipline. She saw that the discipline contained many of the elements she'd expected after the discussions on the previous Wednesdays. There were matters of witness to Christ by word and deed, issues of stewardship of time and money, and concerns about appearance and dress. She noticed too that there was a line for a signature. This represented a new level of accountability in church discipline.

She sat quietly as she watched the four ministers take the counsel of the congregation. They went from bench to bench, beginning in the front of the congregation. Each minister moved from the aisle toward the center of the bench, conversing with each member.

Emma glanced around to take note of the people who were prospective charter members. She observed that they were mostly people who had supported the mission movement and the weekly Bible studies, so she knew them well. Further, she was related to at least one of the marriage partners in nearly every household, including the ministers. There were many first or second cousins. It felt so different from the congregation in Iowa, where she had often felt like an outsider. Blood kinship brought a certain comfort and connection that augmented the bonds of church membership. But having relatives in church could at times bring discomfort. Tobe had borrowed money from a number of her relatives in the fellowship, and she could not escape their gaze.

Quietly Emma read through the proposed discipline, written entirely in English. She was eager to see what changes were proposed to be made. With pleasure she noted that women would now be allowed to wear a broader range of clothing, that "front and side zippers or snap fasteners may be used." That would be an improvement over the current practice of allowing only straight pins to fasten a dress together.

She noticed also that full beards for men would still be required. But they could be trimmed short, unlike the long beards of the men in the Old Order fellowship.

Telephones would be allowed in members' homes, although they were never to be used for practical jokes or foolish talk.

Automobiles would be allowed. The chief guiding principle in the purchase of automobiles was a concern for Christian stewardship. To that end, used automobiles should be purchased, depreciated to no more than one-third of their original sticker price. They must also be modest in appearance, not "two-toned" or "loud colored." Whitewall tires and loud mufflers would not be acceptable.

Cameras could be used, as long as such use did not offend the conscience of those who considered them unscriptural. This change was not likely to extend to the display of photographs in members' homes. Hanging or setting out individual or family portraits could easily lead to vanity. Emma recalled that as a child, even the use of mirrors had been considered vain in many homes.

Preacher Willie Wagler moved down the aisle toward the place where Emma sat. "Emma?" The expression in his eyes and the tone in his voice invited comment.

"I'm in favor of the discipline as it is written," she said. "I can support it."

"Thank you," Willie said as he made a mark on the card in his hand. Then he moved on to the woman to Emma's right.

In their summary of the counsel that evening, the ministers reported strong agreement on the proposed discipline. Yet Emma wondered if some members might be hesitant to sign their names.

The ministers also informed the group that they were seeking a broader affiliation for the new fellowship. On the one hand, they were considering the possibility of joining the fellowship of Beachy Amish churches. But they were concerned that some of the churches in that fellowship showed little concern for mission outreach or holiness of life. Some detractors accused them of having formed new churches just to be able to own cars or worship in church buildings. And some Beachy congregations even allowed members to use tobacco. Those churches were not deemed to be good models to follow.

On the other hand, the ministers were not ready to merge with the Plainview Church and join the Conservative Mennonite Conference, as some had suggested. They worried that many of the Conservative Conference churches were compromising on important issues of nonconformity to the world.

The ministers suggested that the congregation choose a middle way. They suggested that they could remain an independent fellowship with loose connections to the Beachy Amish fellowship.

• • • •

Shortly after the new church formed, Emma decided to buy a car. Following Raymond's advice, she bought a high-mileage 1950 Dodge at the auto auction in Hutchinson for $80. It was a green four-door sedan with a three-speed stick shift. She depended on Mary Edna to drive it, since her daughter had obtained her driver's license not long before. Emma wasn't eager to learn to drive. The stick shift on the column looked too daunting. Even deeper inside, Emma feared the possibility that a mishap with the car could snatch her life away like Tobe's. Then who would care for her children?

Shortly after Emma bought the car, she received a letter from her brother John, who owned a farm in Indiana. John needed a farmhand. John offered to pay $60 per month plus room and board if Perry would come to help him.

Emma brooded over the invitation. Was she prepared to send Perry so far away? He was only fifteen years old. Was it so difficult to find farmhands in Indiana that John had come to her? Or was John just trying to help her out by giving Perry a job? Usually Perry found enough work to do for his uncles in Kansas, although they paid in kind rather than in cash.

Emma broached the idea with Perry, who seemed ready to try a new venture. He said he would enjoy staying with his cousins. After further thought and prayer, Emma wrote John to inform him that she was prepared to send Perry to work at his place.

Yet Emma wasn't about to send Perry that far away via public transportation, so she looked for a chance to send him with someone planning to make a trip. Her opportunity came in October, when she learned that her brother Henry was about to make a trip to Iowa. They were going on behalf of their son David, born with Down syndrome. At six months of age, David was not thriving as they had hoped. So they decided to take him to see Dr. Huls in Davenport, Iowa.

Emma remembered Dr. Huls from the times that he had treated Edith. Indeed, it was the treatments by Dr. Huls that first drew Tobe and her to consider the move to Iowa. She remembered well the doctor's unusual technique for treating children. She had watched with intrigue and some puzzlement as he examined the roof of Edith's mouth with his fingers. He claimed that he was relieving undue pressure on the brain. It seemed strange, but Edith had always seemed better after he treated her. Emma hoped that the doctor might be able to help her young nephew David as well.

Since they were now part of the new church, Henry Nisly's family could purchase a car to drive to Iowa. They wouldn't need to hire a driver, as they had at previous times. They agreed to take Perry as far as the town of Davenport, Iowa, where Dr. Huls had his practice. Emma's brother John agreed to meet Perry there.

As soon as her oldest son was gone, Emma missed him. She had so much appreciated his willingness to work on the farm, as well as his eagerness to please her. Perry always took pleasure in doing the chores and working with farm equipment. In Tobe's absence, Emma had relied on Perry to help with manly tasks around the house.

Emma also regretted that Perry needed to miss the revival meetings held at the new Elreka School in late October. Although it was not mentioned in the new church discipline, the new fellowship now felt free to participate in revival meetings. The traditional Amish looked askance on revival meetings, intended as a way to encourage devotion to God. The fervent preaching culminating each evening in an altar call—a moment of decision—smacked of emotionalism and popular piety, they thought. But the new congregation believed that such calls to discipleship could be appropriate. Consequently, the revival meetings served to widen the gap between the new fellowship and the members who had chosen to stay with the older way.

Andrew Jantzi from Pigeon, Michigan, served as the speaker for the meetings that year. His dramatic stories and preaching style coupled with zeal for the gospel made him a compelling speaker. Each evening after his message, Brother Jantzi invited people to come forward for prayer and confession. Emma watched with gratitude as people, both young and old, made public witness of commitments to Jesus Christ. Through his encouragement, church members confessed their shortcomings and claimed victory over their sins.

Emma was particularly grateful for the effect of the meetings on her daughter Mary Edna. She admired Mary Edna's devotion. Each evening she carried her Bible and paid careful attention to the sermons. On the way home from the services, she often commented about how interesting the sermons were. Each day, she tried to memorize a Bible verse and write the reference in her diary.

On the other hand, Emma worried at times that Mary Edna might be drawn too strongly to new expressions of faith. When Mary Edna attended the Wesleyan Methodist Church the next Sunday evening, Emma began to wonder if Mary Edna would be content to remain in her home church fellowship. Since Mary Edna spent most of her week at the Webb's home, she was regularly exposed to radio, television, and other worldly influences. Might these influences prompt Mary Edna to pursue her spiritual interests elsewhere?

In spite of these feelings, Emma chided herself. "How can I complain about my daughter's fervent interest in spiritual things? Isn't that what the mission movement is about? Isn't that the goal of *Witnessing*? Isn't that the primary purpose of the Christian life? How can I blame Mary Edna for exploring other ways of understanding the Bible?"

The fervency of the revival meetings carried over into the Sunday morning worship of the new fellowship. Emma felt it as she walked down the center aisle of the German Schoolhouse and chose a seat on the right-hand side along with the other women. She glanced around. Nearly every seat was filled.

By now it was clear that the majority of the members in the North and South church districts had chosen to cast their lot with this new group informally dubbed the West Center fellowship. She also noticed that several couples from the East District had joined the group. It seemed clear that the split in the church was not related to geography, but a philosophy of change.

The most noticeable rift came between age groups. Most of the older members, including Tobe's parents, chose not to join the new fellowship. In contrast to her sons, Anna Stutzman had deep convictions about keeping the old traditions. Yet Emma's mother and stepfather enthusiastically identified with the new church, even at sixty-five years of age.

It wasn't as though the worship setting was new. Over the last number of years, the two districts had met biweekly in this same building for Sunday school. Now the new fellowship used the building every Sunday, though they alternated weekly between Sunday school and church services. The members who remained in the Amish fellowship were compelled to find their own Sunday school space.

• • • •

The coming of the portable meat canner in early
November presented the first opportunity for the folks in the
newly separated churches to join hands for a common cause.
The canner was housed in the semitrailer of a large truck
owned by Mennonite Central Committee, a relief and development organization. Several men operated the canner and
moved it from one Mennonite community to another. In each
community, the local churches butchered beef cattle and
donated the meat to be canned for relief. For a couple of days,
men and women gathered to cut up the meat in preparation
for canning it. The meat was put in labeled tin cans that carried the words "In the name of Christ." It was sent to feed
refugees and other poverty-stricken people in distant parts of
the world.

As Emma helped to cut up meat at one of the tables, she
overheard the talk that was circulating among the men who
operated the traveling canner. They commented with amazement that members of the Old Order district, the new Center
fellowship, the Plainview Conservative Mennonite Church,
and the Yoder Mennonite Church were working together. So
far in their travels, they had not seen such cooperation
between members on such a broad spectrum of churches.

Emma felt a sense of pride as she overheard the discussion.
Why shouldn't they work together, even if people disagreed on
some expressions of Christian discipleship? After all, her brothers John, Raymond, and Rufus had chosen to join more-progressive churches than she. So had Tobe's brothers Clarence
and L. Perry. "It wouldn't be helpful," she reasoned, "to cut
each other off over the issue of church membership."

• • • •

About that time, Emma learned that two young men

from the Center youth group were planning to make a trip to Indiana. Both were courting young women from the area where Perry was living. She was so eager to see Perry that she asked if she could ride along. Since there was enough room in the car, they invited Emma to take Glenn and the twins with her. Mary Edna decided to stay at home since Preacher David L. Miller's family needed her to do housework and care for their new baby, John Lowell.

It was a long ride to Indiana, so Emma breathed a deep sigh of relief as they drove into her brother John's farmyard. Perry came out quickly to meet the family. After a few minutes of conversation, Emma sensed that he was homesick. "Perhaps it wasn't wise," she thought, "to have let him come. He's too young to be so far from home."

As Emma conversed with her brother, the boys set off to explore the farm. Perry was eager to show Glenn what he had been doing over the past two months.

"How has Perry been doing?" she asked John and Mary.

"Quite well," John replied. Mary smiled and nodded her affirmation. "He enjoys working with the cows and equipment."

"I wonder if he might not be a little homesick," Emma wondered.

"I think he might be. He talks about home a lot," Mary replied. "But I think he'll get used to it."

That evening as Emma's children joined their cousins in different bedrooms for the night, Emma prepared for bed in a guest room with five-year-old Ervin. As she got into her nightgown, she wondered about the wisdom of leaving Perry in Indiana. She missed him and he missed her. She wondered, too, if it was a good thing for Perry to attend a Mennonite Church every Sunday. He might lose interest in his home church. Her head ached as she asked herself what Tobe would do.

Emma pulled back the covers of the bed and slipped into bed. "*Ich hab en Koppweh*. I have a headache," she commented, mostly to herself.

Ervin was lying in bed. "You have a head hurt," he said, trying out his emerging English.

"*Nee*. No," she corrected him, "I have a headache."

The boy's face fell into a frown.

"'Ache' is the right English word to use."

"*Oh, ich verschteh*. Oh, I understand," he said, satisfied with her explanation.

Emma sensed that Ervin was going to learn English in plenty of time for school the next fall. At home, she always spoke to Ervin and Erma in Pennsylvania German. But Mary Edna was beginning to teach them how to speak in English.

As they were leaving the breakfast table the next morning, Perry and Glenn spoke to Emma in a whisper.

"Mom," Glenn asked, "would it be all right if I took Perry's place here? Perry is ready to come home."

Emma looked at John. "What do you think? Would it be all right if Perry came home with me and Glenn stayed with you?"

John nodded and smiled. "We've enjoyed having Perry here. But if he wants to go home and Glenn wants to stay here, that will be fine with us. Won't it, Mary?"

"Certainly." Mary accented her nod with her typically broad smile.

Emma looked at Glenn, whose face reflected eagerness. Glenn was even younger than Perry. Would he get homesick too? Perhaps not, since Glenn was different from Perry.

Emma nodded. "It's okay with me."

"Yippee!" Glenn yelled as he ran out the kitchen door.

Emma looked at Mary. "He doesn't have much clothing with him."

"That's no problem," Mary said. "We'll see that he gets what he needs."

A couple of days later, Emma prepared to leave her brother's home. She squeezed back tears as she bade farewell to Glenn and slid into the seat. Everyone waved as the car pulled out of the yard and headed for the open road.

On the way back to Kansas, Emma stopped by Kalona, Iowa, to visit Edith for a few days. Meanwhile, Perry found another ride onward to Kansas.

"It has now been two and a half years," Emma reflected, "since Edith came to the Weaver home. She seems to be content enough." The eleven-year-old laughed and played on the small farm, doting over her kittens and romping with the goats.

"She also seems healthy," Emma observed. "Perhaps it's because the Weavers are so health-conscious." Sarah and Arvilla cooked quite different from Emma. Although they were quite poor, the Weavers used vitamins and other health foods. For this reason they shunned cow's milk, which they said was too difficult to digest. They instead chose to milk goats.

More than once Arvilla reminded Emma that the Weavers had loaned a goat to the Stutzmans when the twins were small. Emma admitted that Ervin hadn't been as fussy when he drank goat's milk. She remembered how Arvilla had scolded Glenn and Perry when they romped too vigorously with that nanny. "It's too hard on them," she would say.

Emma observed that Arvilla assumed most of the responsibility for Edith's care. She treated her like a daughter. Arvilla was now thirty-nine years old, just two years younger than Emma. She told Emma that as a late teenager, she had heard a call from God to take care of children. Taking care of Edith was a fulfillment of that call.

Noah and Sarah, Arvilla's parents, felt a similar call in life.

Emma watched with gratitude as Noah disciplined Edith with his deep and gentle voice. She struggled to hold back the tears when she recalled the way Edith had once responded to Tobe's masculine presence. If only Tobe were alive to care for Edith now!

Once while Emma was visiting, Edith had an epileptic seizure. Emma could hardly stand to watch as her daughter was seized and thrown to the ground. The girl writhed and thrashed wildly, seemingly unaware of what her body was doing. When she came to consciousness, she woke up slowly as though out of deep sleep. Even a strict diet of health foods could not stop the seizures.

Emma still nursed guilt that she was dependent on Arvilla for Edith's care. But she couldn't help feeling relieved as she left for home one evening. It would be too difficult for her to manage life at home with both Edith and the twins.

The morning sun was peeking over the horizon when their car rolled into the driveway back home in Kansas. Perry got out of bed to greet her.

"Mom," Perry said, "I'm so glad you traded the Dodge for a '50 Chevy while I was at Uncle John's. I drove it right away when I got home. It starts so much better than the Dodge did."

"Oh?"

"Yeah, and the engine sounds so much better. One time when I drove the Dodge to church, one of the men said, '*Es macht wie en Schippli am Blarre es*. It sounds like a bleating lamb.'"

"I like it better too," Mary Edna said as she joined them. "The clutch works better."

For some following weeks, Perry and Mary Edna both worked around home. Mary Edna was taking a break from her job as nanny at the Webbs, serving instead as needed in the neighborhood. In February 1959, she was invited to help next

171

door at Raymond and Mary Nisly's home when their son Jason was born. Mary Edna scrubbed and waxed the floors while Mary was in the hospital, and then took care of the baby when mother and son arrived home. With some pride Emma noted that folks in the neighborhood readily asked Mary Edna to help when a child was born. They knew she was a good helper.

It reminded Emma of the way she herself had served at Mary Edna's age. As the oldest child in the Levi Nisly family, she'd had plenty of practice with her youngest brothers. This gave her confidence to care for babies, first for uncles and aunts—Ed Nislys, Menno Yoders, Levi Millers—and then for others.

Even now, Emma readily helped others with their housework. She often took the family with her to help at Mother Stutzman's home. Emma felt sorry for Anna, whose hands were crippled with arthritis. It had been that way as long as Emma could remember. To add to Anna's woes, her husband, John, wrestled with illness over much of the winter of 1958. Because Anna had no daughters, she relied on her daughters-in-law to help her with domestic tasks. It seemed that every time Emma dropped by to visit, Anna had something for her to do. Emma didn't really mind, since it always felt good to be able to help someone in need. Yet she was glad that L. Perry lived next door to Grandpa Stutzmans in the trailer house. He and Silvia were available to assist them as needed.

To help treat John's illness, Grandpa Stutzmans traveled to a health clinic in Oklahoma. There, they soaked in the healing waters of the natural mineral baths. It was common for the Amish to travel to the baths, which attracted health-seekers from near and far. Like many of their Amish peers, the Stutzmans were not averse to the use of traditional medicine, but they gravitated quickly to alternative treatments in search of a cure.

In late March 1959, the week after Grandpas' trip to Oklahoma, a tall young evangelist named Myron Augsburger came to Hutchinson. Myron was a Mennonite preacher from Virginia who came to conduct a series of evangelistic meetings in the Convention Hall in Hutchinson. Roy D. Roth, a trained musician who was President of the nearby Hesston College, led the singing. The sixteen-day event, sponsored by Crusade for Christ, galvanized the local Anabaptist community. People from the plain churches joined with other Protestant churches in town to help plan the crusade and provide spiritual counseling at the event.

The youth from the church were particularly drawn to the young evangelist, who spoke rapidly, in a deep and authoritative voice. Each evening, Mary Edna came home to tell Emma about the sermon theme. Drawn by her enthusiasm, Emma attended too. She was impressed by Augsburger's ability to preach with force and freedom of expression.

During the second week of the special meetings, Mary Edna began complaining about a sore throat. It grew so bad that Emma sent her to visit Dr. Cowan, a chiropractor who lived in the *Grossdaadihaus*, the grandparents' house, next door to Raymond's home. He recommended that she see a medical doctor. The next day, Emma accompanied Mary Edna to a doctor in Hutchinson, who diagnosed her with scarletina. Two days later, Mary Edna broke out with symptoms of the measles. She would have to stay in bed and miss the remainder of the meetings.

Emma felt sorry for her daughter and a bit frightened too. She herself had never had the measles. Would she get them now? She'd heard said that the measles were much harder on adults than on children. But there was little she could do now that she'd been exposed.

While Mary Edna was in bed with measles, Emma ordered

a telephone installed in her home. Although she dreaded the monthly fee, she longed for the convenience of contact with her family. Now that six months had passed since the break with the Old Order Amish church, many fellow church members had installed phones.

Emma watched as the telephone worker put the last screw into the black telephone case mounted on the end of the kitchen cabinet.

"You've got a dial tone, Ma'am," the man said as he hung up the receiver. "Your phone number is written right here on the dial—Mohawk 21570. Just remember that you're on a two-party line. When it rings once, it's for your neighbor Raymond Nisly. When it rings twice, it's for you."

"Did you hear that?" Emma asked the twins, who watched wide-eyed.

They nodded eagerly.

That evening at suppertime the family crowded around the phone.

"Who shall we call first?" Mary Edna asked.

"Let's call Mrs. Gillock," Perry suggested. "We can tell her that we have some rabbits ready."

"I think Mom should call," Mary Edna said. "Let me find the number."

Emma picked up the phone and dialed.

"Hello," a voice at the other end answered.

"This is Emma Stutzman calling."

"Oh, you have a phone?"

"Yes, we got one today. I wanted to tell you that we have rabbits ready for you. I believe that we have six of them in the brine."

"Thank you for calling. I'll be out tomorrow to pick them up."

After supper, Mary Edna dialed her cousin Dorothy's number.

"Don't talk too long," Emma warned. "Remember that we have to share the line."

Emma listened as Mary Edna chatted. How good it was that her daughter had a chance to talk with her friend after being in bed for several days. The two of them had much in common, born just months apart as the two oldest grandchildren in the Nisly family. Now Mary Edna could call Dorothy from home instead of needing to go to Raymond's house, as she had done before. Raymond and Mary were always gracious, but Emma hated to take advantage of their generosity.

Nevertheless, Emma did ask to borrow Raymond's phonograph for a few days while Mary Edna was recovering from the measles. Emma's church didn't allow radios or phonographs. But Emma reasoned that the ministers wouldn't mind if Mary Edna listened to sacred music on Raymond's record player. Mary Edna reveled in the music of four-part harmony. It also lent a good spirit to the quiet house.

On Sunday evening, Emma also borrowed a reel-to-reel tape recorder so that Mary Edna could listen to Augsburger's recorded sermons in bed. Throughout the day, she listened to the sermons on tape.

Just as Mary Edna was recovering, Ervin began showing similar symptoms.

Mary Edna noticed it first. "Mom, Ervin Ray has red spots on his arm."

Emma looked closely at the small welts. "I wonder if he's getting the measles. The twins got measles shots two weeks ago. I wonder if Erma is getting them, too."

Mary Edna grasped Erma's arm. "Yes, she's getting them, too. I'm afraid it won't be long until they have to stay in bed."

"Perry, please play Uncle Wiggly with me," Ervin begged. It was a favorite board game.

Emma nodded encouragement. The game would help to distract the child.

Emma smiled with pleasure to hear the two brothers play the game together, even though neither was feeling well.

The next morning, both Perry and Emma woke up with spots on their arms as well. Now everyone had the measles. Emma soon grew more ill than the rest. As the week wore on, Emma called on Mother Nisly to help. She couldn't remember ever feeling so ill.

Mother Nisly walked quietly from room to room, caring for the ones in bed. She stroked Emma's brow with a damp washcloth. When evening came, she said to Emma, "I'm going to stay overnight. I'll sleep on the couch."

"You don't need to do that," Emma murmured.

"I think it would be best," Mother Nisly replied. "I don't want to leave Mary Edna to do all the work by herself."

"Thank you," Emma replied.

Two days later, as Mother Nisly cooled Emma's brow, she noticed strands of hair on the pillow. "You're losing some hair," she whispered quietly to Emma. "You must be very sick."

Emma nodded and groaned, too ill to reply.

After several days, Perry and the twins were up and about. But Emma remained in bed for another week. Mother Nisly came by from time to time, helping with the twins and giving comfort to her daughter.

Emma regained her strength just in time to attend the church counsel meeting and spring communion. In addition to the regular communion ceremony, there were two ordinations scheduled—one for a deacon and the other for a bishop. As always, the person to be ordained would be chosen by lot.

The communion was held on Sunday morning in the gymnasium of the new Elreka schoolhouse. The deacon ordination was held in the same place that evening. Emma was particularly interested in the ordination since her brother Fred was in the lot along with six other men.

As it turned out, the lot fell on Mahlon Wagler. He would follow in the footsteps of his father, Peter, who had served as deacon up to the time of his death several years earlier. Mahlon would now serve on the ministerial team with his older brother Willie.

Now that the deacon ordination was over, Emma looked forward even more to the bishop ordination. It was scheduled for the following Tuesday evening, again at the Elreka School. The man chosen in this ordination would serve as the lead elder of the church. Ever since the division in the previous September, Bishop Elam Hochstetler of Middlebury, Indiana, had served as an interim bishop. More than once, Emma heard the members of the new church fellowship referred to as "Elamites." Emma resented the term. Perhaps after this ordination, people would stop speaking of them in that way. Until they had their own bishop, the church could not be truly autonomous.

As was the custom, two visiting bishops took charge of the service. Bishop Hochstetler was joined by Bishop David A. Miller of Thomas, Oklahoma. All three of the ordained ministers were in the lot: Willie Wagler, David L. Miller, and Amos Nisly. Each had been named by at least three church members in the *Stimmen*, the nomination process, as being qualified for the role of bishop.

Emma knew that any of the three men could serve well if chosen. Of course, each would bring a different personality and a particular way of doing things. Bishops who served for a long period of time could deeply influence the long-term direction of the church. Their way of "keeping house" would shape the church discipline.

The convening bishop invited all of the nominees to sit on

the bench at the front of the men's side in the congregation. Then he took a slip of paper on which was written a verse from the book of Acts. He gave it to two men, who moved to a separate room with instructions to hide the slip within the pages of one of the three identical hymnals. They were to mix the order of the books until neither knew the placement of the slip.

A few minutes later, they returned the hymnals to the bishop with an elastic band around the outside of each one. It wouldn't do to have the pages open even slightly while the men were choosing a book.

The bishop stood the books on edge on a table in front, for everyone to see. Then he led in prayer, asking for the Lord to guide the right man to choose the book with the slip in it. The nominees were seated in order from the oldest to the youngest. "Now brothers," he said, "we are ready. Please come forward to choose a book."

Willie Wagler stepped forward first. Not only was he the oldest; he also had been ordained the longest. Then David stepped forward, followed by Amos. They stood beside each other with the books in their hands.

The congregation fell silent as the bishop stepped from behind the table and moved toward the men. Emma leaned forward with bated breath. In whose book would the lot slip be found?

10

Beachy Amish

Bishop Elam Hochstetler stepped up to Willie, who proffered the book in his hand. The bishop solemnly took the band off the book and leafed through its pages. There was no slip in it. He handed it back to Willie and stepped over to David, who handed him the book in his hand. Again, there was no slip. Then he stepped to Amos and took his book. When he removed the band, the book readily fell open to the place where the slip lay. He removed the slip from its place and said, "The lot has been found in Brother Amos's book."

Bishop Hochstetler then proceeded with the ordination. After inviting the first two candidates to be seated, he opened a small black book and asked several questions about Amos's commitment to the church. Amos answered each in the affirmative. Then Bishop Hochstetler read the charge of ordination. Following the charge, Amos knelt for a prayer of consecration. All of the ordained men who were present in the congregation gathered around and laid their hands on him.

As the bishop led in prayer, Emma heard subdued weeping among several in the women's side of the congregation. The calling to be a bishop was a heavy burden. He alone would have the authority to ordain other ministers and deacons, including his successor as bishop. The bishop would be responsible to enforce the church discipline as agreed to by the preachers and deacons, in consultation with the membership of the church. The bishop was ultimately responsible to stand before God to give an account for the state of God's flock, the church.

Unlike his predecessors, Amos would also govern the use of a meetinghouse. Eight months had now passed since the division, and a building was now being erected for worship. It stood on two acres of ground purchased from Levi Miller. The early stages of construction had already begun for a forty-by-eighty-foot Butler steel frame, to be closed in with concrete block and covered with a brick veneer.

When the $32,000 cost estimate was first announced, some felt the price was too high. Why spend so much for a house of worship to be used only one day a week? For generations, their ancestors had worshipped in homes, without any such expense. Now the members would pay the cost of not only their own homes but also the church house as well. Each family head would need to donate $625. Each single man 21 years and older was to donate $100. In addition, each man would need to donate 50 hours of labor to the project.

Everyone agreed that the building should be modest in appearance. It would not do for a plain people to have a fancy meetinghouse. It should also be affordable. In the end, the church decided to borrow money, which would in time be repaid by donations.

Emma felt tightness in the back of her neck as she considered her suggested share of the cost. She decided that she, as a widow, might give what a single man would give. It would need to wait until after the wheat harvest.

Early the next morning, Emma sat down to pen a few lines to keep Glenn abreast of the important changes taking place at home. "I am finally over the measles," she wrote. "I had to miss the baptismal service two weeks ago last Sunday. Bishop Dave Miller was here from Oklahoma to baptize 15 young converts. They joined us in communion on May 10.

"Mahlon Wagler was ordained as deacon on Sunday evening, and Amos Nisly was ordained as bishop on Tuesday evening at Elreka.

"Melvin Yoder came with his tractor and cultivator to work up the garden. We planted radishes and onions right away. Perry planted asparagus along the fence on the north side.

"Perry and Mary Edna went with the young folks on their annual picnic last Tuesday. They were at the park in Pratt. They got back just in time to change clothing and get to the ordination."

She leaned back to muse. What might she say about Glenn's stay at John's farm? She leaned forward and wrote: "I hope you'll want to come home before too long."

There, she had said it. He needed to know that he couldn't stay indefinitely. After all, he was only fourteen years old.

After adding a few closing words, Emma sealed the letter and addressed it. Then she rummaged through the little cardboard box where she kept her stamps. There was only one left.

Emma stamped the letter and then walked briskly to the mailbox in the dim morning light. She stepped carefully across the plank that bridged the ditch between the yard and the edge of the road. Flipping open the front of the large mailbox, she placed the letter on the right-hand side. With a flip of the wrist, she put the red flag on the outside into its upright position so the mail carrier would know that he needed to stop.

• • • •

Now that Perry was sixteen years old, Emma muscled up the courage to suggest to Raymond that she could now take the responsibility to farm her forty-acre plot. Perry was eager

181

to do the farming and to get Emma's place ready to keep her own livestock. Raymond agreed, so she set out to buy the necessary farm equipment. She had saved sufficient cash from the older children's earnings to buy an old tractor and worn implements that had enough life remaining to till her small acreage.

With assistance from Raymond and others, Emma added a section onto the barn to store hay for the cow. Then she strung up a barbed-wired fence for a corral. She also moved a wooden shack from Raymond's farm and strung up a woven wire fence to make room for a couple of hogs. Then she brought in a brooder house for chicks and a small chicken house from another neighbor's farm, with room for two dozen hens. To make it possible to haul livestock, she got Perry to install a hitch on the 1950 Chevy. It would serve to pull a two-wheeled livestock trailer.

After Perry built a milking stall for a cow and constructed a wooden bin for ground feed, Emma purchased a feed grinder, to be powered by a drive belt from a tractor. Then she bought a used tractor, a 1937 Model D John Deere. Perry loved the unmuffled "pop-pop" sound of the two-cylinder tractor and drove it home from Hutchinson in high gear, a pace just slightly faster than he could walk. A few days later he drove it to Henry Nisly's home to fetch a used two-bottom plow. Although most farmers used bigger plows, Emma was satisfied that its two sixteen-inch plowshares would turn over the soil fast enough for her small field.

Along with the development of the small farm, Emma decided to expand her garden space as well. "Those Russian olive trees along the south side are dying anyway," she told Perry, "so we might as well make use of that space. It will be a good place for sweet corn." Perry helped to clear the trees for a plot just south of the house and another one further east, beyond the new hog pen. Then Emma bought a rototiller to work up the ground in her three garden plots. It would be a compliment to the gas-powered lawn mower, which now replaced the mechanical push mower she'd brought with her from Iowa.

Emma surveyed her garden with deep satisfaction. A variety of flowers separated the garden from the driveway: cockscomb, tiger lilies, peonies, and a large rose bush. Beside the opposite fence, raspberry bushes and asparagus grew alongside the strawberry patch. In between, there was room for all manner of vegetables in addition to the ones in the new plots.

How Emma wished that Glenn could be part of the action around the farm. Although she appreciated the sixty dollars sent by her brother John for Glenn's pay each month, she wished that Glenn could earn it at home in Kansas. After church one day in late summer, she discussed the matter with Mother Nisly.

"Mom, I don't like having Glenn gone so long. He doesn't write much, and it doesn't seem as though he has any interest in coming home. I feel like writing him and telling him to come home."

"I think that would be a good idea," Mother Nisly agreed. "If he stays there too long, it may be hard for him to come back into our church."

"That's what I'm afraid of. I think I'll write him today."

Mother Nisly went on: "You know that Harmon Yoders are going to Indiana. They might be willing to bring him back with them."

Emma pursed her lips. "I think I'll ask them today."

That afternoon, after speaking to Mrs. Yoder, she wrote a letter to Glenn, asking him to come home with the Yoder family.

That same week, the twins started in the first grade at

Elreka School. Emma watched with mixed feelings as they got onto the bus. It was the first time in seventeen years that she wouldn't have a child to care for at home during the day. "Perhaps I should bring Edith back home now," Emma thought. Yet as she contemplated it, her spirit had no peace. It would be too stressful.

The children had been in school for a couple of weeks when Glenn arrived home from Indiana. Through an open window, Emma heard the car pull into the gravel lane. She beamed as Harmon Yoder stepped out of the driver's side and her son opened the backdoor.

Emma slipped on some old slippers and hurried outside. She greeted the Yoders in the front seat.

"Thank you for bringing Glenn home. Feel free to come inside and visit for awhile."

"I don't believe we'll take the time to come in now," Harmon responded. "We're eager to get home."

"Can we pay you something to help with the trip?" Emma asked Harmon as he closed the trunk.

"No, we're just glad we could be of help," Harmon said.

"Thank you. I'm much obliged," Emma said with a smile.

As Harmon backed rapidly out of the driveway, Emma picked up one of Glenn's suitcases. She couldn't help but notice that Glenn was wearing his hair parted on the side. Didn't he realize that this hairstyle was not allowed by the church discipline? Or was he simply challenging the *Ordnung*?

Emma also learned that Glenn had earned money for himself by working overtime as a farmhand for John's neighbors. She wasn't happy that he'd used the money to buy jeans and other worldly clothing. They didn't conform to the church discipline any more than his hairstyle did. Emma didn't say much about it. What good would it do? Glenn already knew the right thing to do.

Glenn quickly adapted to the rhythm at home. Along with his work on a neighboring farm, he helped Perry finish some tasks around the home. Emma was pleased when the boys ran a water supply line from the house to the barnyard. The boys dug the trench by hand, deep enough so they could bury the supply pipe below the frost line. They finished the job by building a wooden form and pouring a concrete water tank for the cow.

By this time, Emma had faced into her fears of driving and had a driver's license. Perry had coached her through the motions of shifting the on-column three-speed stick shift on the old Chevy, which sometimes got stuck in first gear. Whenever that happened, she had to shut off the car, set the emergency brake, open the hood, and pull up on the faulty shift rod. Driving brought a feeling of independence that Emma had not felt for years. Now she no longer had to depend on someone to drive her from place to place.

She also relieved Raymond of the responsibility for keeping her financial accounts. Emma learned to keep entries in a columnar account book. And when she paid her accounts by check, she no longer signed her name as Mrs. Tobe Stutzman, but used Mrs. Emma Stutzman instead. To continue to seek her identity in her deceased husband would hold her suspended in the past. By slow and painful steps, she was learning to live in the present.

• • • •

The maize was ripe in the fields in late October, when Perry went to work at Albert Miller's shop. Albert was the owner of the window-making business that Tobe had started some ten years earlier. After purchasing it from Stutzman Brothers, he moved the business into a wooden building on his own property and called it Reno Fabricating.

Emma was delighted to see Perry take the job. Perry had often helped Tobe in the shop and would easily be able to learn the work. Perry was well suited to work with Albert's easygoing pace.

The next day, when Emma came home from a trip to town, the twins came running to greet her. "Mom, you must come in right away. Mary Edna's burned her face with the stove."

"Oh my, where is she?" Emma's face mirrored her alarm.

"Resting in bed."

Emma hurried inside and stepped into Mary Edna's room. "The twins said you burned yourself."

"Yes. I was canning apples."

Emma wrung her hands as she examined Mary Edna's blistered face. "How did it happen?"

"I had put the glass jars of apple sauce in the oven to finish processing them. I kinda forgot them until I opened the oven door. I guess when the cold outside air hit the jars, it made one of them explode. The hot applesauce hit my face. It burned terribly. I'm so lucky that I had my glasses on so it didn't go into my eyes. Right away I rinsed it off with cold water from the sink."

Emma nodded her approval.

"No one was home, so I called Uncle Raymond right away. He took me to the doctor."

"What did the doctor say?"

"He put some ointment on it and told me I should get some rest. He wants me to come in again tomorrow morning." Mary Edna was stoic about the incident and didn't seem upset.

"I'm glad it's not worse."

The anxiety of the moment was lightened an hour later when Perry arrived home with the used car they'd bought that day. He explained, "It's a 1949 Chevy with a lot of miles on it."

"It looks a little funny. Why does the top go so far back?" Ervin asked.

"It's what you call a fastback."

"I'm glad we have another car," Mary Edna told Perry. "That way you'll have your own car to go to work at Albert's place. I can't always come to get you like I did yesterday."

• • • •

The next two weeks were exciting as the congregation finished the church's new building. On two occasions, Perry stopped by at the Stutzman Greenhouse to help make hymnal racks for the church pews. It was a heated space with plenty of room to work.

Emma also got involved in the project. As part of her commitment to the new church facility, Emma helped to strip varnish off the used pews the church had purchased. She joined other volunteers who came and went for several weeks at her brother Henry Nisly's shed. When all of the pews were stripped, they stained them blond and gave them a coat of varnish.

On the third Sunday in October, the congregation used the new building for the first time. It was a council meeting to continue a discussion begun earlier in the week. There was much to decide at the meetings, including the use of the building. Although the blueprint included a kitchen in the basement, it was not equipped that way. Some felt that it would not be appropriate to prepare meals in a church meetinghouse. Others reasoned that it was quite appropriate to serve food in the worship space. For generations, they had eaten communal meals in their homes immediately following church services. Yet this seemed different. It would take more discernment before the congregation would move ahead with a kitchen.

At times, council meeting could be a time of wrangling

between different opinions. But this time the meeting was touched by grace. A number of people made heartfelt confessions. Emma knew that the transitions over the past year hadn't been easy for everyone. She hoped that confession and ample forgiveness would smooth the road ahead.

The first snow fell a few weeks later, in early November. The wind blew so hard that Emma worried as Perry left for work. What if he got stuck in a snowdrift?

That evening, her fears were confirmed at the supper table. As Perry finished the table grace, he turned toward Emma. "I thought you should know that I had a little accident with the car today."

"Oh no!" Emma said with dread in her voice.

"I got stuck in a drift close to Enos Miller's place this morning. The road was really covered where the north wind blows off Merle Kent's land. I saw that I wasn't going to be able to get out, so I walked over to Enos's house. Enos came with his 620 John Deere to pull me out."

Perry glanced over to Glenn. "You know how that hub sticks out from the rear axle on the tractor?"

"Yes," Glenn said.

"Well, Enos got too close to the driver's door, so the hub scraped against the door. It made a pretty good-sized dent."

"Can we straighten it out?"

"No. We'll need to have the body shop fix it."

Emma knit her brow. "That will be extra expense."

A couple of days later, Perry drove into the lane with a different door on the car. Emma anticipated an explanation as he came into the house.

"Did you see that I got a new door on the car?" he asked.

"Yes, but the color doesn't match."

"The body shop picked it up at the junkyard. All they had was a white one."

"Now we'll need to get it painted."

"Yes, we'll do that after New Year's Day."

"Did they say what it will cost?"

"Maybe $25."

Emma shook her head in disgust. Perhaps she should have asked Perry to stay at home when the snow was drifting so badly. Or at least she could have asked him to be more careful. Now that she had a small amount of discretionary cash from her children's earnings, she hated to spend it for accidents that could have been avoided.

• • • •

In January 1960, Perry and other volunteers joined hands in a frolic to put up a greenhouse that Tobe's brother Ervin J. had disassembled in Hutchinson and moved to his place. As a cautious entrepreneur, he was building a greenhouse business on a cash basis. Both Clarence and L. Perry now had other employment, so Ervin J. changed the name of his business from Stutzman Brothers to Stutzman Greenhouse. From watching Tobe, Ervin J. had learned that it didn't pay to go too far out on a limb. And since he lent his property free of charge to the relief canner each fall, he didn't mind asking the community for assistance on occasion.

With the twins in school, Emma felt free to help at the greenhouse from time to time. February was the peak of the transplanting season for the greenhouse, so Emma worked there several days a week. Since the greenhouse property adjoined the schoolyard, the twins walked to the greenhouse rather than riding the bus.

One day, because of the workload at the greenhouse, Mary Edna, Perry, and Glenn all joined Emma in the transplanting effort. All of the workers sat on stools around a large plywood table. With a small wooden jig, they pressed twelve evenly spaced holes into the soil in each plastic container, eight containers to a wooden flat. Then they separated the seedlings in the seedling flat and transplanted one small plant into each of the twelve holes.

Since the workers got paid by the flat, they sometimes engaged in friendly competition. Each time they finished a flat, they made a mark on the record sheet. By the end of the day, the weary workers watched as Ervin J. tallied the marks for the day. Eleven thousand, two hundred plants!

• • • •

On the week before Valentine's Day, Emma invited friends and relatives to help her stitch a quilt top that Mary Edna had embroidered. The cover was made of forty-eight blocks pieced together, each depicting a state bird and flower for one of the forty-eight contiguous states. (Alaska and Hawaii became states the previous year.)

In preparation for the quilting, Emma and Mary Edna moved furniture to make space in the living room for the quilt frame and then set it up. First they laid the four sides of the wooden frame on the floor and clamped them together with screw clamps, forming a rectangle the size of the quilt. Each took hold of one end and lifted it onto the four corner leg stands.

"It'll be a little tight to work in this room, but I think it will work just fine," Mary Edna said.

Emma nodded approval as they stretched the quilt backing into the frame, fastening it at intervals with straight pins to the strips of fabric on the four wooden sides. Then they laid batting onto the backing and spread it out carefully so that there were no gaps or overlaps. Finally they laid the quilt top onto the batting and fastened it with pins, to keep it from shifting while quilters stitched the quilt.

Emma stroked the quilt top. She was proud of her daughter's embroidery work, a project that had taken months. The quilt would make a wonderful addition to Mary Edna's hope chest, a collection of items with which she could start a new household. It could well become a family heirloom.

The next morning the first guests arrived soon after the twins left for school. Others dropped in later on. As each one arrived, Emma invited them to a place at the quilt. By noon there was hardly enough room for everyone to work at the same time.

As Emma took the count for the noon meal, she looked with satisfaction at the four generations of guests. Mother Nisly was present, along with four sisters, including one who was visiting from Missouri. Emma's sister Barbara was also helping, along with four sisters-in-law, a niece, five cousins, and a couple of other friends—nineteen guests from four different generations.

Emma was thankful that differences in the church didn't keep Mother Nisly and her sisters from enjoying fellowship around the quilt. Now that the new church had gotten started, the sisters belonged to four different fellowships—Old Order Amish, Beachy Amish, Conservative Mennonite, and Mennonite. In spite of their differences, they got together to quilt every month or so.

"You did such a nice job of embroidery, Mary Edna," Mother Nisly said. She stroked the image of a cardinal as she spoke.

"Oh yes," several women chimed in.

"I like the state bird and flower pattern. It makes so many different colors, with no two blocks the same," one of Mary Edna's aunts added.

"And you've made such a nice border," commented another.

"Thank you," said Mary Edna, blushing slightly.

"Thread," Mary Edna's cousin Dorothy called out. Mary Edna reached for the spool of white thread and tossed it across the quilt. Dorothy pulled about a yard off the spool and then tore it with her fingers. She twisted the frayed end of the thread between her wet lips and deftly pushed it through the eye of her small needle.

"It looks like we're ready to give this side a turn," Emma suggested.

"Yes, I only have a couple of inches left here, and then I'll be ready," Barbara replied.

"I'll thread a couple of needles while we wait," Dorothy volunteered.

Emma rose and moved to one end of the quilt. Mary Edna went to the other. Each loosened the clamp and turned the wooden frame board one full turn; then they fastened the clamp back on. The women on that side leaned back into the work.

Emma reveled in the conversations around the quilt. Quilting was one of the best ways to catch up on the latest news in the family and congregation. It could also be a time for teasing. Both Mary Edna and her cousin Dorothy had just started dating, so they were the most vulnerable to light-hearted ribbing.

"What's this I hear about a group of young people going to Temple Baptist Church a couple of Sundays ago?" Barbara asked.

Dorothy and Mary Edna looked at each other. "What did you hear?" Dorothy asked with a grin.

"I heard that some interesting things happened that day," Dorothy's mother said, mischief evident in her voice.

"Well, several of us worshipped there in the morning and then went to the singing in the evening."

"Who all went to Temple Baptist?"

Dorothy responded, "Oh, Mary Edna and Perry, Menno Yoder, Rosa Yoder, and I. It was an interesting service. In the evening, we went to the singing at Menny Yoders."

"And afterward?" Barbara was relentless.

"Oh, several people came to our house," Dorothy replied.

Dorothy's mother laughed. "I think she's avoiding the question."

The whole group burst out in laughter as Dorothy blushed.

"They had a double date at our house," Dorothy's mother volunteered. "Daniel Miller had Dorothy, and Perry had Erma Yoder. Three of the other boys and Mary Edna came over to 'help' serve the food." She rolled her eyes to make the point. It was sometimes difficult for young people to find much privacy on dates.

The women laughed again. This time, Mary Edna and Dorothy joined in.

"It sounds like you had a nice time," Barbara said. "Those are nice boys you were with."

The conversation lulled as the women rolled up the other side of the quilt a bit. Then the talk turned to a couple of neighborhood women who were suffering with cancer.

"I guess you know that we're making Levi Clara a scrapbook," Mother Nisly said.

"I made a page for it this week," Mary Edna volunteered.

"She's pretty much bedfast these days. I'm sure that it will help to cheer her up."

"I feel the same way about Raymond Fannie," said Emma. "It seems she hasn't quite recovered from her brain surgery. She just hasn't gained the way that we had hoped."

"Both Clara and Fannie seem so young to suffer in this

way." Mother Nisly lamented. "But we have to leave it in the Lord's hands."

"What did Daniel Miller tell us in the topic Wednesday night?" Dorothy reminded the group. "He said that longsuffering is one of the fruits of the Spirit. The Spirit helps people to be patient in their suffering. But it must still be very hard."

"I often think how Abe Sarah has been such a good example of patience in suffering," Barbara said. "She's bedfast year after year without getting better. But I don't hear her complaining."

"I don't get to visit her as often as I should," Mother Nisly confessed. "But I'm glad to know that the young people sing for her sometimes."

"Yes, and we need to keep remembering to visit Noah Bevly," Barbara suggested. "Her days get long too."

"The young folks sang for her not so long ago," Mary Edna said. "She seems to be getting a little bit forgetful."

"Yes, there are times when it's hard for her children to take care of her," Mother Nisly observed, "especially when she forgets where she is. It's so sad that some people lose their mind as they get older."

"Dinner's ready," Emma announced. The women finished a few stitches and then moved to the table for the meal. When all were seated, Emma led in a brief prayer of thanks for the food. The mood was festive around the table.

After dinner, several women helped with the dishes while others took their places around the quilt again. The women made such good progress that the group began to disperse by mid-afternoon. There were still a couple of women at the task when the twins came home from school.

Mother Nisly greeted them as they came into the house.

"Hi Grandma," Erma said as she looked at the quilt. "I like this quilt."

"I don't like it that Mrs. Cowan makes us take a nap," Ervin complained. "The second graders don't have to take a nap."

Mother Nisly chuckled. "Someday you'll be glad to take a nap after lunch."

"No," Ervin retorted. "I'll never take a nap in the afternoon. I'd rather read or go play."

Emma grinned and winked at her mother.

"Doesn't that hurt your finger when you poke the needle against it?" Ervin asked as he watched the women quilt.

"A little bit at first, but you get used to it," Grandma said. "When you get a callous like this, it doesn't hurt anymore." She lifted up the forefinger on her left hand.

"Oh." The young boy soon went to the toy drawer and began to play.

• • • •

The month of April was a sad time for Emma, almost frightening. First her aunt Clara Miller died, followed five days later by Fannie Wagler's passing. Both died of cancer. Emma attended both funerals and grieved deeply. It seemed to her that both women were too young to die. Clara was 58, Fannie only 47.

Not long afterward, Arvilla Weaver called to announce that Edith had contracted scarlet fever. Arvilla voiced her fear that Edith might not live through the ordeal, so they discussed tentative funeral plans. It was upsetting to hear that the Weavers thought Edith should be buried in Iowa instead of Kansas. But to Emma's great relief, Edith got better. By the end of May, she had practically returned to normal.

Also in May, Emma was cheered by the dedication of the new meetinghouse for the church fellowship. The beige-colored brick complemented the riverbed gravel in the churchyard. A row of small trees on the east and west sides of the building promised future shade for parked cars. The metal letters mounted on the brick at the front proclaimed the permanent name for the fellowship: CENTER A. M. CHURCH. "Center" was an acknowledgment that the building stood in Center Township. The letters "A. M." stood for Amish Mennonite.

As Emma sat waiting for the service to begin, she glanced around at the new auditorium. A simple pulpit stood behind the rail on the platform, which stood two steps up from the linoleum floor. Above the preacher's bench hung a wooden motto with the opening words of Psalm 91 in old German script:

> *Wer unter dem Schirm des Höchsten sitzt*
> *und unter dem Schatten des Allmächtigen bleibt.*
> He that dwelleth in the secret place of the most High
> shall abide under the shadow of the Almighty.

A microphone stood in front of the pulpit, a silent witness to the move from smaller gatherings in homes to a larger gathering that required amplification. It could facilitate the recording of the services too, if it was deemed appropriate in the future.

Emma glanced out the metal casement window to her right. All the windows stood open to allow for air circulation on the warm May afternoon. Through the window she could see the German Schoolhouse less than a half mile away. The church wouldn't need to use it any longer.

The service began at 3:00 p.m. with singing from the *Church and Sunday School Hymnal*, now available in the hymnal rack on each pew. Most of the songs in the hymnal were English, but there was a German section in the back. This eliminated the need to use the *Ausbund* any longer.

While a few men like Noah Nisly favored German singing, most of the younger members preferred English songs.

The dedication service featured a guest speaker and a litany of dedication borrowed from the Mennonite Church. Preacher Jake Hershberger of Lynnhaven, Virginia, delivered the main message in German. Preacher David Miller of Thomas, Oklahoma, also spoke in German. The two ministers represented a network of congregations who had left the Amish church but preserved many of its traditions.

While some young people preferred English, the sermons were nearly always preached in German. To move completely away from the mother tongue was too radical a departure from long tradition. Abandoning the German would mean a loss of many hymns and treasured writings.

Emma watched with interest as Ervin leafed through her German/English Bible. Now that he had finished the first grade, the boy took interest in following along with the preacher's Scripture references. Emma was relieved that it kept him somewhat quiet. In another year or two, she could send the twins to sit with their peers on the front-row seats.

"Mom, I want some Cheerios," Erma whispered. Emma reached into her purse and pulled out a small plastic bag full of the breakfast food. Erma looked up with a winsome smile as Emma put them into her hand. Erma savored them one at a time, as though wanting to make them last as long as possible.

Late that afternoon Emma left the service with a deep sense of fulfillment. She was confident that she had done what Tobe would have wanted her to do. He would have been delighted to give volunteer time to build the church house. Although it was now four years since Tobe's death, Emma thought of him every day. And, for the first time, she was prepared to consider the possibility that she might someday remarry.

11

Courting Again

One hot day in July, Emma took the family to visit her cousin Lizzie Miller, who was ill at home. Lizzie was Levi Miller's unmarried daughter. Levi was a widower, having lost his wife, Emma's aunt Clara, to cancer in April. Twice during her brief visit in Levi's home, Emma sensed Levi's eye on her. She felt a bit flattered at his show of interest. He was much older than she—perhaps by sixteen years.

Fondly she thought of the time as a young adult when she had worked in the Miller home. She had served as a helper when Levi and Clara's daughter Emma was born, the youngest of their twelve children. Both Emma Stutzman and Emma Miller were named after Clara's older sister.

Emma recalled that Levi and Clara's twins—Harry and Perry L.—were eleven years old at the time. They had played around the sewing machine as she sewed school garments and patched torn clothing. Perry had been particularly curious and plied her with questions: "What do the young people do after the singing? What do boys and girls do on a date?" Emma suspected that he had found her more forthcoming with answers than his older siblings.

Now she blushed to recall that as a young adult, she'd once told the Miller children about the use of a pendulum to predict the future. She couldn't imagine Perry L., now that he was grown, allowing young people to do such a thing. Neither would Levi, for that matter.

Emma mused about the possibility that Levi might soon ask her out. If he did, what would she say?

• • • •

Throughout that summer, Perry and Glenn worked as farmhands for a number of farmers in the neighborhood. Perry's job at Reno Fabricating was sporadic, so it worked well to have other summer work.

In August, Glenn took up a full-time job with his uncle L. Perry. Two years earlier, in 1958, L. Perry had purchased a couple of trucks and a trash route in Hutchinson. Now that Glenn had turned fifteen years old, Uncle Perry invited him to drive one of his trucks. It seemed like a good job for him. He would bring home a steady hourly wage.

The new job called for Glenn to get out early in the morning. So Emma arose before 5:00 a.m. each weekday morning to make Glenn a hot breakfast and pack his lunch. It seemed easier for him to get out of bed with a breakfast aroma in the house.

After working for various farmers in the neighborhood during the summer, Perry again worked for Albert Miller at Reno Fabricating. It didn't promise to be full-time work, but it paid a respectable hourly wage.

Now that all three of the older children had at least part-time jobs, Emma worried less about income. More jobs required more transportation, however. Perry wanted to buy a car for himself, so Emma helped him purchase a 1953 Chevy. She had confidence that he would take good care of the car, a black four-door sedan with a blue interior. Perry was alert to small details, whether for car maintenance or other matters around the farm. Emma depended on him to keep things in shape.

Mary Edna was helpful around the house, too. Like Perry, she took responsibility to see that things got done. Emma wondered how she would manage when Mary Edna got to be of age when she turned 21. She assured herself that by that time, the twins wouldn't require as much work. But Emma would still miss having her oldest daughter at home.

By now, Mary Edna had moved from being a nanny to working for Anna Shaklee in a small personal care home. Emma wasn't entirely happy with the arrangement. Anna wanted Mary Edna to live at the home and work long hours, including weekends. Emma wasn't pleased that Mary Edna practically had to beg to get time off.

Emma observed that Anna recognized Mary Edna's potential and used it beyond the regular routine at the home. When Anna found that Mary Edna had an eye for design, she bought a cake decorating kit to teach her the secrets of cake decorating. Mary Edna soon picked up the art and used it for Anna's residents. She practiced at home, too, so Emma's family benefited from her new art.

On the other hand, Emma didn't appreciate Mary Edna's exposure to the Shaklee's television. From time to time, Mary Edna mentioned the programs she'd been watching. In early November she told Emma that she had witnessed the televised debate between presidential candidates Richard Nixon and John F. Kennedy.

Emma wasn't interested in politics. From her youth she'd been taught that political voting belonged to the ways of the world. Except on special occasions, the Amish didn't vote in elections beyond the local school district. However, the 1960 presidential campaign stirred up some old worries about Catholics in government. At home Emma didn't say much about her political worries, but at work the older children all heard it talked about.

In the end, none of Emma's family registered to vote, but they were disappointed when Kennedy won the election. Perhaps because they clung to the painful memory of a Roman pope ordering the persecution of their Anabaptist ancestors in the sixteenth century, they feared that the pope might try to use his enormous influence over a fellow Catholic to the disadvantage of other faiths.

It was during the election campaign that Levi Miller did in fact speak to Emma about cultivating a friendship. "Might I come to see you next Sunday evening?" he asked.

Emma blushed. "Yes," she said, with a bit of hesitation. "But I don't want the children to know."

"That's fine. I'll come by after everyone is in bed."

"I'll be in bed, but I'll watch for you."

Over the next couple of days, Emma brooded over the invitation. What was she getting herself into? How would she keep the children from finding out? What would she tell them if they did find out?

She wondered what Tobe would think about her seeing Levi. While it wasn't unusual to marry someone so much older, she wondered about the wisdom of such a move. His oldest son was only five years younger than she was.

Emma lay in bed on Sunday night when she heard a gentle scratching on the screen at the south window. She turned to see Levi's silhouette in the moonlight.

She sat up in bed, hoping that she wouldn't wake the children. She reached for her covering in the dim moonlight and then paused in silence as she heard Erma stir in her bedroom.

Quietly Emma stepped into the hallway and closed the door behind her. She made her way into the living room, turned on the light, and welcomed Levi into the room. He proffered his hand, so they shook warmly. She motioned toward the sofa. "We can sit down," she said softly. After a brief time of conversation, she heard a bedroom door open into the hallway. She turned to see who was out of bed.

Levi sprang up and clicked off the wall switch. Emma felt her muscles tighten as Levi moved to the far edge of the sofa. Her eyes adjusted to the darkness as Erma made her way past the couch into the bathroom. They sat wordlessly. Soon the bathroom door opened again. The bathroom light cast a glow onto the sofa before Erma turned off the light and walked back to the bedroom. Emma pondered what to say if Erma questioned her the next morning.

It was hard for Emma to relax, knowing that the children might well be eavesdropping. Levi and she spoke quietly in casual conversation. She was relieved that he didn't stay too long.

Erma didn't bring up the matter the next morning, so Emma said nothing. "If something comes out of the relationship," she reasoned, "I can explain it then." She wasn't ready just yet to discuss the matter with the children, especially the twins.

Emma knew that it might not be possible to keep the matter secret. She recalled with chagrin what had happened to her mother just six years earlier while being courted by a suitor. Not long after Emma's father Levi died, Noah Nisly had come to see Mother Nisly at the home farm under cover of darkness. On one of his first visits, he forgot to extinguish the lantern on his buggy, parked behind the barn. When Emma's brother Fred came out to investigate the flickering light in the barnyard, the secret leaked into the family circle.

Now the tables were turned and she was the one who had been discovered. Emma hoped that Erma hadn't recognized Levi's face. Would Erma tell her friends? Emma hoped not.

She had enough hesitancy about the matter that she didn't want rumors to spread around the close-knit neighborhood.

Two weeks went by before Emma heard from Levi again. She tried not to look in his direction at church. It wouldn't do for him to think that she was pursuing him.

Meanwhile, Emma watched with intense interest as her three oldest children all had dates. She was particularly interested in Mary Edna's relationship with Menno Yoder. Menno was a soft-spoken young man from the youth group who sang with Mary Edna and Perry in an octet. Emma had watched him interact with Mary Edna from time to time. He seemed to have more than passing interest in her. Emma fully expected that he'd ask Mary Edna out for a date soon. She wasn't sure, though, that Mary Edna shared the same admiration for him that he did for her.

Menno worked for Reno Fabricating, the same place that Perry had employment. He installed windows and doors. On the last day of the year in 1960, Menno came to install a storm door on Emma's front porch. She was pleased with Menno's work. He seemed pleasant and respectful. She was happy to see Mary Edna get to know him.

Emma tried not to press her children regarding their affections. It was better to be reserved than to be too curious. Hence, several days later she learned from Mary Edna that Glenn had experienced his first date on New Year's Day. She wasn't surprised since he'd turned sixteen in August. But she was surprised that he had a date two evenings in a row. He wasn't talking about the matter, so she hadn't yet learned the girl's name.

The night before Mary Edna's first date with Menno, Mary Edna spent the night with her cousin Dorothy, talking about dating. She reported to Emma that they had talked about wholesome activities to do on dates. Since Menno was coming to Mary Edna's house, she felt responsible to plan something interesting to do. Of course, the twins would have to stay in their rooms. It wouldn't do to have them come out into the living room or eavesdrop from the nearby bedrooms.

Emma sympathized. Should she tell Mary Edna about what had happened when Levi was there? She decided not to say anything for now. It would be better to let the matter rest unless something further developed.

Soon thereafter, Levi called again. This time when he came to visit, he invited Emma to sit in the front seat of his car to talk. He wasn't eager to have the children wake up during the night and investigate the presence of a stranger. It was midnight when Levi wished her goodbye and drove away. She walked to the house and quietly made her way to the bedroom. As Emma slipped into bed, Erma stirred but did not wake. Emma sighed with relief.

It felt strange to be dating at the same time as her children. Dating didn't carry the same novelty as it had when she was a teenager. She felt the gravity of the relationship from the beginning. Even though they'd seen each other just several times, she was confident that marriage was on Levi's mind.

Emma lay quietly, but her mind was in a whirl about the visit. Would she want to be married to an older man with a large family of his own? How would her children adjust to a new father? Levi seemed a bit nervous. At his age, would he have the patience to deal with her energetic twins?

Certainly there would be big advantages to marrying Levi. He seemed to be financially well off, or at least much better off than she. Already she could feel the relief it would bring to no longer worry about money. And Levi's companionship could relieve the loneliness that often gnawed at her heart.

What would Tobe say about her friendship with Levi? She could almost hear Tobe comment that this man wouldn't be his first choice for her. But she couldn't tie herself to Tobe's opinions. He was gone—out of the picture. That's why she was seeing this man in the first place. With these thoughts in her mind, she dropped off into a troubled sleep.

As Emma went about the chores the next morning, she pondered what it would really be like to marry Levi. Since he was still active on his own farm, she would likely need to move there with him. What would she do with her house? She was becoming increasingly attached to it. She found comfort in having her own small farm.

As Emma looked around the neighborhood, she observed that nearly all of the men who had lost a spouse had remarried. Yet there were many widows who remained single and other women who had never been married. Should she take this opportunity, or risk the possibility that she might be alone for the rest of her life? What would be best for the children?

Emma toyed with the idea of asking Glenn how he would feel about her marrying Levi. She could always trust him to be honest and straightforward, even though she might disagree with his ideas. As she had feared, Glenn had never felt at home at the Center Church after returning from Indiana. Perhaps it was because he missed a crucial stage in the young church's development. But more likely, he longed for the freedom of expression he had seen in Uncle John's church. Glenn wanted to fit with the crowd; being a part of the Beachy Amish kind of church made him feel like he stuck out among the many people he met in town every day. Now he was attending, at least sporadically, at the Plainview Conservative Mennonite Church.

One day when Emma was alone in the house with Glenn, she asked, "What would you think if I got married to Levi Miller?" Now that she heard herself say it aloud, she could feel her heart beat faster.

Glenn arched his left eyebrow. He then responded in a somber tone. "I don't care if you marry him. But if you do, I won't turn over my paychecks anymore. He has enough money to support you."

Emma was taken aback by the tone in Glenn's voice. It was true that Levi could support her without the boys' income. But what if Levi insisted that the boys surrender their paychecks until they were of age, that is, they had turned twenty-one? Or what if he insisted that they help with his farm operation? What would happen if they refused? The last thing she wanted to do was to create an ugly confrontation.

Not long after Emma spoke to Glenn about Levi's interest, Harry Miller came to speak to her. Harry was Levi's son, the fifth of twelve children. They chatted for a time before Harry revealed the nature of his mission. "I understand that you've been seeing my father."

"Yes."

"We children wish that Dad would have waited a little longer before showing interest in another companion. But we understand that since Mother had cancer, he had some time to grieve before she died. It was not a sudden thing, like the way you lost Tobe."

Emma nodded.

"Now Dad is very lonely."

"It's lonely to live without a companion. And the children need a father."

"*Brauche sie awwer en Grossdaadi im Haus*? But do they need a grandfather in the house?"

Emma fell silent for a few moments. Levi was indeed a grandfather; he already had thirty-five grandchildren, with the potential for many more.

Harry continued. "As you know, Dad is quite a disciplinarian. I wonder if the twins might get on his nerves."

Emma wrung her handkerchief in her hands. "We haven't decided anything yet," she said.

After Harry left, Emma pondered his words. It was true that Levi was known for the way he disciplined his children, even more so than Tobe's father and others with a similar reputation. The biblical warning—"Spare the rod and spoil the child"—served as the watchword for many a father in the neighborhood. Levi would certainly be stricter with the twins than she was.

Another matter niggled in the back of her mind. If she married Levi, would they bring Edith back to Kansas to live with them? If the twins made Levi uneasy, surely Edith's nervous manner would make things even worse. But if Edith stayed at Weavers, she and Levi would be able to pay for her care without church assistance.

Edith seemed further away than ever, since the Weaver family had recently pulled up stakes and moved to Middlebury, Indiana. They made the move in response to a plea from their daughter Lula. Among other children, Lula had a young girl who was so developmentally disabled that she required total care. So the Weavers agreed to move next door to Lula and help care for the child. They purchased a ten-acre plot and moved into a trailer house, with the plan to construct a small house and barn. What bothered Emma the most, however, was that the property fronted on Road 13, a busy highway. She worried that Edith might not be safe so close to fast-moving traffic, especially since she loved to go to the mailbox.

• • • •

Since Perry didn't have full-time work at Reno Fabricating, he accepted an invitation to drive a truck on the garbage route for Menno Nisly. Like Glenn, Perry soon discovered that wasteful people threw away items that still had good use. He brought them home to be used around the house.

Each week, Menno picked up a large collection of day-old bread at local grocery stores and dumped the loaves onto the smooth concrete floor of his storage shed. There he sold it for ten cents a loaf to all comers. It sounded like a bargain to Emma, so she drove by one day on the way home after a day of transplanting at the greenhouse. The twins were with her since they had dropped by the greenhouse after school.

Emma got out of the car and walked into the large tin shed. On the far end lay a large mound of day-old bread. She walked around the pile, inspecting the loaves. Emma selected several loaves and handed them to Ervin to hold. Erma walked around the pile as well, looking for whole-wheat bread. After Emma found six loaves that suited her, she stopped at the small desk in the front of the shed. She dropped a few coins into the box. It didn't seem fair that Menno got paid to haul off the bread and then charged other people for it. But she was willing to pay a small price. At least it was cheaper than the fresh loaves at the store.

Emma felt a little guilty about buying white bread since she'd learned from Raymond that white flour wasn't as healthy as whole-wheat flour. Following Dr. Cowan's advice, Raymond had purchased a small stone mill to grind wheat from the farm. And he'd started farming grain the organic way.

After Mary Edna heard a TV broadcast at Shaklee's, she showed new interest in health as well. On the broadcast, Art Linkletter lamented that so many youth in the United States were not as interested in sports as youth from some other countries. They were too attached to cars, whereas youth from many other countries had to walk or ride their bicycles.

Hearing that, Mary Edna started walking for exercise. She got Ervin to join her in some exercises, and Perry even went on a run with her one evening. After talking to Raymond about her interests, she ground some wheat on his stone mill and used the flour for baking organic oatmeal cookies. Emma was intrigued. She hadn't yet decided that health foods were so important.

• • • •

At the same time that Emma was wrestling with the decision about Levi, Mary Edna had second thoughts about dating Menno. She told Emma that she had asked him to slow things down a bit—not to date regularly for a time. Emma sensed that Mary Edna was thinking about many things—not only courtship, but also her faith commitments and her vocation. Anna Shaklee was pressing Mary Edna to get training as a nurse's aid, but Mary Edna wasn't sure it was what she wanted to do.

For Mary Edna, working for Anna was like walking a tightrope. Since it wasn't easy for Anna to find good help, she leaned on Mary Edna harder than either Mary Edna or Emma thought was right. One evening when Mary Edna planned to attend a local church, Anna accused her of shirking her duties at the home.

Church was important to Mary Edna. She dreamed of being a missionary and talked about going to Africa. She dreamed of becoming a nurse like Emma's cousin Vera Mae or Mother Nisly's stepdaughter Rosa. But they were single women. Married women in the church didn't usually have careers such as nursing. They stayed at home to raise a family. It didn't seem likely that Mary Edna would be single. Menno wasn't the only young man who showed interest in her.

Emma observed that Mary Edna stretched her wings by trying new things, beyond what her brothers would attempt. She memorized Bible verses, wrote essays on Bible topics, taught herself to type, decorated cakes, drew pictures, sang in an octet, and constantly read books. Now she was talking about taking singing lessons with Mrs. Silvers. "Where did she get such energy? It must have come from Tobe," Emma thought.

Emma worried a bit about Mary Edna's interests in so many different churches. On one level, she was pleased. "But if Mary Edna showed such interest in other churches, might she lose interest in belonging to her own church? Would she be satisfied to dress plainly and follow other rules for non-conformity?"

Meanwhile, Emma was grateful that their own church was providing many more interesting things for the young people than the Amish congregation had when she was a youth. The winter Bible school, summer vacation Bible school, tract distribution, and visitation at the Broadacres Nursing Home—all were new since Emma's days as a youth.

Emma knew that Mary Edna wouldn't have been satisfied to stay in the Old Order Amish fellowship. The recent vote at Center to hold both Sunday school and a preaching service each Sunday, rather than alternate between Sundays, created more variety. And more of the service was held in English. Although Emma missed the German language, she knew that the young people liked English better.

In early May, Mary Edna decided to quit her job at Shaklee's and be at home full-time for the summer. Emma and twins went to Anna's home to fetch her, along with her things.

The following week, Mary Edna confided in Emma that Menno had asked her to go steady. Although Mary Edna had some hesitancy, she consented. But Menno agreed that they'd go slowly at first, not spending too much time together. He recognized that Mary Edna needed more time to think through the relationship.

Emma wrestled with ambivalence as she thought about

her own situation with Levi. She sensed that he was soon going to ask for a decision. It was as hard for her to decide as it was for Mary Edna to decide whether or not to say "yes" to Menno.

12

Single by Choice

In the early morning, Emma swung her feet out of bed, aware that there was plenty of work to do that day. The mournful sound of a dove drifted through the window as she got dressed. The first rays of the summer sun shone through the east window as Emma moved into the kitchen. She glanced out the north window toward the garden. "Those weeds are getting away from me," she lamented aloud. "I should get out there and take care of them. The rain we just had will make it a little easier."

Emma first checked the rain gauge. "An inch and two-tenths," she murmured with satisfaction. "We really needed that." As she moved toward the garden with a look of determination, a toad hopped across her path. First she staked the tomatoes, which had outgrown the gallon-sized tin cans she had used to protect them from the cool weather. She stripped off the cans, which had both ends cut out, and strung them onto the long wire suspended along the side of the garage.

Emma fetched the collapsible tomato stakes from the garage that Tobe had made in the shop back in Iowa. She swatted at the swarm of midges that moved past her face as she pushed the four-sided wire cages into the moist soil around the plants. As she stood back to survey her work, she remembered the time when Tobe had come into her garden to take and sell some of the stakes already in the ground. He'd made a promise to someone, he said, and hadn't had time to get enough new stakes made. That was hard for her to accept. Why did Tobe make promises that he couldn't keep? Surely the customer could have waited.

Now that the tomatoes were staked, she moved toward the melon patch. After an hour of hard work, she stood back and eyed the garden with delight. The ripening melons were fully visible now beside the pile of weeds.

The sound of the vacuum pump for the milking machine on Raymond's farm broke the morning stillness as Emma leaned her hoe against the side of the garage. It was time to do the farm chores.

Emma went to the washroom, grabbed the slop bucket in one hand, and took the stainless-steel milk pail in the other. She divided the slop between the hogs and chickens and then headed for the barn. On the way, she flipped up the red handle of the hydrant by the corral and listened with satisfaction as the water rushed into the square concrete tank. Josephine, Emma's Guernsey-Holstein cow, sauntered up to the tank and drank deeply of the cool liquid.

When the tank was full, Emma turned off the water and moved into the small barn. She turned on the light and swung open the small wooden door to the feed bin. With the galvanized scoop she dug out some feed and dumped it into the manger of the milk stall. Then she dipped a small tin into the galvanized container of molasses and poured it like syrup onto the small pile of feed. She savored the sweet tinge of molasses in the air as she swung open the small wooden gate of the milk stall, stepped through the stall, and swung open the larger outside door that opened onto the concrete platform.

"Come, Josephine," she called softly. Then she stepped back to make way for the large bovine. As soon as the cow put her head into the manger, Emma pulled shut the wooden stanchion and locked it with a wooden block.

Tiny drips of milk spattered onto the straw as Emma wiped Josephine's large udder with a rag. She hummed a tune as she sat down on the small one-legged stool and began to stroke the milk out of Josephine's large front teats. Streams of liquid gold sang against the bottom of the pail and flecked the sides. As the milk rose in the pail, Emma reflected on how lucky she was to have such a good cow. Josephine's Holstein lineage made her an excellent producer. She gave plenty of milk for the whole family as well as the farm animals. Her Guernsey lineage added the rich butterfat that made it well worth the effort to separate the cream from the milk.

Half a dozen cats gathered around as Emma coaxed the last drops out of the front teats and moved to the back two. Within minutes the milk had risen within two inches of the rim of the four-gallon pail.

Emma shooed the cats as she rose from the stool and set the pail safely outside the stall. She released the stanchion and stood back as Josephine turned and walked out of the barn. Then she poured some of the milk into a small porcelain pan and watched as the cats lapped wildly at the creamy liquid. Nothing on the farm drew cats more quickly than fresh warm milk.

As Emma carried the pail toward the house, she mused that if she were married to Levi, she wouldn't need to milk the cow. Since he was moving toward retirement, there might not be many chores of any kind. Life would be much simpler.

Emma carried the milk into the washroom of the house and poured it through a strainer into the top of the cream separator. Then she began to turn the crank. Each time the hand grip came to the top of its cycle, she heard a clink against the tin at the other end of the hollow cast-iron handle.

The disks inside the separator rotated in a steady whir as the machine gained momentum. When the handle turned fast enough that the handle stopped clinking, Emma turned on the valve that released the milk from the tank into the body of the separator. She watched with satisfaction as the milk passed through the separator and emerged from two spouts. A large stream of skim milk splashed from the lower spout into the container on the floor. Cream swished from the smaller, upper spout into a raised container. When all the milk had flowed through the separator, she put the milk and cream into the refrigerator.

Emma made breakfast for the children and then headed back to the garden. As she pulled more weeds, her thoughts again turned to Levi. She sensed that he wanted an answer soon. Might she ask him to wait for a couple years, until Glenn was gone from home and the twins were a bit older? Perhaps she could tell him it wasn't the right season.

It didn't seem likely that he'd wait, especially since he'd started dating so soon after Clara's death. She observed that men seemed impatient to get married after the death of a spouse. Few widowers in the community chose to remain single. Emma recalled that her grandfather, the esteemed Daniel Mast, had been widowed three times and married to four different women in succession.

"It would at least be worth talking to Levi about it," she thought. She would tell him that she wasn't willing to move ahead now, but perhaps at a later time. Perhaps she could ask him if he'd be willing to wait. She decided to do so the next time he came by to see her.

Emma didn't have long to wait. Late the next Sunday evening, Levi showed up beside her open bedroom window.

"I'm coming," she whispered through the screen. She dressed quickly and closed the bedroom door behind her.

By moonlight she made her way to Levi's car. The dome light shone on Levi's face as she opened the door and slid into the passenger seat. He seemed more nervous than usual, tapping his fingers on the steering wheel.

They made the usual small talk about family, church, and neighborhood. A breeze flowed through the open windows. Then Levi paused and cleared his throat.

Emma held her breath. This was the moment of truth.

Levi cleared his voice again and spoke slowly. "I've been thinking that maybe we should decide about our future together."

"Yes?"

"I would like to know if you are interested in going forward."

Emma's heart raced. She pinched her lips tightly for a moment and then said, "I think it might be best if I would wait for a while. Maybe wait until the twins are older." She paused. Should she tell him that she feared how he might treat the twins? Or that Glenn was so opposed to the idea? She remained silent, waiting for his response.

"I see," Levi said. He turned from her gaze and looked out the windshield of the car. He paused. "I don't think I want to wait."

Emma sat quietly, looking out the windshield at the outline of the house in the dim moonlight.

Levi breathed deeply and said, "Well then—I'll say goodnight."

Emma reached for the door handle. "Goodnight," she said, avoiding his eyes. She closed the door gently and turned toward the house. The porch door closed behind her as Levi backed out of the driveway onto the gravel road. She watched through the porch window as he turned on his headlights and headed south. It was not likely that he'd come back.

Over the next weeks, Emma often replayed that scene in the car. Had she done the right thing? How might he have responded if she had said it differently? At times when she felt particularly alone, she questioned the rightness of her decision. At other times, when she thought through the tensions that the marriage would have introduced for her children, she was convinced that she had done what was right. She pondered the matter at some length the day when Glenn decided to buy a car.

It was late in the morning when Emma glanced out the west living room window to see a '57 Chevy two-door hardtop pull into the driveway. The bright red body was accented by a white top, white sidewall tires, and chrome polished to a sheen.

"Who might this be?" Emma wondered. "Certainly not anyone from among the plain people." She looked more closely as the car came to a stop. "Was that Glenn at the wheel?"

She watched as Glenn got out of the driver's side and beckoned to her through the window. Emma leaned her broom against a wall and made her way outside. A middle-aged gentleman wearing a suit swung his legs out from the passenger side, stepped forward, and proffered his hand. Emma greeted him and then looked down at her faded dress. She hadn't expected company.

"I saw this car on the lot at A. D. Rayl this morning," Glenn said. "I have almost enough cash saved up to buy it, but I need you to loan me a little to cover the sales tax. Will you do that for me?"

Emma pursed her lips for a moment. The salesman walked to the back of the car as mother and son conversed.

"It's my money," Glenn said. "If I buy this car, you'll have the use of the family car for someone else in the family."

218

Emma nodded in silence. Glenn had a point. He had worked long overtime hours to earn his own cash. "How much are they asking for the car?"

"$995 plus tax. I only need to borrow $100. It's a solid car that should last me a long time. Please, can you loan me the money?"

Emma took a deep breath. "How soon do you need it?"

"I want to buy the car today. I don't want someone else to get it."

Emma turned toward the house. "I'll have to see how much I have in the checkbook."

Glenn glanced at the salesman, who winked and nodded.

A few minutes later Emma emerged from the house and handed Glenn a check for $100.

"Thank you, Mom," Glenn said as he put the check into his pocket and headed for the driver's seat.

Emma watched in silence as the two men got back into the car and headed for town.

That evening Glenn pulled into the driveway with his new car. "Anybody want a ride?" The family crowded around; then Perry and the twins got in.

Emma took a deep breath as Glenn sped off. Why did he have to pick such a sporty car with such a bright color?

At the supper table, Glenn joked about the car salesman who had come with him. "I told the man that I needed a little more cash. So when we got close to our place, he asked if we'd need to sell a cow or something."

The family joined in laughter. They wouldn't be likely to do that.

Emma worried about how Glenn would use his car. He was already spending a lot of his time in town with his job. Wouldn't a sporty car make him more likely to associate with worldly people? What would people in the church think?

Often when women gathered for the monthly sewing at the church house, they talked about such things. The sewing was coming up in two days.

On the day of the sewing, Emma milked a little early. She washed up and fixed a few things to take along for lunch. She slipped into a clean dress, exchanged her brown work scarf for a covering, and got into the car to head for the church house.

Emma glanced at the clock as she made her way down the concrete steps into the church basement. Although some arrived by 9:30 a.m. or earlier, women were free to come and go throughout the day. Most of the married women from the church participated whenever possible. It was understood that some of the unmarried women had day jobs that prevented their involvement.

Emma put her lunch on the table in the room that had been designated as a kitchen. Then she looked around at the various table stations to see where she was most needed. A dozen women were stitching on the quilt near the center of the large open area. Others worked on projects at sewing machines around the perimeter of the room.

Emma joined the ladies making bandages for relief. She picked up a worn bedsheet that was draped over the back of a chair. It was to be cut into strips to make bandages. Emma laid the sheet on a table and marked off the edges into two-inch strips. Then she took a scissors and cut a slit through the hem at each mark. She took hold of the fabric on each side of the first slit and pulled it apart, tearing the fabric along the weave. Through long practice, she could easily tear the whole length of a sheet in a straight line. By the time she was finished with the sheet, she had a pile of two-inch strips ready to be joined. Emma sat down and sewed the strips end-to-end until there were enough to be rolled into a large coil.

As Emma sewed, she recalled seeing pictures of people

who used such bandages. Through slide lectures and church newspapers, relief workers sponsored by the Mennonite Central Committee shared stories of ministry to victims of illness and war. The rolls would first be taken to the regional relief center in Newton, Kansas, some forty miles to the east. From there, they would be distributed to hospitals and clinics in needy places around the world.

As she worked, Emma chatted with Levi Miller's daughter Lizzie. Emma wondered if Lizzie knew that her brother Harry had come to see her. Had Levi confided with any of his children about his relationship with her?

Lizzie paused as she finished the last seam on a strip of bandages, flipped the handle to the presser foot on the sewing machine, and snipped the white thread. "It seems to me that I heard something about Ervin being sick. What seems to be the problem?"

"We're not sure," Emma replied. "He said his chest hurt so I took him to Dr. Cowan. The doctor thought maybe something isn't quite right with his heart—maybe rheumatic fever. He had to stay in bed for a week."

Lizzie arched her eyebrows. "I don't suppose that was easy for Ervin. He doesn't sit still for long."

"Oh, it was terribly hard on him. The one good thing is that he likes to read. He reads lots of books. And the children at school had a card shower."

"So Dr. Cowan wasn't sure what was wrong?"

"That's right. He sent us to a specialist for children."

"A pediatrician?"

"Yes, that's it. So we went to Dr. Orthwein in Hutch. He wasn't sure what the problem was either, but he gave Ervin some medicine. It tastes bitter, so Ervin hates to take it. Now he's in school again, but he's not allowed to play sports this year."

"I hope he gets better soon."

"Thank you." Emma stood up to get another large sheet.

"I also heard that you got a new garage," Lizzie said.

Emma smiled as she began cutting the sheet. "Yes, L. Perry and Silvia bought a house in town and moved it to their place. They didn't need the garage, so they offered it to me at a good price."

"It's nice that you'll have a place to put your car inside."

"Yes, the boys are happy about it, too. Alvin Yoder helped them dig a pit for it."

"You mean like they have at Fairview Station?"

Emma nodded. "You can go down underneath the car to drain the oil or work on the engine."

"That's nice if they can do their own work on their cars. It'll save money too."

Emma smiled and nodded. "I'm glad they take an interest in those things. We had to widen our driveway to make space for the garage. Raymond helped them pull out some of the hedge trees to make room for it."

"That was a lot of work."

"Yes, but I'm glad we did it. I think the garden will do better now. Those trees took a lot of moisture."

Lizbet Nisly came alongside the two women. "Have you heard about the man who recently escaped from prison and lived with Elam Hochstetlers?" she asked.

"No!" Emma raised her eyebrows. Elam was the bishop who had helped get their church started.

"I saw it in *The Budget*. The man called himself William Souza. He lived with Elams and helped on the farm for five weeks before they found out who he really was."

"No!" Barbara Yoder joined the conversation.

"Yes, he escaped from a prison somewhere in Rhode Island. Maybe he figured that no one would come looking for him on an Amish farm. He attended the Woodlawn Church with the Hochstetler family."

"Maybe he was trying to change his ways," Barbara said. Emma nodded.

"That's what Elam thought," Lizbet continued. "They were ready to baptize him last Sunday night. But on Sunday morning the Elkhart County police got a call from the FBI. When the family came home from church at Sunday noon, the Elkhart County sheriff was there waiting for them. They said the man's real name was Eddie. I can't remember his last name. So he didn't get baptized after all."

"I wonder if he was sincere or just pretending," Barbara asked quietly, compassion softening the edges of her voice.

"I guess it's hard to know. But if he was just pretending, it's a good thing that he got caught," Lizzie declared.

Emma shuddered to think of a criminal on the loose so close to the place where Edith lived. The Hochstetler farm was less than a half mile from Noah Weaver's new place. But again, if the man was sincerely converted, it was a good thing. Time would tell.

A few weeks later the extended Stutzman family gathered to celebrate L. Perry's birthday. Since they hoped to surprise him, the family parked in the area behind the shop and gathered in their newly built garage. Together they sang "Happy Birthday" and marched into the house with the carry-in supper.

Silvia grinned broadly. Perry hadn't even suspected it.

All through the evening, Emma kept glancing toward Beverly, the young woman Glenn had invited to the party. Beverly's bright red lipstick accented her slender cheeks, pink with the warmth of the September evening. Her slender legs beckoned Emma's eyes to scan the hem of her short red dress with disapproval.

"I imagine she likes to ride in Glenn's bright red car," Emma mused. "I was afraid he was going to get into trouble with that car. I don't know why he would date a town girl. He wouldn't get by with that if he were a member at Center."

Emma couldn't help but notice that Glenn and Beverly sat closer to each other on the sofa than Mary Edna and Menno, who were going steady. Emma's eyes kept flitting between the couples as the group watched a Billy Graham telecast. It wasn't hard for her to imagine how Grandpa and Grandma Stutzman felt about their son having a television in his home. L. Perry hadn't grown up with a TV, but when he met Silvia, he left the Amish church and made some changes in lifestyle. Now that Glenn worked closely alongside his uncle L. Perry, Glenn would likely be drawn to make more changes.

That evening before Emma climbed into bed, she pled that God would somehow show Glenn the error of his ways. It wouldn't do much good, Emma reasoned, to talk to Glenn about his dating habits. Only God could bring about a change in his heart.

Emma was working at the kitchen sink when Mary Edna arrived home from Shaklee's the next weekend. After Mary Edna had been away from the care facility for a time, Mrs. Shaklee had talked her into coming back to work there again.

"Hi, Mom," Mary Edna said as she set down her purse. "We got a new resident yesterday. Her name is June Sewell. She's seventeen years old."

"Is something wrong with her? Why does she need to live in a nursing home?"

Mary Edna glanced toward Erma playing in the living room and lowered her voice. "She's pregnant. Her parents didn't want her to stay with them in Kansas City, so they brought her here till the baby is born."

"Oh my," Emma murmured. "She got involved in some wrong activities."

"Yes, but she's fun to be with," Mary Edna said. "We played Concentration till late last night." Mary Edna enjoyed table games.

Emma laid down her peeler and reached for the food grater. "When will the baby come?"

"She's about four months along." Mary Edna counted off the remaining months on her fingers. "I suppose about the middle of February."

Mary Edna pulled a drinking glass out of the cabinet and moved toward the refrigerator as Emma started to grate the carrots. "Could June stay at our house on the weekend? She could go to church with us. She doesn't want to stay with all those older people at Shaklee's every weekend."

Emma stopped grating and pursed her lips as she pondered how to respond. "I suppose that would be all right. It would be good for her to go to church."

"Good," Mary Edna said as she finished her glass of water. "I'll invite her next weekend. I don't think Menno will mind if she spends some time with the two of us."

Late that Friday afternoon, Emma watched from the sink as Mary Edna brought her new acquaintance into the house. Emma dried her hands on her apron as the brown-haired young woman followed Mary Edna through the washroom into the kitchen.

"Hi, Mom, this is my friend June Sewell," Mary Edna said.

Emma reached out her hand. "Welcome." Her eyes met June's and then dropped toward June's waist. Her dress fit tightly, with no belt at the waist.

"Thank you, Mrs. Stutzman," the young woman replied. "I'm going to enjoy being here with your daughter."

Emma smiled broadly and nodded. She watched as Mary Edna led June to her room.

As the weekend progressed, Emma was pleased with the way things worked out. Their guest accompanied the family to church without seeming unduly self-conscious. She sat with Mary Edna and the other single young women in the third bench on the women's side.

Emma looked up with anticipation as Bishop Amos Nisly approached the pulpit to bring the morning message.

"I greet you this morning in the name of Jesus Christ," he began.

"English again," Emma mused. "It seems that he's preached in English most of the time recently."

Amos continued. "You might have noticed that we ministers have been preaching in English recently. Some time ago we made a decision that we would preach in English whenever we have visitors who cannot understand the German. Because our young people have been inviting their friends to church, we've needed to be prepared to preach each Sunday in English as well as German. We know that some of you would prefer that we always preach in German. Others would prefer otherwise. But we have now decided that we will preach in English except for special occasions."

Emma glanced over to where Mary Edna was sitting. That would certainly suit her well. June Sewell was far more likely to attend at Center if the sermons were in English.

Mary Edna's friendship with June grew over the next months. In the middle of December, June's parents stopped by Emma's home on a weekend trip from Kansas City to visit their daughter.

"Thanks for being such good friends to our daughter," Walter Sewell said as the couple rose to leave after a brief visit. He gripped Emma's hand tightly and held it, then brushed away a tear as he turned toward the car. Emma watched pensively as the couple backed out of the driveway.

"What will happen to the baby after it's born?" Emma asked Mary Edna.

"She's giving it up for adoption. There's a Christian couple in St. Louis who have asked for the child. Their names are Bill and Gertrude Walls."

"Will June move back home?" Emma wondered.

"Yes, she wants to finish her schooling."

"What a shame that it happened this way," Emma thought to herself. "Young women should learn to stay out of trouble. But it sounds like her baby will have a good home."

When Mary Edna came home the next Wednesday evening, she stood with Emma at the sink. "Mom, Bill and Gertrude would like for me to come to St. Louis to help them when the baby is born."

Emma wrinkled her brow. "Why would you want to do that?"

"I'd like to make sure the baby gets off to a good start. I've had more experience with newborns than the Wallses. They would like for me to spend several weeks with them."

"I don't like for you to be gone so long by yourself," Emma said. "Are you sure you want to move into the big city to live with someone you've never met?"

"Sure. They sound like nice people on the phone. But we don't have to decide right now."

"We'll see," Emma said as she drew a deep breath. She put the last dish into the rinse water and pulled the drain stopper. Then she dried her hands on the small hand towel hanging from the cabinet door pull.

Emma slipped off her apron and hung it on the hook in the washroom. "Do you think that Menno will be able to finish installing our storm windows soon?"

"Yes, Menno said he'll finish this week," Mary Edna replied. "He wants to have them done in time for Christmas."

"It will be so nice to have them all done." Emma smiled. "Then the bedrooms won't be so cold anymore."

Since Perry worked at Reno Fabricating, Emma was able to buy storm windows at a discount. And Menno agreed to install them outside his regular hours. These two factors convinced Emma that she could afford the project.

Mary Edna continued, "Menno said he'll help me assemble the Christmas boxes and deliver them too. We'll get a list of names of the people who need them a couple of days before Christmas. I suppose most of them will go to people in Hutch."

Emma nodded in affirmation. The Christmas boxes were a way to share with those less fortunate. And it gave Menno and Mary Edna something wholesome to do together.

Christmas came and went with the usual family gatherings. Emma hosted the extended Stutzman family at her home for a big noon meal on Sunday, Christmas Eve. Afterward Perry and Mary Edna delivered Christmas boxes and went caroling with the youth group.

The next morning, Mary Edna was bubbling with excitement. "Mom, it was so wonderful to sing last night. The moon was so bright we hardly needed to use our flashlights to see our music. I helped start some of the songs. We went to about thirty places. It was a perfect time to be with Menno."

Emma's face glowed as she went to bed that night. She was grateful to see her daughter so happy. Yet as she replayed the scenes of the last year in her mind, she felt a sense of loneliness. She rolled onto her side and looked outside at the evergreen trees in the bright moonlight. She could almost see Levi's shadow and hear him tapping on the window screen. But that relationship was no longer a possibility. Levi had recently married someone he had met in Florida. It still wasn't easy to be alone. But if God willed it, Emma resolved, she was willing to keep living this way the rest of her life.

13

Arkansas Mission

One morning not long after, Emma lay half awake as the mantel clock chimed the three-quarter hour. She glanced at the Big Ben alarm clock; the luminescent hands showed 4:45 a.m. Glenn would be expecting his breakfast in less than thirty minutes.

She yawned noisily and blinked her eyes as she swung her legs out of the bed. Emma dressed by the light of the small lamp on the dresser and then stepped into the dim hallway. Glenn's alarm rang as she passed the boys' bedroom on her way to the bathroom. He was good at getting up; she didn't need to remind him as she did the twins.

Emma stepped into the bathroom and pulled her dentures out of the cup where they had soaked overnight. She brushed them and slipped them onto her gums. She put her toothbrush back into the wooden cabinet that Tobe had made to hang over a sink. Then she made her way to the kitchen and stirred up a generous helping of tomato gravy at the same time as she prepared French toast. "Good morning," she said quietly as Glenn came into the kitchen.

"Mornin'."

Emma placed a hot pad on the table and set the kettle of steaming gravy on it. She scooped two pieces of French toast out of the skillet and flipped them onto his plate. Glenn bowed his head briefly and then ladled the gravy onto his toast. Emma put the skillet back on the burner and sliced some cold mush out of the porcelain dish. "Do you want two or three pieces of mush?"

"I'll take three."

Emma sliced three pieces out of the pan and placed them into the buttered skillet. She turned on the switch to the exhaust fan as a puff of steam rose from the edge of the golden mush. The mush sizzled and spattered as she flipped it over. Emma reveled in the sound and smell of frying mush. It gave such an at-home feeling.

"Did you hear that Levi Miller got married?" Emma asked.

"No. Who did he marry?"

"A woman from Florida."

"I hope they're happy."

"Me too." Emma stepped over to put the mush onto his plate. "Do you want some of that canned meat for your sandwich?"

"Yes."

Emma reached into the refrigerator and drew out a jar of canned meat. She slathered mayonnaise onto a couple pieces of bread, cut two slices of meat to put on them, and put it all together with lettuce and cheese. Then she stuffed the sandwiches into Glenn's aluminum lunch box alongside fresh carrots and a dish of potato salad.

"I put some of that hot tomato soup in your thermos. Did it stay hot enough yesterday?"

"Yes, it was okay."

Emma closed the lunch box to the sound of Glenn scraping his plate clean. She set it on the table as Glenn put on his work jacket. It was still dark outside as he picked up his lunch and walked out the door.

Emma rinsed the dishes, put them beside the sink, and then sat down on an armchair to rest for a few minutes. It had been a short night. Before long, she drifted into sleep.

When she awoke, it was light enough outside to go about her chores. She put on her coat and headed for the barn. As she milked the cow, she pondered again what had happened between her and Levi. "I may have missed my only chance to get married," she fretted aloud. "It would be so nice to have a companion." Although it was more than five years since Tobe's death, she still thought of him often. She wondered if the hole in her heart would ever heal.

"I still think it's best for the children that I didn't marry Levi," she said aloud to herself. "I have to think of them first. Someday they'll all be gone from home."

"The most important thing," she reminded herself as she finished coaxing the last streams of milk from the cow, "is to raise my children for God."

Of Emma's six children, Mary Edna spoke most readily about God's mission for her life. She dreamed of being a mission worker, perhaps even to serve overseas as a missionary nurse. She watched Christian films and attended Youth for Christ rallies. Just last summer, she'd convinced a group of young people to accompany her on a trip to St. Paul, Minnesota, to attend a Billy Graham crusade.

Since Mary Edna loved adventure, working at Shaklee's was boring at times. But June Sewell's coming brought new excitement. The young teenager looked up to Mary Edna. Mary Edna saw their friendship as an opportunity to be a witness for Christ.

June gave birth to her baby on Saturday evening, February 17, 1962. On Monday morning, Emma accompanied Mary Edna to Grace Hospital, to visit June and baby Michael David. After a few days of worry about the baby's health, the doctor declared the infant fit for immediate adoption. June agreed that Bill and Gertrude Walls could adopt the child. The couple pleaded for Mary Edna to come and help them. Meanwhile, Mary Edna cared for the baby at the Shaklee home.

"Mom, can't I go to help the Wallses with the baby?" Mary Edna begged. "You know I'm good with babies."

There was no question in Emma's mind about that. Over the last few years, Mary Edna had cared for a dozen newborns around the neighborhood.

Emma pondered. She didn't like to let Mary Edna work so far away with no support from her own people. But her heart went out to the young couple who were adopting the child. They would surely benefit from Mary Edna's help. "All right," she agreed, "you can go."

"Thanks, Mom," Mary Edna said as she stepped to the phone to make arrangements. In early March, Mary Edna accompanied Bill and Gertrude Walls and the two-week-old infant to St. Louis, Missouri.

Two weeks later, Emma got her first letter from her daughter. She learned that things were going well except that the baby attached itself to Mary Edna rather than bonding to his new parents. "They're a little worried about what they're going to do when it's time for me to leave," Mary Edna wrote.

Mary Edna told about playing chess, shopping at the Shopping Fair, and eating prime rib at the Congress Hotel's Town and Country Room. She had plenty of time to read, so she finished *How to Stop Worrying and Start Living* and *How to Win Friends and Influence People*, both by Dale Carnegie.

Mary Edna also told about being with the Walls's friends. "I accompanied them to their Baptist church and attended the Training Union for soul-winning."

Emma was delighted to know that the Wallses were

Christians but somewhat worried over too much talk about soul-winning and witnessing. If Mary Edna got too involved in that kind of witnessing, would she be satisfied to come back to Center Church? Emma observed that people sometimes used "mission" aspirations as an excuse to leave the Amish Church. Wasn't it possible to be good witnesses while remaining Amish? Did people really become better witnesses by joining a more-progressive church?

Hence, Emma was relieved to hear that Mary Edna planned to come home for the biannual communion service. That event was too important to miss.

Mary Edna arrived home from St. Louis late on the last Saturday in April, just in time to attend the communion service the next morning. Emma joined Mary Edna and Perry in the usual fast from breakfast on communion Sunday, but made breakfast for Erma and Ervin, who were not yet members of the church.

"I'm nine years old now," Erma reminded her older sister as they prepared to go to church.

"Yes, you and Ervin had a birthday. I'm sorry I missed it," Mary Edna agreed. "I'm so glad to be home again. The last two weeks in St. Louis kinda dragged along."

Ervin piped up. "That's how it was at school. Time went real slow. Now we're out for the summer. Next year we're going to be in the fourth grade."

Mary Edna nodded. "That means you'll be in the fourth grade in Bible school too."

Emma nodded. "I'll be helping with Bible school all week."

Unlike the traditional Amish pattern, the communion services at Center Church weren't much longer than a regular Sunday service. So Emma arrived home from church that day in time to make a late dinner for the whole family. Then Mary

Edna accompanied Menno and others to attend a service at the county jail.

The next morning, Emma let the twins sleep longer than usual. "Remember that we're going to Bible school this morning," she said as she knocked on the door to wake them at eight o'clock. The event for school-aged children met each forenoon, Monday through Friday, for two weeks.

The twins were soon at the table with Mary Edna, who had slept in as well. Emma had served Glenn earlier that morning and now made a second round of tomato gravy and mush. This time she sat down for the meal. By the time the breakfast dishes were done, it was time to head for Bible school.

Emma assisted in the second-grade classroom while the twins attended the fourth grade. After classes were over, she stepped outside to watch the children at play. She observed that the group games attracted the children as much as the classroom lessons. Most of the boys, along with some of the girls, played a popular game they called Andy-over. The size and shape of the church facility made it an ideal place to play.

"Andy-over," yelled Oren as he threw a softball over the top of the roof to the team on the other side. A few moments passed as his team waited to see if a member of the other team had caught the ball.

"Not this time," Emma thought as she heard the cry from the other side: "Andy-over." She smiled as she watched the ball bounce off the roof into LaVerne's eager hands. He held the ball behind his back and darted around the south side of the building. The whole team followed suit, some around each end of the building. Soon the other team came running from the opposite side. The point of the game was to capture members of the competing team by tagging them with the ball. The element of surprise lent some advantage.

"Did he get anybody?" asked Philip, hoping his team hadn't lost any members.

"Nope," Leon assured him. "We're too fast for them."

Emma motioned to Ervin and Erma, who were on the same team. "It's time to go."

"I have to go now," Ervin told his teammates as he made his way to the car.

"*Bischt du net bissel kalt mitt ken Wammes*? Aren't you a little cold without a jacket?" Emma asked.

"*Nee, ich bin net kalt.* No, I'm not cold," Ervin replied.

"I don't know why you'd want to go without a jacket," Emma mumbled as she started up the car and headed for home.

By the end of the week, the weather was balmy, perfect for a belated birthday party for the twins. The Alvin Yoder family surprised them by bringing a cake in the shape of a pony. It wasn't always easy to draw the line between plain and fancy in the church, but decorated cakes didn't seem to enter the equation. Mary Edna and others developed the art.

Decorated clothing or jewelry was quite another matter. These fell under the rubric of nonconformity to the world. Although the folks at Center Church were less strict than the Old Order Amish, they still thought of themselves as plain people. And it was very important to dress at variance with the surrounding culture.

The next Sunday morning, Willie Wagler addressed the issue of nonconformity in his sermon based on Romans 12:1-2. He began by reading aloud from the King James Bible: "I beseech you therefore, brethren, by the mercies of God, that ye present your bodies a living sacrifice, holy, acceptable unto God, which is your reasonable service." Willie cleared his throat and then continued: "And be not conformed to this world, but be transformed by the renewing of your mind, that

237

ye may prove what is that good, and acceptable, and perfect will of God."

Emma leaned forward in her seat as Willie began to expound on the biblical text. She recalled how Tobe used to enjoy hearing Willie preach. He spoke with sincere conviction and filled his messages with vivid illustrations. He spoke with confidence, not fearing to offend.

"As plain people, we believe that God calls us to be separate from the world," Willie declared. "The apostle tells us not to be conformed to this world. That is why we believe in nonconformity. If people are living holy lives according to the Bible, it should not be difficult to tell who are Christians and who are not."

Emma nodded. If Christians dressed and acted like everyone around them, what kind of witness would that be?

"Some churches teach that Christians can dress any way they want to," Willie continued, "just as long as they are modest. But that does not provide a uniform witness. That's why we have a discipline in our church. Many companies ask their employees to wear a uniform. People can tell that they are a part of the company because of the way they dress. In the same way, we believe that we should have a uniform witness in our dress. We have examples of plain churches who allowed individuals to dress however they wanted. Before long, they lost the principle of nonconformity."

"It's the same way with our cars or other things we own," Willie continued, his eyes sweeping the congregation. "It is a great temptation to drift into worldliness. Without us realizing what is happening, we can be drawn downstream, to be like the world. Many worldly people have simply drifted to the place where they are today. That's why we need to be careful to draw the lines in our fellowship."

Emma hoped Mary Edna and Menno were listening well.

Recently, she'd caught wind that the two of them were debating whether or not it was essential for women to dress plainly or wear the prayer covering. It worried her too that Mary Edna was reading books reflecting a popular understanding of Christian faith. Perhaps Willie's message would convince them of the need to keep following the discipline of the church.

It wasn't easy for Emma to share her concerns with Mary Edna. There were so many ways that Mary Edna demonstrated a growing Christian faith. Furthermore, she was a hard worker. Emma watched with appreciation as Mary Edna painted the ceiling and walls in several rooms and cleaned out the kitchen cabinets. Mary Edna didn't need to be nagged. She sought out work and pursued it with vigor. It wasn't easy to criticize the faith of such a dedicated daughter.

Mary Edna reflected her enthusiasm as she told Emma about the introduction to a Dale Carnegie course that she and Perry had attended. "Mom, it was such an enjoyable evening. The people gave testimonies about how much difference it made for them," Mary Edna said. "Harold Abbott, the sponsor from Kansas City, told us how much his home life has changed since he took the Dale Carnegie course. It made me anxious to take the course this fall."

Perry echoed Mary Edna's enthusiasm. "Three of our ministers took the course, and some other members from Center Church, too. I signed up to take it. It only costs $150.00. I'll pay for it with my own money."

Emma frowned. Why would people pay that much money to learn how to speak better in public? Was it really that important for plain people to learn how to be more expressive?

Perry continued. "Amos Nisly said it really helped him. He said next to salvation in Jesus Christ, this is the best thing that ever happened to him."

Emma shrugged her shoulders. Amos was the bishop.

He should know the value of the course. Perhaps it would be okay if it helped Perry to be a better witness. "I don't mind as long as you use your own money," she assented. Through bonuses, overtime, or odd jobs, Perry had the chance to earn his own cash.

Perhaps it was like singing, Emma reasoned. In the Old Order church, people worshipped by singing slow tunes in unison. Things were different at Center. Both Perry and Mary Edna learned to sing voice parts and joined an octet. There were many opportunities for them to sing; a half-dozen different *englisch* (non-Amish) churches invited them to sing for their special music. If Mary Edna and Perry were right, maybe more-expressive worship would help to draw "outsiders" into the plain church.

Emma wholeheartedly approved of missions to win new people to Christ. The testimonies at church and the stories in the *Witnessing* paper tugged at Emma's heart. For some time, she had been pondering the possibility of teaching as a volunteer at the summer Bible school sponsored by the Shady Lawn church in Arkansas. The mission outpost was supported by the Center church, with Amos Nisly serving as their bishop. The Bible school would be held not far from the little town of Mountain View, about a nine-hour trip by car.

Emma worried just a bit about leaving the twins at home for two weeks. But Mary Edna assured her that she would take care of them.

In early May, Emma took a step of faith. She notified the church that she was available to teach at the vacation Bible school. In the third week of May, she bid the family farewell and left with a carload of other workers headed for Arkansas.

The carload made its way to southeastern Kansas, through the southwest corner of Missouri, and into the northern part of Arkansas. Emma watched with wonder as they entered the land of the Ozarks. She marveled at the mountain bluffs, tall trees, and narrow winding roads. The steep wooded hills stood in stark contrast to the level prairie that surrounded Hutchinson. At several points along the way, the travelers stopped to enjoy the scenic views. Emma held her breath as the group stepped to the edge of a bluff with a steep drop to a river far below.

The group arrived in Harrison, Arkansas, in late afternoon. Emma sighed with relief as the car made its way up the steep driveway onto the grounds of Hillcrest Home, some hundred miles from their final destination at Mountain View. They took a few minutes for refreshment. Eli Helmuth, the administrator for the home, volunteered to show them around the grounds.

"This place was first known as the Boone County Poor Farm," Eli Helmuth explained as they walked around the perimeter of the first building. "But it got a bad name because they gave such poor care. Finally they had to close the doors. Then they heard about the work that the South Central Mennonite Conference was doing over in a neighboring county. So the Boone County board asked if the plain people would be interested in operating this place. In 1953, the MIC took over the operation and reopened the doors. The county board is really pleased with this arrangement. They provide the buildings and the grounds, and we provide the administration and the workers. Because we use young people from the plain churches as volunteers, we can provide Christian care and still make a profit. We send money each year to Amish Mennonite Aid, or AMA as we call it, which uses it for mission projects in other places."

Emma nodded. It was a wonderful thing to have a place where the young people could serve without leaving the plain church.

As Eli took them inside the building, he said, "We eat supper early around here, so we have lots of time to put the residents to bed. You'll see some of them heading for the dining room. We'll join them there in a few minutes."

Emma followed Eli eagerly. She hoped for the opportunity to see Elmer Nisly, a volunteer worker from Center Church. The group walked slowly through the hallways, smiling at the people in their rooms or stopping to speak briefly to them. Eli greeted each of the residents by name.

"Just find a seat at one of the tables," Eli told the visitors as they moved into the dining area. Emma scanned the room briefly before taking a chair opposite an elderly resident. Everyone grew quiet as Eli lead in prayer for the meal. Emma looked around at the young volunteers who were assisting residents seated around them. Her heart throbbed with pity as she observed a young resident named Jesse Leatherman. He was half sitting, half lying in a wheelchair with tall sides. His head was thrust into a corner of the conveyance. Jesse couldn't speak, so he made his will known through a small repertoire of sounds accented by the arching of his large dark eyebrows.

A tear trickled onto Emma's cheek as she watched a young volunteer feeding the disabled young man. The task required persistence, since Jesse didn't swallow well. "How good it is," Emma thought as she ate, "that our young people learn to serve those who are less fortunate than we. It will teach them to be grateful for what they have."

After supper, Emma left with her group for Mountain View. As they drove into the town, she understood how the municipality got its name. It was surrounded by mountains on three sides. They proceeded through town on Route 14 and turned south onto Route 5, a gravel road. They made their way more slowly now as rocks pinged against the car's belly. White dust enveloped the car and trailed behind them. It was dusk as they pulled to a stop in front of the mission.

Abe and Lydia Mae Schwartz assisted the group with the luggage and showed them up the stairs to their sleeping quarters. When people were settled in, they briefly oriented the volunteers to their task. Emma learned that the Mission Interest Committee had started the Bible school in 1955 as part of the groundwork to build a church. Two other couples served alongside the Schwartzes as core workers in the mission, assisted by a half dozen other volunteers. After eight years of mission work based in home fellowships, the emerging congregation was building its own meetinghouse.

Emma looked forward to assisting with Bible school. There was plenty of support work to do as well: gardening, canning, and cleaning. Not least, there were meals to cook for the workers who were building the new church facility. The 24-by-42-foot block structure was nearing completion.

After a week at the mission, Emma was delighted to receive a letter from Mary Edna. Since there was no telephone service in the rural area, letters were the only way to communicate. Emma tore open the envelope and glanced over her daughter's letter.

"Oh my!" she said aloud as she came to unexpected news. "We had a bad hailstorm here on Thursday, the 24th," she read aloud to herself. "I never saw hail like this before. The hailstones ranged in size from marbles to baseballs. Delilah Nisly found one hailstone ten inches in circumference. Some of them had fringed edges and looked like a handful of marbles frozen together. Some looked like flowers. The Stutzman Greenhouse was badly damaged."

"The hail was even bigger in Hutch. The Flower Shop was completely destroyed. Many cars had their windshields broken and tops dented in. Fortunately, our cars were inside."

"A tornado went through about a mile west of here, but it didn't do any damage till it got to Hutch. There it picked up a trailer house and smashed it to pieces."

"We worked in all three gardens. I tilled two of them. The children helped."

"The twins and I finished shelling the hickory nuts. It's a relief to be done."

Emma smiled broadly. She could always count on Mary Edna to work hard while she was gone.

The next morning, Emma woke with the early morning light. She quietly got dressed and made her way past her sleeping roommates in the dormered upstairs room. In the dim light of the wooden shed, she found a hoe and made her way into the garden plot that supplied the mission with vegetables. "With all the guest workers here," she thought, "Lydia Mae doesn't have time to keep up with the garden." As she closed the door to the shed, she was delighted to see a deer bounding across the nearby clearing.

Emma started in by hoeing around the beans. "The soil is different here," she observed out loud. "It's a little harder to hoe with all these stones."

As she moved down the row of beans, Emma reflected on how much she enjoyed the rhythm of life at the mission. It was much the same as life at home, she reasoned, except that the church was located in a community where people weren't familiar with the Amish. And, certainly, the mission needed to manage with fewer members available to do the work of the church. That's why dozens of volunteers came from scattered communities to help the small church with their summer Bible school.

By breakfast time Emma had weeded all of the vegetables. With a sigh of satisfaction, she put the hoe back in the shed and washed up just in time to eat with the other volunteers.

After breakfast, she got ready to meet her class, a group of children aged four to seven. Together with the other workers, she made her way several miles up the gravel road to the Arbanna Church and school building. It was a wooden structure with a tin roof, its clapboard siding begging for paint. Three wooden steps led up to the small porch. A few small square windows stood high, near the eaves.

As Emma took the class roll, she reflected on the children's last names—Swafford, Goins, Roberts, and Berry. She wondered what an Amish church might look like if all of the church members had names like these students. They sounded so different from that of the typical volunteer teacher or mission worker: Burkholder, Nisly, Stutzman, King, Schwartz, Swartzendruber, Yoder, or Gingerich.

Since the mission taught and modeled nonconformity to the world, the workers anticipated that people from the neighborhood would be slow to join. But they forged ahead with the hope that through witness and good deeds, the church would eventually grow. Already a middle-aged native Arkansan named Marie Billington had joined and was bringing her three teenage daughters. The four of them stepped over the tall threshold into the disciplined life of the Beachy Amish Church, with its strict rules.

When Emma greeted Mrs. Billington with a kiss at the Sunday service, she felt a strange warmth well up inside. It was the first time she could recall giving such an intimate greeting to anyone who hadn't been Amish from youth. "What an affirmation of our way of life," Emma thought as she took her seat, "that this woman should choose to join this fellowship."

One of the things that Emma enjoyed most about her brief time in Arkansas was the connection with other workers. Unencumbered by the care of the twins, Emma relished the hours spent alongside young people the age of her oldest children. They too seemed to enjoy the chance to make her acquaintance. As their two-week commitment came to an end, the volunteers agreed to stay in touch with each other by circle letter.

As Emma was preparing to leave for home on Monday morning, Lydia Mae grasped her hand and gave her a kiss of parting. "Thank you so much for helping us these two weeks," she said. "I feel like the house and garden work is all caught up now. It isn't always that way when our workers leave."

"Thank you," Emma said, her face flushing at the compliment. She had observed that some workers spent more time talking than they did working.

When Emma arrived home on Monday evening, she took a quick look around all three gardens before supper. After the children were in bed, Emma chatted with her oldest daughter until late, trying to catch up on all that had transpired in her absence. She was pleased that Mary Edna had managed so well in her absence.

Seeing that Emma had had such a good experience at the mission, Mary Edna agreed to volunteer as well. A few weeks later, Mary Edna left to assist at the Arkansas mission for a three-week stint. A week after her daughter left, Emma received a letter from her. She sat down at the dining room table to read it.

"Got up early and went down the road a ways and into a grove and picked blackberries for an hour or so," Emma read aloud. "We girls froze Dairy Queen. Then we went to a beautiful place not very far from here to have our late picnic dinner."

"Lena and I had a real good talk on Wednesday evening— 'tender subjects'! Wrote a letter to Menno afterward."

Emma nodded approval as she read. Lena would have good advice on love and marriage.

"We killed a Copperhead (we think it was) on Thursday evening. Anew we realized many times that 'all things work together for good to them that love God. . . .' His hand was over us all through the day."

Emma frowned. That was one of the bad things about the woods and rocks in Arkansas—dangerous snakes. After breathing a prayer of thanks for Mary Edna's safety, she kept reading.

"We started out early Sunday morning to pick up different people for the services. Good attendance in the morning and evening. The Hillcresters conducted most of the morning services, and then our other company had most of the evening service."

Emma read the rest of the letter before laying it on the hallway dresser. She would reply on Sunday. The letter she had written yesterday had crossed this one in the mail.

Over the coming weeks, Emma's thoughts often turned to Arkansas. She pictured Mary Edna going about the everyday tasks that kept the mission alive. "Perhaps," Emma wished, "Mary Edna can serve as a volunteer at Hillcrest Home or Mountain View when she turns twenty-one." That milestone was only ten months away.

Shortly after Mary Edna arrived home from Arkansas, Emma took her and the twins to pick sweet corn at the home of Menno's parents, Melvin and Lydia Yoder. Emma often benefited from their generosity. Several others came to Emma's home to help her prepare the corn for freezing. Silvia Stutzman came to help, accompanied by Grandma Stutzman. Two of Menno's sisters brought Mother Nisly with them.

"Did I hear that Menno bought a new car?" Silvia asked Mary Edna as they husked the ears of corn.

"Well, it's not a new one. It's just new for him. It's a '59 Plymouth."

"Do you think you'll get to drive it?" Silvia teased.

"Oh yes, I already did. It has pushbutton drive."

"You mean it's not a stick shift?"

"No, it's an automatic. You push one of the buttons on the dash to choose the gear you want."

"It sounds pretty fancy to me."

"We think it's pretty fancy too." Menno's sister Wilma nodded in agreement. "It has bucket seats in front and big fins sticking out back."

"So you won't be able to sit next to Menno?" Silvia flashed a wry smile toward Mary Edna.

"I guess not. But that's not a problem."

Emma was a little worried about Menno's car. The stylish lines of the light green Plymouth didn't seem to belong in the Beachy Amish-style of church. The car looked expensive, too. She wondered what Menno had paid for it. Was it really depreciated to one-third of its original value, as required by the written discipline? Or was Menno's purchase a telling sign that he wished to contest the church rules? She sensed that Menno wasn't satisfied with Center Church. Would Mary Edna be able to influence Menno to stay at Center?

It seemed fairly certain that the two of them were going to get married. If Menno decided to leave Center Church, Mary Edna would need to go along with him.

It wasn't long before Emma learned that Mary Edna's weeks away from Menno had only served to strengthen their commitment to each other. She was dumping the milk pail into the separator when Mary Edna popped into the washroom. "Menno and I were together again last night and . . ." She paused and smiled broadly as Emma emptied the last drops out of the pail.

Emma sensed the poignancy of the moment. "Yes?"

"We're engaged."

Emma smiled.

"Yes, it was very romantic last night. We went to the cemetery park along Highway 50. It was full moon, and we were sitting there beside the stream. The crickets were serenading us. That's when Menno asked me."

Tears welled onto Emma's cheeks. "That's good," she said, after a deep breath. "Menno will make a good husband for you. He comes from a good family."

"Let's keep it a secret for the time being," Mary Edna said. "Menno and I are planning to find a special way to announce it to the youth group, maybe in the next few months."

Mom agreed to keep mum.

Over the next few weeks, Emma helped Mary Edna and Menno prepare for the wedding. There were plans to be made and dresses to sew. Emma's mind raced ahead to the prospect of grandchildren.

At the last of October, Center Church hosted the annual youth fellowship meeting. More than a hundred youth came from around the country for a series of meetings. In the midst of the flurry, Mary Edna and Menno took time to fashion handwritten cards announcing their engagement to friends and neighbors. Each card was accompanied by a photograph of the couple. They would begin by handing them out at the upcoming youth social.

As Emma watched the proceedings, she reflected that the social customs had changed considerably since her own youth. In keeping with custom at the time, she and Tobe had kept their engagement secret until less than two weeks before the wedding. She grinned as her mind revisited the scene:

At the end of the Sunday morning message, Bishop Jake Miller had announced: "Two weeks from today, we will be meeting at Levi Nislys for our communion service. On the Thursday before, Tobe Stutzman will be married to Emma

Nisly. The wedding will take place here at the Dan Miller place."

Emma felt every eye on her as she and Tobe stood to make their way outside. She stood waiting at the end of the sidewalk while Tobe hurriedly hitched his horse. They hoped to make a getaway before the other fellows came out to razz them. As it was, the young people were making their way out of the house by the time Tobe pulled up to the front walk.

Emma eagerly stepped into the buggy and settled into the seat. Tobe clucked to the horse and slapped the reins. Then the horse balked. Tobe slapped the reins, but to little effect. The bemused crowd grew in size as Tobe slapped the reins harder. Noah Nisly stepped out and tugged on the horse's bridle, again to no avail. Tobe cracked his whip, with the same disappointing result.

Finally Tobe got out and tugged gently on the bridle. To his surprise, the horse suddenly leapt forward. Tobe vaulted into the seat as the buggy shot by. Emma heard the roar of laughter as they sped out the lane, the horse's tail streaming over the dashboard of the open buggy as the horse lunged into a fast trot.

It only made sense, Emma mused, that weddings should be announced further ahead of time. Trying to keep their engagement a secret had made it difficult to make her wedding dress without telling white lies in response to curious questioners. It was much better to prepare things in the open. Mary Edna and Menno were about to announce a June 7 wedding date, still seven months away.

The day after a youth social, Mary Edna explained how they had announced their engagement. "We waited until the very end of the evening. Then we did a skit called 'Courting in India.' As part of the skit, we announced that we were engaged. Then we handed out our engagement cards."

Emma smiled broadly. "Did the young people like it?"

"Oh yes. We got lots of congratulations afterward. Now Menno and I can talk freely about our plans for when we're married."

Emma nodded. She was eager to hear what Mary Edna and her fiancé were going to decide about many things, but particularly their church involvement.

14

Tested by Fire

During the Christmas holiday season, Emma hosted Clarence and Bunny Stutzman for several meals. They had made the trip to the area from San Juan, Puerto Rico, where they were living with their adopted baby, Wanda Jo. On Christmas Day, the extended Stutzman family gathered at Grandpa Stutzman's home for a Christmas gift exchange.

Emma watched with pride as Mary Edna held the new baby, a native of Puerto Rico. "When is her birthday?" Mary Edna asked Bunny.

"March 25, 1962. She's nine months old today."

"How did you get her?"

"Her mother brought her to the Mennonite hospital in Aibonito. She met with one of the social workers. She said she wanted to give up the baby for adoption. She hoped that a couple from the States could get her. A nurse told us about it, and we filled out the necessary papers."

"I'm glad you can give her a good home."

"She's a gift from God."

Emma knew that Clarence and Bunny had moved to Puerto Rico largely because they had hoped to adopt several children. Just before that time, they had owned a restaurant in Sarasota, Florida. The previous owner's policy had been to serve "colored people"—as African-Americans were designated there—only at a side window. When the Stutzmans made plans to serve African-Americans inside, the white waitresses and their customers threatened bricks through the windows and other protests. The tension became so palpable that Clarences sold the restaurant in favor of job opportunities in San Juan.

Emma and the children listened enthralled as Clarence and Bunny talked about life in San Juan. Clarence told of learning Spanish from business colleagues and of joining a Spanish-speaking Mennonite Church. He spoke of his thriving sales distributorship for the AirChem Corporation throughout Puerto Rico and the Virgin Islands.

As Clarence spoke, Emma thought about how well Tobe would have done in that role. More than once, Tobe had been told that he could sell ice to an Eskimo.

Later that day, Emma overheard Clarence talking to Mary Edna.

"You should come down and work in the Mennonite hospital," Clarence said. "They're always in need of workers. You could train to be a nurse."

"Menno and I have often talked about becoming missionaries."

"Then come on down. We'll help you find a place to serve."

Emma wasn't sure she wanted Mary Edna to go so far away. She hoped that Mary Edna would find a place of service sponsored by the plain churches, such as Hillcrest Home. Serving under the General Mission Board of the Mennonite Church, in the area where Clarence's lived, might too easily allure her away from the plain church.

As Mary Edna's 21st birthday approached, Emma listened closely to see what direction she might take. She sought clues in snatches of conversation between Menno and Mary Edna, in the books that Mary Edna was reading, and in the places Mary Edna spoke about visiting. While Emma felt close to Mary Edna, at times she felt like her daughter was slipping away. Was this what it was supposed to be like to have a daughter getting married and leaving home?

In spite of niggling worries about Mary Edna's future, Emma was grateful for the way she kept helping with the work at home. One Saturday in early February, Mary Edna helped to prepare for the youth singing that Emma was to host on Sunday evening. She fixed the carrot salad and fruit salad, as well as the graham cracker fluff, Emma's favorite dessert.

That same day, Raymond delivered a new Tappan range that Emma had purchased. She watched with satisfaction as he installed it. She smiled widely as Raymond demonstrated how nicely the gas burners simmered when the knobs were turned low. It would be wonderful to have the new stove in the kitchen when the young people came the next evening.

Emma felt better prepared than usual to host the singing. With Mary Edna's help, she'd trimmed the trees around the house and painted the walls and ceilings. While Emma wasn't particularly happy about the junk '49 Chevy parked right behind the house, the front yard was in better shape than ever. So Emma was hardly prepared for what she encountered when the family arrived home from church the next day.

When she opened the door to come through the washroom, smoke billowed into her face. "*Es is hesslich*! This is awful!" she cried as she threw back her head in surprise and dismay. After she caught her breath, she tried to peer into the basement. That was where the smoke seemed thickest. The smoke was overwhelming.

About that time, Perry pulled into the yard and got out of his car. "Perry," Emma yelled. "There's a fire in the house."

Perry came running and swung open the door. He tried without success to peer through the billowing smoke. "We'll have to call the fire department," he said. "I'll run up to Raymond's house." He hopped into his car, whipped around the big elm trees in the backyard, and raced up to Raymond's home.

The twins stood in the backyard with Emma, waiting for Perry to return. In a few minutes, he pulled back into the yard and hopped out of the car. "We called the fire station. The fire trucks will soon be on the way."

Minutes ticked by as the family waited for the fire trucks to arrive. Because of the cool February weather, there were no windows open in the house. At least the fire wouldn't spread too quickly without oxygen.

"I hear them," Ervin shouted when he detected the first faint whine of fire sirens several miles to the north.

"It's been twenty minutes since I called," said Perry, looking at his watch. Soon they could see the trucks as they roared down the gravel road from the north. Perry ran to the road to direct them into the driveway. With no road signs or street numbers to guide the drivers, it wasn't always easy for emergency vehicles to find the right homes in the countryside.

There still were no flames visible through the windows as the fire chief pulled on his gas mask and headed into the house with his flashlight. Two firemen followed with an extinguisher. Men from a second truck stood at attention.

In a few minutes, all three men emerged from the smoky basement. "We've got it under control, Ma'am," the chief said to Emma. "You had a fire in some junk under the stair steps. We're not sure how it got started. All I can say is that you're really lucky. The fire melted the plastic water pipe close to your water tank. The leak kept the fire from spreading."

The chief glanced at the children and then spoke to Emma

in a lowered voice. "If that pipe hadn't melted, you could have lost the house."

Emma sucked in her breath. "Oh my!" she said. "Thank you for putting out the fire."

"Is it safe to go inside now?" Ervin asked in a trembling voice.

"Yes, you can go inside."

The chief filled out some papers as the firemen loaded their equipment back into the truck. The family moved cautiously into the house.

"It stinks in here," Erma said. "I can't stand it."

"Let's open the windows," Emma said as she cranked open the casement window in the living room. Then she lifted the sash in the dining room. Ervin ran to open a window facing the back of the house. Soon the cool breeze drew the smoke out through the windows.

"I don't know if we can have the singing here tonight or not," Emma worried aloud. "It smells pretty bad in here."

"We might have to wash the walls and cabinets," Mary Edna suggested.

"Let's make dinner first," Emma replied, as she pulled out a pan and put it on her new stove.

Meanwhile, Perry brought a scoop shovel from the barn and cleaned out the smoky remains of rags and boxes under the stairway. He carried them outside to the burn barrel while Emma made dinner.

After dinner, the family concentrated on preparations for the singing. Mary Edna carried in the sheet cake she had decorated the day before. It had been stored in the washroom. "This cake is ruined," she said. "The frosting is black."

Emma looked at it. "I'm afraid you're right. We can't eat that."

Everyone pitched in to help scrub the inside of the house.

Mary Edna helped for a time and then left for the youth program at Broadacres, the county home for the aged. The rest of them worked until the house seemed presentable enough to host the singing.

As guests arrived that evening, Emma explained what had happened. In spite of the smell and the smoky shadows on the ceilings, the singing turned out well. Everyone seemed to be having a good time. Emma collapsed into bed that night, tired but deeply grateful that the fire hadn't been worse. So easily she could have lost the house. She worried that the firemen hadn't discovered the cause and prayed that it wouldn't happen again.

The following Sunday when the family arrived home from church, Ervin slipped into the house first. He immediately ran back out. "Mom," he yelled, "there's a fire in the basement." Mother and son quickly filled a bucket of water from the washroom and doused the flames. The fire was spreading among the newspapers that lined the canning storage shelves.

Emma was shaken. Thoughts raced through her mind: "How did the fire get started? Why did it happen for the second time on a Sunday? Did someone get into our house and set the fire? Perhaps we should consider locking the house on Sundays to keep an arsonist from slipping in while we're attending church services.

"But why would someone want to start a fire in our house?" Emma asked herself. "We don't have any enemies that I know of."

Emma observed that Ervin was very worried. Several times that afternoon, she saw him check the basement. That evening as the family ate their usual Sunday evening fare of popcorn, Ervin often glanced toward the basement. When he saw a glow on the stairway wall, he quickly put down his popcorn dish. "Mom! There's a fire in the basement!" This time there was a fire burning on the motor of the water pump.

Ervin ran to the electrical fuse box and threw the switch to the water pump. The fire soon went out.

Emma shook her head. She called Raymond to explain what had happened. "What can we do about it?" she asked.

"I wonder if there might be a gas leak," Raymond suggested. "I'll call the gas man out on Monday."

Meanwhile, Ervin kept a close watch on the basement. The family went to bed, troubled. "If only Tobe were here," Emma worried.

The next day, Raymond accompanied a man from the gas company. They looked over the pipes and performed a pressure test. Finally they found a gas leak in the supply pipe that ran from the propane tank to the house.

"It looks like propane gas is leaking into your basement," the gas man said.

"But the pipe comes out of the ground before it goes through the wall into the house," Raymond replied. "That should keep any leak in the pipe from getting into the basement."

"It seems to be getting in somehow," the tester observed. "When the water heater lights up, the fumes burst into flame."

"I saw the water pump on fire," Ervin insisted.

"Maybe the water pump throws out sparks when it lights up."

"It sure does," Raymond asserted. "That could have started the fire under the stairs."

Emma sighed. "I guess we'll have to replace the pipe."

Raymond nodded. "Meanwhile, you have to keep the basement aired out real well so the gas doesn't collect down there."

A few days later, Raymond helped dig up the propane line. "The pipe is very rusty in this spot just outside the house," Raymond observed.

Emma looked it over. "I wonder what would cause it to rust right there?"

"Do you ever pour salty water here?"

Emma pondered for a moment. "I usually throw my wash water out there. Oh yes, I do pour the water out of my ice-cream freezer there."

"That's really salty. It'll make the pipe rust."

"I'll have to learn to throw that water somewhere else," Emma conceded.

Even though the problem was said to be solved, the whole family, particularly Ervin, was wary of another fire. He often checked the basement and showed reluctance to go to church on Sundays.

Although the family remained wary of fire in the house over the next weeks, the problem did indeed seem to be solved. Emma felt assured that no arsonist had been involved. In a small community with unlocked doors, trust was essential.

That's why it was particularly disturbing when the Center congregation found a bullet hole in an east window in their new church building. Since they found large black tire marks on the sidewalk at the same time, they reasoned that it must have been a vandal.

It wasn't unusual to find tire marks around the neighborhood. It was a way for energetic young men with powerful cars to leave their mark without damaging property. Occasionally after a church service, a young man from the neighborhood would draw observers by doing "doughnuts" with his car on the gravel intersection nearby. He would turn his steering wheel tightly to one side, rev the engine, and spin the rear wheels. The car spun in a tight circle, spewing gravel in every direction.

The bullet hole signaled more-sinister motives. Did someone resent the church or one of its members? Some suspected that a disgruntled member of the Old Order Amish Church had done it. For a time after the formation of the Center Church, young men who remained in the Old Order Amish Church poked fun at people who broke away. They called the breakaway members Elamites, after the name of the bishop who helped the fellowship get started.

Perhaps the folks in the new fellowship had underestimated the feelings of the traditional Amish. Those who stayed with the old ways felt that folks in the new fellowship were being goody-goody in their attempts to be more spiritual. But would that have caused sufficient alienation to prompt acts of vandalism? The question caused the church elders to muse on their relationships with the folks left behind by the church division. Meanwhile, they notified the sheriff, who quietly investigated the case.

The closing days of April brought the end of the school year as well as the twins' tenth birthday. The Stutzman family celebrated around the Sunday dinner table.

After dinner, Emma sat down to read in the living room while Perry and Mary Edna discussed what Perry was learning in the Dale Carnegie course. "Look," he said to the family, "they teach us that you have to act the way you want to become. They make us stand up in front of the class and show how enthused we can be." Perry illustrated by jumping up and down several times while shouting, "*Act* enthusiastic and you'll *be* enthusiastic!" With each phrase, he punched the air with his right fist. "The more enthusiastic you are, the more the class will clap for you," he said.

The family watched with glee.

Ervin picked up the little green booklet that Perry had gotten with the course: *How to Remember Names*. "What is this about?" he asked.

"Hey, you're not supposed to be reading that," Perry said.

"Why not?"

"It's just for people taking the course." Then Perry softened. "Well, I suppose it doesn't hurt for you to see it. It just has some memory aids to help you remember people's names."

Ervin perused the booklet. "Some of this looks pretty silly."

"It seems silly, but that's what helps you remember. Now, give the book back to me."

Ervin shrugged his shoulders and handed it over.

Emma listened without comment. For some time she'd noticed that Perry could readily remember names and dates, even better than Tobe. Whenever someone asked about a wedding or anniversary, Perry could tell you when it had taken place. She wondered if the Dale Carnegie course was helping him with that as well.

Emma picked up the book that Perry had brought home from his course: *How to Win Friends and Influence People*. It did seem as though Perry was gaining more confidence in his friendships. Over the last few years, Perry had moved from being quite shy to the point where he often initiated conversation. Emma observed that he was becoming more like Tobe, who'd readily engaged strangers in conversation. It felt good to see Perry following in his father's footsteps.

• • • •

As the time for Mary Edna's wedding drew near, Emma grew ever more interested in Mary Edna's plans for the future. She listened more closely now to the missionaries who came through the area. When Lewis Overholt spoke at Center Church about the outreach in Germany, Emma wondered whether it would pique Mary Edna's interest. That was an outreach of the plain churches through the Amish Mennonite Aid mission committee.

But Mary Edna seemed more interested in a Spanish-speaking country. At her uncle Clarence's suggestion, she had obtained a series of records to learn Spanish. Since Center Church was still debating the appropriateness of owning a record player, Mary Edna listened to them on a borrowed turntable. Emma listened from the kitchen as Mary Edna played the records.

"*Cómo está usted?*" the speaker on the record said.

"*Muy bien, gracias,*" Mary Edna replied on cue.

Ervin and Erma stood by as Mary Edna studied. They were intrigued by Mary's interest in Puerto Rico. To Emma, the Spanish words sounded like gibberish. She had no interest in learning another language.

"*Cómo se llama?*" the speaker asked.

"*Me llamo María,*" Mary Edna replied.

"What is the man saying?" Ervin asked.

"He's asking 'What is your name?' Now you can answer by saying '*Me llamo Ervin.*'"

"*Me llamo Ervin,*" the boy repeated.

Over the next weeks, Mary listened to the language records at work and brought them home each weekend. Meanwhile, she and Menno wrote a letter to the General Mission Board at Elkhart, Indiana, communicating their interest and availability.

Less than a week before Mary Edna's twenty-first birthday, a missionary named John Driver spoke about his time of service in Puerto Rico at the Wednesday night Bible study. To Emma, it seemed like more than a coincidence. Might Menno and Mary Edna soon join Clarence and Bunny in Puerto Rico?

At the same time that Mary Edna was exploring a mission assignment, she prepared for her wedding. Ever since she had learned cake decorating, she had dreamed of making her own wedding cake. So she baked a three-tiered cake a week ahead of time and put it in the freezer. Anything more than a three-tiered cake would have been considered too worldly. However, it was much smaller than the five-tiered cake she baked for someone else about the same time.

Mary Edna also made her own wedding dress, a light blue one with a full cape. In keeping with church practice, it was made to be worn later for regular church services. Wedding dresses always served double duty. It was vain to make a dress that could be worn for only one occasion.

It appeared to Emma that Mary Edna and Menno were more relaxed before their wedding than she and Tobe had been. One big difference was the church house. Having a regular place of worship was much simpler than needing to get her own house ready for a huge crowd. It simply wouldn't have been big enough for all of the invitees.

Furthermore, the Elreka schoolhouse was an ideal place for a reception. Granted, they needed to set up tables and chairs in the large gymnasium, but that could be done a day or two ahead of time.

The June sun was shining brightly through the west windows of the church house when the wedding began early on Friday evening. The wedding party sat on the front bench on the men's side. The rest of the congregation was seated as usual, men on one side and women on the other. The wedding service was much like other worship services except that special music was allowed. An octet sang two songs before the message. At the appropriate moment, Bishop Amos Nisly called the couple forward, along with their chosen witnesses. He read aloud a series of vows, with an invitation for Menno and Mary Edna to answer each one in the affirmative. Then he pronounced them "man and wife."

Menno and Mary Edna led the way in their car to the Elreka school, just over a mile away. Along with their witnesses, they greeted each of the guests as they arrived. The dropped off their gifts at a long table and found a place to be seated in the auditorium.

After everyone had gone through the receiving line, the bridal party sat at a table in the front of the room. The white three-tiered cake stood in the middle of the table. On the top were two symbols: an open Bible and a cross. The pages of the Bible declared: "God hath joined together." On the cake were large yellow flower petals and white artificial sprigs of lily of the valley. Immediately beside the cake was a bouquet of yellow carnations.

Although photos were not allowed at the wedding service, people freely took pictures at the reception. Menno was dressed in a plain black suit, Mary Edna in her light blue dress. The ribbons of her large prayer covering were tied neatly in a small bow under her chin.

The food was served in trays so that people could eat it at their seats. Emma sat in the front row at the reception, soaking in the sight. Next to her sat her daughter Edith, accompanied by Arvilla Weaver. It was Edith's first visit to Kansas since Tobe's death. Emma felt the stares of curious onlookers. She also felt a tinge of nervousness, knowing that Edith could have a seizure at any second. Emma hoped against hope that there would be no such disturbance. It seemed that when Edith was nervous, she was far more likely to have a seizure.

Emma needn't have worried, since all went well. The mood of the event was celebrative, and many guests wished her well as they left. They assured her that Menno and Mary Edna were a wonderful couple.

After a quick reading of a Bible passage late that evening, Emma knelt beside the bed to thank God for his mercies. Within a few moments after she dragged her tired frame into bed, she was fast asleep.

The newlyweds spent the night in a motel at the nearby

town of Sterling and then returned to Emma's home. Emma helped them sort through some of their wedding gifts.

"Mom, I don't feel worthy of all these gifts," Mary Edna commented. "There are so many, and there is such variety."

Emma nodded in acknowledgment. It was indeed a wonderful thing to have such support from others for the formation of a new home.

Over the next two weeks, Menno and Mary Edna wrestled to make a decision about a place of service. In addition to considering Puerto Rico, they had also received an invitation from Frank Claasen of the Union Rescue Mission in Wichita, Kansas. Emma hoped against hope that they wouldn't make that choice since Frank did not support the idea of plain dress. If Menno and Mary Edna served there, they would need to change their wardrobe. Mary Edna might even quit wearing the devotional covering.

When Mary Edna started shopping around for new clothing, Emma sensed that the die was cast. In the midst of the turmoil, Emma and the twins made a weekend trip to Harrison, Arkansas, with Perry.

When Emma returned home, Mary Edna conceded that they were making plans to go to the rescue mission. Unfortunately, they'd earlier notified the preachers, Bishop Amos Nisly and David Miller, that they intended to turn down Frank's invitation. After hearing Frank express deep disappointment, they had changed their minds and were planning to go to Wichita after all. Shortly after sharing this news, Menno and Mary Edna left for a two-week trip to Arkansas with the plan to start service at the rescue mission upon their return on the fourth of July.

Emma felt a sense of urgency that neared panic. It just wasn't right. Surely Bishop Nisly wouldn't have agreed to marry the couple if he had known they were going to leave the church so soon after the wedding. Was there anything to be done to change their minds? Emma took solace in knowing that Menno's parents felt as deeply about the matter as she did. The three of them decided to call a meeting to discuss the matter.

The day after Menno and Mary Edna returned from Arkansas, they agreed to meet with a group at Emma's home that included Menno's parents. Frank Claasen came to represent the Union Rescue Mission, while Preacher David L. Miller and Deacon Mahlon Wagler represented Center Church.

The atmosphere was tense. Frank insisted that the rescue mission was a good place for the young couple to serve. Why should the church try to stop a young couple from doing what they thought was right? He reminded them that the congregation already supported the rescue mission in various ways, donating canned goods and providing occasional leadership for the Sunday evening service. Why couldn't they support a young couple who wished to serve on a full-time volunteer basis?

In turn, the ministers appealed to the covenant that the young couple had made to the church. Hadn't they made a pledge to be loyal to the congregation? Weren't they aware of the many couples who had taken a step away from plain dress only to find themselves and their children drifting toward worldliness?

Menno described examples of churches that were evidently serving God without being plain. It seemed to him that these churches were more faithful in missions and evangelism than the plain churches. Wouldn't God be pleased to see him and Mary Edna serve in a place that regularly invited men off the street to make decisions for Jesus Christ?

Since there were plenty of other people talking, Emma said little in the three-hour meeting. By the time the meeting broke up, it was clear that Menno and Mary Edna hadn't changed their minds. They were still planning to go to the rescue mission. And they were going to leave the plain witness of their home church.

Emma's heart ached. It was bad enough that Glenn had left the Center church to attend Plainview Conservative Mennonite. But who would have thought that Mary Edna, her beloved firstborn, would follow a similar course? Why couldn't she be satisfied with Center Church? The new church was so much more spiritual than the congregation of Emma's youth. Was each new generation compelled to push against the edges? Emma identified anew with Tobe's mother, who sometimes commented, "*Es misse epper Amish bleiwe*. Someone must stay Amish." If each generation joined a more-progressive church, where would it end?

15

Weathering the Storm

The following Monday morning, Mary Edna and Menno prepared for the move to Wichita. Mary Edna showed up at Emma's home in her new clothing—modest but clearly not plain. Emma tried not to show that she was upset. She gave them a proper goodbye but sighed as the couple headed out the drive for their new home in Wichita.

A few weeks later Emma was still grieving the turn of events when she made a trip to Kalona, Iowa. The main reason for the trip was to attend a reunion of widows who corresponded regularly by circle letter. Perry agreed to take Emma in his car. The twins went along, as did Delilah Nisly, a widowed correspondent from Center Church.

Since the Noah Weaver family now lived in Indiana, Emma stayed in the home of her Uncle Fred. Although Fred was somewhat older than Emma, he and Katie had several children about the same age as Emma's children. The twins would feel at home there.

On the morning of the reunion, Perry took Emma and Delilah to the home of Fannie Miller, the hostess for the meeting. Fannie had lost her husband Henry some thirteen years earlier. As the women arrived, the hostess invited them to find a seat in a circle of chairs in the living room. The morning passed quickly as women shared from their lives. Upon the loss of their husbands, all the women had been left with children. Several of the women, like Emma, still had children living at home.

Emma listened patiently as each woman spoke about their lives and their losses. Loneliness, financial struggles, farm accidents, wayward children, discipline problems, lack of support—each woman struggled with different yet similar problems. However, Emma observed that not all of the women carried their burdens the same way. Some complained too freely, in her judgment. Emma hoped others didn't feel that way about the way she handled her sorrows. She remembered the moment not long after Tobe's death when she had determined that she wasn't going to complain about her situation. It wouldn't make things any better and might even drive her friends away. Few people enjoy listening to complaints.

Emma arrived back at Fred's farm to find Ervin soaking his left foot in Epsom salt-water.

"He was out playing with the boys and hurt his foot," Aunt Katie explained. "He chased the cows through some pine trees and stepped on something."

"*Mei fuuss dutt hesslich weh*. My foot hurts terribly," Ervin complained.

Emma lifted Ervin's foot out of the tub and held it in her hand. "It's a very small cut."

"But it hurts something terrible."

"Maybe we should take him to the doctor," Katie said. "Dr. Beckman's office might still be open."

Emma agreed to stop by the doctor's place on the way back to Kansas. Dr. Beckman, who had delivered the twins at birth, looked briefly at the foot and then sent them on their way. He saw nothing to cause alarm. But each time Perry accidentally bumped Ervin's leg as he shifted gears, the boy complained. Emma was worried.

The day after they arrived home, Emma took Ervin to Dr. Orthwein, the pediatrician who had examined the boy two years earlier. The doctor shook his head as he examined the foot. "I don't understand why it's so swollen. We'd better take an X-ray," he said. The X-ray showed nothing unusual. "We'll need to look at it again in a few days if it's not better," he said.

The next days brought no relief, so Emma took the boy back into Dr. Orthwein's office. "I'm concerned about that foot," the doctor said. "If it doesn't get better by next Friday, I'm going to put him in the hospital. Meanwhile, I can get a crutch for him."

"I don't want a crutch," Ervin protested. "I can hop on one foot."

Dr. Orthwein shrugged. "That's okay as long as it works for you."

A few days passed. Emma was doing the wash one day when Ervin shouted from the kitchen. "Look what I found in my foot!" He held up a pine needle about three-fourths of an inch in length. "It feels like there's another one in there too."

Emma swished the wash in her tub as Ervin searched for another sliver in the wound.

"Mom, I'd like to go to Grandma Nisly's house. She might be able to get this big sliver out."

Emma went to the phone and dialed her mother. After a brief conversation, she announced, "We'll plan to go in a little while."

"Okay," Ervin agreed.

Emma hung a load of wash on the line and then announced that she was ready to go. She followed Ervin as he hopped out to the car on his good foot. She couldn't help but grin. Ervin could move as fast on one foot as she could on two.

"Come and sit on the sofa," Grandma Nisly told the boy when they arrived at her home. "We'll see if we can find what's wrong with your foot." She sat on a hassock and held the boy's foot in her hand. "First we'll need to clean it," she said. She rested the boy's foot on the hassock and stepped over to the cupboard, where she pulled out a bottle of denatured alcohol. After daubing a piece of cotton with alcohol, she swabbed the wound. Then she fished around in the wound with a tweezers.

"I think there might still be a sliver in there," she said softly. "Maybe some *Zuck-Schmier*, pull salve, might help bring it out."

Grandma mixed up a plaster that included fresh manure from the corral and applied it to the wound. Like some other home remedies, the concoction would have raised grave medical concerns about tetanus or other infections if she had consulted a doctor.

"Let's let that work for a little while," she told the boy. "Just sit here quietly, and we'll see what it does. If you want, you can read something while you wait."

Emma joined her mother in the kitchen. "When we visited the doctor, he told us that he would put Ervin into the hospital if it doesn't get better in two weeks," Emma said. "That would be this weekend. I don't see how I could afford it."

"We hope the good Lord will help us," Grandma replied. After an hour passed, Grandma again took the boy's foot in her hands. With each probe of her tweezers, the boy protested in pain. "I believe there's something in there, but I can't really seem to get ahold of it," Grandma announced. "I believe we should get the menfolks in here to help."

Within a few minutes, Grandpa Nisly and his son Amos joined the group, with a large tweezers from the dairy barn. "I know this is going to hurt," Amos said.

"It will be worth it if you can get it out," Ervin said.

"We're going to need to hold you still so I can get it out," Amos explained.

"Okay," Ervin said as he squeezed his eyes shut and took a deep breath.

"Dad, you grab this leg and hold it tight so that it won't move," Amos said. "Mom, you can hold Ervin's arm on this side. Emma, you can hold the other side."

"Hold on," Amos said after a few moments of tugging. "I've got 'hold of something!"

"Look at that!" Emma exclaimed as the man drew a large splinter out of the foot.

Ervin sighed in relief.

"Let's measure that thing," Amos declared.

Grandma handed him a ruler. Amos measured the piece and then declared, "One inch by a half inch by three-eighths inch."

"And the doctor said there was nothing in there!" Emma exclaimed. "He even did an X-ray."

"Doctors don't always know everything," Grandma said.

Emma nodded in agreement. "Let's go home and see how he does."

Within the hour, Ervin was walking on the injured foot.

"I'm going to show that sliver to the doctor," Emma declared. Two days later when Emma made a trip to town, she took the vial with her. With a smile of triumph on her lips, she slipped into the lobby of Dr. Orthwein's office. "Look what we found in my son's foot," she said when he came to the waiting room. She held out the vial. "There was a pine needle too."

The doctor shook his head with amazement. "How's the boy doing now?"

"He's walking on his foot as though nothing had happened," Emma assured him. "As soon as we got that out of there, he was able to walk on it again."

"It must have lodged in the muscle and then broken off," the doctor suggested. "But I'm not sure why it didn't show up up on the X-ray. Maybe it was turned sideways. Or maybe it swelled up inside there. At least the boy's doing better." He handed Emma the vial.

She put it into her purse and moved toward the door. When she got home, she displayed the vial and sliver in the china hutch beside the dining room table. What could be a clearer exhibit of the truth that simple folks sometimes know more than medical doctors?

• • • •

Emma never paid much attention to the press, regardless of whether it was local, national, or international in scope. With no regular daily paper, radio, or TV, she didn't try to keep up with the news. Yet the *Capper's Weekly* provided some perspective.

When Glenn left Center Church and started listening to the radio every day, he occasionally shared the news. From time to time, he brought home news magazines from the trash route. "Look at this one," he said to Emma, as he showed a story of captured American soldiers being tortured in Vietnam. The Cold War between the Soviet Union and the United States was heating up in Southeast Asia.

Emma wasn't prone to worry about world affairs, but when Glenn reported on the tensions surrounding the Bay of Pigs debacle, she began to worry that the Cold War would eventually lead to a (USSR) Communist takeover. A few months later, when President Kennedy was shot by an assassin, some saw it as a Communist plot. The Cold War escalated, fueled by worries that Communists were gaining the upper hand in world affairs. The heightened pitch of the war rhetoric was accompanied by the military draft.

Emma was worried that Perry and Glenn would be drafted into the service. Glenn particularly was itching to leave

leave home. If he was drafted, he might end up in a place where she didn't want him to be.

Emma was happy to see Glenn visit the Bible School in Berlin, Ohio, at the beginning of the 1963 year. He provided a ride for Jonas Yoder, one of the ministers at Glenn's church. More than a hundred young people from around the country traveled there to take short courses of several weeks each. For a time, Glenn had pursued his General Equivalency Diploma (GED) through correspondence. It proved to take more time than Glenn wanted to invest, so he abandoned his studies. Emma wouldn't have minded if Glenn had attended Bible School for several weeks. She was confident that Bible School had a positive effect on young people. She'd heard the testimonies that it had helped steer young men in a good direction. But Glenn was tied down to his job with his uncle L. Perry on the trash route.

She was relieved that Glenn's relationship with Beverly had ended. Now he was dating Joyce, a girl from the Yoder Mennonite Church, where L. Perry and Silvia attended. Glenn had Joyce's picture in a frame on his dresser. Glenn's was the only room in Emma's house with photographs on display. He had his own portrait displayed on one of the two shelves over the head of the top bunk bed. He displayed his guns, too. On the wall above his bunk, they hung on metal pegs mounted on a pegboard frame. His Remington shotgun hung on top, a rifle with a scope just below it, and a pistol at the bottom of the rack. Two boxes of bullets sat on the shelf alongside a piggy bank, a clock radio, and a few books.

Glenn slept on the top bunk, with the guns within easy reach. Ervin slept below Glenn, in the bottom bunk. Emma sometimes worried that the boys slept too close to the guns. She worried too that Glenn's lackadaisical attitude toward the church would have a bad affect on Ervin. She wasn't happy about some of the books and magazines Glenn brought home from work. Ervin was such an avid reader that he might too easily be drawn to bad reading material.

She also worried about Glenn's influence on Ervin when he bought a loud motorcycle. It was a stripped-down racing bike with quite small fenders and hardly any muffler. Although it had no lights, Glenn sometimes rode it at night. One night, Glenn took Ervin for a ride on his bike. Emma watched in dismay as they roared south on the gravel road, lit only by a waning moon. Neither wore a helmet. What would happen if there was something on the road they couldn't see? What if a car came along? At times the boys seemed oblivious to danger.

• • • •

When Glenn returned from Bible school, he talked to Emma about the possibility of doing I-W service in Toledo, Ohio. Emma wrinkled her brow as she heard Glenn talk about his interest in moving to a city in the east. She'd heard too many stories of I-W men who lost their way in the cities.

She wished that Glenn would choose some form of voluntary service to fulfill his draft requirement, if indeed he was drafted. Since Glenn was part of the Conservative Mennonite Conference, she couldn't expect him to serve at Hillcrest Home. But she was quite certain that the Conservative mission board would have something similar for him to consider.

Emma's worries about the draft were well founded. First her son-in-law, Menno, was drafted. Shortly after his notification, he took the train to Kansas City for the Armed Forces physical exam. Emma was relieved to learn that since he was already serving at the Union Rescue Mission, he could count it as his place of alternative service.

Not long afterward, Perry was conscripted, so he made the same trip to Kansas City. The next evening at the supper table, the family was eager to hear about his experience.

"What do they do to you when you go up there?" Ervin asked.

"They do a lot of the same things you do in a doctor's office. They make you take your clothes off, except for your shorts. They listen to your heartbeat, check your blood pressure, and so forth. They want to know how healthy you are, to see if you can survive on the battlefield."

"Were you scared?"

"No. But the men talked pretty rough. They swore a lot. I went on the same train as Mervin Keim, who's from Yoder," Perry explained. "On the way up, he told me that he hopes he doesn't pass the physical. He wants to stay on the farm. I told him that I hoped I would pass."

"So what happened?" Emma asked.

"We both got our wish. I passed and he didn't."

"That means you have to go into service?"

"Yes."

Perry was able to delay his entry into service until he turned twenty-one. The day after his birthday, he left to work as an orderly at Hillcrest Home in Arkansas. Emma wasn't happy that Perry chose to attend the youth singing before he left. It meant that he'd need to drive alone all night without any sleep and report for work on the morning shift.

Emma was pleased, however, with his choice to serve at Hillcrest. Somehow, Perry didn't seem motivated to push the edges like Glenn, Menno, and Mary Edna. So it wasn't easy for Emma to see Perry go. Who would maintain the small farm property? No one took interest in the tractors and other farm equipment as Perry did.

Perry hadn't been gone long when misfortune struck in a way that made Emma wish he were home. Emma was first alerted to the sign of trouble while driving home from town late one afternoon. As she drove along, she noticed a darkening weather front. "It looks pretty bad up north," she commented to her friend Sadie Mast, who was riding with her.

"Yes, it does. It looks like it might be moving our way."

Emma grimaced. "I told the children I'd pick them up at the greenhouse after school," she said. "I hope they remembered." She steered her car out of town and onto Highway 61.

"I wouldn't be surprised if we get some hail," Sadie commented as Emma's car jolted along a section of washboard road near her friend's home. "Hey, it's about time for the road grader to go through here."

Emma breathed a prayer for safety as she dropped Sadie off at her home and headed the car toward the Stutzman Greenhouse. She was relieved to see the children playing outside when she arrived. She got out of the car and walked toward the basement house that she and Tobe had built. It looked different now that Ervin J. was building a house on top of it. The walls were up now, but there was no roof.

As Emma approached the house, Silvia Stutzman stepped out of the basement door. "Emma, the radio sent out a tornado warning, so we all went to the basement for awhile."

"I'm glad everyone is safe."

"Me, too. The weather came up pretty fast. We were afraid it might blow these walls over since they're not really fastened yet."

Ervin J.'s wife, Emma, came to the door. "Someone just called," she told Emma. "They said there's some storm damage to your garage. They were worried about some electric wires that were down."

Emma grimaced and motioned to the twins. "Come. We'd better go home."

As Emma got into the car and drove the two and a half miles to her home in silence, her mind was deep in thought. She worried about what she might see. They pulled into the driveway to see that the detached garage lay in ruins. She walked around the yard with the twins, surveying the extent of the damage. The garage roof lay in large pieces, carried some hundred yards southeast by the wind. The four walls were strewn across the driveway in a way that no one could pass through. Part of the wreckage had torn off the corner of the house roof. In the backyard, tops of the elm trees were ripped off, along with the top of the feed grinder.

When Glenn arrived home, he took pictures of the storm damage to share with Perry. "If Perry were home," Emma reasoned, "he would take the lead to get things back in order." But she needn't have worried. Over the next week, Raymond and a group of volunteers from the church helped to clean up the damage and rebuild the garage. They were able to reuse some of the building material. Emma was relieved to see the garage back on its foundation within weeks of the storm.

A couple of days after the storm, Raymond found a porcelain insulator in a wheat field about a mile northeast of her house. It looked like one that had been in the garage. Raymond figured that only a tornado or whirlwind could have carried the heavy insulator that distance. How else would it have gotten there?

Emma learned that tornadoes had touched down the same day at a number of places in the area. Besides tornadoes and strong winds, there had been heavy hail. "How fortunate I am," Emma thought, "that the damage to my place was not worse."

She accepted it as a part of what it meant to live in Kansas, with the most changeable weather in the nation. But it was more than compensated for by the sights of the trackless blue sky on most days, the indigo-black sky with star-holes punched through on clear nights, and the mesmerizing metamorphosis of the clouds in changing weather. To willingly surrender to those forces beyond one's control, she thought, may instill a depth of character unique to dwellers on the central plains.

• • • •

Not long after the storm came through, Glenn got official notice that he too had been drafted. He passed the physical exam and began looking at options for service as a conscientious objector. Since Glenn was a member at Plainview Church, he decided to serve with the Conservative Mennonite Board of Missions and Charities, based in Ohio. Emma prayed that he'd choose to serve in one of several locations where there was a Voluntary Service unit with proper supervision.

While Glenn was still trying to make up his mind where to go, William Stutzman, an evangelist from Ohio, came to Plainview Church for the fall revival meeting. Emma and both of the twins accepted Raymond's invitation to ride along to the meetings on the last evening. At the end of the evening, both Ervin and Erma went forward in response to the evangelist's altar call. Emma's heart beat with joy when they made their way to the front. Glenn stepped forward to serve as a counselor and pray with Ervin.

"What a change has happened lately," Emma thought, "that Glenn is helping in the revival meeting. Now that Ervin has decided to become a Christian, he isn't likely to balk at going to church either."

As though to underscore Emma's sense that things were changing, Glenn brought home religious signs to post around the home property. The signs were produced en masse by a church organization and marketed throughout the country. Each sign was blue, with white reflective letters and edging. When Glenn asked to mount them around the property, Emma readily gave her consent.

"Come, look at them, Mom," Glenn announced after he had them all nailed in place.

Emma followed Glenn outside. Migo, Glenn's German shepherd dog, tagged close behind.

"I put the smallest one out by the road," Glenn explained. "It fit the best on the telephone pole." "OBEY GOD'S WORD," the sign announced.

"Then I put the biggest one on the garage." Glenn pointed at the sign: "REMEMBER THE SABBATH. GO TO CHURCH."

"That's good," Emma thought to herself. "Glenn hasn't always felt that way."

"And the third one I put on the barn," Glenn said, leading Emma back into the driveway. He pointed to the sign above the large door that opened into the barn: "JESUS SAVES."

Emma nodded her approval. Now anyone who visited their place would know that theirs was a Christian home.

By late October, Glenn made up his mind about a place to do alternative service. He learned that the mission board had an opening at the Hudson Memorial Home in El Dorado, Arkansas. He agreed to serve there as a maintenance man.

Emma breathed a prayer of thanks. It would be so good to have both of the boys serving in Arkansas.

Glenn left in November, some nine months before his twenty-first birthday. Emma watched with mixed feelings as Glenn pulled his '57 Chevy out of the driveway and headed toward the south in a cloud of dust.

She reflected that Glenn's leaving marked a change of season in her own life. Now that the three oldest children were gone from home, the twins would need to take more responsibility for the house and farm. As it was thus far, they hardly helped with the farm chores in the morning.

The next morning, as Emma came in from the chores, she looked at the clock only to realize that if Ervin didn't get up right away, he was going to be late for school. She knocked loudly on his bedroom door. *"Du misse uft schteh. Du bischt schpot fer die Schul.* You have to get up. You'll be late for school," she said. Hearing no response, she knocked again, more persistently this time.

After a few moments she pounded on the door. "You must get up. You'll be late for school." Not hearing any action, she opened the door and went to the side of the bed. "Ervin, you have to get up. The bus will be here in fifteen minutes." She shook the boy's body and pulled off the covers. "If you didn't read so late at night," she lamented, "you wouldn't be so sleepy in the morning."

Ervin groaned. "I'm getting up," he said, wiping the sleep out of his eyes.

Emma turned to the other side of the hallway. "Erma," she warned, "if you don't get up, you'll miss the bus." She walked in and shook her daughter before heading back to the kitchen in disgust. Why must it be so difficult to get the children out of bed?

When the children got onto the bus in the nick of time, Emma groaned with relief. "It isn't as though the children are trying to be irresponsible," she reflected. "It's just that they have a hard time waking up in the morning." It was quite the opposite for her. She found it hard to sleep after 6:00 a.m. Like Tobe, she usually awoke with duties pressing on her mind.

Emma knew that Tobe would not have stood for the children's tardiness in getting out of bed. She recalled times when Tobe had seemed a bit too strict with the children, but she would gladly welcome it now. When Tobe spoke, the children moved quickly. At times it seemed that they were "mother deaf," afflicted by a selective hearing loss that allowed them to sleep even through her shouting.

But then, Emma figured it wasn't right to expect too much of the children. They needed time to grow up. In the meantime, others would have to fill the gap—like the times when the cows broke through the gate and got into Donald Epperson's wheat field. Epperson was a gentle man but not from among the plain people. Emma worried that it was a bad witness to have cows running into his field. But with both Perry and Glenn gone, she didn't have anyone to fix the gate.

At times such as these, she hated being a widow, needing to call on men for every little thing. In the case with the cows, Bishop Amos Nisly heard about the problem and came by to fix the barbed-wire gate.

It wasn't that Ervin didn't take interest in the farm. One day he surprised Emma by making her a milking stool for the cow. "Look, Mom," Ervin said. He handed her a one-legged stool.

"Oh," she smiled. "It looks nice."

Ervin's face beamed. "I used material from the backseat of the '49 Chevy." The car had been parked in the backyard ever since the engine failed. Occasionally it yielded a junk part.

Emma turned the stool upside down and surveyed its construction. The twelve-year-old had stretched cotton padding and plastic over the top of a board to form the 6-by-12-inch seat. She was pleased that he had found something worthwhile to do with the junk car. This new stool would make a comfortable seat for milking the cow.

That evening Emma lay in bed, pondering the changes that she was going through. In the last year and a half, all three of the oldest children had moved out. Not only did she miss their companionship and help around the house; she'd also lost their income. She would need to make some adjustments.

What was she to do? The income from the wheat crop on her 40 acres would not be sufficient for the family. The transplanting work at the greenhouse was only seasonal. The twins still needed her at home when they returned from school. She would need to do something soon.

The next morning as Emma prepared to do her morning chores, she pondered the best way to earn some more income. She picked up the new milking stool and made her way into the barn. "Ervin should be using this stool himself," she reflected as she dumped feed into the manger. "He's old enough to milk."

More than once, Mother Stutzman had chided her for doing the milking herself now that the twins were adolescents. "But Mother Stutzman is different," Emma thought to herself. "She was always more strict with children than my mother. That's probably why the twins always preferred to go to Mother Nisly's house."

As Emma stroked milk into the pail, she mused that cleaning houses for townspeople might be the best way to earn a bit of cash. She could arrange to leave home after the twins got on the school bus and get home about the same time as they did.

She knew that not everyone in the church would approve of her working outside the home with school-age children at home, but what was she to do? It wouldn't be hard to find a cleaning job. She had heard that many townspeople preferred to have a woman from the plain churches clean their houses. Emma determined to get started.

The next week she made a new dress that was suitable for working in town. When it was finished, she hung it on the hook behind her bedroom door.

That evening, Erma spied the new dress. "Mom, what's this?"

"I made a new dress to work in town," Emma replied.

"What are you going to do?"

"I'm going to clean houses for people," Emma said. "I need to do something for cash. But don't tell anyone. People don't need to know that I'm doing this."

Erma dropped her eyes. "I won't tell anybody," she promised.

Emma decided to start cleaning each Friday. One of her clients was a middle-aged man named Mr. Zent, who lived by himself. She began by sweeping the floors, scrubbing the bathroom, and washing his kitchen floor. It took most of the morning. He paid a dollar an hour for the service.

Another client was an aged widow named Mrs. Smith. Emma soon learned that Mrs. Smith needed company as badly as her house needed cleaning. The lady followed Emma around and chatted as Emma dusted, scrubbed, and swept. When Emma was finished with her work, the woman asked her to sit for a spell. Emma sat and listened. When she rose to go, Mrs. Smith asked, "Would you like to take the newspaper with you? I'm finished with it."

"Sure," Emma said, holding out her hand. "Maybe the children will want to read it."

As Emma moved toward the door, Mrs. Smith asked, "Since you live in the country, do you know of anyone who has eggs for sale?"

"I could bring you a dozen or two every week," Emma volunteered.

"Then bring me a dozen next week."

Since Emma was driving down South Main on the way home, she stopped in at the Dillon Food Market. In the back of the store, she found the rack where they kept day-old bread and other food with reduced prices. She picked up a bunch of bananas whose skins had turned quite brown. "These look like they're still good," she thought. Then she cashed in some coupons she had gotten through the mail.

After paying at the counter, Emma made her way to the nearby Smith Market for fresh fruits and vegetables. Then she went to Marion Davis Meats, a store that sold odd cuts at low prices. Emma looked over the bargain shelf and bought two pounds of minced ham before heading home.

As she prepared supper, Emma reflected on the day's activities. It was clear that cleaning houses wasn't going to make much money. It would provide money for groceries and gas money, but she wished for more. Eventually she would need to seek other means of income.

After supper, she sat down beside Ervin on the sofa, who was reading an entry in the *World Book Encyclopedia*. She reached for the small green vibrator on the stand beside the sofa and ran it back and forth across her neck and upper back. Emma wondered if the housecleaning didn't aggravate the soreness. At least the gentle vibrations brought some relief to her tired muscles, which seemed particularly sore in the evening.

"Maybe you should get a treatment from Dr. Knackstedt," Ervin suggested. "I'd like to get a treatment too. Can we go over there this week?"

"We'll see. I think he's open on Tuesday nights." Emma didn't care to make the twenty-some mile drive to the small town of Inman. But unlike Dr. Cowan, he used a machine to give small electric shocks to the skin before making spinal adjustments. The treatments brought her some relief, and Ervin seemed to benefit as well.

One day as Emma pondered some alternatives for income, Raymond dropped by to make a suggestion. "There's a man in Hutch named Frank, who sells chinchillas," he told her.

"Chinchillas? What are they?"

"Well, they're little animals you raise for fur. It might be a good business for you. It would give the twins some chores and make some money for you."

Emma wrinkled her eyebrows. "How much would it cost to get started?"

"They're kinda expensive, but then you sell the furs for good money, too. They say some of the big ranchers make big money."

"How would I get started?"

"They're having a meeting in Hutch next Tuesday evening. The salesman will be there to give a demonstration and tell us how to start a business. If you want, you can ride with me to the meeting."

Emma thought about it for a moment and then agreed to consider the idea. After Raymond left, she pondered long and hard. Should she spend her hard-earned savings on a business investment? What if it didn't work out, like some of Tobe's business ventures? Could she run a business better than he?

That night as Emma retired to bed, she breathed a prayer for guidance: "Lord, give me wisdom to know what to do."

The next Tuesday evening found Emma seated with her twins and Raymond among a dozen other prospective investors at the home of a man named Frank. Emma watched with keen interest as he demonstrated the exotic nocturnal rodents. Squirrel-like in physique, the silver colored chinchillas balanced themselves with their long bushy tails. When Emma held one in her hand, she was surprised to find how little it weighed. The long fur made its body look deceptively large.

Before the evening was over, Emma decided to invest in the new venture. Frank agreed to deliver three males and nine females to her home within a week.

"Where are we going to put them?" Ervin asked.

"We'll have to keep them in the house. They have to stay warm and clean," Emma said.

"Where in the house?"

"In Erma's room. She'll need to move into the bedroom with me."

"I want to stay in my room," Erma protested. "I didn't get to have it very long—just since Mary Edna left."

"Maybe later. But for now, we need it for the chinchillas. On Saturday, we're going to move our bedrooms around."

287

True to his word, Frank delivered the chinchillas the following Monday evening. The twins helped Frank set up the three cages, each capable of housing three females. A vertical wire runway connected the stack of three pens in each cage. "The male can go between the cages," Frank explained, "but the females can't. Look at this." He showed them a large plastic ring that encircled the neck of a female in his hand. The animal's heavy fur nearly obscured the collar.

"I see," Ervin said. "The collars are too big to fit through the hole on the side of the cage. Since the male doesn't have a collar, he can go in and out of the cages when he wants to."

"That's right. You have to let the male in with the females so they can have babies. That's how your chinchilla herd will grow. When the babies get big enough, you put them in their own cages."

"I want to help take care of the baby chinchillas," Erma said, visibly excited.

"Be careful how you reach into these cages," Frank warned. "They can give you a nasty bite. Or sometimes they spray at you."

Frank picked up a galvanized tin container. It looked to Emma like a large tin can turned on its side with a rectangular opening on top.

"Watch this," Frank said as he opened the wire mesh door to the middle cage. He set the container onto the wooden shavings, closed the door, and stepped back.

"It's called a dust bath," Frank explained as the young female snooped into the container.

"A dust bath?" Erma asked. "Who wants to take a bath in dust?"

"Just watch," Frank said, with a smile crinkling the corners of his eyes.

As he spoke, the chinchilla hopped into the container

and rolled vigorously in the silvery powder. A cloud of silver dust rose from the container.

The twins crowded in closer. "That's neat," Ervin exulted.

The foursome watched a male cautiously make its way into the cage from the runway.

"The male wants a bath too," Ervin observed aloud.

"Each of the animals should have a lava bath twice a day," Frank instructed. "It helps to keep their fur dry and healthy."

Erma moved the dust bath from cage to cage as Frank went on to demonstrate how to hang the water bottles on the front of the cages. The glass bottles were suspended on a wire hanger. A bent glass nipple reached from a rubber stopper into the front of the cage.

"You should change the litter at least once a week, but oftener is better," Frank explained. "If the wood shavings get wet or dirty, it will make their fur less valuable."

"How do we sell their fur?" Erma asked.

"You have to skin them for the pelt," Frank explained.

"You mean you have to kill them?" Erma asked, her forehead wrinkling.

"I'm afraid so," Frank said.

"Do you eat the meat?"

"No, these animals are just good for the pelts. We sell them to the furriers in New York City. They make fur coats with them. Here, let me show you," he said as he reached into his attaché case.

"Oh, I'd like to have one of those," Erma exclaimed as she looked over the portraits of women modeling the exotic coats.

"I'm afraid they would be a bit expensive for you," Frank said. He pointed to a model with a floor-length coat. "This one would cost well over a thousand dollars. After your chinchillas have babies that are grown up, I'll show you how to pelt them."

Emma saw Ervin shrink back. He didn't like to help butcher animals. He might not be ready to skin these animals. If they became pets, it would be even harder.

Over the next few weeks, the twins took up the rhythm of chores with the chinchillas. Each Saturday when Emma cleaned the house, the twins changed the shavings in the large galvanized pans that rested on the bottom of the cages.

"I'm looking forward to them having babies," Erma told Emma as she finished sweeping the room.

"Me, too," said Ervin.

• • • •

Now that the older children were gone from home, Emma was grateful that the twins had been born some years after the others. It felt better now to have them around the house, helping with various chores. It would be lonely without them. "After two more years of school," Emma reflected, "they'll be free to work full-time, as their older siblings have done. That would help with the finances."

In midsummer, however, Emma learned that the Kansas legislature had passed a law requiring all students to attend school until they were sixteen years of age. "It doesn't seem right," Emma complained to Mother Nisly. "First they pass a law to lengthen the school year from eight months to nine months, and now they make students go to school until they're sixteen."

Mother Nisly nodded her head in sympathy.

Not all of the decisions made by the government went against the wishes of the Amish people. In July, President Lyndon B. Johnson signed into federal law a statute that released the Amish from paying Social Security tax. Emma didn't pay much attention at the time, although she overheard the talk at church and family gatherings. It only seemed right that if the Amish were conscientiously opposed to collecting Social Security for themselves, they shouldn't need to pay into the system. The new law reminded Emma that she'd foregone the opportunity to collect after Tobe's death. Although the decision had been difficult at the time, it now seemed as though things were working out. If the chinchillas did well, she would be able to manage without having to work in town more than a couple of days a week.

Emma cut back her work in town during the summer. There was too much work to do in the garden, and she didn't like to leave the twins at home by themselves. As it was, the twins spent long hours with their cousins at Raymond's home. Emma hoped Raymond and Mary didn't mind. There were weeks when Ervin and Erma spent the greater part of their time on Raymond's farm. Sometimes they even slept there overnight. There was much to do and see on the farm with their cousins.

That summer, Raymond made it even more attractive for the twins to spend time at his house. As part of a new irrigation system, Raymond dug a well in his pasture. Then he dug a pond. By means of a dike, he was able to make part of the pond almost six foot deep. Thanks to the irrigation system, he could easily keep it full. The twins, as well as Raymond's children, loved it. Nearly every afternoon when the necessary farmwork was done, they went swimming in the pond.

"Mom, you should come and see it," Ervin said. "Raymond built a diving board for us."

"Uh huh."

"He used a big wooden plank for the board, and the front springs from one of the junk cars makes it bounce. Nevin and I are learning to dive through the middle of an inner tube."

Emma grinned. Between their time at Raymonds and the Stutzman Greenhouse, the children kept themselves well occupied. Ervin had always enjoyed playing with his cousin Mahlon. Now Ervin J. and his wife, Emma, had taken in three foster children, siblings to each other. The foster children called each other by nicknames, but Ervin J. and Emma soon dissuaded the children from using them. Junior might have been an appropriate name for Don, but Fats and Skinny weren't the kind of names that would help Florence and Virginia develop respect for themselves.

• • • •

In the midst of the busy summer, Emma learned that Glenn was coming home for two weeks of vacation. It would be his first visit since leaving for voluntary service. "I'm going to drive home," Glenn said in a phone message, "but I'd like for my friend Miriam Kinsinger to visit too. She works at the Hudson Memorial Home where I do. She only has one week off. Is it okay if she comes to stay at our house for a week?"

Emma assured him that she was eager to meet his friend and that Miriam would have a place to stay. "I wonder what she's like," Emma thought. "I hope she's the kind that would make a good wife. He'd hardly be bringing her to visit if he wasn't quite serious with her."

Everything worked out as planned. A couple of days after Miriam arrived, Glenn confided that the two of them were engaged to be married. Since she'd only met Miriam, Emma wasn't sure how to respond at first. But several more days around Glenn's fiancée confirmed Emma's impression that he had made a good choice. She watched as the couple carried their luggage outside and put it into the trunk of Glenn's car.

Miriam seemed stable and sensible. She might help Glenn to settle down. And Glenn talked as though she seemed willing to come and live in Kansas.

Emma bid them goodbye as Glenn opened the door on the driver's side. Miriam got in and scooted toward the middle of the bench seat. Glenn followed after. The two sat tightly against each other as the car rumbled out the lane. Emma held her hands folded in front of her as she watched the Chevy head south, trailing a cloud of dust.

"I wish you'd tend the chinchillas before we eat supper," Emma said to Erma when she came back inside. "And Ervin, you go and fetch the cow from the back of the shelterbelt."

The two embarked on their assignments. Ervin headed out the backdoor, and Erma went to the chinchilla room. A few minutes later, Erma called out, "Mom, come look!"

Emma walked toward the room. "What is it?" she asked.

"This one has babies!" Erma said, pointing to two tiny creatures in the wooden shavings.

"Sure enough." Emma said as she peered into the cage.

"They're so tiny," Erma said. "Can I hold one?"

"It's probably best to wait until they're a little older," Emma cautioned. "It looks like they were just born a few minutes ago. Maybe in a couple of days you can hold them."

"Okay." Impatience tinged her voice.

Emma reached to close the galvanized slide to the run. "Remember that Frank told us to close the gate when they have babies. You don't want the male to come in and bother them."

"That's right," Erma agreed.

Within the next week, two other chinchillas gave birth.

Emma breathed a prayer of thanks that the animals were reproducing. Perhaps there was some hope for this new venture.

But in the meantime, there were setbacks. One evening, Emma's cow didn't show up at milking time. Thinking that the cow must have lingered in the back of the shelterbelt, Emma sent Erma to fetch her.

She returned with a somber look and reported: "Mom, Josephine's dead."

"What!"

"Josephine's dead. She's lying on the ground right next to the fence."

"Now what do we do?" Emma wrung her hands. "At least we have a heifer. She'll soon be freshening."

The next morning, Raymond brought his tractor and dragged Josephine's body up to the farm buildings. A truck from the rendering plant took the carcass without charge. Not long afterward, Emma learned that her neighbor to the east had been spraying the fencerow for weeds.

"So that's what happened," Emma mused aloud. "Josephine ate some of the grass in the fencerow and got poisoned. Should I call him and say something?"

She pondered the question for a couple of days. "I can't really prove anything," she thought, "and besides, what difference would it make? He'd just feel bad. Things like this happen." She remembered how Josephine had gotten into a different neighbor's field. "Sometimes things just don't go the way that we hope." She decided to let the matter drop.

Emma tried her best to live at peace with others. Once when she felt she deserved more money for cleaning one of her client's homes, she wrote a little note and left it on the table. She asked for a small raise but added the disclaimer: "If you feel this is not fair, we can leave it as it is. I would rather clean your house for the lower price than to cause bad feelings."

To some extent, Emma's aversion to conflict reflected the church's teaching about nonresistance, as emphasized in the baptismal instruction the twins received that summer. Each Sunday afternoon for some weeks, Emma accompanied them to the instruction class at the church house. Each time, Deacon Mahlon Wagler or one of the ministers led the eight members of the instruction class through the study of a small booklet called *Instructions to Beginners in the Christian Life*.

The doctrine of nonresistance was based on the character of Jesus as the Prince of Peace. Jesus taught that one must not resist an evil person, but turn the other cheek. On this basis, the church members at Center Church were expected to be conscientious objectors to war. The church didn't believe that one could follow Jesus' command to love one's enemies while serving in military combat.

The doctrine of nonconformity was a close complement to nonresistance. In its teaching the church observed that when the plain churches lost their emphasis on nonconformity to the world, they soon lost their nonresistant stance as well. So, at Center Church, the doctrines of nonresistance and nonconformity were joined like Siamese twins. The baptismal candidates were taught that those two teachings must stay together.

The baptismal instruction class was also a time to review the church's written guidelines for Christian conduct. The church believed that Christian discipleship was very practical, touching on matters of everyday life such as speech, use of the telephone, and even how one should chew gum. Each member of the class promised to cooperate with the church's standards.

Shortly after the beginning of the new school year, the church announced that it was time for the candidates to be baptized and publicly embraced as church members. Bishop Amos Nisly led the service of baptism. Emma watched attentively as Amos called the eight members of the instruction class to stand in the front of the church house and make their vows to the church.

Ervin stood on the left end of the line, beside Phillip Nisly and Carl Buril. The other five members were girls. Emma listened as Amos spoke their names: "Valetta Miller, Grace Nisly, Janette Miller, Rosetta Nisly, and Erma Stutzman."

After each made their vows, Amos invited them to kneel in a slight semicircle. Then he baptized each one in turn, cupping his hands above each one's head and reciting the ritual words. At the proper time, Deacon Wagler poured a small amount of water from a pitcher. Then the bishop extended a hand to each of the young men, beckoning them in turn to stand to their feet. When they did so, he greeted them with a light kiss to the lips, the kiss of love commanded by Holy Writ. He extended the hand of fellowship to the young women as well, but when they stood, it was his wife, Ann, who stepped forward to welcome them with a kiss.

When the ceremony was complete, the eight returned to their seats. Emma watched with deep joy. It was good to know that all of her children were members of the church—all except Edith. Emma didn't worry that Edith would never be baptized. The church taught that handicapped people like Edith did not have sufficient reasoning ability to make an informed decision to follow Christ. They were like children who had not yet reached the age of accountability. Emma was confident that when Edith appeared someday before God's throne of judgment, she would be covered by the grace of Jesus Christ.

Not long after the baptism, Emma received a copy of the formal invitation to Glenn and Miriam's wedding, planned for the weekend before Thanksgiving. Perry agreed to take Emma and the twins to the wedding in Ohio, along with a couple of other passengers. During his time in voluntary service, he'd traded in his '53 Chevy for a '59 Pontiac Catalina. It was spacious and comfortable, with a three-speed automatic transmission. It would provide a very nice ride for six or seven people.

Emma was pleased to find that Miriam's family was friendly and welcoming. Miriam's parents, John and Mattie Kinsinger, greeted her warmly. She found that Miriam was indeed an identical twin. Emma could not distinguish Miriam from her sister Martha.

The wedding service was quite simple. The Maple View Mennonite Church in Burton Station, Ohio, was simply furnished, with oak pews. Matching oak paneling served as wainscoting on the sidewalls, and its top edge angled up toward the front, to where paneling touched the ceiling. A reproduction of Sallman's portrait of Jesus in Gethsemane adorned the front wall above the preacher's bench.

Miriam wore a small prayer covering and a satin knee-length gown sewn for the occasion, with white shoes. As the only bridesmaid, her identical twin sister wore a blue dress made on the same pattern.

Glenn wore a black suit with a lay-down collar and a white shirt buttoned at the neck. A white carnation was pinned to the left lapel. Perry was the only groomsman. He wore the Amish regulation suit, his black jacket fastened shut with hooks and eyes all the way to the stand-up collar.

The service was so short that the wedding party remained standing the entire time. Emma was used to much-longer services. The wedding services at Center were much too long for the couple to stand during the whole service. The protocol of the Conservative Mennonite Conference had some of the same restrictions as those at Center. There was no exchange of rings, no unveiling of the bride, no nuptial kiss.

The reception afterward was a festive occasion. All of the guests were served a simple meal at tables. Ervin and Erma collected the gifts from the guests and placed them unwrapped on a table, for all to see.

Emma was satisfied that Glenn had married into a good family. While she wished Glenn would have stayed with Center Church, she was satisfied. Glenn's experience of service at Hudson Memorial Home was doing him good.

16

Venturing Out

Emma woke up to the first hint of the January sun through the frosty window of her bedroom. She yawned and looked at her alarm clock. Since Glenn was in voluntary service, Emma no longer had the early morning task of preparing his breakfast. "I must get up and get going," Emma commented out loud. "It's butchering day."

She quickly dressed and did the morning chores before she got the twins out of bed. Emma was preparing their breakfast when Raymond drove into the lane, pulling a trailer. "Ervin, go help Raymond get that hog loaded," Emma said.

Ervin grabbed a coat and headed out the backdoor. In a few minutes, the squealing hog was loaded, and Raymond drove back out the lane.

Emma sat down to eat a hurried breakfast before seeing them off to school. As they made their way to the bus, she pulled out a couple of knives, to sharpen them for the day's task. Her butcher knife sounded a raspy tune as she swished it against the edge of the sharpening steel, first on one side, then the other. She tested the sharpness of the blade with her thumb. She swished it again and followed suit with two other knives.

When she was finished, Emma gathered her knives and

pans and headed for Raymond's home. She saw a thin cloud of smoke rising from the chimney as she approached the butcher house. "Good, Raymond has the fire going," she thought.

Emma walked through the frozen barnyard and swung open the door into the butcher house. It was a frame building with wooden sheeting on four sides, wooden shingles, and a concrete floor. She smelled the dull odor of fat and smoked meat as she stepped inside. The sights and smells of this outbuilding on the home farm were very familiar. For as long as she could remember, this was the place where the Nisly family had butchered meat. As custom butchers, they used the building through much of the winter, butchering meat for their neighbors as well as for their own household. They also butchered meat for sale, peddling it on the streets of Hutchinson.

Although the fire was burning, the building was still cold as Emma stepped inside. She grabbed a bucket and made several trips to the stock tank, fetching water to fill the large pot used to scald hair off the hog's hide. The pot would also be used to render the lard, some of which would be used to make the lye soap Emma used for her weekly laundry. As the fire grew hot under the cauldron, the water began to steam. Meanwhile, Raymond's wife, Mary, joined the group, along with Grandma and Grandpa Nisly. There were only two hogs to butcher today, one for Raymond's family and one for Emma's, so they could easily do the work in one day.

Emma was cleaning up the sausage grinder when she heard a rifle shot just outside the east wall. In a few minutes, the men dragged the hog, drained of its blood, into the building. Before long, they were scalding and scraping the hair off the hide. The tangy rhythm of the metal scrapers against the hide almost made Emma shiver. But they were soon done, and it was time to hang the carcass on the overhead metal track.

As soon as the hog was disemboweled, the women began their work in earnest. Emma took the small intestines and emptied their contents outside the building. Then she rinsed and scraped them clean in preparation for making sausage. As she worked, Emma reflected on her upcoming birthday. Next week, she would turn fifty. If he had lived, Tobe would be forty-seven. Unlike the first years after his death, Emma didn't think of him every day. But birthdays and anniversaries brought vivid reminders of him.

Emma glanced over at the men who were cutting the carcass into sections and laying it on the worktable. "Tobe never enjoyed butchering," Emma recalled. "But he did enjoy fresh meat. If we'd have had a hog in Iowa, we would have eaten better."

Then Emma moved to join the others as they cut up the meat into smaller portions. She listened as others conversed, but her thoughts drifted to Mary Edna and Menno, who had given her the first grandchild. Merrill Dean was now nine months old. Emma lamented that he would never know his grandfather.

Now that Menno's two-year term of service was finished, the couple lived in their own large old house, a fixer-upper in Wichita. With only slight hesitation, Emma had loaned them some cash to help renovate the place. After years of frugal stretching to put a bit into savings, Emma felt fortunate to have any money to loan out. "I must share some of this meat with Menno and Mary Edna," Emma told herself. "The meat they buy in the store just isn't as good as fresh pork."

After lunch, Emma prepared to stuff the sausage. She dumped a large portion of meat into the stuffer and clamped down the lid. Then she slipped the intestine casing onto the tube that protruded from the sausage stuffer. Grandpa Nisly turned the crank that squeezed the sausage down into the container and out the small tube into the casing. Emma held the casing as it filled with sausage. As the meat flowed into the casings, she coiled them into a galvanized tub. When she was finished, the large galvanized tub was half full, enough for a whole season. Now that the twins were the only children at home, the meat supply lasted much longer.

The winter sun had dropped to kiss the western horizon by the time all the meat was wrapped and ready to go to the food locker in town or home to the freezer. Emma breathed a prolonged sigh of satisfaction as she headed for home.

• • • •

Over the next three months, Emma watched the calendar with keen anticipation, knowing that Perry's two-year term of service in Arkansas was coming to an end. She hoped to visit the Hillcrest Home again and see Glenn and Miriam in El Dorado as well.

When the time came, Emma found a ride to Harrison, Arkansas. She brought Ervin along as well, notifying the school that he would be missing for a couple of days. Emma made arrangements for Erma to stay at Raymond's house overnight.

During her short stay at Hillcrest Home, Emma was gratified to see the way Perry bid goodbye to the residents whom he had come to love. She could tell that he had become quite attached to the residents as well as the staff. Ervin helped Perry load his belongings in the trunk and backseat of Perry's Pontiac Catalina. Then the three of them crawled into the front seat and headed for El Dorado, not far from the Louisiana border.

They arrived at the Hudson Memorial Home late in the afternoon. For his first year of service, Glenn had lived with several other voluntary service workers in a dorm. Now that he was married to Miriam, they lived together in a small apartment.

Emma followed Perry up the wooden outside steps to the second-floor dwelling. Glenn answered their knock on the door and invited them into his sparsely furnished apartment. It was neatly arranged, with everything in its proper place. After a few moments of small talk, Glenn took them on a tour around the nursing facility. As at Hillcrest Home, volunteer service workers provided primary care for aging and infirm residents. While they walked from room to room, Emma reflected on how good it was for Glenn to be at this place.

That evening Emma helped her daughter-in-law prepare a simple supper. The three brothers played a game together and talked about Glenn's work at the nursing home.

The next day, when Glenn took Ervin to harvest cypress knees in a nearby swamp, Miriam confided to Emma that she was pregnant. Emma's face lit up with the promise of a second grandchild.

On the way back to Kansas the next day, Perry asked Emma if he could live at home for the next while. Although he was of age, he preferred to live at her home. Emma saw no good reason to refuse. In fact, there were advantages. In exchange for a place to stay, he could help farm the forty acres. He was better than any of the other children at keeping the small farm in shape. If he had been at home, the family wouldn't have forgotten to drain the water in the John Deere D, causing the engine block to crack.

"He could also help keep Ervin in line," Emma thought to herself. From the time of Tobe's death, Perry had felt some responsibility for the discipline of the younger children. Perry had his father's resolve to make children behave.

Because the chinchillas took up one of the bedrooms, having Perry live at home meant that the boys would need to share a double bed or sleep in a bunk bed. Ervin wasn't enthused about giving up his own room. It was a privilege he'd enjoyed ever since Glenn had left for service in Arkansas. But at Emma's urging, he consented.

A few days after he arrived at home, Perry started working full-time at Reno Fabricating. His earlier work record and the growing demand for aluminum storm windows provided much employment for him. The pace at the company had picked up speed, so they were eager to hire him as a production worker.

Emma was particularly interested in Perry's pursuit of a romance with Dorothy Wingard. The tall, slender woman from Thomas, Oklahoma, was the picture of neatness, with her dress and hair as prim and proper as anyone whom Emma had met. A few weeks after he started his job back home, Perry took a full week off to take Dorothy on a long trip east to the wedding of a friend in Pennsylvania. Accompanied by another dating couple, they stopped to visit friends in Indiana, Minnesota and Nebraska. When they returned home, Emma sensed that the relationship was deepening.

She and her family felt a special connection to Dorothy's home community, since it was the place of Tobe's birth. A number of Tobe's relatives lived in the area, including Tobe's uncle David A. Miller, the bishop who had preached at his funeral. It was David who had first suggested to Perry that he pursue a relationship with Dorothy.

Grandma Stutzman, who was David's sister, didn't share his perspective. "*Die Wingards sin net wie uns.* The Wingards are not like us," she told Perry. "*Sie hen Geld.* They have money."

Grandpa agreed: "You might be wearing out your car and still not get that girl."

Since she had lived in Oklahoma for a time, Grandma felt keenly the status differences among the plain people around Thomas, Oklahoma. The Wingards were relatively wealthy. The Stutzmans were dirt farmers, with little to show for their efforts.

In spite of his grandparents' reservations, Perry made several trips to Oklahoma through the next months in pursuit of his romance with the girl. How could Grandpa and Grandma Stutzman be so sure that it wasn't going to work out?

In early December, Grandpa and Grandma Stutzman marked their own romantic milestone, the celebration of fifty years of marriage. Along with the rest of the extended Stutzman and Miller families, Emma brought her family to celebrate the occasion. She observed that Grandpa was his usual quiet self, shunning attention as much as possible. Grandma, on the other hand, delighted in the arrival of guests who dropped by to give greetings. She used the occasion to call for a hymn sing. For an hour, the room rang with Anna's favorite hymns and gospel songs.

Throughout the day the extended family gathered in various clusters, catching up on news and talking about the future. Emma overheard Tobe's brothers discuss the recent news that Highway 61 was to be widened. It had implications for the Stutzman Greenhouse, since their buildings were close to the right of way. The two shops that Tobe had built would need to be moved or taken down.

"Will the highway people tear down the shop, or do you have to do it?" L. Perry asked his brother Ervin as they sat in a small circle in the living room.

"Oh, they'll tear it down, all right. I just need to get ready by building something else."

"What are you planning to do?"

"We're going to build a bigger shop south of the house."

"Is the shop you have now too small?"

"Well, you know our motto: 'Our business is growing.'"

"I know your motto. I just wondered if it was still true."

The men in the circle laughed.

"It's always true. Our business is growing plants," Ervin J. retorted.

"Are you selling more of them lately?" L. Perry snickered with delight.

Ervin J. grinned. "Yes, we can hardly keep up. The wholesale division is doing really good these days. How about your business? Is it still picking up?" His voice reflected the mischievous nature of his question.

L. Perry laughed. "That's what our motto says: 'Our business is picking up.' It's always true. We pick up trash every day except Sunday."

"Are you picking up more trash lately?" Ervin J. grinned.

"Yes, as a matter of fact, we are. Now that Glenn is back from service, we should be able to pick up more trash than ever."

"So Glenn is back from Arkansas?"

"He got back last week. When he left, I promised him that I'd keep a job for him. It's hard to find anyone else who works like he does."

Emma listened with interest. She was pleased that Glenn and Miriam had decided to move back to Kansas with their daughter, Janet, who had been born a few weeks earlier. It was sometimes difficult for people from further east, like Indiana or Ohio, to choose Kansas as a home. Many complained that it was too hot, too dry, or too flat for their liking. Kansans, on the other hand, often thought many Easterners were too soft to live with the changes in weather. And people of Kansas preferred to think of the landscape as level rather than flat.

Emma observed that the conversations at the anniversary celebration steered away from any references to the tensions that had at times plagued John and Anna's marriage. She recalled snippets of talk with Tobe about the tensions in his childhood home. Emma was confident that some other homes had similar tensions. But the biblical prohibition against divorce, coupled with the strong shame it evoked in the church community, kept married couples from seeking divorce as a way to escape problems. Thus, there were no couples in the plain church community near Partridge who had ever sought a divorce.

Tobe had always sympathized with his mother, who watched her siblings prosper on large farmsteads while John's efforts at tillage came to naught. When Tobe's parents lost their Oklahoma farm during the dust-bowl days, Tobe had vowed someday to get away from farming in pursuit of a different dream, so as to never leave his family stranded. "Yet his ambitious dream," Emma mused, "eventually led him to lose everything, just like his father. How could it be that Tobe, so ambitious and energetic, ended up at the same place as his father, John, who paid so little attention to getting ahead?"

• • • •

In March of the following year, Emma obtained the land deed for the property she'd been living on for more than a decade. For whatever reason, no one had ever thought it necessary to make the legal transaction. It had simply remained in Mother Nisly's name, along with her second husband, Noah.

The new deed increased Emma's acreage to include all of the shelterbelt, not simply the road frontage where the house was built. The plot included ten acres in all.

With great satisfaction Emma carried home a copy of the quitclaim deed. It was more land than she and Tobe had ever owned together. "Raymond still has the deed for her forty acres in his name," Emma reminded herself. "Is he worried that I or one of my children might lose it if I have full ownership? Am I not trustworthy?" The thought weighed on her mind.

Now that the deed was in hand, Emma decided to erect a separate building for the chinchillas. The herd was growing too large for the one room in the house. Besides, Erma was eager to have her own bedroom. It seemed right to construct a building specifically for the animals. Meanwhile, Dr. Ralph Cowan agreed that, until the new building was complete, Emma could keep the chinchillas in his basement level (in the *Grossdaadihaus* beside Raymond's home).

Emma's brother in law, Alvin Yoder, took charge of the construction. He laid the footer for the 20-by-40-foot building in an excavation about four feet deep. Emma watched as Alvin set up his water level to set the four corners of the building. A large plastic jug with blue-colored water stood in the center of the large rectangle. Clear plastic tubes forked out from the jug and ran to the four corners of the rectangle. Since water seeks out its own level, Alvin knew that the colored water was the same level in each corner. He set a stake at each corner to mark the top of the wooden form for the footer.

After he finished pouring the footer, Alvin built forms in which to pour the concrete walls. After the concrete was dry, he laid up several courses of block and poured concrete steps for an entry on the west side, facing the house. The west end of the building sat just fifteen feet away from the east side of the house.

To help Emma save costs, Alvin constructed the ceiling joists and rafters out of wood rescued from an outbuilding torn down on the John B. Yoder farm. He then shingled the roof with interlocking asphalt shingles. When Alvin was finished on the inside, the building had one large room on the east end and two smaller ones on the west.

Alvin finished the project by piling dirt from the excavation against the wall, so that the ground rose to within two feet of the roof's edge. The windowsills stood just above ground level. With the building mostly underground, it would stay cool in the summer and require less heat in the winter.

When Emma moved the chinchillas into the new quarters, the family dubbed it "the chinchilla house." This move freed up space to rearrange the bedrooms in the house. Erma now had her own room back, and the boys got a bedroom big enough for two separate beds.

Not long after the chinchilla building was completed, the school year came to an end. With it came Ervin's graduation from the eighth grade. Emma was grateful since graduation from grade school usually signaled a move from school into the workforce. Having a son earning again would help to bring in some cash to replace her investment in the chinchilla house.

Emma anticipated that Ervin would serve as a farmhand for Willie Wagler. Earlier in the spring, Willie had voiced an interest in having Ervin work for him on the farm in the summer of 1967.

"We can provide transportation," Willie offered. "If he's got a driver's permit, he can drive one of our older cars."

"Yes, he got his permit as soon as he turned fourteen."

"That means he can drive back and forth to work as long as it's not too dark. We'll try to send him home in the evening before it gets dark."

Meanwhile, Emma learned that a new state law required farmhands under sixteen years of age to be trained in tractor operation before being hired out. Emma thought it unnecessary in Ervin's case, since he had been operating tractors for several years on Raymond's farm. But she dutifully sent him to the Extension Office for the obligatory three days.

Emma took Ervin to work on his first day. That evening, he came home with Willie's green Dodge.

"Willie's car drives funny," Ervin explained to the rest of the family at the supper table.

"How's that?" Erma asked.

"It has a fluid-drive transmission," Perry broke in. "It's a stick shift that acts like an automatic. It has fluid between the gears, so there is some give when you start out."

"What's it good for?" Erma asked.

"You don't have to worry about grinding the gears or jerking when you pop the clutch," Perry replied. "It takes off gradually. You could start out in third gear if you wanted to. The fluid just slips a little more until the transmission catches up with the engine. Of course, you can't lay rubber or spin your wheels very easily."

"It sounds like a good car for young boys to drive," Emma thought to herself. "Too many boys tear around with their cars."

Over the next weeks, Ervin settled into the rhythm of the work on Willie's farm. He complained, however, that the hand clutch on Willie's Model M Minneapolis Moline was much too hard to handle. To keep the worn-out clutch from slipping, Willie adjusted it so tightly that the boy could hardly engage the lever. He had to yank with the whole weight of his small frame in order to stop the tractor.

Part of Ervin's pay was a hot meal at noon with Willie's family. He spoke glowingly of Willie Alma's cooking and the lively meal conversations.

Willie irrigated much of his acreage, so he was expecting a good crop of wheat. Neither he nor others anticipated the long spell of wet weather that arrived just as the farmers were moving their combines into the ripe fields. The rains fell intermittently, with little time for the ground to dry. Even though there were a few hot days, the fields had large spots much too wet for the large machines.

"Mom, you wouldn't believe how hard it is to get into the fields," Ervin told Emma one evening. "I have to keep the tractor close to the combine all the time so I can pull it out of the mud holes. Willie got so tired of getting stuck that he put dual wheels on the combine. He mounted the extra tires with the treads backward so it has better traction in reverse. That way he can always back out when he gets into a mud hole."

"I see." Emma nodded.

"It works fairly well, but I still needed to pull him out a couple of times. Willie says this is the wettest summer we have on record here. It looks like we're going to lose some of the wheat. It's lodging [flat on the ground] so badly that it's really hard to pick up with the combine. Some of it is already sprouting in the heads. He might be able to feed it to the cows, but it's not worth much for anything else."

Emma grimaced. It was hard to lose a crop. Fortunately, Raymond had been able to get most of her wheat out of the field. Now it was safely stored in the Eaton bin that Raymond helped her put up near the back of her small property. The prices were sure to rise within a few months, particularly if some of the wheat was being lost in the fields.

One evening Ervin told Emma that Willie thought Ervin's hair was too short, with too much of a shingle. To taper the hair in the back was considered worldly. But Raymond, who generally cut Ervin's hair, had the habit of tapering it the way he did his own.

"I told him that's the way that Raymond cuts it," Ervin lamented.

"I know," Emma sympathized. "Raymond always does it that way." She recalled that Raymond had resisted the traditional bowl haircuts that characterized their childhood home. Now she heard talk about a rock band named the Beatles, who let their hair grow longer than the Amish. Some of the young people from the Mennonite Church were starting to imitate the British band. Maybe it was a good thing if Ervin wore his hair a bit too short for Willie's taste. At least he wouldn't look like one of the Beatles.

One evening at the table, Ervin explained that Willie had taught him how to tell the difference between barley and wheat. "Willie says that the barley heads have Amish beards and the wheat heads have Beachy beards." Everyone laughed. Although Center Church required the men to wear beards, they allowed them to be much shorter than those of the Amish. The Amish church took more literally the Mosaic command not to "cut the corners of their beards." The Beachy Amish Church interpreted the command as part of an earlier era, not binding on Christians. Yet along with the Amish Church, they forbade the men to wear a mustache. Hair on the upper lip still evoked images of men in the military who many years earlier had tried to force their ways upon the nonresistant Amish, who refused to go to war.

Near the end of the summer, Perry invited Emma and Ervin to accompany him for a visit back to his place of service at Hillcrest Home in Arkansas. The three of them spent the weekend visiting with friends that Perry had made during his two-year stay.

As they were preparing to return home, Perry learned that a volunteer worker had a '57 Chevrolet for sale. Ever since Perry first heard the sound of a '57 Chevy, he had longed to buy one. This opportunity seemed too good to pass by. Yet to buy it would mean that someone else would have to drive the Pontiac back home. "Would you be willing to drive the Pontiac home?" Perry asked Emma. "Or maybe Ervin could drive it."

Emma hesitated. She didn't feel comfortable driving such

a big car for such a distance. Ervin had a driver's permit, but he was only fourteen years old. By law, she would need to be in the front seat with him. Was it wise to ask the young boy to drive the winding roads through the Ozarks?

"How about taking the car out for a drive?" Perry asked. "I'll let Ervin drive to see how he does."

"All right," Emma agreed. She waited until the two returned fifteen minutes later. Perry seemed cautious about entrusting the Pontiac to his younger brother. "Mom, are you sure you don't want to drive?" he asked, his eyes begging for an affirmative response. "You can have the car for yourself when we get back home."

Emma could hardly believe her ears. It was much nicer than the old Chevy she was driving now. Power steering, power brakes, automatic transmission—it seemed too luxurious to be true.

"I can try," she said.

"I can drive," Ervin begged.

"I think it would be better if Mom drove," Perry said.

Ervin looked crestfallen.

The sun was setting when they embarked on the long drive home. Perry led with his Chevy while Emma followed with the Pontiac. Emma was greatly relieved when they finally pulled into the yard back home. The mantel clock chimed 4:00 a.m. as Emma prepared for bed. At least she could get a few winks before it was time to chore.

Three hours later Emma awoke. She shook off her grogginess and went about the morning chores. Although she didn't see much sense in Perry buying an older and sportier car, she was grateful for the way she would benefit. The Pontiac would be much nicer to drive than any of the cars she'd owned before.

At the same time, Emma felt a bit self-conscious. It might raise a few eyebrows in the church to see a widow driving such a large car, with such prominent fins on the back. As a widow receiving assistance from the church, Emma felt the need to test the effect of each such acquisition on communal perception. Especially since the congregation was assisting with the cost of Edith's care, she couldn't afford to have them think that she was using her money unwisely. The safety net that kept widows from sinking into ruin also restricted their movements.

• • • •

As the summer school vacation came to an end, Emma braced herself for Ervin's entry into the public high school. Since Erma had been held back a year in school, it would be another year before she started. With the new law mandating school attendance until age sixteen, Emma had little choice but to send Ervin to high school. Although she had written a letter to a congressional representative when the matter came up for a vote, she wasn't going to protest now that the law had passed. But who could know what temptations the boy would face?

Galen Garber, Ervin's good friend and classmate from Elreka, wasn't going to be allowed to go to high school. His father, Leroy (Shorty) Garber, a member of the Old Order Amish church, voiced deep convictions about the right of parents to keep their children at home after grade school. Two years earlier, when Leroy's daughter Sharon had finished grade school, he had sent her to the small Harmony Parochial School near Yoder, Kansas. When county officials charged him for sending his daughter to an unaccredited school, a sympathetic lawyer stepped forward to help him plead his case in Reno County Court. He was fined a token five dollars and asked to comply. By this time, Sharon was sixteen and the law no longer applied to her. It wasn't that Garber was opposed to learning; he supported Sharon in completing high school by correspondence courses. Rather, he felt that Sharon's way of life would be compromised by her interactions in the public high school environment.

Now that Galen had graduated from grade school, Leroy suspected that the boy would become the focus of new controversy. Leroy appealed to the state courts, who upheld the earlier conviction. By this time, several conservative groups had gained an audience with Kansas State Governor Robert Docking. They expressed their aversion to forced attendance in state-sponsored education on the high-school level. Sympathetic Protestants, Catholics, and Jews aligned with the National Committee for Amish Religious Freedom to press the issue. Money poured in from various sources for Garber's defense, so he appealed to the U.S. Supreme Court.

In November 1967, a few months after Galen should have been in school, his father learned that he had failed to win the hearing of the top court. He felt somewhat vindicated, however, since Chief Justice Earl Warren and two associate justices voted to take the case. Garber licked his wounds and put his farm up for sale. He decided that it would be better to move to another state than to keep fighting a losing battle in Kansas.

A number of families from Center Church sympathized with Garber's concerns. Even so, they complied with the new law. Some seemed to welcome the opportunity to send children to high school. Emma's neighbors, Enos and Mary Miller, had sent their son David to Central Christian High School in Hutchinson. Perhaps it made a difference that Perry L. Miller, a member of the church, had gained his master's degree in teaching. His work as principal of the Elreka School touched the lives of many members at Center Church.

The ministers at Center seemed to have a relatively neutral stance on higher education. Willie Wagler's son David was just completing a college degree at nearby Bethel College.

Preacher David L. Miller had himself spent a year at Eastern Mennonite College in Harrisonburg, Virginia.

Emma took some comfort in knowing that Partridge High was a small rural school. It would not have some of the bad influences of large city schools. And since there were a number of youth attending from the various Amish and Mennonite churches, Ervin could depend on having support for his convictions.

At first it seemed a bit strange to see the twins off to school on two different buses, but Emma soon got used to the rhythm. Erma won the nod to pitch for the girls' softball team, so she looked forward to going to school every day that fall. Over the years that the twins played sports in grade school, Emma rarely took the time to go to the games. The schedule for games often conflicted with her work schedule in town. Besides, sports were not a high priority in her mind. But when the girls' softball team showed competitive play, she came to watch Erma pitch. The Elreka team faced a disadvantage since the girls from the plain churches had to wear the same long dresses to play softball that they wore to class. Whenever a breeze came up from the wrong direction, Erma's skirt threatened her underhand pitch. In spite of this handicap, her team won first place in league play.

Ervin seemed to enjoy high school as well, although the Amish boys faced considerable razzing from their *englisch* peers at school. Because high school teams played their games at night, the church did not allow the youth to participate in extramural sports.

Emma didn't mind that the twins didn't fit in with the normal patterns for sports in school. Sports were only for a limited time, while participation in the church was for a lifetime. It was part of the price to be paid for being separate from the world. If the church didn't draw the line somewhere, the

Amish youth would soon accommodate to worldly ways. She trusted the church to make wise decisions about such issues.

Emma particularly trusted the judgment of Preacher David L. Miller, who had the most philosophical bent of the ministers at Center Church. When he preached on the first Sunday of 1968, David L. expressed his approach to the many outside influences that threatened the life of the plain community. Emma listened intently as he spoke.

"I think we would all acknowledge that change is not only good, but it is often necessary, and to say that we will not change is to say that we will not grow, because growth is change and likewise deterioration is change. But we need a philosophy of change.

There are two alternatives to a philosophy of change. The first is the absence of a philosophy that lets things take care of themselves. I think the end result of this is that we are moving along without any predetermined boundaries or direction. When we have no philosophy of change we are drifting."

Emma suspected that David was talking about the neighborhood churches who had no written discipline. They simply let their members do as they wished. He may even have been referring to some more-progressive Mennonite churches who were somewhat careless with membership issues.

She listened as he continued. "The second alternative is a philosophy of no change, which says: 'Here we stand, and we will not under any circumstances consider change because change is drift.' This likewise is not realistic. It is probably as disastrous as the other alternative because it is not open to the principle of growth."

"That's like the Old Order Amish," Emma thought to herself. "They refuse to buy cars."

David went on, "We are in a world of change, but what should be our attitude toward change in relation to the

Word of God, which doesn't change; in relation to a God who doesn't change; and in relation to a human nature that is still the same as when Adam and Eve were driven out of the garden of Eden? I believe there are certain basic principles in our Christian experience upon which we build. We approach change against the background of the elementary things of salvation: the basics of repentance, faith, grace, works, and discipleship, in that order.

"Certainly it would be out of order for us to stand in judgment against others who arrive at different conclusions, but on the other hand, it would be unfaithful for us to overlook demands of obedience that are upon us as the Scriptures speak to us."

Emma reflected on David's words. She found assurance in his confidence that the church was finding a middle way with change, between traditional reaction and undue accommodation. Still, Mary Edna and Menno had left Center Church, unsatisfied with the slow changes it was making. She wondered if Ervin's exposure to high school would lead him along a similar path.

The following Sunday morning, Emma knocked on Ervin's bedroom door. "It's soon time for church," Emma told the boy.

"I'm not feeling well," Ervin moaned. "I have a bad stomachache."

Emma paused then moved toward her bedroom to finish getting dressed. Perhaps he'd feel better a bit later.

Thirty minutes later she knocked again and then stepped inside the room. Ervin responded in a similar manner. "I want to stay home from church today. I'm not feeling well." He turned over in bed.

"Where does it hurt?" Emma asked.

"Down here," Ervin replied, pointing to his lower abdomen.

"Okay," Emma said. "You can stay at home today." A few minutes later, she left with Erma for the church service.

When Emma got home, Ervin was working at the dining room table. "I'm feeling better now," he said.

Emma looked askance at the materials laid out on the dining room table. Ervin was assembling an Estes model rocket. Mr. Neally, his science teacher at Partridge High, had introduced him to rockets. Emma watched for a moment as Ervin glued a fin onto the cardboard body of the small rocket.

"I'm going to send this one up after dinner," Ervin said. "I have the launcher almost ready to go."

Emma grimaced. How was it that Ervin was so sick that he couldn't go to church but felt well enough to send off rockets? She felt like saying as much, but held her tongue.

Glenn's family joined Perry and the twins for dinner, so the three brothers talked about rockets during the meal. After dinner Ervin took the launcher and his newly formed rocket outside into the frigid air. He wore a light jacket. "Mom, I want you to see this," he said. "Erma, you come too."

The whole family watched as Ervin set up the wooden launcher with a long copper rod to guide the blastoff. Once the six-inch rocket was on the launcher, Ervin connected two electric clips to the small wires protruding from the small engine. The energy would flow from a battery, heat up the wire element, set off the rocket fuel, and launch the rocket into the air.

"Everybody ready?" Ervin asked. "All right, here we go: 10, 9, 8, 7, 6, 5, 4, 3, 2, 1, blastoff."

Emma watched with amazement as the small rocket shot into the air and out of sight. The three stood looking up at the sky. "We should see it tumble down in a minute," Ervin said. "It's made to land softly."

Soon a full minute went by, with no sign of the rocket. "I think it's pretty windy up there," Ervin said. "It must have blown a little ways downwind." He set out to find the stray rocket, but without success. "I think I used too powerful an engine," Ervin said. "It went too high."

"We can't afford to buy rockets and then lose them," Emma thought to herself as she pulled her jacket more tightly around her body. When she saw that Ervin was gathering up his things, she took the lead to go inside. Ervin was probably disappointed enough from losing his rocket that she didn't need to rub it in.

She became worried, however, when Ervin complained of illness the next Sunday as well. Similarly, after staying home from church and joining the family for dinner, he felt well enough to demonstrate his rockets to a friend who dropped by. She hoped Ervin wasn't trying to avoid going to church just so he could work on his own projects.

17

Abundant Harvest

One day the following week Ervin barely made it to the bus in time, so Emma checked the chinchilla feed for herself. "We're going to need feed for this evening," she said aloud to herself. "Ervin will have to do it when he comes home from school." She also noticed that a couple of the chinchillas looked quite sick. One had its head pushed into the corner of the cage as though it was about to die.

That evening when the twins got off the school bus, Ervin came to the kitchen for a snack. "I have some cream that needs to be used," Emma said. "I want you to churn it. You can get the butter churn down from the top shelf."

"Okay," Ervin agreed. He stood on a kitchen chair and pulled down the glass churn from a high shelf in the kitchen cabinet. Then he unscrewed the metal lid and waited as Emma poured three quarts of cream into the gallon container. After fastening the lid back on, he began to crank.

"I saw a chinchilla that looked sick," Emma told Ervin as he cranked the churn.

"I think it's too cold down there in the chinchilla house for them," Ervin said. "I have to wear a jacket when I feed them."

"They should be able to take a little cold," Emma said.

"They have thick fur. Besides, it's expensive to heat that basement."

A few minutes later she emerged from another room with papers in her hand. "I need a little help to do the taxes. You're the one who likes to use the adding machine."

"I can try," Ervin said, cranking vigorously. "But I don't understand all those tax forms. You may have to get Uncle Raymond to help you."

"We need to do it soon," Emma worried aloud. "I don't want to keep Uncle Ervin's adding machine too long. He needs it for his business." She paused. "Maybe I can take my tax papers up to Raymond's house while you grind some wheat for the chinchillas."

"That's fine with me," Ervin said as the sound of the churn changed from a solid stirring to a splashing sound.

"Hey, it's turning into butter!" he exclaimed soon afterward. "Another two minutes, and it will be done." The splashing sound gradually increased as the butter separated from the buttermilk. "*Do, es is faddich. Du kannscht's hawwe.* Here, it's done. You can have it."

Emma emptied the buttermilk into the slop bucket for the hogs and put the hunk of butter into a stainless-steel bowl. Ervin leaned over to watch for a few moments as she worked the buttermilk out of the butter with a wide wooden paddle.

A few minutes later, mother and son headed for Raymond's home. Raymond started up the wheat grinder and set the millstones at the proper tolerance to crack wheat. Then he beckoned Emma into the house while Ervin poured wheat into the hopper.

Raymond's family was so health-conscious that they ground all of their flour from their own certified wheat. Mary used only whole-wheat bread in her kitchen. Emma used whole-wheat flour as well, but she supplemented it with enriched flour from the grocery store for baking.

Some time back, Raymond had suggested that they grind wheat for the chinchillas as a substitute for the expensive feed from the manufacturers. It seemed to be a logical substitute. So far, it hadn't curbed the sickness that had plagued the animals for several weeks. But then, the prescribed medicine hadn't helped either. Each day that week, Emma listened anxiously as Ervin reported on the health of the chinchilla herd. Unless they could lick this problem, she would lose her investment.

Over the next two weeks, a number of chinchillas died. Although the family regularly put the recommended medicine in the water, they couldn't seem to stop the plague. They watched the herd carefully and separated the sick ones from the rest. On several occasions, they brought them into the house to nurse them back to health. Nothing seemed to help.

• • • •

In mid-February, when Erma arrived home from school, Emma told her, "It's Grandma Stutzman's birthday. I need you to help get things ready to take over there." Erma put on an apron and pulled out the ingredients for a cake and a batch of cookies.

When Ervin came into the kitchen, Emma asked him to make some ice cream with the new mixer the family had bought for her recent birthday. Ervin pulled a couple of large chunks of ice out of the chest deep freeze and put them into a gunny sack. Then he picked up a sledge hammer and whacked away at the chunks in the sack. Before long, the ice chunks were reduced to small pieces that would surround the canister in the hand-cranked freezer. He poured the ice around the canister, poured some salt on the ice, and began to crank.

As the smells of fresh-baked cookies rose from the counter, Ervin said, "Hey, I'll take one of those cookies."

"You can get one," Erma teased.

"I'm freezing the ice cream," he said. "I can't stop now."

"Okay," she conceded. She brought a cookie and laid it into his outstretched hand.

"Thank you," he said.

When the ice cream was done, Emma pulled the stirrer out of the ice-cream container and put it into a stainless-steel bowl. She scraped large portions off the stirrer and then handed it to Ervin. He grabbed it with eager hands, hurriedly licking the stirrer to beat the melting of the ice cream. Then Ervin poured the saltwater out the backdoor, taking care to avoid the spot where the gas pipe came near the house. The memory of the gas fire still loomed large in his mind.

The three of them loaded the ice cream and baked goods into the car and headed for Grandpa Stutzman's home.

It was a happy celebration. After the meal, Emma sidled up to Grandpa, who was chewing on a toothpick. "I was wondering if you could help Ervin to set up an electric fence tomorrow," she asked.

Grandpa blinked his eyes and stopped chewing on his pick for a moment. "I guess I could," he said. "What time would you need me?"

"I could come get you at 9:00 o'clock," she replied.

John nodded his head in silent assent.

The next morning, Emma picked up her father-in-law and watched as he joined Ervin to set up the electric fencer. Meanwhile, she sent Erma to burn the paper trash in the burn barrel out back.

Erma carried the two large wastebaskets from the house and dumped the contents into the fifty-gallon barrel, with vent holes slashed in the sides. Then she lit a match and held it to a piece of paper. She stood back as the fire consumed the lighter material. When it seemed safe to get close to the barrel, she stirred the fire with a stick, exposing unburned material to the flame.

When the men came in at noon, they reported that they had strung all of the electric wire and connected it to the new fencer. Now they could let her cow and a couple of calves graze on the young wheat on the north side of the shelterbelt. After the meal, Emma thanked her father-in-law for his work and took him back to his home.

Emma was pleased with their work. Nothing boosted the cow's milk production like grazing on young wheat plants. As long as the ground was not too soft, the cows could graze for several months without damaging the prospects for a good crop. The tender leaves kept growing like freshly mown grass. After April 1, if you wanted a wheat crop, you had to let the wheat grow without being grazed.

The wheat in the field was forming heads when Ervin announced that his friend Dave Hess from school had a Honda motorcycle for sale. Emma was dismayed when Perry showed strong interest.

"Mom, you don't understand," Perry assured her. "This is one of the smallest motorcycles they make—a Honda 90 cc. It's more like a scooter."

"Why do you need a motorcycle?" she asked, trying to calm the tremor in her voice.

"I need something to ride to work. I could park it inside Grandpa Stutzman's shop during the day. That will save me from having to park my '57 Chevy in the hot sun. The black paint gets so hot that I can hardly touch it."

Emma wasn't convinced, but Perry went ahead and bought it. At night, he parked it in the lean-to garage north of the barn.

It wasn't long before the news of Perry's purchase reached the ears of the ministers. They warned him that the matter should be brought to the fall council meeting. Perry wasn't happy to hear that, but he decided to keep the bike until he was told he had to sell it.

. . . .

As soon as school was over, Ervin returned to work on the farm for Willie Wagler. On the first evening he returned with good news: "Mom, Willie got another tractor. It's a 4010 John Deere. It's not brand new, but it's a lot better than that old Model G." Ervin obviously preferred a John Deere to a Minneapolis Moline.

Emma nodded in acknowledgment.

"He ordered a cab for it, too. I hoped it would have air conditioning, but it won't. It should be here by next week. I'm going to help put it on. That will help to keep the dust out when I work in the field."

Over the next few days, Emma sensed that Ervin was enjoying his work at Willie's home more than the previous year. The new tractor seemed to make a big difference. The spring had brought plenty of rain, so there were high hopes of a good wheat harvest.

The early weeks of June, however, delivered an unusual amount of rain. Some of the tall wheat began lodging, knocked to the ground by wind and rain. For a time it looked as though the harvest might be delayed, as it had been the previous year. The long spell of wet weather had stretched the 1967 wheat harvest into August, the longest harvest season in memory.

By the end of June, however, the weather turned hot and dry. It was perfect harvest weather. The machines moved through the fields from early morning till late at night. After church on Sunday, Emma overheard men in the anteroom talking about the harvest. No one could recall such a time of abundance in the wheat fields. Long lines of trucks waited at the grain elevators to unload their golden cargo.

The timely rains had nearly balanced the scales between those who irrigated their crops and those who did not. Most farmers reported yields of 40 bushels to the acre, with many getting 50 bushels or more. The good weather and the extraordinary yields were a bonanza for the custom wheat harvesters, who made their way from Texas to North Dakota each year. With earnings of $3.50 per acre, and 5 cents bonus per bushel on yields over 20 bushels per acre, they had never seen a better year.

The harvest brought only one note of sadness into Center Church. Some lamented that so few professing Christians let their threshing machines rest idle on the Sabbath. Even respected neighbors from the Partridge Community Church made their way into the fields on Sunday afternoon. It had not always been so. In earlier times, only those who did not profess Christian faith would have dared to show such a public disregard for the Lord's day.

Emma was grateful for the abundant wheat crop on her land. With her new Eaton bin, she didn't need to wait in line at the elevators. More important, she could wait to sell her wheat until Raymond advised her that the price was right. With a glut of wheat at harvesttime, prices were sure to take a dip.

Emma learned from Ervin that Willie irrigated much of his land and fertilized it generously. Unlike Raymond, Willie used popular commercial fertilizers, including anhydrous ammonia. Raymond was displeased that a fellow Christian— more, an ordained minister—applied the poisonous substance to the soil. Raymond told anyone who would listen that the use of anhydrous ammonia put excess nitrogen into the earth. It seeped into the groundwater, raising the percentage of nitrogen to dangerous levels. A test of Raymond's own well water showed enough nitrogen to cause the birth of blue babies, infants born with inadequate oxygen. He was convinced that the high level was caused by liquid fertilizer applied on adjoining farms. How could one who claimed to be God's steward pollute God's good earth that way?

Willie believed otherwise. He had no scruples about applying the product on all of his crops at planting time. Ervin explained to Emma that the handling of liquid fertilizer worked much the same way as butane for tractor fuel.

"Mom, you just have to wear a mask when you fill the tanks," Ervin said. "And you have to use gloves to make sure that you don't get the stuff on your bare hands. Once you have it in the tank on the chisel plow, you don't have to get close to it."

Emma shrugged her shoulders. What was she to know of such things?

Ervin continued. "I often get a whiff of it, though. The stuff smells terrible, like that ammonia in the plastic jug in the kitchen. Willie wants me to turn on the liquid gas sometimes when the chisel is out of the ground, so I can check to make sure that all of the tubes are open. If the wind is blowing in my direction, it really stinks. And I hate to dig the dirt out of the nozzles on the chisel points when they get stopped up with dirt or something."

Emma grimaced. It wasn't as though Willie didn't care about health. He was very health-conscious. Hadn't he insisted that a factor in her father's, Levi Nisly's, death was their household practice of cooking in aluminum pots? Willie and Alma insisted on using stainless steel. Emma cooked mostly in stainless-steel cookware as well, but she found it hard to believe that cooking in aluminum had contributed to her father's early demise.

Although Emma felt no need to stand in judgment of Willie's choices, she used the same fertilizer as Raymond. It was produced by Harlan Stubbs, Tobe's customer and friend from back in Kalona, Iowa. Stubbs branded it Veldonna, after his two daughters Velma and Donna. Raymond bragged that its "electrical balance" was best suited for the organic nature of the farm.

At Ervin's request, Willie agreed to loan his new tractor to plow Emma's wheat field. Emma watched with some excitement as Ervin pulled into the lane with Willie's 4010 John Deere pulling a four-bottom plow. This would make quick work of Emma's field. It was likely to take only half as long as it did with her John Deere D and the two-bottom plow. Emma watched with a twinkle in her eye as Perry joined Ervin to set off for the field in the late afternoon. They assured her that the tractor's lights made it possible to work into the night.

Emma was sleeping when they returned. At the sound of the diesel tractor in the yard, she glanced at the luminous hands on her alarm clock. It was 12:45 a.m. In the July moonlight, she could see her sons pull the rig around the back of the house. The smell of diesel exhaust drifted through her open bedroom window, along with the exuberant sounds of their voices.

"Boy, that went fast," Perry said.

"Yeah, a lot faster than when we used the D," Ervin agreed.

She heard the backdoor slam, and then the sound of the refrigerator door opening.

"I wonder what's here to eat," she heard Perry say.

"Maybe Mom will make us something," Ervin commented.

Emma blinked her eyes and swung her legs over the side of the bed. It wouldn't take long to fix something to reward them for their hard work. She straightened up her sleeping cap, shuffled into the kitchen, and blinked for a moment in the bright light.

"I can make some milk soup," she said.

"Good," Perry replied.

Emma quickly prepared broken pieces of homemade bread covered with strawberries and slices of canned peaches. She set the two heaping bowls on the dining room table and poured milk on top. The mother watched with silent satisfaction as her two sons bent over the food. They never seemed to tire of the simple fare.

Emma went to bed happy that Ervin and Perry had worked so well together. There were too many times when they were at cross-purposes with one another. Perry often played the role of a father, and Ervin resented it. He staved off Perry's advice with his sharp mind and quick tongue. She was disgusted with their arguments. Why couldn't they just get along with each other?

She mused, "It might not have been the ideal arrangement to have put them in the same double bed when Perry returned from voluntary service. At least they each have their own bed now. The house is simply too small for everyone to have a private bedroom." She drifted off to sleep with a prayer of thanks that things could go so well at times.

• • • •

A few months later, when Center Church asked for volunteers to help start a new outreach, Perry stepped up to help. In January 1969, the volunteers opened worship services in an abandoned church building north of the small town of Arlington. Perry agreed to serve as the primary song leader. The new center for worship would serve a number of current attendees who lived on the western edge of the church community, giving them a shorter distance to drive. Since the present building was often crowded, the new location would free up space for growth. The fellowship also hoped that a new location would be more likely to draw newcomers. In that sense it was a mission outreach.

When Perry started attending at the Arlington outreach, Emma wondered if this might be Perry's way of seeking fresh air. New churches on the edge of the community sometimes had less stringent rules than the mother church. At least that's the way it was in the outreach church in Arkansas. Mary Edna and Glenn had sought more-progressive congregations. Was Perry seeking more freedom as well?

Affiliation with the new congregation didn't insulate Perry from criticism when he traded in his '57 Chevy for a red '63 Chevy Impala. Emma was surprised at his choice of color. Didn't he realize that the church discipline warned against such bright colors? Or was he making up for his disappointment at needing to sell his motorcycle after the church council meeting last fall?

Emma kept her tongue as Perry defended his choice of color: "I bought the car under a cloudy sky, so I didn't really notice how bright it was." At the time, it seemed about the same hue as the dark red color of a fellow member's car. To Perry's knowledge, no one had approached the other person about his car.

Emma wasn't surprised to learn that Willie Wagler had spoken to Perry about the color of his car. "You're not taking that car back east, are you?" Willie asked.

Willie's question confirmed Perry's suspicions that part of the problem was the Center Church's reputation among stricter sister congregations in Indiana and Ohio. Since ministers were often judged by their ability to "keep house," Perry suspected that they were guarding their reputations by approaching him about his car.

Perry brought up the matter of the other person's car color. Wasn't it red, too?

"Well," Willie replied, "we hope he sells it soon."

Perry tried to show sympathy for Willie's concerns. "I don't want to be a stumbling block," he said. "What if I painted my car white? Would that be okay?"

His eyes widened at Willie's response: "The Bible says, 'Though your sins be as scarlet, they shall be as white as snow.'"

Perry could hardly believe his ears. Willie's playful interpretation of Isaiah's (1:18) prophecy had paved the way for him to have a white car, even though both colors were forbidden by the church discipline. A couple of weeks later, Perry came home with his car painted white.

Emma was pleased. This solution would not have worked just a few years earlier, but it brought peace now. That was the most important thing.

18

Holding On

"Mom," Ervin said to Emma as he prepared to go to school one day. "I need to do a welding project in my VoAg class. Would you like to have a loading chute?"

"How much would it cost?"

"Just the money for supplies. We can get them at a good price through the school."

After discussing the matter further, Emma gave him permission to proceed. The chute would be portable, functioning both as a trailer and a loading chute. She wouldn't need to borrow Raymond's trailer anymore. "At least one class in high school is practical," Emma thought.

"I'll let the teacher know," Ervin said as he and Erma headed for the bus.

Both of the twins were in high school now. Erma didn't really enjoy the studies, but she loved being with her friends. She enjoyed the home economics class and seemed to be benefiting from it as well. Emma noticed that she took greater interest in domestic tasks such as cooking and sewing.

That Saturday, Emma asked Erma to help her butcher chickens. "I promised Mary Edna that I'd bring chicken along for the meal tomorrow," she said. Emma made her way to the henhouse carrying a rusty number 10 paint can, pressed into service as an egg carrier. A layer of wheat straw in the can's bottom cushioned the eggs.

When Emma swung open the door of the small henhouse and switched on the overhead light, a few chickens flew wildly toward their nests.

"*Schicket eich. Schand eich.* Behave yourselves. Shame on you," she said with some disgust as she stepped toward the group of nests where the chickens were to lay their eggs. She laid the eggs gently into the can, counting them as she went. Glancing around, she spied an egg lying on the roost. She grimaced as she picked up the egg, soiled with droppings. "Why must chickens lay eggs outside the nest?"

She gathered only sixteen eggs, less than usual for the small flock of two dozen hens. It was time to cull out the ones that were no longer producing eggs. One by one, she reached for the chickens on the roost. With her left hand and arm, she cradled the hen against her chest. With two fingers of her right hand, she felt the bones below its tail. "This one's not laying anymore," she told herself after checking the third hen. With the bones so close together, it wasn't likely to be laying eggs.

Emma handed the chicken to Erma, who was now standing behind her. Emma found three more chickens to cull and then moved to the task of butchering them. Just outside the chicken house, a metal pipe hung suspended between two trees. Five loops of twine hung from the pipe, about a foot apart from each other. She took each of the four hens from Erma and looped one of the twines around their feet. Soon all four chickens hung quietly suspended by their feet. With quick dispatch, Emma moved to cut off their heads. She grabbed each one's head with her left hand and stretched out its neck, severing it with a swift stroke of the butcher knife in her right hand.

Mother and daughter stepped back as the four birds

flapped their wings, spraying blood in every direction. When all were still, Emma unfastened the twines and dipped the chickens into a bucket of scalding hot water she had heated on the stove. Erma joined her to pluck the feathers from the birds, pulling them in bunches and throwing them into a bucket. Next they took the naked birds into the house and held them over the open burner on the gas stove. It was the fastest way to make sure that the hair on the skin was removed. The smell of singed hair tinged the air as she rotated the birds over the flame.

Emma pulled out the pin feathers, scrubbed the skin of the birds, and doused them in cold water in the kitchen sink. She sharpened her knife and quickly cleaned the inside of the birds, saving the hearts, livers and gizzards. She put the rest of the intestines into the slop bucket. When she had finished with all four, she said, "Erma, take this slop to the hogs, please. And don't forget to pick up the heads and put them in too."

Erma nodded.

As Emma worked, she mused that the twins would soon be sixteen years old. Then they could join the church youth group and start dating. She worried that Erma might run into trouble, since her attractive figure and outgoing manner were already gaining several fellows' eager attention. One of the older boys had already asked her out. Perry, who still lived at home, had called the date to a halt and spoken to Emma about it.

"Did you hear that Jonas Bontrager asked Erma for a date?"

"No!" Emma reacted in disbelief. Jonas attended the Plainview church and drove a Chevelle Super Sport with a big engine.

"Yes, I told her that she wasn't allowed to date until she's sixteen."

"What did she say?"

"She said it was already planned and that Jonas was coming to pick her up. I told her that it didn't matter what they had planned. I wasn't going to let her leave the house."

Emma could hear Tobe's determination in Perry's voice. She thanked him for taking the initiative. She worried about Erma's sense of judgment. Didn't she realize how easy it was to get into trouble with the boys, especially older ones? She certainly didn't want Erma to be boy crazy, as some called it.

Yet Emma worried about Ervin's friendships too. He spoke of many new friends in high school, all outside Center Church. His after-school job on the O. J. Packebush farm also served as a conduit for connections to community youth.

The Packebushes had hired Ervin to help with chores after their son Randy crashed his motorcycle into the back of a school bus. During Randy's six weeks in traction and his ongoing recovery, Ervin had helped them with the evening chores. Even though Randy was better now, Ervin worked there evenings and Saturdays. Sometimes after the chores were finished, he and Randy drove around together. Emma hardly dared imagine where all they might be going. Randy had the reputation of being a wild driver. Randy drove a '57 Chevy. Now Ervin wanted one too. His birthday was only a few weeks away.

Emma looked out the window to watch Erma stroke a couple of kittens before she stepped into the house. "I'll finish these chickens if you want to do a little sewing for me," she told Erma. "I have the dress cut out and ready to go."

"Sure. I love to sew."

Emma pulled out the material and helped Erma get started before going back to the kitchen to finish the chickens.

"That's a relief," Emma thought to herself. Emma preferred to butcher rather than sew any day. Sewing was a duty to be performed, not a delight to be enjoyed.

Emma was pleased that Erma was planning to quit high

school after her first year, shortly after turning sixteen. She would be free to help around the house, assist her with cleaning jobs in town, or work at the Stutzman Greenhouse.

With Ervin, it was a different story. He was insisting that he be allowed to finish high school. When he explained that he could take all his courses in three years instead of the usual four, Emma agreed. She found it hard to understand why anyone would want to keep going to school when they could just as easily stay at home.

• • • •

A couple of weeks before Ervin's birthday, Emma bought him a black '57 Chevy for $400. It was a four-door sedan, not as sporty as the ones that Glenn and Perry had owned. But Ervin was happy. He started driving it to school each day. And he celebrated his sixteenth birthday by taking a car full of friends from high school to a coffeehouse in Hutchinson. It meant he had to miss attending the youth group at Center.

Emma felt some relief when Ervin joined the church youth group not long afterward. He took Erma along to the singing each Sunday evening and went to the occasional social gatherings.

It wasn't long before Erma was asked for a date, this time by a young man named Jim Toms. Erma knew Jim quite well since he hung around her uncle Raymond's farm. Jim was the one who had accidentally backed a tractor into Nevin Nisly's legs. It was a serious accident that had sent Nevin to the hospital for skin grafts and a long recovery.

Erma said she wasn't eager to go out with Jim but didn't want to risk the danger of refusing the first invitation to a date. Emma wasn't happy about it either. Jim was from the Plainview Church, the more-progressive church where Raymond's family attended. Though it wasn't uncommon for the two youth groups to spend time together, it was less common to date across those lines. Why were those boys so eager to date her daughter?

Emma was anxious all evening while Erma was gone. She hoped that Erma would keep her wits about her if the young man tried to do anything foolish. When Erma returned home, Emma was in bed.

Erma came to Emma's bedroom door, which stood slightly ajar. "Mom," she said, "you wouldn't believe what happened tonight." She giggled as she spoke.

Emma sat up in bed. "What happened?"

"Jim told me he wanted to go miniature golfing, but he wanted to take something over to his aunt's house first. So we stopped at her place."

Emma nodded in the dim light that came from the hallway.

"The thing he wanted to do was to pick up his parakeet. So he put the cage between me and the passenger door. I think he planned it that way so that I'd have to sit right next to him. He said that it needed to be on that side. Well, we're driving along, and guess what?"

Emma shrugged her shoulders.

"The parakeet got out of the cage. It started flying around inside the car. Jim said it was all right. He could catch it when we got there. Well, you know what happens when birds get excited. Mom, it landed on my shoulder and pooped right on my white sweater. I was so embarrassed."

"Oh my!" Emma exclaimed.

"We finally got rid of the bird. I cleaned the spot off my sweater as best I could. Then we went miniature golfing." Erma's face brightened. "I got back at him. I beat him so bad at golf. I hope he wasn't too upset. I think he was trying to beat me, but he couldn't."

Emma smiled. "So it turned out all right?"

"Yes," Erma said. "But I'm never going out with him again."

"Good," Emma thought. "Maybe she can start dating the boys from Center Church."

Emma's wish soon came true. One Sunday afternoon in December, the twins invited a number of friends from church to Emma's house. Emma watched with interest as they played Dutch Blitz, a card game she hadn't seen before. While the church forbade regular playing cards, this activity was accepted as a good pastime for youth. Designed for four players, the game depended partly on the luck of the draw but also on coordination and speed. Players did not take turns laying out cards. Rather, they tried to rid themselves of all their cards by placing them on numerical piles built during the fast-moving game. When placing a card, a split second sometimes made the difference between winners and losers. Emma giggled as she watched the youth immersed in the game, hands flying to place cards on piles.

Not long afterward, the twins arranged to go to the formal youth Christmas banquet with four friends who often played as partners in Dutch Blitz. The three couples decided to call the event a triple date. Erma was paired with Phillip Nisly, Ervin with Naomi Wagler, and Oren Yoder with Dolores Wagler. The Christmas banquet was the most formal youth event of the year.

Emma was pleased. She mused about how much fun it would have been if she and Tobe could have played such a game in their early courting years.

"It won't be long," she mused, "before the twins will be leaving home. Then I'll live all alone." Even now that the twins were attending the youth activities, Emma felt a new sense of freedom to pursue her own social activities on Sunday evenings. She found the most satisfaction in being with a group of single women. Some were widowed, others never married. What she liked most was the absence of the sense of awkwardness she sometimes felt around married couples. She felt companionship with others who lived without a husband. If it was God's will, she could be content to be single the rest of her life.

• • • •

Over the holidays, Emma didn't make her regular trips to town to clean houses. Instead, she enjoyed the time with both of the twins at home. But life returned to its normal rhythm the second week in January. As usual, she stopped to pick up her friend Sadie Mast on the way to clean houses in town. Sadie was a maiden lady from the Old Order Amish church who depended on Emma for a ride each week. Emma looked forward to their weekly conversations. Sadie's dry wit often prompted spontaneous laughter.

"I notice the schools are back in session," Sadie said as they started out. "A bus went past our house this morning."

"Yes, I wish Ervin would take the bus, but he thinks he needs to drive. It saves him some time if he can drive straight to work after school."

"Is he still working for O. J. Packebush?"

"Yes, he likes it there. Since Packebush used to run the Partridge Garage, he has interest in cars. Ervin was pretty tickled when he gave him some used tires for his car."

"I would think he would be," Sadie commented. "What is Erma finding to do now that she is not in school?"

"Today she's sewing a dress for me. You know I never liked sewing very much."

"I wish I had someone to sew my dresses," Sadie remarked. "I'm like you; I don't enjoy it that much. I'm glad for the people who do."

"Did you hear that my brother Raymonds are planning to move to Arkansas?" Emma asked.

"No. What are they going to do?"

"They're going to help with a little mission church at Calico Rock."

"I see. Might Raymond feel called to preach?"

"I believe he might. He's never been called through the lot at Plainview. But in the mission churches, people can volunteer. There's always a need for more workers."

"Who's going to take care of the farm while they're gone?"

"Paul Nisly—my nephew. That's Henry's Paul."

"I don't suppose it will be the same as having Raymond there."

"That's right. We depend on Raymond quite a bit. The twins will miss their children too."

Just then, Emma pulled up to the place where Sadie was to clean. Emma bid her goodbye and headed for the place she was to clean. As she went about her work that day, she reflected on Raymond's plans to move to Arkansas. It would seem very different to have them gone. Ever since she'd moved to Kansas, she'd relied on Raymond for counsel and for equipment to carry out tasks on the farm. It was a little worrisome to see them move away. On the other hand, she was feeling much more confident in making her own decisions than she once had. And Perry was close by to help when needed.

After cleaning two houses that day, Emma worked together with Sadie to clean a third. By 4:30 p.m., the two of them were finished with the joint venture. They split the pay and headed for the car.

"I wouldn't mind if we could stop for a few groceries," Sadie said.

"Yes, I'd like to stop at Dillons. I have some coupons I want to use."

"I have some coupons too."

Emma pulled into the parking lot at the grocery store just

as a John Deere tractor with an enclosed trailer was pulling out. The popping sound of the two-cylinder row-crop tractor seemed oddly out of place.

"It looks like your neighbor," Emma said.

"Yes, that's Abe Garver, with his wife in the trailer. I'm rather glad I don't have a husband who hauls me around that way. One time, she sat in there waiting so long that she finally got out of the trailer and asked him what he was waiting for. He said he was waiting for her. He didn't realize that she was inside the trailer."

Emma laughed as she parked the car. After a short time at Dillons, Emma said, "I'm going to go over to Smith's yet. I'll meet you back in the car."

Ten minutes later, Emma got back to the car.

"Did you find anything on special?"

"I got some ripe bananas that were real cheap," Emma commented. "I can use them to make slush for the children to drink. And I got some minced ham at half price—ends and small pieces." Emma put the car into gear and pulled out onto South Main.

"Would you mind if we stopped at Salvation Army yet?" Emma asked. "I'd like to see if they have anything there I might need." Emma always stayed alert for ways to cut costs, especially on household goods.

When Emma got home, she was pleased to find that Erma had finished her dress and had started supper. It was gratifying to see her pick up responsibility. Erma sometimes helped to clean houses in town as well, but sewing sometimes was more important. And it would soon be transplanting season at the Stutzman Greenhouse, where both Erma and she would work for a couple of months. Erma particularly enjoyed jobs where she could interact with people. Her quick smile and pleasant manner attracted friends wherever she went.

Ervin had many friends as well. During his last semester of school, Emma sensed that he was spending more time than ever with his friends at school, especially a sophomore named Pam Cox. One morning Ervin voiced the words she had hoped never to hear: "We're going steady," he said as he prepared to leave for school.

Emma's face fell. Ervin was repeating what Glenn had done—dating a town girl outside the church community. As Ervin was about to walk out the door, Emma went to her room and threw herself down beside the bed. She poured out a prayer of lament, pleading for a change in her son's heart. She prayed that his graduation from high school would bring an end to his interest in the young woman.

About the same time that Ervin started dating Pam, he told Emma that he was planning to attend the Yoder Mennonite Church. Emma did not think that Pam was interested in any church, but she did fear that the only reason Ervin had for going to Yoder Church was so that he'd have more freedom to date girls like Pam.

Then she mused that it could be for other reasons. She recalled Ervin's anger one Wednesday evening after the regular Bible study at Center. The ministers had announced their decision to break up an emerging women's group. The women's group had announced their intent to study the Scriptures, share prayer concerns, and pray together. The ministers gave two reasons for their decision. First, they felt that it was not appropriate for women to teach the Bible to adults, even other women. Second, they questioned the organizers' motives. Why were they exerting themselves in this way? Were they hoping to influence the spiritual direction in the congregation?

The ministers' reasoning was both traditional and familiar. For similar reasons, the stricter Amish preferred that laypeople not carry their Bibles to church or participate in study groups.

Without the supervision of ordained men, things could take an inappropriate turn. It made sense to Emma, so she hadn't objected.

But Ervin didn't seem to understand. "I can't believe they would do such a thing as that," Ervin yelled at Emma. "Whatever could be wrong with women wanting to study the Bible for themselves?" In his rant, he insisted that it was for such reasons that he was leaving to attend the Yoder Mennonite Church.

Emma had just listened. It didn't pay to argue with her son, although she didn't believe the ministers' decision was just cause for Ervin to leave the church.

Glenn and Miriam were attending the Yoder Church, too, having moved from the Plainview Church. Miriam liked it better, since it was more like her home congregation in Ohio. Emma had hoped that Ervin would follow in his brother Perry's steps rather than his brother Glenn's.

Emma spoke to the ministers about her concerns, particularly Ervin's relationship with Pam. They promised to speak to Ervin about it. A few days later, Preacher David L. Miller came to Emma's home to see Ervin. It was past 9:00 p.m.

Emma watched as Ervin climbed into the front seat of David's car. She could barely distinguish their form by the light of the moon. When Ervin returned to his room, she was in bed. She didn't dare to ask about the conversation, but hoped against hope that Ervin would at least end his relationship with Pam.

Ervin seemed pensive the next morning but said nothing about the conversation. Emma decided to let him bring up the matter in his own time. His graduation from Partridge High was only a few weeks away.

At Ervin's graduation ceremony, Emma felt pride mixed with worry. She noticed that along with a few others, Ervin wore a gold cord for achievement. She'd expected him to do do well. Studies had always been easy for him. Yet as she watched Ervin receive his diploma, she wondered if he would be satisfied with his high school education. Or might he want to go on to college?

As July turned to August, Ervin informed Emma that he was hoping to register for college in the fall semester. Norman Terrill, the high school guidance counselor, had spoken to him about a scholarship to Hutchinson Junior College, often called Juco. Norman had encouraged Ervin to enroll.

Emma was eager to have Ervin take up a job rather than go to school. She asked her brother-in-law Alvin if he might be willing to talk to Ervin about the problem. Emma feared that she wouldn't be able to withstand Ervin's persuasive ways by herself.

Alvin agreed to take up the challenge. He and his wife, Barbara, stopped by Emma's house one Sunday afternoon in late August. Emma called Ervin from his room. The four sat down in chairs at the dining room table.

"Your mother says that you have interest in going to college this fall," Alvin started out. "Is that correct?"

"Yes, I'd like to go," Ervin said. "Norman Terrill says that I can get a scholarship to go to Juco. He says I could be a teacher."

"We think it would be best if you could go to work now," Alvin said. "Your mother needs the income."

"But I can work after school," Ervin protested.

"She needs you to work full-time. You owe that to your mother," Alvin came back. "That's the way our people do it."

Emma looked down as she listened to Ervin's protest.

"But some of the others from our church went to college, like David Wagler. And Paul Nisly at Messiah College."

"Yes, but they waited until they were of age," Alvin replied. "If people want to go to college, they should do it on their own. Their parents shouldn't have to pay for it."

"You mean it's okay to go to college as long as you wait until you're twenty-one years old?" Ervin asked.

"It's certainly better that way. There are many temptations in college."

"But high school worked out okay for me."

"College is different. You need a good reason to go to college. When you're older, you know better whether or not you need college."

"But if I wait, I'll lose this scholarship."

"You can save up for school."

Emma glanced back and forth as the two carried on the debate.

Finally Ervin asked, "Are you saying that I'm not going to be able to go this fall?" He looked around in anger.

"That's what we believe is best for you," Alvin said.

Emma nodded silently.

Ervin stood up in disgust. "All right, then, I won't go to school if that's what you want."

Emma took a deep breath as she watched her son stalk to his room.

"Thank you," she said to Alvin and Barbara as they rose from their seats. "I'm glad that's settled." She sighed with relief as the Yoders got into their car and drove away. It was so good to have a man around the house when hard things needed to be said.

Shortly after Alvin and Barbara left, Ervin came out of his room. He wasn't ready to drop the matter. "Glenn and Perry spent money on guns and cars and things like that. I'd much rather spend money for school. If I can't go to school, I'll spend money on other things like cars."

Emma remained silent.

Ervin turned and went outside. Emma rose and looked out the kitchen window as her son headed for the garage.

When Migo came bounding toward him, he reached down and scratched the dog's ears. The dog's long tongue lolled in the August heat.

He knelt down by the cardboard box that served as the home for the five small pups that Migo had sired. His face relaxed as the young pups wagged their way onto his lap. After a few moments of holding the pups, Ervin took a walk up the road, with Migo panting at his side.

Emma watched him go. At least Ervin wasn't one to hold grudges. Taking a walk with the dog would help him get over his disappointment.

The next week, Glenn and Miriam dropped by for a few minutes after supper. Their two children begged to see the new puppies.

"You can't go outside by yourself," Miriam told the two girls. "It's not safe for you to be with Migo."

"I believe that Migo went up to Raymond's house with Ervin," Emma said. "He went up there to get something."

"Do you mean Paul's house?" Miriam asked.

"Well, yes, I mean Paul's house." It was hard for Emma to adjust to Raymond's absence now that he and his family were in Arkansas on a mission assignment.

Janet and Norma made their way outside into the warm evening sunlight, with Glenn and Miriam close behind. Emma glanced out the kitchen window. She could see the box that housed the five puppies. Misty, the canine mother, lay beside it with the puppies nuzzling at her nipples.

A few moments later, Emma heard a growl and a snap, followed by a scream. She ran to the door to see Glenn scooping two-year-old Norma into his arms. Blood dripped from her face.

"Migo bit her," Miriam screamed. "Let's go to the hospital."

Emma ran to get a towel. She wet it in the sink then ran outside to put it on the girl's face. Glenn handed the screaming girl to Miriam as they headed for their car.

Emma stood back as Glenn hurriedly backed out of the driveway. She watched with bated breath as Glenn gunned the engine while heading north on the gravel road.

"Keep them safe, Lord," she prayed as the car raced toward town. Her face was drawn.

A few minutes later, Perry and Ervin returned from the neighbor's house. "Mom, why was Glenn driving so fast?" Ervin asked. "He must have been going eighty miles an hour. Is something wrong?"

Emma looked sober. "Migo bit Norma in the face. I thought he was up there with you."

"He was, but he started fighting with Paul's dog, so Paul sent him home. Migo was quite upset."

"Norma was trying to pet the puppies. Migo snapped at her."

"How serious is it?"

"We don't know yet. Glenn is going to call when they're finished at the emergency room."

Later that evening, the phone rang. Emma eagerly reached for the receiver. "Hello."

"Mom, it looks like Norma is going to be okay. But the doctor put forty-five stitches in her face."

Emma grimaced.

"Migo must have bitten her twice 'cause she has four sets of teeth marks on her face."

"Did the doctor say anything about rabies?"

"Yes, he said we have to keep the dog tied for a couple of weeks to make sure that he doesn't have rabies."

Emma motioned to Ervin. "Go tie up Migo. We have to see if he has rabies."

"What's going to happen to him?" Ervin asked in a worried tone.

"We'll see. If he has rabies, Norma will have to get shots."

Ervin's face dropped. "Come, you naughty dog," he called as he stepped outside. Emma watched out the open window as Ervin got hold of the dog's collar and fastened his collar to a chain. He had a worried look on his face.

Two weeks later, while Ervin was at work, Glenn dropped by Emma's house. He was carrying his .22 caliber rifle. "I guess you know what we need to do with Migo," he said. "Perry was willing to do it, but I told him I'm the one who got the dog and he bit my child."

Emma nodded. She watched out the kitchen window as Glenn untied the dog and led him by the collar into the corn field north of the house.

Emma grimaced as she heard a single shot. Ervin was going to miss his dog. But what else were they to do? The safety of others had to come first.

Emma was grateful that the older boys were available to do some of the hard things around the house. Perry wasn't going to be around home much longer, she reminded herself, since he was buying his own place. He seemed eager to settle down.

Perry had signed an agreement to buy thirty-nine acres with farm buildings from the Henry Schrock family, who was planning to move to Minnesota. The farmhouse was a bit small for the Schrock's family of six, but it would be a good place for Perry to set up housekeeping. The Schrock farm had rich black soil. The wooden barn and outbuildings needed paint, but Perry would get around to that in due time. When the farm sale was held in November, he would have the opportunity to buy some of the farm implements.

Perry had called off the relationship with Dorothy Wingard some time earlier. She spoke of eagerness to work as a missionary nurse; he hoped to settle close to home to be able to help Emma when needed. Now Perry was going steady with Judith, the oldest daughter of Melvin and Fannie Nisly. Perry was nearly eight years older then Judith, who was not yet twenty years of age. Emma suspected that age difference was the only reason for delaying an engagement. Although they hadn't been dating long, Emma suspected that the couple would get married shortly after Judith's next birthday.

The Schrock farm sale took place on November 6 as planned, so Emma dropped by to watch the proceedings. She was proud that Perry had managed his money so well that he was able to buy the land. Unlike his father, Tobe, Perry exercised caution in all his purchases. He was quick to save and slow to borrow money.

Emma joined the circle of people standing around the auctioneer as he called for bids on a farm disk. She glanced at Perry, who was absorbed in the action. Unlike his father, he thoroughly enjoyed auctions.

"What am I bid for the disk?" the auctioneer cried. "Seventy-five, seventy-five, who'll bid me seventy-five?"

Two hands went up.

"I've got seventy-five, who'll give me eighty-five? Eighty-five, eighty-five, eighty-five?"

Emma turned and made her way toward the food stand, where Mrs. Schrock was standing. She frowned as she recalled that Migo had bitten Lizzie's daughter Mildred some time earlier. The children had been playing in Emma's yard after dinner on a Sunday afternoon. It hadn't been as serious as Norma's injury. Nevertheless, the nip on the young girl's leg had taken a few stitches. "Perhaps we should have gotten rid of Migo then," Emma thought. "But I remember Mildred's father saying that we shouldn't get rid of the dog just yet."

"How is Norma doing?" Lizzie asked in her gracious way.

"Norma is healing slowly," Emma said. "Miriam puts salve on her face every day to keep the skin soft. But she will probably have scars for the rest of her life."

"Oh, I'm sorry to hear that."

"And I'm so sorry that Migo bit your daughter. We just didn't realize that he was so apt to bite children."

"We understand."

Emma chatted with Lizzie for a few more moments. After excusing herself, she sidled up to her sister Barbara, who was looking over some of the household items for sale.

"I see that Perry is bidding in the auction," Barbara said.

"Yes, he was hoping to get a few farm implements. He won't have to move them."

"Now all he needs is a wife," Barbara grinned. "I hear he's dating Judith Nisly. I believe she'd make a good wife for him."

"Yes, I believe so." Emma's face showed her satisfaction.

Nearly four months later, Perry and Judith publicly announced their engagement to a gathering of youth at a pop-corn shelling. Perry began to prepare in earnest to take up farming on the property he had purchased.

Later, according to custom, their wedding date was announced in the church service at the Center Church. Although Perry usually attended the church near Arlington, that service was canceled due to heavy snow that had not yet been removed from the parking lot. After the church service, the couple joined Emma for dinner.

"We had quite the attendance at Center today," Judith observed as they washed the dishes after dinner. "Not having services at Arlington makes a difference."

"It was a good day to announce your wedding date," Emma commented. "A lot of people were there to hear it."

"Yes," Judith agreed. "When were you able to get out of your driveway this week?"

"The caterpillar went through here on Wednesday evening. Ervin borrowed Raymond's tractor from Paul Nisly and got the lane cleared out on Thursday morning. So I did my cleaning in town on Friday like usual. Ervin and I were the only ones at home for several days. He was working on his car, so he didn't mind being snowed in. He borrowed a space heater from Fred Yutzy so he could stay warm in the shed. He helped me figure the taxes, too."

Erma spoke up. "I was at Ralph and Virginia's house all week. I didn't come home on Wednesday night like usual. The service was canceled."

"What all do you do for the Hedricks?" Judith asked. "I know she had polio, but I don't know what kind of help she needs."

"I do just about everything that a woman of the house would usually do. Virginia really can't do any of the housework by herself. But she does have strong opinions about how it should be done."

Judith laughed. "She's like me. I know how I like things done."

"Yeah," Erma said, "she tells me what groceries to buy, what recipes to cook, how much water to put in the bucket, how much soap to put in the water—those kinds of things. She pretty much looks over my shoulder all the time."

"I think that would make me feel *griwwlich*, creepy" Judith said with an exaggerated shiver.

"That's not the hardest thing, though," Erma said. "The thing I hate the most is the suction machine. Because she had polio, she can't cough. She has a tracheotomy, so I use a machine to suction out her lungs. It's a little gross, but it has to be done."

"Can she feed herself?"

"Yes, she puts her forearm into a special thingamajig that she clamps onto the table. That way she can use her shoulder to push her arm down and swing her hand up toward her mouth. It looks strange, but it works." Erma demonstrated with her arms as she talked.

"Ralph must be pretty patient."

"Oh, he is. He works two jobs to support her and pay for a helper."

"He does?"

"Ralph's a mail carrier for his main job. He gets up early in the morning to deliver the mail. In the afternoon or evening, he tunes pianos."

Judith watched as Emma wrapped the leftover bread in a plastic bag.

"I really liked your bread, Emma," she said. "Perry said that you baked it."

Emma smiled broadly. "Yes, I started using everlasting yeast. That way I don't have to buy yeast every time."

"How does it work?"

"You have to get some live yeast in a bit of dough from somebody. You put the *Deegich*, doughy starter, in the refrigerator. Whenever I want to bake bread, I get out the *Deegich* and tear off a lump to mix it with my other ingredients. Some people say it tastes a little more yeasty than regular bread."

"I like it that way."

Erma washed the last dish and pulled the strainer in the sink to let the water out. As she opened the door to dump her food scraps into the slop bucket, she could hear the waste water gurgling through the drain in the washroom.

Judith dumped the pan full of rinse water down the drain in the kitchen sink and wiped her hands on the small towel hanging on the cabinet door pull. Then they all moved into the living room. Perry was snoozing in the armchair. Ervin was warming himself at the propane heater that stood in the living room. He sat against the front and top, the porcelain grill bending under his weight.

Perry opened his eyes as Judith walked by his chair. Emma smiled as Judith brushed Perry's cheek with her hand and then sat in the chair next to his. She would make a good wife for Perry. Judith spoke forthrightly about her opinions and feelings, but in a deferential way. Emma looked forward to having her as a daughter-in-law.

19

Letting Go

Perry and Judith got married two weeks later, just before Perry's twenty-eighth birthday. Although Perry moved into the farmhouse on his own place, he promised Emma that he could assist with farming her forty acres as well. He hoped eventually to have enough acreage to be a full-time farmer. He also worked for Stutzman's Refuse Disposal as a truck driver.

Now that Ervin was out of high school, he worked for the Stutzman's Disposal as well, driving the truck for recycling cardboard and assisting his brother Perry on occasion. What he enjoyed most, however, was to work on cars. By hanging around with guys who worked on their own cars, he soon got the knack for mechanical work.

In the summer of 1971, Ervin tackled a complete engine overhaul on his '57 Chevy. With his uncle L. Perry's permission, he used the engine lift and other tools at the Stutzman's maintenance shed. He parked his car just outside the shop while working on the engine inside the shop. One day while it was parked there, L. Perry painted the truck bed of his large packer truck in the driveway. Although there was only a slight breeze outside, it carried particles of white paint spray onto Ervin's parked car. He came home from work to find tiny dots of white paint covering his black car.

"I don't mind," Ervin told Emma when he got home that evening. "I was hoping to repaint the car anyhow."

Meanwhile, Ervin agreed to overhaul the engine in Alvin Yoder's 1964 Chevy. Emma watched with approval as Ervin pulled the V-8 engine and disassembled it in the backyard. She observed with pleasure that Ervin had Tobe's can-do attitude as well as his ability to figure out how things worked. She didn't mind that Ervin got a lot of grease on his overalls. The ability to work on engines was a practical skill. A good mechanic could always find a job.

Emma was pleased, too, that Ervin seemed to be doing well at the Yoder Church. In spite of her disappointment that he had left Center, she was grateful for his growing involvement in the new youth group. He'd broken off his relationship with Pam and no longer spent much time talking about his old high school friends.

Late one Saturday afternoon as Emma was pulling a pan of freshly baked bread out of the oven, she heard the revving of an engine in the driveway. She looked up to see an older model car rumble past the kitchen window. Emma glanced out the east window and watched as the car came to a stop. Two young men got out of the car. One was LaVern Yutzy, Ervin's cousin and friend from the Yoder Mennonite church. The driver was a stranger.

The gentle breeze pushed the light curtains against her face as she stepped closer to the window. "Hi, Ervin," she heard LaVern say as her son stepped out of the garage. "This is my friend Dennis Ediger. I met him at Juco."

"Hi, Dennis," Ervin said, extending his hand.

"That's a nice car. What model is it?"

"A '39 Pontiac."

"What engine do you have?"

"A 327 Chevy."

Emma watched as Ervin stroked the rounded front fender. "May I open the hood?"

"Sure." Dennis opened the hood, and the three of them looked into the engine compartment. After some animated conversation, they closed the hood and walked around the car. The dark green paint glinted where the sunlight shone through the leaves of the tall elm trees.

"We came to see if you might help us do some work on the car," Dennis said.

"Sure. What do you need?" Ervin replied with enthusiasm.

"I need to change the third member on the drive train. The rear axle came out of a car with a three-speed tranny, so the ratio is wrong." "Tranny" meant "transmission."

"I'll trade you mine, since I went from an automatic to a four-speed transmission in my '57 Chevy."

After LaVern and his friend rumbled out of the lane, Ervin came in for a drink of spearmint tea. He poured himself a glass and helped himself to the oatmeal cookies Emma had baked earlier in the day.

"I'd love to have an old car like that," Ervin said as he munched.

Emma's shoulders dropped. "Wouldn't it take a lot of work?"

"I could do the work myself," Ervin said as he popped a second cookie into his mouth and moved toward the door.

Emma watched as he headed toward the lean-to garage he and Glenn had built onto the side of the barn. She hoped he'd abandon that idea soon.

• • • •

It was summertime, the season for family gatherings, when Emma and Erma set out to can peaches with Mother Nisly's assistance.

357

"I'm looking forward to the Dan Nisly reunion," Emma said as she picked several handfuls of overly ripe peaches out of the bushel basket and put them in a stainless-steel pan on the table. Mother, daughter and grandmother pulled their chairs up to the table and began preparing peaches for canning.

"I am, too. But this year we'll be missing one who would usually be here."

"Which one is that?" Erma asked as she cut the pit out of a particularly large peach.

"My uncle Fred Nisly from Iowa," Emma replied. "Remember, he died last October. My dad was the oldest of that family. Fred was next to youngest in the family. There were nine children in all. Four are still living."

"Do I know them?"

"Of course you do: Ed Nisly, Menno Lizzie, Junior Dan, and Jake Edna."

"I didn't realize we were related to them."

Emma gave a knowing nod to her mother. "That's why we need reunions, isn't it?"

"Yes," Mother Nisly replied. "And that's why we need a book like Clara Nisly just put out."

"Yes, I just got my copy," Emma said. "Here, Erma, I'll show it to you." She wiped her hands on her apron and went to the living room. "It's called *Family Record of Abraham C. Nisly and His Descendants*. Abraham was my great-grandfather." She held out the book for Erma to see.

"Maybe you could show Erma who Dan Nisly's family was," Mother Nisly suggested.

Emma thumbed through the pages. "Here it is—Daniel A. Nisly, Family No. 173. It says he married Elizabeth Mast and it lists their nine children. Then it says, "Elizabeth, three of her daughters, and one son—Rebecca, Emma, Clara, and Fred—died of cancer."

"They had a daughter Emma?"

"Yes, she was my aunt. I'm named after her. Right, Grandma?"

"Yes."

"Do I know her?"

"No, she died young."

"It's really sad that four people in that family died of cancer."

"Yes, Fred was the latest one to go. He did live to be sixty years old, though."

"I think I heard someone say that he thought God was going to heal him," Erma reflected.

"Yes, some of the people from one of the Pentecostal churches felt that if he had enough faith, God would heal him. He ended up joining that church, but it didn't help," Mother Nisly said with sadness in her voice.

Since Fred had been a preacher in the Amish church, Emma imagined that the congregation must have felt somewhat abandoned by his leaving. His wife Katie also felt the tension, since she had chosen to remain loyal to the Amish church. Had the Amish church been more adaptable to new ways, Emma mused, perhaps Fred and several of his children wouldn't have felt the need to join Church of the Living Word. Fred had always been a spiritual man who longed to make changes in the Amish church. She knew her sister Elizabeth, along with her husband John Bender, claimed to enjoy a greater spiritual depth in teaching than was available in the Amish church in the Kalona area. So were a number of other members of the charismatic fellowship who had once worshipped in Amish and Mennonite churches.

From the scuttlebutt in the neighborhood, Emma knew some thought of the Church of the Living Word as a cult. The minister, Bob Stevens, had come from California. He claimed special revelations from God to help people get ready for the end times. The church stored up food against possible shortages in a time of war and prepared to live in a fort-like structure.

Mother Nisly paused, held up a peach and said, "Now this one's pretty soft. Maybe we should put it aside to eat rather than canning it."

"Yes, we'll use it for milk soup tonight," Emma agreed. "Just put it in this container over here."

"Did you hear that they're going to have Dan Nisly's old meat box at the reunion? And his wooden churn too."

"What's a meat box?" Erma asked.

"It's the wooden box that grandpa used when he peddled meat in Hutch. In the winter, he sold meat from house to house in Hutch. He made a good living with that."

"Levi and I did a lot of that too," Mother Nisly said to Erma. "Your mom helped butcher a lot of hogs, both for Grandpa Dans and for us."

Emma pushed back her chair. "I'm going to start making the syrup," she said. She moved toward the stove and started heating up the water in a stainless-steel kettle.

When all of the peaches were cooling in jars, Emma took Mother Nisly home. Then she sat down to read the latest copy of the *Calvary Messenger*. It was a new magazine produced by the Beachy Amish church. As she paged through the journal, her eyes lit on a short article by Marie Billington entitled "The Christian Salutation." The writer began by listing the five scriptural references to the Christian kiss of greeting. Then she explained the importance of this greeting.

"There are many excuses afloat trying to bypass this command," Emma read. "Even the small things are important, if we expect God's blessings." She commented, "It's sad to see that many church groups neglect the Christian salutation. To me this is a serious matter. Isn't it dangerous to neglect any of God's commandments, or to perhaps limit it to Sunday morning?"

Emma nodded. To be a Christian certainly implied a willingness to follow all of the commandments in the Bible, including women's wearing of the prayer covering and greeting one another with a holy kiss. As Marie expressed it, "Where Christian people 'love one another with a pure heart fervently,' it is only natural for them to 'salute one another with a holy kiss.'"

Emma was grateful that a new Christian in one of the mission churches could so clearly instruct others in the way of Christian love. Perhaps because she had joined the Arkansas mission church as an "outsider," she could see the truth more clearly.

• • • •

Since Erma was staying at the Hedrick's home, Emma occasionally asked Ervin to help get the braids started in her long hair. "Mom, you're getting kinda gray," Ervin commented as he parted her hair and started to braid it on one side."

"I know. I'm fifty-five years old."

Ervin paused for a moment. "Mom, I found just the car that I would like to buy."

"What's that?"

"Do you remember that red '40 Chevy that we borrowed to drive from Perry and Judith's wedding to the reception?"

"Yes."

"Andrew Miller owns it, but he's living in Washington, D.C. I think he'd sell it for a couple hundred dollars."

By the time Emma was finishing braiding her hair, she'd agreed to arrange for the purchase through Andrew's mother. The old car was stored at her home.

Ervin towed the car home and kept it in the lean-to garage.

Using nearly every spare moment after his day job as a welder at Murray Manufacturing, he converted the old Chevy into a street rod. At the end of several months, it was ready for the road with a V-8 engine, a new drive train, and a newly stitched interior, which included bucket seats.

Meanwhile, Ervin's friend LaVern Yutzy bought the '39 Pontiac he'd earlier shown Ervin. Emma sighed as she watched Ervin and LaVern drive their two street rods down the road together. At least they weren't skipping out on church activities to work on their cars.

As though to defy Emma's worries, both Ervin and LaVern soon got so involved in church activities that their interest in cars took second place. At the invitation of a church in Hutchinson, the pair moved into an apartment in South Hutchinson as part of an outreach program. The Belfry, so called because it was located in an abandoned church building with a bell tower, was an outreach to youth. Ervin and LaVern helped to staff the center in return for free rent. Several nights a week, the building was open for youth to play pool, ping-pong, basketball, and other games. Once a week, Ervin taught a Bible study for youth. Emma couldn't have been more pleased.

• • • •

The following May, following LaVern's graduation from Juco, the two young men packed their things into a little camper for a trip to the west coast. Emma watched with a bit of worry as Ervin got into the driver's seat. As she walked slowly into the house, she breathed a prayer for protection.

Two days later, she got a call from Susan Yutzy, LaVern's mother. "I just wanted you to know that the boys got to Oregon safely," Susan said. "LaVern called to say that they had arrived at about 7:00 in the morning. They drove straight through without stopping except for gas—thirty-two hours."

"They must have been really tired."

"They took turns sleeping and driving," Susan said. "LaVern said they plan to go up to Portland this weekend for the Bill Gothard Seminar."

"Yes, that's what Ervin told me. I feel like the one in Kansas City really helped Ervin. I know that Ervin is more respectful of me now."

"Oh, I think it helped LaVern, too. He and Ervin are memorizing parts of the Bible together. The youth group is memorizing the book of James."

"Ervin is memorizing Matthew. He reminds me of Mary Edna. She used to memorize so many Bible verses."

"That's true of LaVern too. I was so glad they helped at the Bill Glass crusade last fall. Now they're thinking about going to Bible school someday."

• • • •

As the sun rose on New Year's Day, 1973, Emma glanced into Ervin's empty bedroom. He was gone to Rosedale Bible Institute, the first day of two six-week terms. She glanced at the books on the stand beside Ervin's bed. Her eyes lit on the hardbound red diary dated 1967. She opened the diary to the page where Ervin had made his first entry. She noted that he had crossed out 1967 and replaced it with 1968. He had also crossed out "Sunday" and replaced it with "Monday." "He must have found it in the trash and used it a year later," she thought.

Emma's eyes were drawn to Ervin's first entry. "We went down to Menno's in Perry's car and traded back for unsatisfactory chinchillas at Harvey Crabels." She sat on the bed and leaned back. "Yes, I remember that day. Has it been five years already? My, how time has flown."

Emma still wasn't happy with the chinchillas. They still were not doing well. The herd had never multiplied the way the salesman had claimed it would. Hers wasn't the only herd with problems. Menno Nisly was having trouble with his herd, too. If Menno couldn't make it work with all his business experience, how was she to manage?

She glanced at the rest of Ervin's diary page. The bottom half was blank. Surely he wouldn't mind if she made an entry of her own. It would be a shame to let all of that good paper go to waste. She sat down at Ervin's desk and began to write. First she jotted the date, "Monday, '73." Then she wrote, "I worked for Mrs. Hockaday before I came home, since I stayed there for the night."

That evening as Emma was tending the chinchillas, she mused about what it would be like when both Ervin and Erma would leave home. In just a little over a year, they would turn twenty-one and be of age. Then she'd need to manage the chinchilla herd alone. She flirted with the thought of selling them.

Her resolve to part with the herd grew after Erma left for a few weeks of Bible school in Calico Rock, Arkansas. With Ervin in Ohio and Erma in Arkansas, Emma needed to care for them by herself.

• • • •

Emma watched as an unfamiliar car pulled into the yard. It came to a stop under the shady elm trees at the end of the front sidewalk. A young man got out of the driver's seat and came around to the passenger side. Erma got out of the front seat when he opened the door. The two of them strolled toward the house. The young man was about the same height as Erma. His thin blond hair was combed back over his head.

Erma introduced the young man as Ray Zook, a young man she'd met at the Calvary Bible school in Arkansas. After a brief welcome, Emma watched them walk hand in hand around the small farmyard, pausing here and there to talk. She was eager to learn more about the young man with a quiet manner and a wide smile.

Ray stayed for a couple days. Just before he left for Pennsylvania, Emma recalled that she'd met Ray's parents, Amos and Linda Zook, in a visit they'd made to Kansas. Their daughter Marie had served alongside Perry at Hillcrest Home. She had been impressed by Ray's mother, who seemed so kind and friendly.

"Mom, what do you think of Ray? Do you think we make a good couple?" Erma asked when Ray had gone. Emma sensed the eagerness in Erma's question.

"He doesn't say too much, does he?"

"No, he's a good listener. He's a little shy when you first get to know him."

"You think he'd want to live here someday?"

"I think so. I'd like to visit his place in Pennsylvania this summer."

"How would you get there?" Emma asked.

"I'm sure there'll be other young people driving that way sometime. I could get a ride."

"Maybe it would be good to write each other for awhile first. It's good sometimes to be apart for a little while to see if you still like each other."

"I'd still like to go to Pennsylvania to see him sometime."

"We'll see. Maybe it can work out."

• • • •

When Ervin arrived home from Rosedale Bible Institute, he announced that he had a special friend as well. The young woman named Bonnie Haldeman was from Pennsylvania, less than an hour's drive from Ray Zook's house. Like Erma, Ervin hoped to spend part of the summer in Pennsylvania.

Emma agreed that if they caught up with some of the work around the house and yard, they might leave by June.

During the month of May, Erma worked at the Stutzman Greenhouse while Ervin worked around home. At Raymond's suggestion, Ervin put a coating of preservative on the wooden shingles of Emma's house. He also painted the house and enclosed the main garden with a wooden fence. It seemed a bit extravagant to build a fence mostly for looks, but Emma was quite pleased with the results when it was finished.

At the end of May, Emma agreed to let the twins spend the summer in Pennsylvania. She reminded them, however, that they must send their paychecks home. Emma asked Ray's father, Amos Zook, if Ervin could stay at their home. Amos said it would be alright as long as Ervin didn't mind sleeping with Ray in a double bed. He also agreed to let Ervin work on his construction crew. Emma was happy about the arrangement. It could be a good influence for Ervin, and he would get to know the Zook family.

Erma made plans to stay with a friend, confident that she could find work as a waitress. Restaurants in the Lancaster, Pennsylvania, area were busy with tourists in the summertime.

Emma bid the twins goodbye with the usual handshake and then watched as they got into the car and headed south on the gravel road. She took a deep breath and breathed a prayer for their protection as they disappeared from view. It bothered her to think that both Ervin and Erma might soon choose to live in Pennsylvania. She hoped that their eventual marriage partners would be content to live in the Hutchinson area.

The first weeks with the twins gone seemed to drag by. The house felt empty. Emma didn't enjoy eating alone. She relished the times each week when she ate with friends at the Dutch Kitchen, the new restaurant next to the Stutzman Greenhouse. In return for cleaning up after closing hours, she got her choice of entrée from the menu along with occasional leftovers.

Even though there were fewer people to eat meals at home, Emma kept cultivating a big garden. She loved to till the soil, and there were plenty of people ready to receive her produce. On her trips to town, she often dropped off fresh produce at a private home for the handicapped, or shared it with the people for whom she cleaned.

In the meantime, she finally got rid of her chinchillas. After years of tending them with little return, she had never been able to make a profit. Raymond helped her to find a place for them.

Emma hoped that the children would write occasionally. They clearly weren't minded to write the way she did. Besides regular correspondence with friends, Emma kept four circle letters going. The first circle included her mother and all of her siblings. The second one was the widows' friendship letter. The third was the Arbanna letter, which circulated among the friends who'd taught with her at the vacation Bible school in Arkansas. And the fourth was a letter that circulated among a number of women who were her first cousins.

Erma did write to say that she had gotten a job at Good and Plenty. It was a restaurant not far from Route 30, the main highway running through Lancaster city. A lot of Amish girls worked there, Erma said, but they didn't leave a good witness. The Lancaster Amish smoked, danced, and caroused in ways that would not have been allowed in Kansas.

She also wrote about the good times that she was having with Ray. Emma sensed that they were on their way to marriage and anticipated that they would announce an engagement by the end of the year.

Ervin called from Amos Zook's home one evening to announce that he had been invited to Camp Swatara as a camp counselor for junior high boys. It was a Church of the

Brethren camp, Ervin told her. His friend Bonnie was invited to work in the kitchen and help with the junior high girls. He could stay at the Haldeman house on weekends. The invitation meant, of course, that he would need to leave the construction job with Zooks. Amos was supportive of the idea, since the work crew had less work than usual that summer.

Emma agreed that it would be a good experience for him. She sensed that his relationship with Bonnie was also headed for an engagement.

Her hunch was strengthened when Ervin called home in late July to ask if it would be okay to bring Bonnie back to Kansas with him to stay for awhile. With Emma's approval, they worked out an agreement whereby Bonnie could take up the role that Erma had left at the Hedricks. Erma, when she returned to Kansas, would pursue a job that allowed her more freedom in evenings and on weekends.

Emma was hoeing in the garden when Ervin and Bonnie drove into the yard. Ervin parked under the shade of a tree in the backyard. Emma watched with eager eyes as Bonnie got out of the car and walked toward the house.

"What a long dress," Emma thought to herself. Bonnie's highly patterned maxi-dress swished around her ankles in the Kansas breeze. Her long straight brown hair was gathered by a scarf and hung nearly to her waist.

After a brief greeting, Emma invited them to take seats at the table for refreshment.

"I'm just as happy to stand," Bonnie said. "I've been sitting for a long time. This is a long way from Pennsylvania. I've driven it before, though. My brother Barry married a girl named Colleen from Quinter, Kansas."

"Did you drive there often?"

"Just once. To the wedding. Barry and Colleen go to Kansas pretty often, though. Her family lives there."

After chatting for awhile, Ervin suggested to Bonnie, "Let's go for a walk. I want to show you around here." A few minutes later, when everything was unpacked from the car, Emma watched as the two of them took a walk up toward Raymond's house. The sun was dropping on the horizon and a gentle breeze stirred the leaves in the elm trees. It was a lovely time to enjoy the beauty of the prairie.

Later, when the couple returned, Ervin was grinning, "You wouldn't believe what happened to Bonnie. A big grasshopper jumped up under her dress. It couldn't get out," he told his mother.

"I hate grasshoppers!" Bonnie exclaimed. "It was a big one, too. I finally squeezed it through my dress."

Ervin laughed. "We have lots of grasshoppers in Kansas. You'll have to get used to them."

"Well, I don't like them. They can just stay out from under my dress."

"I wouldn't want them under my dress either," Emma sympathized. But it wouldn't have happened, she reflected to herself, if Bonnie had been wearing a knee-length dress.

The next morning, Emma was pleasantly surprised when Bonnie volunteered to help in the kitchen. She cleaned up after the meal and then offered to help Emma clean the shelves in the cupboards. Bonnie worked most of the morning, scrubbing the cabinets and cleaning up the counter. Emma was thrilled that Ervin had befriended such an industrious young woman. It seemed to bode well for their relationship.

"I'll be doing some wash this afternoon," Emma said to Bonnie at noon. "Do you have things you want me to wash?"

"Yes, I have some things from the trip."

"I can hang it up for you," Bonnie said when Emma finished the first load of wash.

"We'll need to wash the lines off first. They get dusty here in Kansas."

Bonnie picked up the wash basket full of wet clothing and followed Emma to the front of the house.

Emma took a damp cloth in each hand, gripped one wash line wire with each hand, and walked the full length of the lines. On the return, she cleaned the other two wires. "There you are," she said. "Now you can start hanging clothes."

"They should dry really fast in this weather," Bonnie said. "It's so hot and dry."

"Oh, yes. It should only take about fifteen minutes."

"I'm amazed," Bonnie said to Emma after hanging up the first batch. "By the time I got everything hung up, the first pieces were almost dry."

"That's Kansas for you," Emma said. She went back to scrubbing a grease stain on Ervin's coveralls. "He's like his dad," Emma said aloud. "Men just don't think about keeping their clothing clean."

About a week later, Ervin appeared at the door as Emma swished the wash in the rinse tub. She nodded a greeting.

Ervin stepped up close and watched her rinse the wash. "Ervin doesn't usually stand still that long," Emma thought as she ran the wet clothing through the wringer. "He must have something on his mind." She looked up with expectancy.

"Bonnie and I would like to get married," Ervin said. "What would you think about that?"

Emma smiled broadly. "I think that would be just fine."

"When do you think would be a good time to have the wedding?"

Emma thought for a minute and then said, "How about next February? About six months from now."

Ervin paused. "I was thinking that we should wait until I turn twenty-one. That won't be until the end of April. Maybe I could make it on my birthday."

"It would be fine to get married on your birthday."

"Thanks, Mom. Bonnie and I will talk about it and decide."

Emma smiled as her son walked toward the garage where his '40 Chevy was housed. "Bonnie will make a good wife for Ervin," she thought to herself. Even though Bonnie didn't come from a plain family, Emma liked Bonnie. She wasn't standoffish in the way that Kansans sometimes visualized people who lived in the East. She was a hard worker who readily pitched right in to help where it was needed. Besides, by this time Emma had given up on the idea that Ervin would marry someone plain.

20

A *Daadihaus*

The next day, Ervin came to the breakfast table with a suggestion. "Mom, what would you think about me remodeling the chinchilla house? You could live in it, and Bonnie and I could live in this house."

Emma pondered for a moment. "You mean like a *Daadihaus?*"

"Yeah."

Emma was intrigued. "Would you want to rent the house from me?"

"No, we'd want to buy it."

"That might work out. I wonder what Raymond would think about it." Raymonds were back on the farm again after a two-year stint at the mission in Arkansas.

"I'll go up there and ask him today," Ervin offered.

That evening at the supper table, Ervin could hardly contain his excitement. "Raymond says that he thinks it's a great idea to remodel the basement house for you. We could just write in the deed that you have a lifelong lease on the basement house. He can help us work out the details."

"That sounds good." Having a married child living nearby was more than Emma had been hoping for. She was now fifty-seven years old.

"I'm ready to start planning," Ervin suggested.

Emma nodded with delight.

As they made their way to the basement, Ervin said, "I'm going to clean up all the old cars around here, too."

Emma's face brightened. Over the years, the family had retired a number of vehicles by parking them in the backyard or shelterbelt. With the addition of the cars that Ervin had purchased for restoration or junk parts, she figured the number had risen to a dozen or so.

By the end of the evening, Ervin and Emma had sketched out a floor plan for Emma's new dwelling. The basement house would have a living room, bedroom, kitchen, bathroom, utility room, and pantry, with two sets of steps to the outside. The attic area could be used for storage.

Emma watched with pride the next morning as Ervin made a list of building materials he would need. "He learned a lot from Amos Zook," Emma said to herself. "It was worthwhile for him to spend some time in Pennsylvania."

Early that afternoon Emma accompanied Ervin to South Hutchinson to buy materials at Mills Lumber Supply on South Main Street. She felt a lump rising in her throat as they drove into the lumberyard. Tobe had often ordered lumber from this same supply house twenty-five years earlier. Might Ervin become a builder like his father?

The lumber company delivered materials the next day. Ervin borrowed a few tools from Raymond and got some advice for plumbing and electricity. Raymond, who often did electrical work, agreed to install a new electrical main.

Over the next weeks, Ervin worked on the project full-time. Emma dropped by to watch the progress several times a day as Ervin built the partitions and ran the electrical wiring. Under Raymond's guidance he dug a hole for a sump pump and ran all of the plumbing for the kitchen and bathroom.

On several occasions, Emma accompanied Ervin to Hutchinson to purchase supplies. Since she paid cash for all of the items, Emma was delighted to find bargains on walnut-grained paneling, kitchen cabinets, and appliances.

One evening she came home from town to find Ervin working with a big bandage on his right thumb. "What happened?" she inquired.

"I cut off the end of my thumb with the power saw," he said sheepishly.

"*Oh, es is hesslich! Wie hoscht's sell geduh?* Oh, that's terrible! How did you do that?"

I was ripping a two-by-four in half with a power saw. I used my left hand to hold the saw for the last part. The grain bound and the saw kicked back where I was holding the board with my right thumb on top. It just got the tip. The blade still sprayed blood on the ceiling. See?"

Emma shuddered as she looked at the streak of blood on the drywalled ceiling. "Did you bandage it up by yourself?"

"No, since you weren't home, I called Raymond Mary. She came and helped me clean it up and bandage it. It thumps quite a bit unless I hold it up."

"I'm so glad that it wasn't worse," Emma worried aloud. Tools could be so dangerous. She recalled that Tobe cut his thumb so badly with a saw that the doctor planned to take it off. Only after Tobe begged to keep it did the doctor consent to try to save it.

"I should probably have gone to the doctor to get it stitched, but I didn't want to take the time," Ervin said. "Since I just cut off the end, I think it will heal up by itself. I'm going to be more careful with the saw, though."

Emma nodded her agreement.

After finishing the rough-in work, Ervin took on the task of digging for a septic tank. Because the house was set in the ground, the trench and the hole for the tank had to be set quite deep. Ervin dug the hole by hand with the help of a couple of friends. He set up a dirt elevator to carry the clods out of the hole. As Emma watched, she recalled how Tobe used to dig basements out from underneath houses, using a dirt elevator.

The hole for the septic tank was not quite finished when the sky dumped a long hard rain on the project area. Early the next morning, Emma went into the basement house to find an inch of muddy water on the floor.

"I hope this never happens when I live in here," Emma thought to herself. Then she checked the basement under her house. It had water too!

When Ervin got out of bed, he assessed the situation. "Mom," he said. "I think we need a little wall on the east side to keep the water away from the house. The house is just built too low. When water comes down this slope, it has nowhere to go but into the landing and down the basement steps."

"I agree we have to do something," Emma said.

With Perry and Glen's help, Ervin mixed concrete for a retaining wall about eighteen inches high.

"Come to think of it," Glenn said as they worked, "it would have made it a lot easier to dig this basement if we'd have laid the grade a foot higher. It was so hot and dry when the man dug it out that he could hardly get his digger to go in. We could have saved him some time and effort."

Emma sighed. "I'll just be glad if this wall keeps the water away from the house."

"We'll have to wait until we get another big rain," Ervin said. "That will tell us whether it's going to work or not."

Now that the wall was done, they poured the concrete for the septic tank. When it was finished, Ervin went back to finish other aspects of the project.

Much of the work was done when Ervin asked for permission to go back to Rosedale for another term of Bible school. "We'd like to go for the November-December term," he said. "We'll probably be back here by New Year's Day."

"Aren't you going to finish the house before you leave?" Emma worried aloud.

"I can finish it when we get back," Ervin promised.

Emma consented. Bible school was a good thing.

• • • •

As Ervin and Bonnie prepared to leave, Bonnie's youngest sister, Sylvia, came to stay for a few days. The next day, Emma accompanied Ervin and the two Haldeman sisters to the Sunday morning worship service at Yoder Church, where Ervin was scheduled to preach. Emma wondered why Ervin had been chosen for the task. It seemed unusual to ask a twenty-year-old to preach on Sunday morning. Perhaps it was because he'd recently attended Bible school and showed potential for pastoral leadership. Whatever the reason, she was eager to hear Ervin preach.

After the service, a number of women went out of their way to shake Emma's hand. They complimented Ervin's sermon and Bonnie's ability to sing with the women's quartet at Yoder. Emma smiled with pleasure. Perhaps some good was coming from Ervin having joined Yoder Church.

The next day, Emma made an offhand comment to Bonnie that she was planning to do some sewing when the cleaning was finished.

"Sylvia and I will do the cleaning for you," Bonnie volunteered.

"Well," Emma hesitated, "if you really want to."

"We'll be happy to clean for you. And Sylvia can do some baking, too. She likes working in the kitchen."

"Ervin is lucky to have such a hardworking girlfriend,"

Emma thought as she sat down at the sewing machine. "She's a good housekeeper."

As Ervin and the two Haldeman sisters packed their things for the long trip, Emma asked Ervin when he planned to come home.

"I suppose we'll go to Pennsylvania for Christmas at Bonnie's house. Then we'll come back here. We'll be here until our wedding in April."

"Ralph and Virginia Hedrick are expecting me to come back soon after Christmas," Bonnie said. "So I'll work there at least until we get married."

"And I will finish the house," Ervin said.

True to their word, Ervin and Bonnie returned shortly after New Year's Day. However, Emma was disappointed to learn that their interest in buying her house had waned. During their time at Bible school, Mark Peachey from Rosedale Mennonite Missions had invited Ervin and Bonnie to go into voluntary service as a couple.

"So you aren't interested in buying the house after all?" Emma asked.

"I don't think so. The mission board wants us to go to Cincinnati, Ohio. They'll let me go to school at the same time I'm in VS. That way I can go to college," Ervin said. "We might come back to Kansas after that."

Emma swallowed her disappointment. What was she going to do with the house? "Perhaps," she thought to herself, "I can rent it to somebody. Or Erma may decide that she wants it, if she and Ray decide to get married."

In spite of the change in plans, Ervin determined to finish the basement house before the wedding. Emma lent her hand as well, helping to paint and stain the trim and the doors. Ervin installed the kitchen cabinets and hooked up the appliances.

Emma wasn't worried about the deadline. There were

plenty of people who could help to put on the finishing touches, perhaps Menno Yoder or even Ray Zook, if he came to visit.

Shortly after Ervin and the Haldeman sisters left for Pennsylvania, a storm dumped five inches of rain on the area. The waters on the nearby roads rose so high that Erma asked a neighbor with a pickup truck to take her to work for the early morning shift at the Friendship Manor. The stormy weather continued all day, with clouds roiling overhead in mid-afternoon.

When Erma arrived home from work, she rushed into the house. "Mom, come look out west. There's a tornado in the sky. I took a picture of it down at the corner."

The two of them stepped outside to see a tornado funnel hanging from a cloud nearly due west. "It looks like it's going to pass north of us," she said, "but we'd better go to the basement." As the two of them huddled downstairs, Emma prayed that God would spare her home and keep everyone safe. When they emerged from the basement some minutes later, the darkest clouds had moved further north. Emma thanked God that the twister hadn't come through her place. The destruction of her garage in 1964 had amply proved the power of a whirlwind to destroy.

• • • •

A few minutes before Emma left for Ervin and Bonnie's wedding in Pennsylvania in late April, she planted a row of beans in the garden. With the warm sun shining on the wet soil, Emma reasoned, the beans should be sprouted by the time she got back.

When Emma arrived in Pennsylvania and met Bonnie's mother, she learned that she too loved to work in the soil. She glanced around the living room at the Haldeman home to observe a great variety of plants. Large windows and a set of patio doors displayed a vista of Lancaster County farmland against the backdrop of mountains to the north. "So this is where Bonnie is from," Emma thought. "This is very different from Kansas."

Ervin and Bonnie had a simple wedding with a small wedding party. Bonnie was accompanied by her sister Sylvia as the maid of honor. Ervin was accompanied by LaVern Yutzy as the best man. Two of Ervin's friends from Center Church, David and Philip Wagler, served as ushers. Erma and Ray, now engaged to be married, served as receptionists. Becker Ginder, the moderating elder of the Brethren congregation, led in the ceremony. Walter Beachy, a guest preacher from Rosedale Bible Institute in Ohio, delivered a sermon.

Emma sat in the second row, taking in the scene. A large painting of Christ on the wall behind the platform framed the wedding party as they stood for the ceremony. She admired Bonnie's sewing skills, obvious in the white eyelet dress she had made for the occasion. She had also made Ervin's suit, constructed of blue polyester with a straight-cut collar. Emma would not have attempted such a project.

After a simple reception at the Penryn Firehouse close to the Haldeman home, Emma rode to the Zook home with Erma and Ray. She spent a few days visiting relatives and friends in the area and then left for Kansas with Perry and Judith. On the way through Indiana, they stopped at the Weaver home to visit with Edith for a day. Edith seemed to be doing well. Edith loved to help around the house and play with the animals on the small farm. Arvilla and her mother Sarah remained as vigorous as ever, cultivating a large garden and keeping livestock.

As soon as she arrived home from her trip, Emma walked around in her own garden. As she had hoped, the beans were up and doing well.

21

Empty Nest

Shortly after Ervin and Bonnie were married, Erma and Ray agreed to live in Emma's home in the same way Ervin and Bonnie had envisioned. Ray moved to Kansas from Pennsylvania and took up a job with a local builder. He helped to put the finishing touches on Emma's basement home. As their August wedding date drew near, Emma started moving her things into her new place.

The Zooks were on their honeymoon when Emma made final arrangements to move out of the house she had enjoyed for nearly eighteen years. She awoke to the sound of rain, with the smell of wet earth wafting through her open bedroom window.

"I wonder if I'll be able to hear the rain through my bedroom window in the basement house?" she mused. "The windows are rather high. And plenty small too."

"This rain will be good for the garden. I should get out and pull some weeds while the ground is wet. I could put in some late lettuce and radishes. Maybe some beans too."

Emma got dressed and padded barefoot into the kitchen. By seven o'clock she was finished with the farm chores, and the sun was peeking through the clouds. After a few bites of breakfast, she moved into the garden. First she picked some spearmint tea and brewed it for the helpers who would come later in the day. Then she attacked the weeds. Weeding seemed less odious in the coolness of the early morning.

She pulled the garden tiller out of the front of the garage and headed it in the direction of the garden. After checking the oil and gas levels, she yanked the cord. She was relieved when it started on the third pull. The tiller bounced along on the front tines and through the garden gate. She dropped the rear shaft and pushed forward on the throttle. She savored the sweet smell of the sandy moist soil as she made her way between the rows. After three full rounds, she was satisfied.

She had just put the tiller back into the garage when a car pulled into the driveway. It was Emma's sister Barbara with her daughter Rachel. Accompanying them in the front seat was Mother Nisly. Emma rinsed off her bare feet under the garden spigot and went to greet them.

"It's so nice of you to help me move," Emma said. "Maybe we could start with the kitchen things. We'll need to empty out the cupboards and carry them over to my new place."

The work began in earnest. Soon more helpers came: in-laws, nieces, and other friends. At midmorning, Mary Edna arrived with her brood of four. The helpers shuttled back and forth the short distance between the two houses, toting articles large and small. It hardly seemed worthwhile packing things into boxes.

Emma mostly stayed in her new place, showing where things should be placed. She watched with pleasure as the helpers brought freshly washed and dusted items to the new space.

By late afternoon, the project was nearly done. Emma's helpers excused themselves and went home. Emma felt very happy. She could easily finish the rest by herself. Besides, it would be good to have a little breather before going to the midweek service in the evening.

On Saturday, Emma finished moving her canned goods into her new pantry. She washed her clothing for the first time in her new utility room. A niece came by to help with the Saturday work. By the end of the day, Emma was content that her house was ready for Ray and Erma to occupy. It was 10:00 p.m. when she crawled into her bed in the new basement room.

A slight breeze pushed at the curtain in the window. The night-light in the bathroom across the hallway cast a dim light through her doorway. She mused that her parents had also moved into a *Daadihaus* at the age of fifty-eight. Somehow they had seemed much older than she did now at the same age.

• • • •

The newlyweds returned on Sunday afternoon. Erma invited Emma to help unwrap their wedding gifts the next day. On Monday morning, Emma watched with delight as Erma unwrapped each of the gifts. To witness the generosity of friends and family stirred gratefulness in Emma's soul. When all of the gifts were unwrapped, she asked, "What will you do with the wrapping paper?"

"Do you want some?"

"I would use some if you don't want it all."

"Take all you want."

Emma folded a dozen pieces that showed promise for reuse. "I guess I'll hoe a little in the garden yet," she said as she put the folded wrapping paper into a bag. She carried it into her new home before heading for her garden.

She kicked off her shoes as she stepped through the tea at the garden gate. "The peas need it the worst," she announced to herself as she surveyed the garden. She hummed as she moved down the row. Peas didn't always yield a second crop as they had this year.

"I wonder if Rays will want to share the garden next year?"

she asked herself aloud. "Or maybe they'll want their own garden."

It was a new thought. There would be things to work out with a daughter living next door.

Several times over the next two weeks, Emma caught herself stepping through the backdoor of her old home. "I'll soon get used to this," she assured herself. "I hope Erma doesn't mind."

Over the next few months, Emma adjusted to life in her new place. On the Sunday before Christmas, Emma sat down in her easy chair to read the *Calvary Messenger* and the other periodicals stacked up on the bureau. It wasn't long before she dozed off. She awoke some forty-five minutes later and resumed her reading. Sunday hardly seemed complete without at least a brief nap.

After the evening chores, she sat down to write a letter to Mary Edna, who now lived in Valley Center, a small town north of Wichita. As she began, it occurred to her that it might be a good time to start a circle letter that included her own children. Now that the children were all married but Edith, it was going to be more difficult for them to stay in touch with each other. A letter could bring news to all of them several times a year. Arvilla surely wouldn't mind writing on behalf of Edith.

She had just finished the letter to Mary Edna when she heard the sound of cars pulling into the driveway.

"It must be the Christmas carolers," she thought to herself. She glanced at the mantel clock. It was twenty to nine.

Emma sat in the easy chair with her hands on her lap. The strains of a familiar carol made their way into the room. "It came upon a midnight clear, that glorious song of old, of angels bending near the earth, to touch their harps of gold."

"The music doesn't carry quite as well here as in the old house," she thought. "But it's just as nice." She got out of her chair, made her way up the stairway into the small porch, turning on the outside light. As she looked through the door, she could just make out the faces of some of the carolers as they sang.

Emma opened the porch door as the last notes of the final carol faded into the night. "Merry Christmas," the young people chorused.

"Merry Christmas," Emma called back. She waved a cheery farewell as they turned to go on their way, laughing merrily in the chill air.

"It's so nice of them to sing for me," she said aloud as she made her way back down the stairs.

A week later, on New Year's Eve, Emma made her way to Glenn's home, where she had promised to babysit for Glenn and Miriam's three girls so they could watch in the new year at a friend's house. "I brought some Pumpkin Whoopie Pies," she told Miriam as she stepped into the house. "The girls always like to eat them when they come to my house."

Grandma and the girls enjoyed a long evening of bedtime stories. Emma held little Penny on her lap as Janet and Norma snuggled tightly against her on each side. Penny pointed to the pictures while Emma read the words.

As Penny's eyes began to droop, Emma finally announced, "It's time to go to bed now." She carried Penny to her crib, kissed her cheek, and laid her on her back. "Goodnight, Penny," she whispered.

She led the other two girls to their room and tucked them into their beds after bedtime prayers. "Goodnight, Janet. Goodnight, Norma." Emma thanked God that Norma's face was beautifully healed after that savage dog bite.

"Goodnight, Grandma," each one said in turn.

Emma closed the door behind her, leaving a small crack for the night-light in the hallway to shine through. She made her way back to the living room and picked up a few toys that had been scattered around the room. "Nothing quite compares with the joy of grandchildren," she thought as she straightened up the room. "They can be a lot of work, but I wouldn't trade being near them for anything."

When the last books and toys were put away, she turned out the overhead light and settled into the reclining chair. Glenn and Miriam would be home late. She might as well get some sleep. Emma leaned back in the chair and pulled on the lever to lift her feet. She glanced at the hands in the soft glow on the face of the clock radio. In about two hours, it would be a new year—1975.

"How the year has flown by," Emma thought. "Yes, there have been hard times, more than I can remember, but God has been good."

In the stillness of the moment, she heard a little girl's voice. "Grandma, when will Mommy and Daddy be home?" It was Norma calling.

"It will be a little while yet," she answered gently. "They expect you to be sleeping when they get home."

Emma sank deep into thought as the house lapsed back into silence. "I am so relieved that my children made good marriage choices," she thought to herself. "I get along well with all my in-laws. Edith seems to enjoy it at Arvilla's house. I have nine grandchildren. Now that Ervin and Erma are both married, I'll surely have more.

"I have a nice new place where I can live rent free for the rest of my life. Erma lives next door, so I will have someone to take care of me when I need it. Tobe would be happy to see how it all turned out."

Emma reached back to adjust her cap so that it wouldn't wrinkle against the cushion. "*Der Harr is gut.* The Lord is good," she murmured as her eyelids fell closed. "*Der Harr is arich gut.* The Lord is very good."

22

Social Security

Emma celebrated her sixty-fifth birthday in January 1981. Not long afterward, she began collecting Social Security benefits from the modest payments she had made into the system through the years. Social Security provided a small supplement to the cash rent from her forty acres and the money she earned through her cleaning jobs. Unlike stricter Amish comrades from other communities, the Amish in the Kansas area now felt free to participate in the Social Security system. The change in their conviction on the matter had come gradually, over a period of several decades.

Emma was satisfied to consider that she would be a widow for the rest of her life. Saying "no" to Levi had emboldened her to turn down a second opportunity that had come later. Saying "yes" to that suitor would have required a move to another state. Emma preferred to live by herself in her small home in Kansas, staying near her family, yet not being overly dependent on them. She looked forward to living a long life, like Mother Nisly, who was now in her mid-eighties and doing well. To live in good health near one's children, grandchildren, and great-grandchildren might well be the ultimate blessing. Emma now had eighteen grandchildren and often spent time with them.

Emma's expectations were curbed four years later in 1985 when she discovered a lump in her breast. Two days after Emma's sixty-ninth birthday, an oncologist confirmed that she had breast cancer. Emma battled the disease by submitting to a radical mastectomy, followed by chemotherapy. She also sought the benefits of anointing with oil when her gathered community prayed for God's healing touch. For two years, the cancer lay in remission.

The cancer returned with a vengeance, however, and metastasized into her bones. In 1988, Emma submitted to further chemotherapy and explored alternative forms of treatment. But over time, she came to realize that she would not outlive the savage advance of cancer cells gone wild inside her body. She reflected often about her children and grandchildren. On the whole, she was pleased with the way things were turning out in their lives.

Emma still worried at times about Edith, who continued to live under Arvilla Weaver's care. Although both of her parents had passed on, Arvilla lived at the home place and kept membership in an Amish district near Middlebury, Indiana. Edith had already far outlived the doctor's predictions. Who would care for Edith if and when Arvilla was no longer up to the task?

After mulling over her questions at length, Emma invited her son Glenn to serve as her power of attorney. She also appointed him to serve as the official guardian for Edith. To make the transaction legal, she arranged for Arvilla and Edith to appear before a judge in Hutchinson. Glenn then sought Social Security benefits for Edith, drawing on the payments which Tobe had made many decades earlier. He learned that the monthly checks, supplemented by Medicaid, would make it possible to double the monthly allowance they were giving Arvilla for Edith's care.

At first, Arvilla balked at the proposed plan. Her congregation would not look with favor on her receipt of Social Security benefits, particularly if they arrived by official post from the Social Security Administration. Arvilla had always perceived her care for Edith as a response to God's call, not as a job to make money. But she agreed that she could live with her convictions if Glenn would receive the payments at his home and forward the funds to her.

Once those arrangements were made, Emma felt a deep sense of peace. She relaxed, confident that Edith's care was assured beyond her lifetime. Emma was also relieved to know that after thirty years of providing financially for Edith's care, her relatives would no longer need to take their turn in the cycle of monthly contributions to be matched by the Center Church.

Emma mused too, about the legacy she would leave through her children, scattered in several places. Mary—who now preferred not to use her middle name—and Menno lived in Kansas City, where Menno worked as an installer of doors and windows. Mary was a full-time homemaker and served as a volunteer at the independent Baptist Church, where they attended. The youngest of their four children was fifteen years old.

Emma was at peace too, with their choice of a church fellowship. Mary's whole family felt at home with a fundamentalist expression of Christian faith, yet they showed respect for Emma's beliefs and way of life.

Perry and Judith now lived on Emma's home place, having purchased it when Ray and Erma moved to Pennsylvania to assist Ray's father in his business after a heart attack. Perry worked out a land swap with a neighbor so that he now owned a forty-acre property just across the road from Emma's home place. He also worked at Reno Fabricating, assembling aluminum windows and other products. Judith stayed at home as a full-time mother, looking after their four children aged eight to sixteen. Perry was the only member of Emma's family who attended the Center Church.

Glenn and Miriam lived two miles away, just a few houses up from the site where Grandpa Stutzmans once lived. Glenn still worked for Stutzman's Refuse. As a pastime, Glenn raised hogs and calves on their six-acre place. Miriam worked as a homemaker, as well as a bus driver for the local school district. The youngest of their three girls was fifteen years old. Together they attended Yoder Mennonite Church.

Ervin and Bonnie lived in Mount Joy, Pennsylvania, where Ervin served as a bishop in the Lancaster Mennonite Conference, with responsibility for five congregations. He also served half-time in the Home Ministries office of Eastern Mennonite Missions, assisting with the planting of new churches. Bonnie worked at home, looking after their three children aged five to ten and providing daycare for a few neighborhood children. They attended Mount Joy Mennonite Church, just a short walk from the large brick home they were restoring.

Erma and Ray lived near Gap, Pennsylvania, with their four children, the youngest being four years old. Ray worked in construction with two of his brothers as part of a joint business venture called Zook's Utility Sheds. Erma worked full-time as a homemaker. The family attended the Millport Mennonite Church.

Emma reflected too on the businesses that Tobe's brothers had established. Stutzman's Greenhouse had grown to become a large enterprise, selling both wholesale and retail. They employed many dozens of workers from the neighborhood, especially in the spring season. She observed that Ervin J. and his wife, Emma, worked closely together in the growing venture. She sensed that they made decisions as a couple, with Emma serving as a vital partner in the work.

It seemed to work the same way with Stutzman's Refuse Disposal, owned by L. Perry and his wife, Silvia. Silvia worked full-time in the front office, contributing daily wisdom to the business, which had expanded beyond anyone's dreams. They now operated out of a large location in Hutchinson, with dozens of employees.

"What would it have been like," Emma mused, "if Tobe and I had worked that closely together? What if he would have asked me to help him with the books and with making business decisions?"

She hardly dared linger on the next thought that came to mind. "Maybe that's how Tobe would have become a millionaire, as David A. Miller had suggested at his funeral."

• • • •

Emma watched with alarm as her left arm swelled while the rest of her body shrank in size. She sat in her glider chair in the living room most days with a gown hanging loosely on her emaciated body. She wondered how much longer she could hold on to life.

Judith Stutzman proved to be a loving in-law, an ideal caregiver just next door. Emma relied on her for many weeks. Then, in the spring of 1989, they decided it was time to call for the assistance of the local hospice center. Emma welcomed the hospice workers into her home each week. The drugs they dispensed brought relief for the growing pain that constantly wracked her body. Even more, she valued their understanding and listening ear.

Emma was happy to have her two oldest sons living close by, with Mary Edna only a four-hour drive away. But she missed seeing the twins on a regular basis. Knowing her health was declining by the week, she invited Erma to come see her. Erma came with her daughter Kim and stayed for a week in mid-February.

Ervin was far away though, living in Wales, U.K. with his family as part of a sabbatical assignment. He was assisting Tell Wales, an ecumenical evangelistic program that was to culminate with a six-week visit by the international evangelist Luis Palau. Emma stayed in touch with Ervin through letters, but she longed for him to come visit her. She was distressed by the thought that she might die before seeing him again.

Emma started putting her request in a letter, but decided to make a phone call instead. "It doesn't matter if it's expensive," she reasoned. "Sometimes it takes a long time for a letter to cross the ocean. What if it gets there too late?"

Emma made sure she understood the difference in time zones, and then dialed the number. She was delighted when Bonnie answered the phone. Ervin soon joined from an extension.

"The cancer is getting worse," Emma told them after a bit of small talk. "It's in my bones now."

"Oh, Mom, that's awful."

"Ervin, I wish you would come home to see me."

"I wish I could, but I don't know if the mission will let me. And I'm not sure how we can afford it."

"I'll pay for the ticket."

"I'll ask my boss tomorrow," Ervin promised.

"I hope you can come soon."

Emma breathed a quick prayer as they ended the conversation. It would be far better for Ervin to visit now than to come later for a funeral. Surely the people in the missions office should understand that.

Ervin called back a couple of days later to confirm that he would come shortly and stay for a week. Emma was thrilled.

She made arrangements for Mary Edna to come down from Kansas City. With Glenn and Perry living nearby, at least four of her six children would be together with her at the same time.

Ervin's flight brought him into town after midnight, but Emma determined to stay up to greet him. Her heart quickened its pace as she heard the sound of a car slowing to turn into the driveway. She heard the backdoor open and the sound of Ervin's footsteps as he walked quietly down the stairs.

"Mom," he whispered softly as he came to the bedroom door, "are you awake?"

She slowly sat up in bed. "Yes, Ervin, I'm so glad you're home."

Ervin stepped to the edge of the bed and then wrapped his arms around her shoulders. They held each other for a long time.

Again she repeated, "I'm glad you came."

"It's so good to be home," Ervin said as he looked into her emaciated but shining face.

"I have the hide-a-bed ready for you," she said. "There's an extra blanket on the chair."

"Thanks, Mom. I hope you can sleep peacefully now. Good night. I'll see you in the morning."

Over the next few days, many people came by to see Emma or her son. There were well-wishers, a hospice caregiver, family, and friends. Although it was tiring, Emma thrived on the opportunity to engage people in conversation.

One afternoon, Ervin asked, "Mom, have you made any funeral plans?"

"No."

"Would you like for me to help you?"

"Yes, I think that would be good." Emma was relieved that he had asked. As an ordained minister, he was familiar with such things. Although she had been sensing the inevitable end, she hadn't yet allowed herself to think about the specifics of a funeral. That afternoon, she sat down to talk about her wishes. While it was painful to think about her impending death, she felt some relief in the openness of the conversation. "What a privilege," she mused, "to be able to plan my own funeral. Tobe never had that opportunity."

When Mary Edna arrived from Kansas City that week, she assisted Emma by labeling dishes and furniture with the names of children or grandchildren to whom she wished to give specific pieces. By the time the week was over, all but a few pieces in the house had labels on them. The children could decide among themselves who would get the remaining pieces.

As Emma prepared for bed on Saturday night, she felt relief that her house was in order. "At least the children will get something when I die," she thought to herself.

The next morning, Easter Sunday, Ervin took a four-mile-long walk around the section. "Mom," he said when he returned, "I was thinking about Dad this morning. I feel like I don't know much about him."

"It's probably true," Emma thought to herself. "I've not talked much to the children about Tobe, especially to the twins."

"I have to leave soon to catch my plane, but could you write down some things about Dad and send them to me?"

Emma agreed. It was a good thing for Ervin to show interest in his father.

She watched as Ervin called up his uncle Ervin J. to plan for other ways to get information about his father. She could see that he was serious about his quest. The elder Ervin agreed to provide a contact list of people who had known Tobe well.

Over the next few days, Emma jotted down several pages of recollections. She told of the places they had lived in Iowa, the church districts, and the products that Tobe had made. Emma mentioned too that he had once taken tomato racks out of her garden to satisfy a customer. She chose to say nothing about the bankruptcy. "There's no need to stir up worries about such things," she thought to herself, "and it might be difficult to explain."

Emma passed on her jottings to Mary Edna, who typed up four pages of notes and sent them off to Wales. Meanwhile, Emma learned that Ervin J. had assembled a mailing list of people who knew Tobe well. Ervin sent them all a memo, seeking further information in his quest.

The anniversary of Tobe's death had just passed when Emma found that she could no longer get out of the hospital bed her children had set up for her in the living room. By this time, she was straining for each breath. Friends and relatives dropped by to say their last farewells.

After a night of struggle with her life ebbing away, Emma opened her eyes for a moment. She saw her two oldest sons and daughters-in-law standing at the sides of her bed. She reached out to Glenn, who grasped her hand in his. As she closed her eyes for the last time, it was as if the strains of a gospel song penetrated the hush of the room:

> Death shall not destroy my comfort.
> Christ shall guide me through the gloom;
> Down he'll send some angel convoy
> To convey my spirit home.

Emma Nisly Stutzman ca. 1962

Emma's twins, Erma and Ervin, outside her temporary residence in August 1956. All captions are identified from left to right.

Emma with her mother and siblings (with spouses) in 1962:
Mary and Fred Nisly, Mary and Raymond Nisly, Henry and Elizabeth Nisly (standing behind Emma), Rufus and Emma Nisly, John Nisly, Barbara and Alvin Yoder, Mother Mary Nisly, John and Elizabeth Bender, and Noah Nisly.

Emma and five of her children in 1963:
Erma, Mary Edna, Perry, Emma, Glenn, and Ervin.

Emma with Vacation Bible School class in front of Center Church building in
1964: Rene Wagler, Arthur Nisly, Beulah Nisly, Michael Miller, Philip Nisly,
Irene Yoder, and Christina Nisly.

Emma with her twins by her garden in 1965: Ervin petting his dog Migo, Emma, and Erma.

Emma with her siblings at the funeral of Emma's niece Orpha Bender in August 1966: John Nisly, Elizabeth Bender, Fred Nisly, Emma's mother Mary Nisly, Raymond Nisly, Barbara Yoder, Henry Nisly, Emma Stutzman, and Rufus Nisly.

Emma with children at daughter Mary Edna's home near Valley Center, Kansas, circa 1970: Mary Edna, Edith, Perry, Emma, Ervin, Erma, and Glenn.

Wedding reception for Emma's son Perry on March 13, 1971: Yvonne Miller, Erma Stutzman, Joyce Nisly, Judith Nisly (bride), Perry Stutzman (groom), Ervin Stutzman, Paul Yoder, and Ben Lapp.

Four generations in 1975: Mary Edna Yoder holding daughter Judy, Emma, and Mary Nisly.

The Author

Ervin R. Stutzman was born into an Amish home as a twin in Kalona, Iowa. After his father's death a few years later, his mother moved her family to her home community near Hutchinson, Kansas. Ervin was baptized in the Center Amish Mennonite Church near Partridge, Kansas. Later he joined the Yoder Mennonite Church near Yoder, Kansas.

Ervin married Bonita Haldeman of Manheim, Pennsylvania. Together, they served five years with Rosedale Mennonite Missions in Cincinnati, Ohio. In 1982, they moved to Lancaster, Pennsylvania, to serve with Eastern Mennonite Board of Missions. Ervin served as a bishop in the Landisville District from 1984 to 1999. Ervin was Moderator of Lancaster Mennonite Conference from 1991 to 2000, when he moved to Harrisonburg, Virginia, to serve as Dean of Eastern Mennonite Seminary.

Ervin holds a BA from Cincinnati Bible College, an MA from the University of Cincinnati, a PhD from Temple University, and an MAR from Eastern Mennonite Seminary. He is a preacher, a teacher, and author of *Tobias of the Amish* (2001), *Being God's People* (1998), *Creating Communities of the Kingdom* (with David Shenk, 1985), and *Welcome!* (1990), all published by Herald Press. Ervin and Bonita have three children, Emma (1978), Daniel (1981), and Benjamin (1983).

More information relating to this book is on the web at www.ervinstutzman.com.

"Ervin Stutzman exhibits a patient interest in letting small details reveal a large moment. Describing his father's funeral service, Stutzman captures a baby's fussing, a passing train, the flicking tail of a horse by a waiting wagon. Likewise he shows us mother and son, sharing early morning breakfast a decade later: contented, eating, mainly silent. These pictures, doggedly mundane, give us real life.

"Through patient narration of everyday events, Stutzman reveals and honors the priorities of this community: hard work; financial accountability; family obligations; discernment as a congregation; restraint that hinders embrace between friends until someone dies. All of these values, of course, shelter foibles and pathos as well, gently exposed in the course of the story. Emma herself exhibits compassion, stoicism, trust—a dignified representative of her people."
—*Susan Fisher Miller, Northwestern University*

"Ervin R. Stutzman's Emma invites us into the life of an Amish Mennonite community in Kansas at a time of great social change. Through Emma—who is quiet throughout, submissive yet strong, caring for her family and devoted to God—I understand what Gelassenheit, the ultimate yielding to the will of the Lord, means for the Amish."
—*Karen M. Johnson-Weiner, The State University of New York Potsdam and author of* Train Up A Child

"Emma Stutzman was my first cousin. I knew almost all of the persons in the story in Kansas and Iowa. The story is not only credible, but very interesting."
—*David L. Miller, Amish Mennonite Church*

"It's an amazing feat. Woven into the life of an Amish widow, in *Emma* you will discover a substantial amount of history on

the Amish and the Amish Mennonite settlements in Iowa and Kansas including their sentiments toward the eastern Anabaptist communities."
—*Verna Schlabach, Berlin, Ohio, Amish and Mennonite Heritage Center*

"*Emma, A Widow Among the Amish*, is a son's love story for his mother. It is also a keenly observed, at times self-conscious, thick description of Amish folkways and the domestic ordering of life in an Amish community in Kansas. For scholars interested in Amish women's lives his long and very detailed descriptions of gardening, meal preparation, socializing, quilting, funerals, courtship and weddings are a treasure trove."
—*Kimberly D. Schmidt, an editor of* Strangers at Home: Amish and Mennonite Women in History

"Ervin Stutzman, Emma's youngest son, sensitively traces his mother's efforts to find her way alone through issue after issue to ever increasing independence. She rejects the stability of Social Security payments to return to her Amish roots in Kansas and the promise of friends and relatives to help her in traditional ways. Emma's story offers the reader an excellent detailed insider's view of how the struggle within one Kansas Amish community."
—*Katie Funk Wiebe, author of* Alone: A Widow's Search for Joy